FOREST'S FALL

Book 6, Angel Fire Rock Romance series

ELLIE MASTERS

JEM Publishing

Editor: Erin Toland

Proofreader: Roxane LeBlanc

Published in the United States of America

JEM Publishing

This is a work of fiction. While reference might be made to actual historical events or existing locations, the names, characters, businesses, places, and incidents are either the product of the author's imagination or are used fictitiously, and any resemblance to actual persons, living or dead, business establishments, events, or locales is entirely coincidental.

ISBN: 978-1-952625-01-5

Dedication

This book is dedicated to my one and only—my amazing and wonderful husband.

Thank you, my dearest love, my heart and soul, for putting up with me, for believing in me, and for loving me.

You pushed me when I needed to be pushed. You supported me when I felt discouraged. You believed in me when I didn't believe in myself.

If it weren't for you, this book never would have come to life.

Books by Ellie Masters

The LIGHTER SIDE

Ellie Masters is the lighter side of the Jet & Ellie Masters writing duo! You will find Contemporary Romance, Military Romance, Romantic Suspense, Billionaire Romance, and Rock Star Romance in Ellie's Works.

YOU CAN FIND ELLIE'S BOOKS HERE:

ELLIEMASTERS.COM/BOOKS

Military Romance

Guardian Hostage Rescue Specialists

Rescuing Melissa

(Get a FREE copy of Rescuing Melissa

when you join Ellie's Newsletter)

Alpha Team

Rescuing Zoe

Rescuing Moira

Rescuing Eve

Rescuing Lily

Rescuing Jinx

Rescuing Maria

Bravo Team

Rescuing Angie

Rescuing Isabelle

Rescuing Carmen

Rescuing Rosalie

Rescuing Kaye

Cara's Protector

Rescuing Barbi

The Dark of You

Military Romance

Guardian Personal Protection Specialists

Sybil's Protector

Lyra's Protector

The One I Want Series

(Small Town, Military Heroes)

By Jet & Ellie Masters

EACH BOOK IN THIS SERIES CAN BE READ AS A STANDALONE AND IS ABOUT A DIFFERENT COUPLE WITH AN HEA.

Saving Abby

Saving Ariel

Saving Brie

Saving Cate

Saving Dani

Saving Jen

Rockstar Romance

The Angel Fire Rock Romance Series

EACH BOOK IN THIS SERIES CAN BE READ AS A STANDALONE AND IS ABOUT A DIFFERENT COUPLE WITH AN HEA. IT IS RECOMMENDED THEY ARE READ IN ORDER.

Ashes to New (prequel)

Heart's Insanity (book 1)

Heart's Desire (book 2)

Heart's Collide (book 3)

Hearts Divided (book 4)

Hearts Entwined (book5)

Forest's FALL (book 6)

Hearts The Last Beat (book7)

Contemporary Romance

Firestorm

(KRISTY BROMBERG'S EVERYDAY HEROES WORLD)

Billionaire Romance

Billionaire Boys Club

Hawke

Richard

Brody

Romantic Suspense

Changing Roles Series:

THIS SERIES MUST BE READ IN ORDER.

WITH JET MASTERS

Book 1: Command Me

Book 2: Control Me

Book 3: Collar Me

Book 4: Embracing FATE

Book 5: Seizing FATE

Book 6: Accepting FATE

Romantic Suspense

EACH BOOK IS A STANDALONE NOVEL.

The Starling

~AND~

Science Fiction

Ellie Masters writing as L.A. Warren

Vendel Rising: a Science Fiction Serialized Novel

Warning

This story contains sexually explicit scenes and adult language and might be considered offensive to some readers.

This book is for sale to adults ONLY, as defined by the laws of the country where you made your purchase. Please store your files wisely and where they cannot be accessed by underage readers.

Grab the First Book in The Guardian Hostage Rescue Specialists Series for Free

https://elliemasters.com/RescuingMelissa

Chapter One

FOREST

I PULLED AT THE COLLAR OF MY JACKET TO WARD OFF THE CHILL. Water pooled on the streets and splashed beneath my boots. Most of the streetlights were out, and very little traffic flowed down the dimly lit streets. Those cars which passed didn't slow, and they never stopped.

Not in this part of town.

Decay seeped from the walls and flowed with the litter on the streets down the gutters where it swirled down the drains. Far too few lights lit up the buildings. Those few locals who remained huddled in their apartments and waited for the dawn to make their neighborhood safe again.

In the hours after midnight, murderers, kidnappers, rapists, and thieves reigned supreme. Drug deals went down in narrow alleys where prostitutes made a living, one John at a time.

Wise men stayed off the streets.

Except me.

I braved the night and walked down the fetid streets as if I was on a morning stroll.

A few prostitutes gathered beneath the safety of a streetlight, braving the night to make a quick buck. They shrank away, eyes widening with fear when they noticed me. One grew bold enough to approach.

I gave a sharp shake of my head, sending her scrambling back to the safety of her friends.

I wasn't here for something like that.

I came for the children.

Kids the prostitutes kicked to the shadows. That's where their young spirits broke, and the fire died in eyes.

I searched the darkness, peering into narrow alleyways.

The light plink, plink, plink of water dripping down drains sounded loud in my ears. A light breeze kicked up, and an empty can rattled down the street.

The smell of rot had me wrinkling my nose as I tried not to gag against the fetid stench. This street was not the place for a stroll. It was a place steeped in the worst humanity had to offer, but I walked with purpose.

I steered away from desperate prostitutes and sent those few drug dealers brave enough to approach running with my cold stare.

Then I heard it, someone scurrying out of sight.

Someone small.

I angled over to the alley and paused at the entrance.

The padding of small feet disappeared into the darkness as they scrambled for safety.

I held up my hands, palms out, knowing the child could only make out my silhouette. My size would frighten him because I was a mountain of a man.

Standing at six-foot-eight, I towered over most. To a defenseless child, I would be a monster. It killed me to think one so young had only seen the worst in men.

"I just want to talk." The low rumble of my voice vibrated in the still night air. I was going to do a whole lot more than talk. Tonight would be the last night this kid lived on the streets.

I wondered, however, how many Johns had said the same thing to this kid and then did far more than just talk. My stomach churned with what this kid must have endured.

The deep rumble of my voice did nothing to soothe the child in the dark. I didn't think this alley had a back way out, but I could be wrong. The kid was trapped, and that would increase his fear.

Now that I found the kid, it was time to let Sara talk him out of the alley. She was soft, sweet, and kids loved her. For some reason, they trusted her implicitly.

Pure as an angel, and as beautiful as the dawn, Sara was sharp as a tack and a royal pain in my ass, but in times like this, the purity of Sara's soul became a most useful tool.

"My name is Forest."

Still nothing.

"I want to help you."

The darkness didn't speak.

What the hell did I expect?

When I had been that age, would I have run into the arms of a giant?

I never ran. I couldn't.

I had been too small.

Too weak.

Too afraid.

Huffing out a breath, I forced those memories back where they belonged.

I took a step, then sat my ass down on the wet pavement and crossed my legs in front of me. It was the only thing I could think of to make myself look smaller than I was. Maybe I would look less intimidating too. Who knew?

Reaching into the breast pocket of my jacket, I pulled out a candy bar.

Was this kid stupid enough to take candy from a stranger?

Those kinds of kids didn't last long on the street, but from the quick glimpse I had, this one might be hungry enough to risk it.

I tossed the candy bar down the middle of the dank alley as a gust of wind blew a noxious odor out from the darkness. I nearly gagged and coughed into my fist. No child should have to huddle in such a place.

"My friend, Sara, wants to help you. We both do. But we want to help your friends too."

A new pimp in town was peddling young flesh. Kids as young as six were on the streets. Forced to satisfy the appetites of monstrous men, it was a death sentence. I peered down the alley, trying to get a glimpse of the kid, but couldn't make anything out. I pulled out my phone and sent a quick text to Sara.

Found a kid. Need you.

A few seconds passed while three tiny dots danced on my screen. Sara's message popped up.

Be right there. Don't scare him!!! And WTF with the ringtone, boss!!!!!

I huffed a laugh. Don't scare him? Might as well ask a giant to shrink to average size. As for the ringtone? What was wrong with "Flight of the Valkyries?" It was perfect for swooping in to save the day. Sara had no humor.

Much like this kid, I'd been tiny as a boy. Skye had called me her beanpole, and for many years she called me Bean, but I'd grown out of the name and was simply Forest now.

Sara hated my evening strolls. She claimed I put myself in danger when I could hire men for this. She was a worrier, but there was very little that scared me. Crowds parted before me. Men shrank in my presence. And women stared with open admiration.

In this world, there was little for me to fear.

The boy in the alley made no move to snatch the candy bar.

Smart kid.

I reached back inside my pocket and pulled out a granola bar. "Not a fan of chocolate? How about this?"

I ripped off the plastic wrap and held it up. The kid wouldn't be able to see, but that was okay.

"It's perfectly safe to eat." I broke off a bite and made a show of putting it in my mouth. "See?"

Still nothing from the darkness.

Behind me, the hiss of tires over the wet asphalt had me turning my head. A dark town car pulled to a stop, and a beautiful woman climbed out.

A creature of habit, Sara smoothed the fabric of her pencil skirt as she approached. It hugged her curves and drew a man's eye. Her heels clicked on the pavement, and the swish of the fabric captured my attention. Why she didn't wear something more practical escaped me, but she liked her skirts. And I enjoyed watching her walk.

Sara gave a curt nod; irritation dripped from her words. "Stop messing with my phone. I hate that ringtone."

Sara interned for me years ago. A graduate of Rice University, she had studied aeronautical engineering and should be working in that field. Instead, she hung on and never left, which worked out well for me.

I hated training new people.

"Evening, Sara." My response sounded like a rumble to my ears.

She spared one look at me, then gave a dismissive shake of her head at my lack of further communication.

What was the point? Small talk was a waste of time. She knew what to do, and there was no reason to discuss it ad nauseam.

Her attention shifted to the alley.

"Congratulations, you trapped a kid into an alley." She pitched her voice low so the kid wouldn't hear.

I said nothing. Sara always had more to say, and if I kept quiet, she'd carry the entire conversation on her own, thus relieving me of the burden of the tiresome exchange.

She pulled out her cell phone and flicked on the light. Rather than pointing it down into the alley, she shined the light on her face.

"Hey there." Soft and friendly, she cooed into the darkness.

Unlike me, Sara always knew what to say, and she said it with an angelic voice.

"My name is Sara, and this is my friend, Forest. We want to help you."

The darkness responded with a scuttling noise.

"Looks like you're scaring him away." I couldn't help the snarky comment.

"Him?" She arched a brow and glanced at me. "Could be a girl. Did you see him?"

"No."

"So, you don't know." Her angelic face, ethereal voice, and eyes which had seen and endured too much pain, tunneled deep inside me where they didn't belong.

Sara made me feel things I didn't want to feel.

"Fifty-fifty chance." I gave a dismissive snort.

"You're impossible." She turned the light from the phone off her face and toward the alley. Her lilting voice pierced the darkness and pushed it aside. "I have chicken fingers, fries, and a soda in the car. You can have them if you want. I have a sweater, shoes, and a blanket too, but only if you want them."

"A blanket?" A tiny voice responded.

Not a boy. It was a little girl.

"I do."

"You can watch...if you want." The tiny voice seemed to fade a little. "But it costs extra."

"Extra?" Sara cocked her head, but I understood.

The kid sniffed. "Fifty for him to f-f-fuck. Twenty for you to watch." The little voice tripped over that word.

It wasn't the first time it had spilled from that innocent mouth. How hard had this child been used? And out here alone? Brokering her ruin?

It was all I could do to hold back a growl. "She thinks I'm here for...to do..." My stomach clenched at what the poor girl thought I wanted.

Sara's eyes widened, but she didn't otherwise react. "My friend, Forest, doesn't want to hurt you...or do those kinds of things to you. And I'm not here to watch."

"You're not?" Shock and distrust filled the kid's words.

"No, sweetie, I'm not, and Forest doesn't want that. We want to help you." Sara's words were breathing things, filled with hope and light. They were soft and sweet, like her. Sara made me believe evil didn't exist in this world.

But it did.

She'd experienced it.

I'd experienced it.

And the tiny waif in the alley had too.

We were all victims.

I shifted on the damp concrete and cleared my throat. "My name is Forest, but do you know what my sister used to call me?"

The darkness didn't answer.

"She used to call me her little beanpole."

"You're not little." I could almost see the little girl's mouth twist, and her brows pinch together as her face screwed up in confusion.

No one believed I had once been little.

"No, I'm not. Not anymore, but when I was a kid, I was very, very small. And bad men got a hold of me. They did bad things to me."

"To you?" Awe filled her voice. "But, you're a giant."

"There was a time when I was tiny, and bad men did bad things to me. Sara and I...we don't want that for you. If you want...if you can trust us, we can give you more than chicken fingers and a blanket. And if you let me help you, we can do the same for your friends."

"He won't like that."

"He?"

"Ronald."

The kid shifted a little closer, but I couldn't make anything out other than the sounds of her scrambling. The light from Sara's phone wasn't that bright. It penetrated only a few feet, casting shadows on top of the darkness.

The thick mist coalesced into spitting rain. Little girls didn't belong on the streets in the darkness, in the rain, or in alleys where men bruised their flesh, and took what didn't belong to them.

Sara didn't seem to notice the chill, or that it had started to rain. She entered the alley without fear.

"Ronald doesn't sound very nice," Sara said.

"He's not." The kid answered almost too quickly. "And he smells. He smells real bad, and he's mean. Meaner than the J-johns."

My heart skipped a beat. This kid spoke with far too much knowledge about what should be something only adults knew.

"Well, I'm bigger now." I tried not to rumble, but my voice had grown to match the size of my body. I hoped it didn't scare the little girl too much. "I take care of bad men."

"You do?"

"I do, and if you tell me where Ronald is, I'll make sure he never hurts anyone again. Sara will take you someplace safe, and we can take your friends too. We don't want Ronald to do mean things to them."

"Y-you'll help them?"

"Yes, dear." Sara took another step into the alley. "We'll help all of you, but you need to trust us."

Something shifted behind what I could now see was a dumpster. Sara continued to walk into the alley while I remained seated on the concrete getting my ass wet.

"What's your name?" Sara held her phone up high, trying to shine as much light as she could into the alley.

I prepared to leap to her defense if something other than a child came out of the darkness. I'd learned to trust nothing and expect the worst.

But nothing stirred in the narrow alley except for the fluttering of trash when the wind kicked up.

Wait a second. That wasn't trash.

A tiny waif covered in tattered remnants inched out from behind the dumpster.

"My name is Sara," the little girl said.

"Like mine!" Joy filled my Sara's voice. She squatted on her heels and held out her arms. "We're like sisters."

"Sisters?" Awe filled the little girl's voice.

"Sure," Sara said. "I don't have a sister. Come here…Sara. What a beautiful name for a beautiful girl."

The kid tucked her chin to her chest. "I'm not pretty like you."

"Hun, you're gorgeous, and you're going to be safe. Forest and I are going to make certain of it. Now, how about you come here? Let me hug you." Sara held out her arms.

To my surprise, the little kid vaulted into Sara's arms. All I could think about were lice and fleas. I'd have to decontaminate both

Saras. The little girl shifted her attention to me; fear and wariness flickered in her gaze.

I understood her fear.

I peeled my wet ass off the concrete and stood to the side while Sara led little-Sara by the hand to the car. When I didn't move to join them, my Sara glanced over her shoulder.

"You're not coming?"

I gave a sharp shake of my head, then tried to soften my voice. But there was no softening a sound this big.

"Sara…" I spoke to the little girl. "Where do I find Ronald?"

Little-Sara's eyes widened, and she clutched at my Sara's hand.

"It's okay. Forest is going to take care of things." My assistant held the girl's hand, pulling her close and wrapping an arm over her shoulder.

"I'll take care of Ronald while you tell Sara where to find your friends. We want them to be safe."

The kid looked up at Sara and whispered. Sara nodded then turned to me.

"He's at Old Grady's bar." Sara turned to the kid. "What does he look like?"

The kid drew a line from her eye to her ear. "He has a scar."

I walked them to the car, held the door while they climbed in, then made a note to have the vehicle fumigated.

"Okay, got it." Knocking on the driver's window, I waited for my driver, Reid, to roll down the glass. "Take care of her, and don't let her go off without backup. Call in the others."

"Yes, sir." Reid didn't bother with small talk. It's one of the reasons I liked him.

I stepped back and let Reid take both Saras to safety.

I should be happy with another rescue, but there was still too much evil to stamp out. And to date, we hadn't found a way to get to the vilest man on the planet. John Snowden, the elusive bastard, continued to evade my attempts to take him down.

After decades of preparation, I was tired of setting up the chess pieces. It was time to put them into play. But I needed Snowden to sit at the table. Once I found him, I would make him pay for all the crimes he committed.

For now, I had kids to save, a small-town pimp to put behind bars, and my demons to dismiss.

I could do this alone, but Sara would have a fit if I didn't go in with backup. A quick tap-tap-tap on my phone and I had a team inbound to meet me at Old Grady's bar.

Chapter Two

SARA

A LOW SIGH OF FRUSTRATION ESCAPED MY LIPS AS FOREST WANDERED into the office. He sported a split lip and a cheeky grin, shoving both of them in my face with far too much pride.

He wanted a reaction, but I'd be damned if I played along.

He knew what I thought about taking chances and putting himself at risk.

I wanted to slap that smug expression off his face, and I would have if it didn't require chasing after him with a step stool in tow.

I sported bags beneath my eyes, a bra left on far too long, and despite finishing my second coffee of the day, my yawns had yawns. I was getting too old to get by on two hours of sleep, but I was here.

At work.

On a Sunday.

Because Forest worked every damn day of the week and couldn't understand how others might want a day off from the hectic hours he kept.

The man didn't do leisure time. To him, that was a waste of time.

"Get Xavier on the line." Forest rarely asked, said please, or

God forbid let a thank you slip out of his mouth. Generally, he barked or growled and expected me to jump at his command.

But I was too tired to jump today or play his games.

I lifted the nail file I hadn't been using and slowly, deliberately, filed my nails.

"I said get Xavier on the line." His deep rumble vibrated the air and sent shivers down my spine.

"You do realize it's three in the morning where he is?"

"So?"

"I'll call him in a few hours."

"I want to talk to him now."

"Then, you call him."

"What the fuck do I pay you for?"

"Technically, you don't pay me. Skye does."

He snorted, but it was true.

There had been a time when he went through executive assistants like water. After I spent a summer interning for him, something clicked between us.

He fired me immediately, but Skye stepped in when she saw how I didn't let him get away with shit. Now, if he wanted me to go, Skye had to fire me.

Not him.

My job security was as tight as Fort Knox because Skye adored me.

"Well, I'm your boss, and I want you to get him on the line."

"Do you have anything new to tell him?"

"No."

"Then I'll wait until he's awake."

"I want to know if he's heard anything."

"If he has, I'm one hundred percent certain he would have called you before he went to bed. And if something happened while he was sleeping, he would have called you as well. You'll wait and talk to him at a reasonable hour, like a normal person, not because you want it now. We're not doing tantrums, Mr. Summers. It's far too early for that."

Teaching Forest about basic civility was a job that never ended. He didn't get people at all.

"Harrumph!" He stamped his foot.

"Don't harrumph me. I'm your executive assistant, which means my job is to assist you and not let you make bad decisions that will piss off your business partners. Unless the sky is falling…" I made a show of leaning toward the window where I stared at the crystal blue sky. "Which it is not, I'll call him at a reasonable hour. In the meantime, you look like shit and smell even worse. There's a set of clothes hanging in your office and fresh towels in your bathroom. Take a hot minute to clean yourself up."

"Don't you want to know what happened?"

"Not really. I'm smart enough to figure it out. At least you didn't go alone this time. I heard you had a swell time at Old Grady's bar."

"Swell time?" He pointed at me. "You're making fun of me."

"Am I?"

"I will fire your insolent ass."

"You can try." I lifted a finger, pointing back at him. "It's rude to point."

"You're pointing at me."

"Only to illustrate a point."

"You're not the boss of me," he said with a grump.

"No, Mr. Summers, I am not, but it's my job to assist you. Take a shower. You're stinking up my office." I flicked my finger toward his office door.

"Assistants don't talk to their bosses like you talk to me."

He was right about that, but most executive assistants didn't work for a man-child like Forest.

"I'll call Skye. You can discuss it with her. And I will call her because she's at least in the same time zone as we are."

"Don't you dare." He took a step toward me, but I just fluttered my lashes. Forest didn't frighten me but having to talk to his sister gave him pause. I won this round, and he knew it.

A veritable giant who towered over the common man, he was impossible to ignore. Rooms quieted when he entered. Crowds parted in his presence. People took notice when he was near.

Monolithic, with tree-trunk legs, arms nearly as thick, and a chest to break men, he was what people called a force of nature, and no one told him 'No'...except me.

I called him something else.

Frustrating.

Irritating.

Annoying.

Amazing and wonderful.

He was perfection.

I called him boss when he wasn't irritating me, and Mr. Summers when he was an ass. And then there were other, more colorful descriptors I used depending on my mood. I never called him Forest, at least not to his face.

That felt too intimate.

Someone to admire as well as fear, I admired him. I feared him, but mostly I adored him. I'd been in love with him since that very first summer when I interned for him. Not that he noticed. Not that he would ever reciprocate. Not that he cared.

Forest didn't date women. He didn't date at all. But he fucked. He fucked a lot of men.

My cause was hopeless.

Which meant, he remained a starring player in my fantasies, while I remained nothing to him.

His piercing, ice-cold stare could make the blood of his enemies freeze while simultaneously melt the hearts of women who couldn't help but swoon in his presence.

I was not immune to his power, but I'd accepted I would never feel his powerful embrace wrapped around me.

There were two people he rarely touched.

His sister, Skye, was someone he used to never touch. Their past carried too much pain, but he was getting better about touching his foster sister.

I guessed time did heal all wounds, but there were deep scars that remained.

Then there was me.

Why he kept his hands to himself around me wasn't something I understood, but he went to great lengths not to touch me. I might as well be a piece of furniture as far as he was concerned.

I took that back.

He would touch the furniture.

Which made me what? Was I that despicable?

He made me think so. And I didn't date either. How could I? I was in love with a man who hated women and fucked men.

"You know…" My tone turned caustic. "If you don't stop with this hero shit, you're going to get yourself killed."

Another snort from him had my shoulders lifting. I held back, not wanting an argument this early in the day. Frankly, I was too tired to get into it with him.

"I'm pretty damn indestructible. Don't forget who saved you."

Like I could ever forget. I owed Forest for bringing me out of the depths of despair. He saved me, and I never got past my hero worship.

He could never love me the way I loved him.

"Would it kill you to begin your little forays with a team?" I wasn't letting this go. If he wasn't going to take care of himself, I would do what I could. "You have an entire security force to back you up."

He ran his hand down his body. "Do I look like I need backup?"

The man could be an arrogant prick.

"Everyone can use a friend, Mr. Summers."

"For the record, I called for backup. I didn't go alone, so get off my case."

"Do they look as bad as you? Or did you tell them to stand to the side and let you take care of things?"

"I'm able to take down one measly pimp on my own."

"That wasn't my question."

He shook his head and refused to answer, which confirmed what I thought.

He brought backup with him, then ordered his men to stand down while he took care of Ronald the pimp.

"Looks like you misplaced your brain again, boss. Do you want me to call Skye and see if she can pull it out of your ass?"

Skye was the only person who could talk to Forest. She took none of his shit, and he deferred to her on nearly everything.

"I do not want to talk to Skye." He shoved his index finger toward me again. "Don't call her."

"You have the manners of an ass."

"Do. Not."

"Okay, how about this. When you see someone for the first time in the morning, it's customary to say good morning instead of picking a fight. Good morning, Miss Brenerkie. How are you doing today? Did you sleep well last night?"

I parroted an appropriate morning greeting, then gave a reply with a little more snark than usual.

"Why no, Mr. Summers. My boss had me up all hours of the night, and I got less than a couple of hours of sleep. I'm tired and cranky and dealing with a royal pain in my ass."

"Whatever," he said with an irritated shake of his head. "Just get Xavier on the phone."

"Not happening."

"I want Xavier." His rumbly voice deepened, but I was immune to his threats. This was why Skye kept me around.

"I want you to stop stinking up my space. Take a shower. Change clothes. And I'll think about getting Xavier on the phone in a few hours."

"You're fucking impossible. I'll call him myself." He gave an exasperated snort and lifted his arms over his head in frustration.

I didn't blink and held back a laugh as he disappeared inside his office. He left the door open while my irritation climbed to an all-time high.

Honestly, I was pissed. Forest had nothing nice to say to me after calling me at oh-dark-thirty last night to go to the worst part of town. He treated me like I was at his beck and call all hours of the day. Like I didn't have a life.

But really, who were we kidding?

I had no life.

But still?

Nothing? No '*Good job!*' Or how about '*How's the kid doing?*' Or '*I can't thank you enough for helping me last night?*'

Was he not interested in how little Sara and her friends were doing?

Nope.

I barely received a grunt. Not that a grunt was unusual. Forest didn't do small talk, and he only used his words when he had something important to say.

My fingers curled in frustration. I had a mind to say a thing or two to him. For one thing, the man did not belong on the streets, tracking down bad guys and rescuing children at all hours of the night. He didn't need to be doing it alone.

Alone!

A man with billions at his disposal, who owned a private security agency brimming with a virtual army of battle-tested soldiers, did not need to be walking the streets by himself where anything could happen.

Summers' Industries could not afford to lose their leader. Despite what he thought, he wasn't indestructible. Not that he cared. Forest should have called his team at the very beginning of the night.

But no.

He went off on his own, the gallant savior with only one thing on his mind.

Save the children.

What exactly did he think was going to happen? Did he think he could swoop in and scoop the kid off the street? To that little girl, his size alone made him the personification of a monster. She'd have PTSD for life.

Knowing Forest, that never occurred to him. Sometimes, his way of seeing the world, black and white with a list of tasks that needed to get done, blinded him to the intricacies of dealing with humans.

His Asperger's clouded his interactions with others—like ignoring my concerns about heading into the worst part of town to save a handful of kids. For a genius, the man had a thick head.

"Sara!" Forest bellowed from his office.

The man never learned what an inside voice was, what it was used for, or why I got on his ass to stop shouting all the damn time. I rolled my eyes because he was incapable of using an office intercom.

Hello! They are called phones for a reason.

I picked up the receiver of our office phone and dialed his desk. It rang and rang. Which meant I had to go into his office. When I stepped inside, I shouted and averted my gaze.

"For the love of God! Clothes, Forest."

He'd stripped out of his clothes and stood in front of his desk stark naked.

If he'd been a flabby-assed bastard, it wouldn't be such an issue. Except Forest had the physique to go with his towering form. All carved granite and chiseled perfection, everything was proportional.

I couldn't help but see his penis…and what an impressive thing it was.

"You told me to take a shower." He responded like there was nothing wrong with calling me in when he was standing buck naked in his office.

Why couldn't he strip out of his clothes within the privacy of his bathroom like a normal person?

"I assumed you could do that without my assistance. What the hell? Put a towel over that…that…"

"That what?" He glanced down and wiggled his toes. The man didn't try to cover his groin. Instead, he glanced down and arched a brow.

I couldn't shift my gaze away from his sculpted physique fast enough.

Having the hots for your boss was one thing. Seeing him naked? I didn't have the strength for this.

My fingers itched to touch him. My mouth watered to taste him. I needed to stop thinking about my boss that way.

Dammit all to hell, I do not get paid enough for this kind of shit.

"Where's my towel?" he asked.

I clamped a hand over my eyes. "I told you. It's hanging in your bathroom, where a towel belongs. Can you at least cover that thing?"

"I didn't see it."

I peeked through my fingers. The bastard made no move to cover himself.

"Did you look?" Exasperated, I headed to the bathroom. Sure enough, two fluffy towels hung right where I had left them. I snagged one then returned to Forest.

He stood at the floor to ceiling windows and stared out onto the city skyline.

"You'll get arrested for that." I tried to keep my tone level, projecting a calmness I didn't have.

Holy hell, but the globes of his ass were perfection.

"For what?" He turned around, bringing him full frontal to me again.

I tossed the towel, which he caught at his waist.

"For flashing innocent people. You can't stand at the window naked like that. If anyone sees you, you'll get arrested."

He scrunched his brow. "No, I won't. No one can see in."

I pointed to the glass and the offices in the buildings across the street. "I can see them."

"So?" He lifted the towel. "They don't have privacy glass like we do."

I snapped my fingers. "Well, I don't need to see you naked. Cover that up!"

"Why? Have you never seen a naked man before?" He moved the towel down. "Didn't think it would bother you."

"Well, it does. Now, if you don't mind, don't call me in here again unless you're decent and dressed. I need to go bleach my eyes...thank you very much."

"That's sarcasm, right?"

"You think?"

"If you say so." He gave another shrug.

I pointed to the bathroom. "Get in the shower, and don't forget to shave. Your scruff is growing scruff. And drag a brush through your hair."

Why were the basics so damn hard?

"I'm thinking of growing out a beard again." He ran a hand over the stubble of his jaw.

Too many of my fantasies centered on that scruffy face doing things between my legs. I had to press my thighs together against the sudden ache. And now that I'd seen the full package, my dreams would be filled with another thing between my legs as well.

Thank you, Forest.

Not.

I hated my boss, only because I was helplessly in love with a man who couldn't love me back.

Leaving him to his shower, I wandered back to my desk, where I sat down and stared at my computer.

Fatigue pulled at me, and all I wanted was to crawl back into bed and sleep like the dead. If I had any other boss but Forest, that's precisely where I'd be. Instead, I closed my eyes and prioritized the tasks I needed to accomplish for the day.

A quick check with Child Protective Services confirmed what we already knew. None of the four kids we pulled off the street had living relatives.

This was good because we could streamline them into Forest's Foster care initiative.

That's what happened to me.

He rescued me from an abusive foster home when I was fourteen. Like little-Sara, I'd been forced to do things no girl should ever have to do.

I was placed with Forest's first foster family and officially became his first rescue.

My name wasn't Sara at the time. Jake and Allison Brenerkie told me I could choose a new name for my new life.

Sara seemed simple, and I needed simple. Little did I know the Brenerkie's would later adopt me. They took in three more of Forest's rescues, adopted them, and turned us all into one of the most unique and loving families on the planet.

I had hope for little-Sara and her friends.

The phone on my desk rang, which surprised me. It rarely rang during the week, let alone on a Sunday.

"Hello?"

"Hello, Sara." A decadent voice rolled out of the receiver. "I need to speak with Forest."

I knew that voice.

What were the odds Xavier would be calling moments after Forest demanded I get him on the line? Sometimes it seemed as if Forest had a sixth sense about the world.

"Xavier, it's nice to hear your voice. It's early for you."

"That it is. Would Forest happen to be at work today?"

"He's here, but he's taking a shower."

"A shower?"

"Yes."

"If it's not too much trouble, I do need to speak with him."

"May I ask what this is concerning?"

"Tell Forest I found him."

There was only one *him*.

Other than rescuing children, Forest had a vendetta against the man who sexually abused both him and Skye when they were foster kids. Skye killed their foster father in self-defense, but John Snowden fled the country. Forest's entire life's purpose was to find Snowden and put the man down for good.

The insides of my stomach did a little flip. It was more of a huge loopy-loop, and I felt a little sick to my stomach.

This was big news.

"Sara?" Xavier sounded concerned.

"I'm sorry, but I wasn't expecting that. Forest will want to know right away. I'll just put you on hold…"

"Don't bother. Tell him to call me back. We need to talk."

"Yes, sir."

I headed back into Forest's office on shaky legs. Snowden had always been a ghost to me. He was the villain nobody could pin down. If Xavier said he found him, everything was going to change.

And knowing Forest the way I did, his obsession with Snowden would consume him.

It would ruin him.

There was a chance it would kill him.

There was no response to my knock on the bathroom door, so I opened it a crack.

Thick steam billowed out, and I pushed the door wide to let the fog out. Waving my hand in front of my face, I tried to clear the air, and that's when I saw Forest through the thick shower glass.

He had his hand on his penis, his head tilted back, and was fisting himself. His arm pumped in time with his heavy breaths.

I covered my mouth, trying to stifle my gasp, but Forest's acute hearing didn't miss a beat.

He slowly turned to face me.

"Sara?"

"I'm sorry. I didn't mean to intrude."

"You didn't intrude. I'm just fiddling the flute."

"Excuse me?"

"You know, relieving some tension. You want to watch?"

"Why would you think I want to watch that?"

"Because you have yet to look away."

Unfortunately, that was true. Damn, but he was impressive. I gave a sharp shake of my head and focused on why I was here.

"I came because Xavier called, not to watch you fiddle the flute."

Seriously, who said shit like that?

Forest did.

"What did he say?"

"He found Snowden."

Chapter Three

FOREST

My guts twisted with the news. Snowden had been found.

I never thought this day would come.

Nervous and a little sick to my stomach, something powerful rose within me; a rage I kept in check most days.

Snowden destroyed my life.

He did unspeakable things to the helpless boy·I had been and had planned to do far worse. He intended to send me to one of his death rings, horrible places where boys went to live or die.

Skye saved me from that.

The only reason I breathed today was that she had taken things into her own hands.

I'd been too weak to save her, but she'd been strong enough to save me.

Skye lived with the repercussions of what she'd done. That blood would never wash clean, and she would carry the burden of taking a life to her grave.

My sweet, darling sister lived with that because I'd been too weak to save her.

An undeniable rage thundered through me, tearing through my guts and slicing through my veins. I bled with the pain Skye endured. If there was an emotion stronger than hate, that's what I had for Snowden.

I hungered to put that man down.

He hurt Skye.

He hurt me.

He destroyed our lives.

And got away with it.

He was still getting away with it.

A feral growl escaped my mouth, and my assistant took a frightful step back.

How many more children's lives had Snowden destroyed over the years?

We put his business partner down. My associate, Joshua Davenport, killed Zane Carson at one of the death matches organized by Snowden and Carson overseas. Carson didn't walk away from that, but Snowden still pissed in the wind.

We'd lost his trail in the aftermath.

I slammed my fist into the shower wall. Tiles cracked and fell to the floor. Blood streamed from cuts on my skin and swirled down the drain as I struggled to control my breathing.

Red.

All I could see was red.

"Forest?" Sara's voice shook.

I tried to keep this side of myself from my assistant. Sara didn't need to see the monster I could become.

"Get out!" I hated shouting, but I needed a moment to get my shit together.

Sara, however, didn't move. She hovered at the door and wrung her hands as she took half a step toward me.

Ignoring her, I slammed my fist into the tile wall again.

"Get Xavier on the fucking phone. Now!" I didn't mean to shout at Sara, and I'd have to apologize later, but too much anger surged within me to care.

"Y-yes, boss." Sara retreated as I tried to rein in the anger surging in my veins.

Then I looked down.

At the erection jutting between my legs.

Sara saw that.

Shit.

Thick, ropey veins sent blood surging to my dick, stiffening it with the filthy desires festering inside of me. I didn't blame her for her aversion. I'd tried to play off her walking in, but from the look on her face, I failed miserably. Not that I blamed her.

My cock wasn't something she needed to see and certainly not in this engorged and needy state. It was a monstrous thing, and it hungered for its cheated release. After the news about Snowden, I didn't have it in me to finish rubbing one out.

But it did.

I had a cock that fit my body.

It never failed to raise an eyebrow with those I fucked. Women might look at me with desire in their eyes, but they weren't built to handle a man like me, not without a lot of pain. They felt things differently, too, with messy emotions that got in the way of what should be nothing more than physical release.

Men were easy.

Built to handle what I had to offer, I didn't worry about hurting them, and there were no emotions.

Men fucked for release.

And we walked away without a care in the world or any emotional attachment.

Clean. Simple. Neat.

It made things…palatable.

But I had a big dick, and it had an insatiable appetite for sex. Which meant I'd be rubbing one out sooner than not. I almost considered finishing, but there were things to do.

I grabbed a towel and hastily dried off. My knuckles were bleeding.

Skye was going to have a field day with that.

With a clean towel wrapped around my thick hips, I headed out to my office, where Sara left my clothes.

The moment I let the towel drop, Sara walked back in, and I

inadvertently gave her the full monty, again. Only this time, my engorged dick stood loud, proud, and hungry for release.

Her attention shifted to my groin, and her eyes widened until I could see the whites all around. But thankfully, her attention cut left to my hand. When it did, her lips twisted.

"You're bleeding." Her words came out flat and emotionless.

I glanced at my knuckles and sighed at the mess I'd made.

"Yeah, you might want to call Skye and tell her to bring needle and thread."

Sometimes it worked to my advantage having a sister who was also an emergency room doc. She patched me up more times than I cared to admit. My attention shifted back to Sara, who stood looking, not at my cock, but rather at the mess of my knuckles.

I didn't ask if she had Xavier on the phone. With the way she shoved her cell phone at me, it was clear he waited on the other end.

Her gaze slipped to my groin, and the raging erection jutting out from between my legs. I swear the beast roared, and those damn veins pumped more blood into it. The bastard gave a little jerk like it was showing off.

Like it was hungry for Sara.

That made my stomach clench.

Sara was an angel, a pure soul, and the last thing she needed was that.

It sickened me to even think of her in that way. I would hurt her without trying, but what I hated the most would be that I wouldn't care. The hunger inside of me wouldn't pause to consider the pain I would cause. It wouldn't care.

And that could never happen.

Not to Sara.

Not to sweet, amazing, and beautiful Sara.

I rolled my eyes and put the phone to my ear. No use in covering my dick. She'd seen everything.

"Xavier…" I kept my voice to a low growl.

"We have a location." The tonal registers of Xavier's voice soothed the raw emotions swirling within me. The man had a presence about him which radiated through the phone.

My unlikely business partner responded with far more control than I displayed. I swore nothing riled Xavier. The man was smooth as silk, a predator who, somewhere along the way, decided he preferred saving the sheep rather than devouring them.

I had a profound respect for the guy, a little bit of a crush, and deep-seated envy for the control he exercised over every aspect of his life.

He'd been saving victims of human trafficking years before I had my hands in the pot, and he was slick about it. Working both in and out of the sickening industry, he bought slaves and freed them.

I had heard whispers about him, did a little digging, then joined forces when I realized what he had to offer. He had something I needed, a veritable army of loyal soldiers waiting to serve his every command, and I had the technical empire to launch cyber warfare on our enemies along with deep pockets to finance our private war.

Like him, I rescued people.

Foster children, trapped in abusive homes, found loving families, new lives, and hope with the foundation Skye and I created.

It was a natural extension to funnel Xavier's slaves through that foundation, not to find new homes and safe families, but to establish new lives with new identities.

It wasn't perfect, but it got the job done.

"Where?" My hand tightened around the phone, and the skin of my knuckles split. I wasn't sure, but I think that white stuff was bone. Skye was not going to be happy.

"Private island off the coast of Manilla, exclusive guest list. High security." Xavier made it easy. He wasted zero time on unnecessary conversation.

He also instilled loyalty on a level that scared the shit out of me.

I felt the pull.

The man had something indescribable, and I almost found myself bending a knee to serve him. I might have, except I vowed never to give someone that kind of control over my life ever again.

Xavier also didn't fuck men.

He had male slaves, but he didn't use them for sex. An odd arrangement, it somehow worked. He also had a wicked-smart female slave, Raven, who I tapped to assist with our cyber warfare. An MIT graduate, Raven lived and breathed code, and the girl knew her way around computers. I admired her skill. That said something, considering my abilities.

Snowden.

He was going down. I lost too much in the basement where Snowden broke me, and while that was years and years ago, the pain remained as raw and fresh today as it had back then.

I woke more often than not sweat-soaked and panic-ridden from the nightmares. Skye, with the help of her husband, Ash, seemed to be healing. I, however, continued living a never-ending nightmare.

"And?" I asked.

Xavier's mention of security didn't bother me. I had teams, ex-SEALS, and Delta operatives, who I recruited and trained with me specifically for this. They were ready to drop everything at my command.

"Our insertion window is short," Xavier said.

"Details."

Was this twenty questions?

I took back what I said about Xavier's communication skills. Why was it so fucking hard for people to spit shit out and just say what needed to be said all at once?

"The event is scheduled two days from now. It'll take your team a day to get here. I have resources inbound. Helicopters you'll need for insertion, extraction, and gear for your team. Entrance is another matter as they have surveillance in play. I'm not going to lie. It's going to be tight. We may lose this opportunity."

"My team can depart within the hour and leave the issue of surveillance to me." I snapped my finger to get Sara's attention.

I needed my hand stitched and my team activated. There was no way in hell we were losing this opportunity.

Whatever it took...whatever the cost, I was bringing Snowden down.

Chapter Four

FOREST

Sara was smart. I liked that.

Intelligence, over any other quality, was something I respected, and she had it in droves.

She was already on the phone, activating my para-military team as well as my medical support team.

I didn't have to tell her what to do; she had it done before I was aware I had the thought. It was one of the reasons I kept her around. People like her were hard to find. I just wished she wasn't so damn annoying.

I gripped the phone, knuckles tight, as Xavier updated me. "Raven is looking into their encryption. Mitzy is helping. I've already sent the tech team ahead. They'll have the basics ready when you arrive. I hope you don't mind a swim."

Mitzy was a relatively new addition to the team. She was the assistant to Kate Summers, a private detective who put her brother-in-law, Joshua Davenport, in jail for rape. Josh came to our operation with a dark past, but his tenacity brought Snowden's business associate, Zane Carson, down.

I wish I'd witnessed that monster's death, but Josh went off-script. He killed Carson rather than bring him in. There was nothing to do about that now.

One monster was down. Another would soon follow.

"A swim?" I needed to focus on what Xavier was saying.

"You'll be dropped offshore. It's the only way to evade their radar. This place is locked up tighter than Fort Knox. I've got DPVs and rebreathers waiting."

I hated the water. With my musculature, I sank like a rock, but I'd trained for virtually every contingency.

Xavier was sending us in underwater with personal propulsion devices to speed our entry and avoid both visual and radar surveillance. The rebreathers would hide our bubble trail from anyone smart enough to watch the waters. It made sense even if I didn't like it.

I trained with ex-SEALS and Delta operatives. It was the only reason I knew how to scuba dive. I hated the confining masks and the feel of the wetsuit against my skin, but my comfort meant nothing if there was a chance of taking Snowden down.

Xavier and I went over the information he had. I held the phone to my ear while yanking clothes over my body, smearing blood all over the clean shirt. He finished, and we ended our call.

Sara's face pinched as her astute gaze ran over my body from head to toe. She, too, was on the phone. "Bring your medical kit. He's bleeding all over himself."

No reason to ask who Sara was talking to; she was on the phone with Skye. As the leader of my medical team, Skye was responsible for activating her team.

"Tell her we leave within the hour." I didn't care about a little blood. It was nothing. "She can stitch me up during the flight."

I waited impatiently for Sara to get off the phone, but she and my sister were being Chatty Cathys, saying a whole lot of nothing while wasting time. I made a show of pointing at my watch, tapping the dial, but Sara rolled her eyes.

"Your brother is doing that tapping thing with his watch." Her eyes twinkled with mischief. "Yes, he's got that scowl on his face…" She gave a soft laugh. "Yes, his face is getting redder by the second."

I could feel blood rushing to my face. I hated it when they teased me.

"I'd better get off before his head blows. Oh, and I'll watch little Zach while you're gone…Yeah, no problem. You know I love the little guy."

They chatted more about what I assumed was my nephew's schedule. Ash was out of town on tour with my favorite rock band, Angel Fire. As lead to my medical team, Skye would be shipping out with me.

It never occurred to me, but someone would have to look after her son.

But then, I tended to miss details like that.

"Did you call the pilot?" I turned my attention to Sara.

She lifted a finger to silence me. "Do you mind if I take him to the zoo?"

It was my turn to roll my eyes, something I did with great emphasis as I gave her my most frustrated 'What the Fuck' look. I mouthed, *'Get off the phone!'*

Sara turned her back to me. "If it's raining, we can go to the aquarium. Zach loves watching the fish…I promise I won't fill him up with too much junk food."

My eyes about bugged out of my head while I listened to Sara's inane chatter with my sister.

Skye needed to be notifying her team and grabbing her stuff, not shooting the shit with my assistant. Finally, I ripped the phone out of Sara's hand.

"Hey!" Sara screeched. She tried to snag the phone out of my hand.

I lifted it high over my head and arched my brow. "You can jump for it if you want," I spoke into the air rather than putting the phone to my ear. Skye could hear my deep, booming voice, and if I held the phone over my head, Sara might just try to jump for it. "Sara is busy, and you need to get your ass in gear."

Sara's pink lips twisted, and she put her hands on her hips. "You'd like to watch me try, wouldn't you?"

I wasn't going to lie. I'd love to see her tiny body jump up and down. From my vantage, I'd get an excellent view of her tits as they bounced.

But then, my guts knotted as I reminded myself not to think of Sara like that.

Filth infested every part of me, and there was no way I'd let any of that touch Sara's perfection.

Skye's crisp voice broke through my thoughts. "My ass is already in gear, Beanpole. Why don't you chill your chops?"

My stomach sank at the nickname.

How long had it been since Skye had used it? Six months? A year? Sometime after she married Ash, that name had disappeared, and she'd reverted to calling me Forest like everyone else.

I think it was her way of putting the past where it belonged, except she brought it back, front and center, using the nickname now.

Maybe I wasn't the only one affected by the news that Snowden had been found. Maybe Skye and I were both regressing to the injured children of our shared past.

The things he made us do...the things I'd done to Skye at Snowden's command were scars that went soul deep.

"My chops are chill." I tried to sound unaffected. Calm, cool, and collected was my M.O., but Skye knew me. She saw right through me.

"Are they?"

"Are yours?"

She vented a deep sigh. "I'm good, Bean."

With great effort, I kept the protective growl from my voice. "Right, my summer sky, you're about as chill as a fucking volcano."

My summer sky was a name I hadn't used in a very long time. Her gasp told me it had been a low blow.

But those words connected us.

They defined the very fabric of who we were. I was her beanpole, and she was my summer sky. Somewhere in the darkness, we found each other and discovered the strength to endure the unimaginable.

"I'm sorry." The words couldn't come fast enough. "I shouldn't have…"

"It's okay, Bean. This is happening, isn't it? We're going after him."

"Yes, we are."

"And?" Her lilting voice warmed my heart.

"I'm as scared as you are."

I wasn't scared.

My entire adult life existed to serve one and only one purpose. I meant to kill Snowden, not that I would tell Skye that.

It was important to her that my soul remain pure, and my hands remained untouched by violence. While I may have never killed a man, I ached to end the life of the one man who had earned the privilege of dying by my hand.

I couldn't tell her that. Skye sacrificed too much to ensure that burden wasn't one I carried.

And I didn't carry that burden. Not yet.

I didn't because I'd been too weak to do what was necessary. My sister killed to keep me safe. She lived with that sin.

And I lived with the incredible burden of everything that came afterward.

I failed to protect Skye. In every way, I failed her.

"I love you, Beanpole."

"I love you too." I needed to speak the words.

My love for Skye was the only thing that got me out of bed most mornings. Her light was pure. Her strength profound. Her love filled me with hope.

She was my light in the darkness, the summer sky, which granted serenity in my moments of deepest despair.

"Now, can I finish talking to Sara and make sure little Zach has what he needs while we're off saving the world?"

I glanced down at Sara. She stared up at me with her arms crossed over her chest. Correction, not over her chest, but slightly below her curvy tits. My mind headed places it didn't need to go, and I slowly dragged it out of the gutter.

"Fine." But before I gave the phone over to Sara, I glared at her over the bridge of my nose. "Did you call the pilot?"

"What do you think, boss?" Her answer came out in a huff.

I shouldn't have asked.

Sara never left a loose end dangling. Somehow, while I struggled to do something as simple as getting dressed, Sara activated my insertion team. She notified my medical team and alerted my pilot to take us to the airport. There, we would hop on a company plane and fly halfway across the world.

Mollified, I handed her the phone. "I think you need to figure out what little Zach likes for supper."

"You don't say." She held out her hand.

"Your brother is a pain in my ass." Her snarky comment brought a grin to my face. Sometimes it was fun to mess with Sara just for the hell of it. I couldn't help myself.

With a flippant flick of her hair, Sara turned her back. She and Skye discussed my nephew's dietary needs while I dug my go-bag out from the closet.

While I went through the contents, double-checking my gear, Sara finished with Skye and fielded dozens of calls as my team called in with their ETAs. Finally, she came to check on me.

"You need anything?" she asked. A blankie? Bib? Something to wipe your ass?"

"Ha. Ha. Not funny."

"How about a Band-Aid? You know, we do have those. Handy suckers. Smart people use them to stop their cuts from bleeding…" She glanced around my office, and her astute gaze landed on my desk and the smears of blood I'd left behind. "But maybe a Band-Aid is too high tech for a nerd like you?"

"Smartass." My cheeky grin came out to play. Next to getting a rise out of Sara, I loved irritating her more.

"Dumb fuck." Her retort had my grin spreading wider.

Out of all my employees, she was the only one who ever called me out on my bullshit. Anyone else would find themselves fired in two seconds flat. Sara didn't worry about her job. She and Skye were thick as thieves, and Skye refused to let Sara go.

Which was for the best when I thought about it.

No one put up with me like Sara did. And, like I said a million times, it's hard work training someone to get the tiniest things right.

Sara had an uncanny knack of reading my mind.

She got all the tiny things right.

I liked that.

I felt connected to her on a level I didn't understand.

"If you're so concerned about me bleeding all over the office, why don't you grab some of these Band-Aid things and patch me up?"

"Really?" Her brows practically climbed up her forehead.

I understood her surprise. I didn't like people touching me. Correction, I didn't want her touching me. The way she made me feel was too confusing.

"Yes. Really." I pointed toward the bathroom. "You've got twenty minutes before people start arriving. That gives you five minutes to patch me up and fifteen to clean the office."

"You think I'm going to clean up all your blood?"

"Yeah."

"Think again, dumbass. You bleed. You clean. I'm not wiping your ass, and I'm not cleaning up your blood. You don't pay me enough for that."

"Technically, I don't pay you at all."

"Which is why I'm still here, but that doesn't mean you can abuse my kind heart."

"Is that so?"

"Yeah, you couldn't find your way out of a paper bag without me."

"I think I could figure that out," I mumbled at that one.

"Right. You'd just rip and shred and use brute force to get out, but sometimes, you need to stop and think. Your brain is big enough, even if you don't use it when you should."

She retreated to the bathroom while scolding me about my brains and lack of common sense. I didn't mind her comments. When you were a man like me, with the wealth I commanded, it was hard to find someone who spoke the truth. It was hard to find someone who treated me like an average person, even if I was far from ordinary.

I didn't agree with a tenth of what Sara said, but she was right about the paper bag. I'd rip the shit out of it, never thinking to take my time to figure a way out without destroying it.

She returned from the bathroom, carrying a first aid kit. Pointing to the couch, she ordered me to sit.

"So, your shower will be out of commission while I get the tiles fixed."

I held back a hiss as she pressed an alcohol-soaked cotton ball to the cuts over my knuckles.

"I'll have someone in tomorrow for estimates. I assume you don't care about the cost?"

"Just do what makes sense. I trust you."

"Really?"

There went the cute arch in her brow, which never failed to bring a smile to my lips.

"Sure." I shrugged, then sucked in a breath as she went to town, cleaning my knuckles.

"So, I have carte blanche in fixing it?"

"Whatever it takes."

"I can change the tiles?"

She hated the bland decor in my office bathroom and had been on me to redecorate for the past year. Not wanting to argue about it, I gave in.

"Like I said, whatever it takes."

Her grin gave me pause.

"Whatever it takes." Sara hummed as she worked on my hand.

The cuts were deep but didn't seem to bother her.

I hated blood.

It brought back bad memories, but I vowed not to let her see how it affected me.

"So..." She let the word stretch out. "Do you want that blankie or not?"

Chapter Five

SARA

Watching Forest was like being inside the eye of a hurricane. Everything appeared calm, but there was a flurry of destruction happening all around. He barely sat still long enough to bandage his knuckles.

Left to himself, he would have bled all over his office.

There was already too much to clean. The stains on the couch probably wouldn't come out. His desk needed a thorough cleaning followed by disinfection. His entire desk suite, the leather blotter, the pen holder, his notepad...they all showed signs of the carnage. The carpets were a speckled mess as well.

How the hell did one person get so much blood over everything from such a small wound?

As soon as he was gone, I was pulling the carpets and installing tile. I didn't care what he said about hating the echoes hard floors made. I'd pour concrete if I could. By far, the easiest thing to clean.

Taking care of Forest was like taking care of a puppy. You had to be proactive because there was always some mess to clean up.

I stood in the middle of the lobby outside his office. We'd turned it into Operation Central.

Forest's team had been trickling in over the past forty-five minutes. The schedule they worked against was insane, but they seemed to be pulling it off. Forest barked orders at six men, something about moving their sorry asses and getting their gear to the roof while I bounced a very sleepy nine-month-old on my hip.

Forest's nephew, Zach, smelled like heaven, snuggled like an angel, and was utterly oblivious to the activity around him.

I tuned Forest's bellowing out about twenty minutes ago and sang a soft lullaby to Skye's son.

Skye's medical crew were the first to have arrived. She'd deposited little Zach into my eager arms then argued with Forest for the next five minutes. She wasn't happy with him going on this mission and wanted him to stay behind where he'd be safe. Forest insisted on taking Snowden down.

I didn't hear all of their argument because they made Zach whimper.

Skye walked out with her face beet red and mumbling about stupid men with no brains.

The two of them worked around each other as Skye's medical team checked their gear. The last of Forest's men reported five minutes ago, and they were similarly going over their equipment.

Through it all, Forest roared.

Everyone moved too slow, had their heads in their asses, or their panties in a wad. Some had both. I couldn't help but smile. There was something he said about their mothers that made my ears burn.

The funny thing was, no matter how much Forest roared, his team didn't step up their pace. They were methodical to a fault, double-checked each other, and moved only when they were damn well ready.

That didn't mean they weren't hustling. I'd never seen men move with such lethal efficiency, and I knew what they had packed in those bags.

The men of Guardian HRS were ready to go to war.

That should bother me, but Forest was more amusing. Besides, I didn't want to think about why they needed all those guns. I focused instead on the hilarity that was a giant of a man stomping around while everyone generally ignored him.

They had to. If they stopped every time he drew close, they'd get nothing done.

I held back more than one or two snickers.

Flustered Forest was fun to watch.

The man had his way with people that didn't match how people worked. He expected them to act like he thought: robotic and lacking empathy. He was oblivious to the camaraderie of his men and the amused expressions they tossed around when he wasn't looking. Forest simply wasn't able to sense that side of people.

"You doing okay?" Skye breezed past me, pausing to kiss little Zach.

Zach was usually a bundle of energy, but he was passed out. In his defense, it was hours past his bedtime. The little sucker was going to keep me busy, but for now, I enjoyed the snuggles and ignored the fact my shirt was wet from his drool.

I had plans and a library full of Disney movies to keep the little guy engaged. Forest thought it was silly to plan for a day at the zoo and another at the aquarium. He said the boy wouldn't remember any of it, and it was a waste of time.

I disagreed. Lights, colors, and sounds fascinated babies, plus they had a touch pool at the aquarium little Zach could play in. Well, hopefully not *in*, but they had horseshoe crabs and spiny starfish he could touch. I think they also brought in some non-stinging jellyfish too. Maybe I was looking forward to it too. It was rare to get a break from work.

Skye lumbered past me, this time with two massive medical packs in tow. A tall, beautiful woman trailed in her wake, followed by a stunning man with the greenest eyes I'd ever seen. The woman was Tia Myers, a certified nurse anesthetist, and the man was Ryker Lyons, the respiratory therapist on Skye's team.

I knew their names but had never met either of them. They had a fourth man on the team, a trauma surgeon. He'd breezed by and headed upstairs to the roof with his pack.

"For the love of God, Skye, let me help you." The deep rumblings of Ryker's voice vibrated with irritation and more than a bit of frustration.

Skye looked over her shoulder. "I can hump it myself."

"You know," Tia said, "people don't talk like that." Tia carried a pack on her back and gripped a duffle bag in each hand. She walked behind Skye, unfazed by her burdens. She was only a few inches shorter than Ryker and as capable as any of the men.

Ryker snickered. "What would Ash say to you humping it yourself?"

"Ryker!" Tia gave a little shout that should have been a reprimand but came out more frustrated than anything else.

Forest told me those two were engaged. From the exasperated but loving look in Tia's expression, that seemed about right.

"What T?" Ryker said with a snort. "She said it, not me."

"But you don't have to be an ass about it." Tia slung one of the bags at Ryker, nearly knocking him over, but he sidestepped with ease.

"Your fiancé is a pain in my ass, Tia," Skye said. "When are you going to tame him?"

Ryker snickered, and Tia's face turned beet red. They shared a secretive glance that spoke to an intimacy I would never share with another.

I held back a deep sigh. Someday, I was going to realize I deserved someone who noticed me, cared for me, maybe even loved me like that.

Forest was a lost cause.

But I couldn't leave him.

He needed me.

At least, that's the excuse I told myself.

"T likes when I'm rough." A grin spread across Ryker's face. "She doesn't want to tame me. She prefers the beast." His brows wiggled suggestively.

Skye gave a huff and turned her back. "Instead of offering to help with my gear, why don't you step it up? There are three more bags downstairs, and if you hadn't noticed, the helipad is on the roof. If you're late, Forest will take off without you."

Ryker gave a low throaty laugh and jogged ahead of the two

women. "I'm on it!" He flashed Skye a cheeky grin and winked at his fiancée.

Skye and Tia moved by me, and I checked Zach's diaper. I'd changed it ten minutes ago but couldn't help but check again. I left the chaos behind and retreated to Forest's office. My desk was too close to the noise. Zach was passed out, and I wanted to put him down.

But where?

I couldn't put him on the couch. He'd roll off. And I couldn't leave him on the floor. One of the Guardians running around might trip over the poor thing. My attention swept around the room while I considered my options. That's when I saw the buffet server against the far wall. The lower drawer was the perfect size for a makeshift crib.

I placed Zach on the floor beside me while I emptied the contents of the drawer. Using pillows from the couch, and clean towels from the bathroom, I padded the inside and placed Zach inside. Kids slept like the dead, and I envied Skye's son. He didn't twitch as I settled him in.

I left the door to Forest's office open and watched Forest's team as they methodically moved all their gear up to the helipad. My phone beeped with a text from the pilot, and I went in search of Forest.

He stood like a mountain, legs spread on a broad base to support his towering form. With his arms crossed over his massive chest and biceps flexed with menace, he looked every bit the part of a Norse god presiding over his subjects.

Three men crouched before him, duffle bags open in various stages of packing. The teams arrived fully kitted out, but Forest demanded they check their gear one last time before heading up to the helipad.

There were three teams in total—Alpha and Bravo, the Guardians, a para-military force, and Skye's special ops medical team.

All of the Guardians had been recruited from special operations forces, ex-military who now found themselves supplied with top-tier equipment and all the technical whizbangs they needed. Forest spared no expense when it came to the needs of his men.

"Hey, boss." I approached from behind him. "The first helicopter is five minutes out."

He didn't turn around or acknowledge me in any way. Instead, he bellowed, relaying my message. "Five minutes. Get your asses in gear, ladies! We leave with or without you."

All bluster, Forest wouldn't leave without his team. I glanced around but didn't see Skye. Surely, she wouldn't leave without saying goodbye. I wanted to look for her, but I couldn't stray too far from Forest's office because of Zach.

I leaned against the doorjamb, anxiously watching the men empty the lobby of their gear. Before long, it was just me and the quiet of a deserted hall.

Forest didn't say goodbye. Not that I expected it. The man barely acknowledged my existence, and only when he needed something. Well, to hell with that.

And what happened to Skye?

It took no time to scoop little Zach into my arms and head to the helipad at the top of the building. I didn't know how Zach would respond to the noise, but he deserved to say goodbye to his mom.

When the elevator doors opened, a very nervous Skye glanced at me.

"Oh, you didn't need to bring him up. I was going to come down to say goodbye."

"I thought this would be easier. Your brother is ready to go, and I knew he wouldn't be happy if you returned to the office."

Skye glanced over her shoulder, where Forest hovered outside the helicopter. They had eighteen total in addition to all their gear. The team would split in two, and a second helicopter hovered waiting for the first to load.

Forest shut the doors to the first helicopter, thumped the metal, then moved to a safe distance on the opposite side of the roof. The first helicopter took off while Skye pulled little Zach out of my grip and into her arms. We turned our backs to the wind kicked up by the helicopter's blades, and Skye cupped her hand over little Zach's ears. Her son didn't even move.

Kids were truly amazing. I couldn't remember the last time I'd slept that deeply.

"You be good to Auntie Sara." Gently, she kissed little Zach's forehead and hugged him hard. "Take care of my boy."

"You know I will." I kept my voice light, hoping my lack of stress would help relieve some of the burden Skye shouldered. Torn between staying with her son and being by her brother's side, she didn't look like she wanted to let her son go, but she reluctantly transferred Zach back into my arms.

"I have tons of fun stuff planned." I wanted her to know Zach would be in good hands. "We're going to have the best time, and you won't have to worry about him at all." I adjusted Zach on my hip and cradled his head against my shoulder.

I was a little surprised she was on this mission. In a support role only, her team was there in the event someone needed emergency medical care. I cringed about what that implied.

Skye's team was trained in surgical special ops and providing life-saving care in the most austere environments. But then, I understood the importance of this particular operation.

"Thank you for watching him. I don't know when we'll be back, but it can't be more than a couple of days. Ash will probably check in with you tomorrow by phone." She fluttered kisses over Zach's eyes and gave him one last squeeze while giving me last-minute instructions I didn't need.

I understood her nervousness. Skye and Ash were new parents. This wouldn't be the first time I watched little Zach overnight, but it would be the first time he was away from his mother for more than a day.

I understood her concern, but I also sympathized with her need to be with her brother. Together, they would be closing out a very dark chapter of their lives.

The second helicopter touched down. The remainder of the team loaded their gear and climbed on board. Wind buffeted me, and the whine of the rotors made it hard to hear, even shouting. However, one sound cut through all the noise.

"Come on, Skye! Get your ass over here. He's a baby. He doesn't even know you're there."

Skye glanced over her shoulder, then turned back and rolled her eyes. "My brother can be a royal asshole at times. He's lucky I love him." She kissed Zach. "Be back before you know it."

Skye wrapped little Zach and me in a hug then jogged over to the waiting helicopter. Forest scowled at her while Ryker extended a hand to help her into the helicopter.

I waved goodbye, but Forest ignored me. Someday, I would train Forest in standard human social conventions. He studied people but didn't understand the nuances of nonverbal communication, or the importance of a wave goodbye.

The door to the helicopter closed, and the rotors spun up. Buffeting winds whipped at my clothes and messed up my hair. How Zach slept through all the noise was a miracle, but the little angel didn't lift his head.

I continued waving. I knew Skye waved back. Forest? He probably forgot I existed the moment I was out of his sight.

Then my phone rang. It rang with the most annoying ringtone on the planet. "The Flight of the Valkyries" blared out of my phone, and I glanced down at Forest's text.

Forest: CU L8R

I laughed. He was always putting that damn ringtone on my phone. I texted him back.

Me: Save the world!

He didn't respond. Not that I expected him too.

"Well, Zach?" I kissed the top of his head. "I guess it's just you and me for the next few days."

I took Zach downstairs and was surprised when the janitorial team called. They were early and were having problems with their access badges. I buzzed them up. Forest and his team had left a mess behind.

Hugging Zach tight to my chest, I went to grab my purse and his diaper bag. We were going to have so much fun.

Chapter Six

FOREST

I hated confining spaces. The shell of the helicopter wrapped around me and shut me in darkness. It reminded me of things that needed to stay in the past. Memories flooded my mind; dark, ugly things that grew and took root.

I tugged at my collar, finding it hard to breathe. With one hand pressed against the inner shell of the helicopter, I gripped my knee to keep it from bouncing.

The fucker wouldn't stay still.

I tried to hold it in place, but that proved impossible.

I felt confined, locked in the darkness where bad things happened to little boys.

"Forest..." A soft voice skittered through my consciousness.

All I could hear was the steady whomp, whomp, whomp of the helicopter as it cut through the sky. The powerful oscillations of the engine worked their way deep into my lungs and smothered me. I tried sucking in air, but the deep vibrations made that impossible.

My mouth opened and closed. A tingling sensation pricked my lips. Like a guppy out of water, I tried sucking in air, but nothing moved into my lungs.

I couldn't breathe.

"Forest?" A voice drew closer. Anxious, the voice clawed at me with its incessant buzz.

My lids pinched together as I struggled to make sense of my surroundings. My chest tried to move, but a steel band encircled it and prevented me from taking in a life-saving breath.

"Forest!" That voice shouted somewhere in front of me. The heat of its breath brushed across my cheeks. It whispered over my lips and tickled the tip of my nose.

"What's wrong with him?" That voice was different; distant, muffled, and barely comprehensible, it spoke of something wrong.

A buzzing irritation scraped at my senses.

"He's flipping the hell out," it said.

"He's fine," the first voice replied. "I've seen this before."

Something touched my leg. A delicate sensation, it was soft, warm, and comforting, but concerning. It was too intimate.

Too close.

Too much in my space.

It did things; things my insides twisted and turned into filth and allowed ugly things to grow inside of me. Ravenous needs. Base desires I craved with a feral hunger.

I pried my lids apart, then jerked back when I realized that voice belonged to Skye. She touched my hand, and I recoiled from the contact. Shaking the remnants of her delicate touch off my body, I tried to clear my head, control my body, and erase errant thoughts.

Skye did nothing to show my actions upset her. She knew what her touch did to me, and my aversion wasn't aimed at her. She wasn't the issue. It was what her touch did to me that I loathed.

Demons wrestled within me, and she accepted what that meant. My sister loved me unconditionally, even when that meant I couldn't stand to have her touch me.

"Bean," Skye screamed at me. "Forest, come back to me. You're safe. We're safe. I'm okay. You're okay. We're okay. Beanpole!" She unbuckled and stood over me. But she was too close. Her fingers snapped in front of my eyes.

Snap. Snap. Snap!

I expected to hear the crisp pop of her fingers, but the droning vibrations overpowered all sound.

Her light floral perfume flooded my senses, and her hot breath fluttered over my skin. Recoiling in horror, my gut filled with self-loathing and disgust with memories of what I'd done to her. I was going to puke. My heart accelerated full-throttle with a panic I couldn't control.

"Ah shit," she said. "Now, he's freaking out."

"What's wrong?" The deeper voice asked with concern.

"One of his fits." Skye's expression softened. She vented a soul-deep sigh and pressed her lips together with determination. "Ryker, can you hold him down?"

"Seriously? You think I can hold down the Viking king?"

"Just do it."

Two vice grips encircled my arms as Skye withdrew. But that was a ruse. She merely shifted to sit beside me, where she could yell into my ear.

I could move if I wanted. I could overpower Ryker and push him away, but I didn't. I didn't because I needed the restraint to ground me. I liked the feel of being overpowered, even if that disgusted me too.

"Breathe, Bean, just breathe. Grab ahold of my voice and follow it to the light. I've got you. Bean...I'll never let anything happen to you again."

Her hand hovered over mine, and the fine hairs on my arms lifted. It was always this way around her. I'd been getting better, but still had problems with her touch.

The horrible things I'd done to her were not my fault. I knew this, but it didn't change the fact there had been a time when I derived pleasure from hurting the one person who loved me unconditionally, flaws and all.

There wasn't another human on the planet who did that.

Above our heads, long rotors cut through the air. We flew over the city with each chop rattling the passenger cabin. It closed in around me like a cage.

"Come back to me. Forest. Come back."

I was in a helicopter.

It was night.

This was not a cage.

I was not in that basement.

My entire body buzzed.

It's not a cage.

But that's not what my mind thought. It believed I was twelve again, locked in the cage in the basement, where I entertained monstrous men with my pain.

Ryker's grip tightened, and I sank into the sensation.

A whole-body shiver overtook me as I struggled to clear my head.

"Bean, come back to me." Skye's voice anchored me, and I began the long climb back to reality by following it to its end.

I was not in a cage surrounded by the impenetrable dark.

I was no longer that scared little boy.

I was in a helicopter with my sister and my men.

And I was a fucking giant who no longer feared other men. I wasn't afraid of Snowden anymore. I was the Viking king, and I would be victorious.

"Come on, Forest." Skye soothed, using her voice to guide me back. "There you go. Come back to me."

The vice on my arms relaxed and then released as the steel band around my chest eased. I took in a slow, measured breath.

My eyes opened, and I stared, not into Skye's eyes, but rather Ryker Lyons' vibrant green orbs which spiked with concern and worry.

I gave a slow blink and took another breath. "I'm good."

I didn't turn my head to glance at Skye. I couldn't face her. Not after the direction my thoughts had traveled. It would take a moment before I could look at her again and not do so with the shame and regret which filled nearly every moment of my life.

Usually, I kept that ugliness locked up tight, but I was off tonight.

Things were leaking out that had no business seeing the light of day; demons I had conquered, or so I thought.

"What the fuck was that?" Ryker backed away and settled into the seat opposite me. A glance around the cabin revealed multiple sets of eyes staring at me.

"Panic attack," Skye explained my reaction to whomever cared while I closed my eyes in shame.

My job was to lead this task force. Now, they doubted my sanity. I'd just lost my ever-loving shit in front of my men.

Skye sat beside me and was buckled in. If anything happened to her during this operation, her husband would have my balls strung up in a sling.

But nothing would happen to Skye.

Her role kept her far from danger. I was the one rushing in, and we hadn't stopped arguing about that. From the look on her face, we'd be having another conversation.

"You don't need to—" she began.

It looked like we were having it now.

"You're not talking me out of this."

"But Forest, you can't even get in the helicopter which is taking you to a plane, which will take you to another helicopter which... will take you to him." She gave an exasperated huff. "Come on. This is an obvious trigger. Your skill set is not a frontline operative. You know this."

I knew it.

Skye was right.

She always was.

It's what I loved about her.

That didn't mean I had to agree. My computer skills pulled us out of the deepest hell. I played the market and turned ten dollars into a hundred.

A hundred into a thousand.

Thousands into millions.

And millions to billions.

I did that.

Me, my computers, and my unique brain.

Next to Skye, computers were my best friends. They didn't leak messy feelings all over the place like people. I understood computers and they understood me.

People, on the other hand?

They confused the hell out of me, and I never got it right.

But Skye wasn't taking this from me.

I'd cracked the code on human emotions by studying people. I felt pretty confident in my abilities to navigate the landmine of nonverbal body language and innuendo in spoken conversation.

My body was a tool I honed to the sharpest edge. I forced Skye to take some of the self-defense classes I took, but I was a master of several martial arts and various fighting techniques.

And I was fucking huge.

My body was a weapon, and I would bring that to the fight against Snowden.

Skye didn't know it, but this wasn't a catch and recovery operation. Snowden wasn't going to meet his end by a jury of his peers. I had every intention of bringing Snowden down and making sure he never took another breath, or hurt another child, ever again.

My sister would not approve.

So, I didn't tell her about my plans.

Instead, I came apart in the back of the damn helicopter on the very first leg of our operation.

Fucking PTSD.

"I'm going." I looked hard into her eyes. "I'll be there when we take him down. I want him to know I'm the one who did it."

"But Forest, you're not trained for this."

"I've spent my entire adult life training for exactly this."

I never served in the military—Asperger's was a disqualifying condition—but that didn't mean I didn't train with the best the military had to offer.

Every man and woman on my team were members of special operations teams. I had former SEALs, Delta operatives, and Skye's medical team, which were a part of the Air Force's Special Ops Surgical team, working for me.

I was the commander of my little army.

"I'm going." I crossed my arms over my chest and turned away. Conversation over.

But she poked me. "We're not done." My sister poked me again.

"We're done." My exaggerated, slow blink brought a huff from her tiny little mouth.

"Are not."

"Are so."

"Dammit, Forest, why won't you listen to reason?"

"When you're ready to accept why I need to be there, I'll listen to the words flapping out of your mouth. Until then, you have nothing to say I want to hear."

She opened her mouth to argue, but I held up my index finger, silencing her.

"You don't get it. I need to do this. I can't sit behind the computer screen while others go in. And I have trained for this. I've trained for over a decade. You don't need to worry about me."

"If that's so, then why did you have a meltdown? You can't do that in front of Snowden. He'll eat you alive."

Snowden had already done far worse.

I had no answer for my sister. She could be right for all I knew. Except, this was something I had to do.

The helicopters took my team to the airport where we offloaded, then reloaded all our gear into one of my corporate jets.

I had my shit together and felt pumped to get started.

That would have to wait because our flight would take over half a day. I preferred the plane to the cramped quarters and the noise of the helicopter, and I liked my company's private jet.

Every seat was one of those first-class pods. We had a sixteen-hour flight ahead of us, and I wanted everyone well-rested. In the middle of the plane, there were two private suites walled off from everyone else. I took one and gave the other to my sister.

At least that was the plan.

Instead, Skye, Ryker, and Tia shoved inside the cramped space of my not so private retreat.

These were more than friends. Skye was family. Tia had been

one of my early rescues—Sara had been the first—Tia went to nursing school, wound up working in Skye's emergency department, where Skye convinced her to become a certified nurse anesthetist.

Against my wishes, Tia refused all scholarships from our foster rescue foundation. Instead, she signed up for the military and went to nurse anesthetist school on the military's dime.

Tia had wanted to see the world.

The military sent her to Afghanistan, where she and Ryker got together.

I met Ryker at Bagram Air Base, where he blew me away with his skill on the bass guitar. Angel Fire had plans to go on tour in the Afghanistan theater, and he saved the day after a bus accident took out Angel Fire's bassist, Bent.

While Ryker carried the tour, the military man who played on stage with the rock legends who were Angel Fire, Bent slowly recovered the use of his busted-up arm. Ryker and Tia hooked up, something that cost Tia her career, but for me, everything worked out perfectly.

I got two top-notch special ops, surgical team members, to anchor Skye's medical team. Bent got better with the help of a perky physical therapist he hated…at least until Piper got ahold of him.

Thoughts of Piper Rains had me thinking about her brother, and I hoped to hell my intelligence was correct. Her brother had been abducted, lost as far as we knew, but I found him and promised Piper I would bring her brother home.

I just hoped he hadn't died in Snowden's death matches. It had taken far too long to get to this point.

All in all, for a boy who lost his parents, I had found a new family along the way. I counted myself lucky and blessed.

They were also a royal pain in my ass because Skye had been talking to Ryker and Tia. This was a last-ditch intervention.

"You know…" Ryker leaned against the doorframe. "Most commanding officers stay in Command and Control, monitoring the troops from there."

"I'm going," I said.

"Ryker has a point." Tia placed her hand on my arm. "You can direct from there, as things change, and they always do, it'll be up to you to react, respond, and redirect."

"I'm going." I practically growled out the words.

"Forest, I think you're letting your emotions cloud your judgment on this one." Skye wrung her hands, wanting to touch me, but knowing she couldn't.

"I don't give a flying fuck what you think. I'm going to be the one who takes him down. I want him to see my face when I do it."

I wanted my face to be the last thing the bastard ever saw.

Skye would want to save me from that. She didn't want my soul sullied by murder.

She should know.

That was the weight she bore every day. Skye killed our foster father to keep me safe. When she learned Snowden planned to take me and put me in the death matches, she did what it took to free us.

I'd let her carry that burden for far too long. It was time I stepped up and took care of the rest.

I crossed my arms over my broad chest and stared down at all of them.

"What I think is that we're getting ready to take off. The three of you need to take your seats, buckle up, and put your tray tables in their full and upright position. Settle in, sit back and relax. Enjoy your damn flight, and leave me the fuck alone. I'm going in with my team, and there's nothing the three of you can say to change that."

Ryker gave Tia a look. "Come on, T, the boss has spoken." He raised his hands, palms out in surrender, and gave a jerk of his head.

"Let's find our seats and strap in. It looks like this is going to be a bumpy ride." Tia gave Skye a sympathetic look, then took hold of one of Ryker's hands.

Her emphasis on that word had me gritting my teeth, and I gave her an irritated look, which she ignored. Tia pulled Ryker to the back to find their seats while Skye stood in the doorway with her tiny fists bunched up.

"We're not talking about this anymore," I said. "I'm going."

"Oh, I know you are, you frustrating, mountain of a man, but I'm allowed to be worried. When was the last time you lost it like that? What's going to happen when you see him again?"

"Skye…"

"I know you're a tough guy now. But Snowden? Seeing him is going to trigger you, and we can't afford anything like what happened in the helicopter to happen during this mission."

She pointed outside my cabin toward our team.

"You have twelve highly trained military operatives who lived and breathed this kind of stuff when they were in the military. You've run them ragged with training, but they know how to dissociate their emotions from the mission. You don't."

"So?"

"It makes you a liability. Why can't you see that?"

"Why can't you have a little faith in me? Why can't you see why I need to be there?"

"I know why you want to go. I do, but I don't see this ending well."

"I'm not that little boy anymore. I'm not afraid of the dark."

Skye took in a deep breath. "I know, Forest. I do. You're not my little beanpole anymore, but that doesn't mean I don't worry."

I did something I rarely did. I reached out and traced the line of her jaw with the back of my knuckles. That was the only kind of touch I could handle without going into cataleptic shock.

"I love that you worry about me. It means a lot. But I need you to have faith in me. Can you do that for me, my summer sky? Can you have faith in me?"

She blew out a frustrated breath and looked up. "I will, Bean. I don't like it, but I'll try."

"Good. Now, try to get some sleep. Once we land, we're going to hit the ground running."

"Promise you'll be safe."

"I'll do my best."

"Promise you won't need me."

She didn't mean her.

Skye meant her medical team.

I didn't think we'd be walking into a firing match. We were prepared, and I didn't believe Snowden would be that paranoid that we would face any real resistance.

We were going to swim in under the radar, sneak into the event, and grab Snowden before anyone could blink.

Then, I would kill him.

I anticipated no problems.

Chapter Seven

FOREST

WE LEFT BEFORE MIDNIGHT CENTRAL STANDARD TIME AND FOUND ourselves halfway around the world in the Philippines sixteen hours later. We'd crossed the international date line, which meant while it felt like early evening to us, the people of Manilla were waking up to a new day.

My team rested on the flight. We were going to struggle with jet lag but would get through it.

Xavier had his men meet us at the airport, and when I glanced out the window, I could see we would be traveling in style. He'd chartered a luxury bus.

I hopped down the stairs and breathed in the humid air as Ben Chambers beamed up at me. Sweat beaded my brow instantaneously. The stifling heat made it hard to breathe.

Standing beside Ben were the members of his team: Chad, Bay, and Mel. Like my men, they were former military special ops, trained to get in and get out without being seen and to fight as dirty as it took to get the mission done.

"Hey, Forest." Ben held out his hand, and we shook. "How was the flight?"

"Not bad."

Skye tried to talk to me after we took off, but I pushed her out of my tiny cabin, popped some melatonin, and fell into a dreamless sleep. My body was well-rested and eager to get things going. I considered that a win.

Chad, Bay, and Mel stepped forward, shaking my hand and thumping my back. I could do without all the back thumping, but it seemed to be a thing with these men.

"We've got luxury wheels for you." Mel gestured to the motorcoach.

"Is Xavier here?"

"He'll meet up with us later." Ben stepped forward and opened his arms wide for Skye. "How've you been, sweetie? How's the kid?"

"He's getting bigger every day. Thanks." Skye went for the hug instead of shaking hands.

"Hey, T." Ben passed Skye to Chad, who buried her in a hug. Tia folded into Ben's embrace while he gave Ryker a smirk. "Your girl smells like heaven."

Ryker pulled Tia out of Ben's grip, then swung out his hand to shake. They did the chest bump thing and followed it with a smack to the back.

I rolled my eyes through the whole thing.

Skye hugged Bay and Mel, stepping back as Tia greeted the men. Ryker followed along behind the women.

Was this a damn reunion or a fucking operation?

The last time we'd all been together had been when we'd taken Zane Carson down.

Josh Davenport had mocked up a snuff operation, pretending to kill his twin brother's slave, Kate Summers, in front of Carson as a demonstration of a new service he planned to offer.

Carson, with Snowden, showed more than a little interest in expanding their business, peddling death for entertainment. Unfortunately for Carson, Josh's invitation to one of their matches resulted in Carson's death. Unfortunately for me, it sent Snowden running for cover.

I would say the whole thing set back my operation, except I had nothing on Snowden before Josh getting involved. He recovered

Carson's cell phone, which, in a roundabout way, finally led me to Snowden.

And I do mean roundabout.

Snowden went to ground after that disastrous event. His death matches stopped, putting a massive dent in his bottom line. The man was hungry, but we found him again, and the bastard was up to his old tricks.

During Josh's operation, we rescued a score of young boys consigned to live or die in Snowden and Carson's sick game, as well as far too many young girls pressed into the slave trade. Snowden had his fingers in a lot of really disgusting shit. All that would end before the sun set.

We were kind of like freedom fighters reuniting to take down the next big bad guy on the list, but that didn't mean we had to do all the chest-bumping and back-thumping crap.

What a waste of time.

"We going to shoot the shit all day?" I glanced at Ben and what seemed the ponderously slow loading of the bus. "Or are we going to get this show on the road? Xavier did say our timetable was tight."

I glanced at my watch and did a little mental math taking into account the length of our flight and the change in time zones. We were going to be cutting things close and didn't have time to dick around.

"Everybody on board!" I shouted to my team, who were unloading the jet and putting everything on the bus.

My team climbed on board the bus while I wiped the sweat from my brow. It was fucking hot in Manilla.

Our ride lasted longer than I would have liked. The roads were passable at best and scary as shit the rest of the time. Eventually, we pulled into a huge compound surrounded by massive cinderblock walls. Mel stopped the bus in a courtyard where two military helicopters sat with their rotors anchored to the ground.

I may have my hand in a lot of shit, but my businesses were above board and legal. Xavier straddled the line between two worlds, and I was curious as shit about how he managed to obtain not one, but two helicopters.

Mel opened the door of the bus, and I was the first to climb out.

Ben followed. "Have your team park their gear over there." He pointed to an open garage. "We'll meet inside and get everyone briefed."

"How long do we have?"

"A few hours to make our insertion. You'll be dropping-in a little over a half-mile offshore."

Everyone went to work. I didn't mess with my gear. Someone would sort it out and bring me what I wanted; there were perks to being the boss.

Skye stuck tight to my side with her disapproving frown front and center. Tia and Ryker, along with their trauma surgeon, Dr. Eli Tool, went with my men to set their gear aside. Strictly support, the chances of us needing their particular skill set amounted to zero.

They were here as a concession to Skye. She told me long ago if there was a chance of bullets flying, she would be there to patch up the damage.

We followed Ben inside and found ourselves gathered around a large dining table. Maps cluttered the top reminding me of a wartime strategy session. I supposed that wasn't far off. However, we had other assets. Computer screens covered the far wall. Radar, weather, and views from the nose cone of our drone, among other things, were continuously updated.

"Where's Xavier?"

"Right here." A voice called out from behind me, and I spun around.

Xavier greeted me with warm eyes and a firm handshake. "How was the flight?"

"Long, but comfortable."

"Good. Your team doesn't have much downtime. We're on the clock." Xavier reached out to Skye and pulled her into a hug. "Skye Dean, you're beautiful as always; positively radiant." His eyes narrowed in thought. "How's the little one?"

Why did everyone keep asking about her kid? I didn't get why they bothered with the extraneous talk.

"Zach is great, getting bigger every day." My sister beamed whenever talking about her kid.

I got it. Little Zach was cute, but he smelled funny, and there didn't seem to be much going on behind his eyes. Maybe when he got older, he'd be more interesting. Not that my sister cared. She thought Zach was a genius because he could blow bubbles with his spit. I'd say the jury was out on that.

"And the husband?" Xavier released Skye from the hug but continued to hold her at arm's length. "Still rockin' it? He's on tour, right?"

"Still rocking it." A smile graced my sister's face. It did whenever she thought about Ash. "He's happy to be playing with Angel Fire, misses his kid, though."

"I'm sure that's not all he's missing." Xavier's gaze cut downward, lingering a little too long on Skye's midsection. Before I could think about that too much, he pulled Skye into a hug and kissed her cheek. He then glanced at me. "Let's get this party started."

"Is Raven here?" Skye glanced around the dining room and craned her neck to look into an adjoining living space. "I don't see her."

"She is." The corner of Xavier's lips pulled up in a smirk. "A bit tied up right now but will be down shortly."

I couldn't help but laugh.

With Xavier, that comment could be taken literally. The man was kinky as fuck, but we needed Raven on this operation, and Xavier wasn't one to dick around.

I was virtually sure Raven was busy elsewhere, but not literally tied up in Xavier's bed, or whatever dungeon he had set up in this godforsaken place.

Skye's face flushed, and she glanced away. She wasn't into that kind of thing. My poor, vanilla sister had no idea what she was missing. Kink was liberating and fun.

I had a few fetishes of my own. Unlike Xavier, I wasn't a strict dominant when it came to sex. I wasn't submissive either. I was what they called a switch, alternating between being the top or bottom. I liked to fight for sex, the more aggressive, the better. And, if another man could best me, then I let him have all of me. If not, things generally didn't work out for long.

Skye worried about my sexual appetite and the number of men who passed through my bed. We agreed on two things. I would get tested regularly, and she wouldn't pry.

It kept things civil between us.

"Well, tell me where she is." Skye glanced at the men streaming in. "There's a little too much testosterone floating around here. I need a break from all the alpha attitudes clotting the air."

The pointed look she gave me did not go unnoticed, although I refused to rise to the bait.

Xavier's head tipped back. He belted out a deep laugh, and then his attention shifted to me.

"I bet it is." He pointed to a set of stairs leading up. "She's in the library upstairs with Mitzy. The two of them are finishing setting up Command and Control. You should go check out the drones we got. Talk about fun toys."

"Boys and their toys." Skye's smile slipped into a tiny laugh. She flapped her hand at me. "See you later, Bean. Try not to be too much of an ass and let your men do what they've trained for."

Skye left us and went to where Ryker, Tia, and Eli had set aside their team's medical gear. She said something, pointed up the stairs, then exited the chaos.

"You ready for this?" Xavier's sharp gaze cut to me. The man was a few inches shorter than me. Most men were, but I felt pinned beneath his cutting gaze.

"I'm ready."

"Good. You've got ten minutes to prep your team, then meet in the ready room to go over details.

"Ready room?"

"Converted ballroom. This place was impressive in its heyday. Your girl, Mitzy, has a rather impressive briefing ready for us."

The mansion Xavier appropriated sprawled across extensive

grounds, encircled by high concrete walls, it was the perfect place to set up our base operations.

I'd already counted more fountains than I cared. They were all dried up with scraggly weeds clinging to life in the muck, which had settled in the basins.

Everywhere I looked, decay greeted my eyes. Plaster flaked off the walls. Shreds of curtains dangled from rods that barely clung to the walls. The marbled floors were chipped and cracked. Dirt and dust covered every surface.

I glanced over my shoulder at the organized chaos that was my team. They didn't need me to tell them what to do.

"I'd like to check out Command and Control."

I'd trained Mitzy in most of the surveillance we needed, and we brought along our VR gear. That was likely what Xavier meant when he said he was impressed by the briefing Mitzy planned.

Before my men stepped a foot on the private island, we would see it in virtual reality.

I wanted no surprises.

Xavier's drones had been collecting the data we needed. Paired with what Mitzy dug up from local records, we should have a realistic set up for a dry run.

Ben Chambers trotted up and stopped in front of Xavier. He gave the slightest of bows in deference to his boss and the man he called Master.

"Sir, we're ready."

"Good job." Xavier gave a slight nod.

I swear Ben beamed beneath the praise.

"Make sure Forest's team is in the ready room." Xavier glanced at his watch. "Seven minutes."

"Yes, sir." Ben pivoted and jogged back to where my guys set up.

His team leaned against the wall, watching the commotion. They would be joining me. Ben, Mel, Bay, and Chad were specialists in covert operations. Their one job was to keep me safe.

Skye wasn't the only one who had concerns about my presence on this mission.

It had been one of the first arguments Xavier and I had.

I won.

He lost.

But I was the one who conceded.

The man had a will about him that defied description.

I had the training, the best in the world, but never served in the military, and I'd never seen combat. These men had. They had experience with the real deal, not the mockups I arranged. To them, I was a pretend wannabe, aka, a liability.

They could keep me safe all they wanted.

They didn't understand the truth.

Chapter Eight

FOREST

Xavier walked with me as we joined the tech team upstairs. I expected the same degree of chaos up there, although I shouldn't have.

Mitzy's OCD wouldn't allow such a thing.

My tech team had arrived ahead of us, courtesy of Xavier. They'd been in place less than a day but looked like they were long-term residents. Power cables snaked through the room, all neatly bound together with pink zip-ties. The tables were straight; monitors placed precisely so. There was no chaos in Mitzy's perfectly ordered world.

Her obsessive nature had everything labeled in a range of pastel pinks and blues with neon yellow, orange, and greens sprinkled through for good measure.

"Forest!" Mitzy's shriek had my shoulders lifting to my ears. The petite pixie with her psychedelic hair ran toward me.

She wasn't going to hug me. The girl was going to hug-hug me, and she did it because she knew how much I hated to be touched by girls.

Mitzy launched into my arms and wrapped her petite body

around mine. Her arms barely wrapped around my midsection, and I had no fucking clue why she had to hang on me like a monkey.

Her stick-thin legs curled around my hips while the clunky heels of her military boots dug into my ass.

I did what any man would do in my situation. My arms wrapped around her, touching without touching anything I shouldn't, followed by peeling the little monkey off my body.

"It's good to see you." I pulled at her waist, trying to get her off, but she buried her head against my chest. I tugged and pulled. I yanked at her ankles while she clung to my neck. Finally, I deposited her on her feet.

"You, boss, are cutting things close." She gave another tiny squeeze. "We're ready to kick some ass."

Skye stood a few feet away, a smirk planted on her face, while a gorgeous woman with raven-black hair looked on with a bemused expression.

Raven took me in from head to toe, then passed right on by me where her eyes smoldered as she looked at her Master.

"We're ready, Master."

"Good girl." Xavier stepped into the room, entirely at ease with being in charge.

He went to Raven, cupped her chin, and dragged his thumb over her lips.

Raven leaned into his touch, and her dark, sultry eyes slowly closed.

"Mitzy," Xavier said, "how about you give Forest a run down."

Mitzy's eyes lit up. "Okay, first communications. Since we're dropping you offshore, I found these amazing earbuds. You won't wear them, obviously, on your dive, but once you hit land, put them in, and we'll be in touch. Snowden's people have radar set up, but they're more concerned with boat traffic. Our drones will be flying above their visibility plane, and your coms will patch through the drones. That'll bounce to us. I also have body cams installed on all the vests. I'll be with you the whole way, boss."

I waited for the poor girl to take a breath, but Mitzy spits it all out fast as lightning.

I wasn't sure if I wanted her watching and in my ear the whole way, especially with what I planned. I could take the body armor off to kill Snowden, but that was something I'd have to play by ear.

"Of course, you have all the things: night vision, laser targeting, etcetera. I'm not in charge of weapons, but I'm told the targeting is spot-on. The VR suite is up and running. It's fucking rad. You have to see what I did." Next to me, Mitzy was becoming a virtual reality addict.

A slow spin let me take in the room. Banks of computers heated the air as their processors churned and crunched through data. The whirring of cooling fans drifted through the room. A deep breath brought a flood of comforting scents to my nostrils.

I'd grown up with computers. They had been my safe space. It was the one thing Clark Preston allowed. Our foster father didn't like his kids playing outside. Skye had her books, and I had my computers. In our rooms, we were safe. When called out to serve his sick depravity, we weren't.

Therefore, computers were my solace. I lost myself in them growing up. I understood them. They never lied. There were no messy emotions. They worked the same way I did. Logical. Methodical. Precise.

For an awkward boy growing up, I'd had no real friends, but I had my computers.

The glow from the monitors gave the space an otherworldly feel, and the ever-present tapping of keys and clicking of mouses floated in the background.

Mitzy took me on a tour, showing me each station as I endured the ritualistic greeting of my tech team.

Unlike the men downstairs, we didn't shake hands, slap each other's backs, or bump our chests to measure our brawn against the other.

There was no bravado, no need to show off our strength and determine the pecking order based on that. Here, our brains were our weapons, and our intellect decided where we sat in our unique pecking order.

I took the throne. Mitzy was my Master at Arms, and Raven proved to be an unexpected treasure. I'd never seen a better hacker.

I smiled and nodded. Not once did I have to shake hands. They were my real team; technical geniuses who would make sure the mission went off without a hitch. I didn't think Ben and his team understood the power this team wielded.

"We need to head down for the briefing." Xavier hurried me along.

Mitzy joined us with a little skip to her step.

"Why are you always so damn perky?" My question came out more of a growl but did nothing to Mitzy. In general, she was unfazed by my size. The girl was fearless.

"Because I can't wait for you to see the VR set up."

I couldn't help but roll my eyes.

In addition to Mitzy, Raven accompanied Xavier and me downstairs. He held her hand, keeping her tucked tight to his side. Skye followed behind us with her lips twisted in a disapproving frown.

When we arrived at the ballroom, I was surprised to see all my team gathered. I had two groups of six, Skye's medical team of four, myself, and Xavier's squad with Ben and his men.

Long tables lined the walls with VR headsets perched on top. Distributed through the room, were unique spheroid treadmills. They would allow us to navigate the VR world; walking, running, and crawling as needed, all while staying in place.

Mitzy clapped her hands together, but when that didn't cut through the noise of my men, she put her fingers in her mouth and gave a long, ear-piercing whistle.

The room quieted between one breath and the next. All eyes went to me, as they generally did, but Mitzy lifted her hand over her head. The tips of her fingers barely reached the stubble of my jaw.

"Hello!" Her high-pitched voice cracked as she spoke. "Welcome to our pre-mission briefing."

Mitzy went to one side of the room, while Raven moved to the other side. They each lifted a VR headset over their heads.

"The briefing today will be conducted in a virtual space. Each of you will need to grab a headset and put it on. Raven and I will come around to help you with the treadmills if you need it, but it's pretty simple. Put the goggles over your eyes first. Lift the strap and settle it over your head. Push the red button to activate it."

Raven demonstrated while Mitzy explained.

"That's it," Mitzy continued. "Everything is set and ready. There are earbuds attached to the headsets. Put those in."

Mitzy grabbed an armful of headsets and passed them out to the men directly in front of her. They took them with brows pinched, looked at me, then put them on when I nodded.

Raven came to Xavier and me, handed us our headsets, then went to distribute the rest to my team.

I settled the device over my head, shoved the earbuds in my ears, and turned the thing on.

Immediately, the world around me shifted. No longer was I standing in a dilapidated mansion in Manilla, but rather on the shore of an island with coarse sand beneath my boots, waves gently lapping behind me, and a twenty-foot wall with serpentine wire coiled at the top standing in front of me.

Tropical plants with big, broad, leaves blew in a soft breeze, and a few palm trees soared into the sky, bending out from the wall. Puffy clouds drifted overhead, and the sound of tropical birds called out in the distance.

I saw an immediate problem if this was our planned insertion spot.

While I checked out the VR environment, people began to pop into the world. They stood in tight clusters according to their team designations. Ben, Chad, Bay, and Mel stood in a loose semi-circle around me. Skye, with Ryker, Tia, and their surgeon, materialized down the beach to my right. To my left, my two six-men teams formed up as they entered the virtual space.

To my right, a man and woman checked things out with wide-eyes and gaping mouths. We'd made incredible strides in improving the realism of our virtual reality space and spared no detail. Xavier appeared behind me.

"Well, this is impressive. I can't believe they were able to create this from overhead photos." Xavier looked impressed.

"Knowing Mitzy, it's a conglomeration of satellite, overhead surveillance, and building schematics she dug up from God knows where."

Xavier sniffed. "I'm surprised it doesn't smell like the beach."

"We're working on that. Scent and sensation are problematic. For our gaming platform, we have a skin suit that emulates most sensations, but smell is a sense which so far eludes us."

"I didn't know such a thing was possible." Xavier spun in a small circle. "It looks so real."

No arguing with him there.

The texture overlays for sand, rock, water, and the plants looked spot-on. If I reached down, I could cup the sand in my hands, and my brain would tell me it ran through my fingers.

Xavier had no idea how realistic we could make this. Mitzy brought her A-game to this simulation. She appeared in front of me with her spiky psychedelic hair and a damn unicorn horn planted in the center of her forehead.

She fisted her hands on her hips and gave me a look as if she defied me to say anything about the damn horn. I wisely kept my thoughts to myself.

In this space, she didn't need to compete to be heard. Mitzy had control over all sound and muted people while she went over a brief introduction of the simulation and what we could expect.

"It's going to be dark when you arrive, but for this simulation, I've kept us in daylight. Once we're done, you'll have an opportunity to walk around and get acquainted with the layout. I believe Xavier has intel about the night's festivities and plan of attack. You'll want to run through that at least once, but you'll have about twenty minutes to move through the space. You do not have to go as a team, although if you want to, that's fine. The headsets will keep up with your movements."

Mitzy gave a few more tips before handing things over to Xavier. He briefed us on attendees, arrival times, what they knew about security, and our timetable. After he finished, he turned the briefing over to me.

I clapped my hands together. "All right. We know what we need to do. You have twenty minutes to look around, and then we'll reset everyone to the beach. Skye, your team is free to look around, but once we get back together, it will only be ops team members. We'll run through things as many times as we can before we load up in the helicopters."

All our dive gear was being loaded on the helicopters as we spoke. All we'd have to do is change into our drysuits and go. Not a fan of water, I wasn't looking forward to the dive.

I set off with Ben while Chad, Bay, and Mel went to check out the security on the walls. For the simulation, Ben and I merely stepped through into the expansive grounds of the estate inside.

A chill ran through me. This was Snowden's lair; only this time, I wouldn't be his victim. I came with an avenging force to take him down.

Music piped into my ears. "The Flight of the Valkyries" brought a grin to my face. Sara hated the song, which is why I changed out her ringtones whenever she wasn't looking, but this was my song.

We were avenging angels coming to enact a profound justice on a monster.

Chapter Nine

FOREST

I LET MY TEAM EXPLORE MITZY'S VR SCENARIO AND FAMILIARIZE themselves with the layout of Snowden's compound. I took one run through the facility, imprinting every room, hall, stairway, and exit into my memory.

It was the best we could do to control the situation. The Fog of War wasn't foggy without reason. Things came up no one expected. That would be our challenge.

Adapt and overcome.

I had the best team in the world by my side to do just that.

We weren't going to adapt and overcome. We were going to be victorious.

After we familiarized ourselves with the layout of Snowden's estate, we went about how to breach the walls, which entrances to take, and where we thought Snowden would be when we got there.

There had been a time when Xavier would have been on the invite list, but his business with Snowden blew up when Zane Carson went down.

"This is a major event for Snowden's enterprise." Xavier shifted beside me.

Xavier and I stood in an inner courtyard where the bulk of the party would take place. I remained in awe of Mitzy's ability to replicate the real thing in this virtual space.

"Seems a risky endeavor," I said.

"It is, but understandable. Most of those on the invite list are clients, and others are business associates being vetted for their potential interest."

Revulsion ripped through me. Sometimes, Xavier had a way of speaking about the slave trade as if it was nothing more than talking about the weather.

Vetted for their interest?

How did that happen exactly? After a board meeting, did these men hang out by the water cooler and casually drop in a mention about Hey, Frank, you interested in fucking a little girl? Or Tom, you like boxing, right? Would you be interested in watching boys fight to the death?

How did that ever come up in conversation?

I knew the answer.

We weren't dealing with sane men. Unfortunately, Xavier understood this world far better than I ever would. I could only see it through the lens of a previous victim.

Xavier and I pulled off our VR headsets and stood to the side while my men ran several drills. Our conversation would be private this way.

"After we sent him to ground with Carson's death, his bottom line took a hit." Xavier scratched at his jaw. "We all but buried his death matches, and he lost business as a result. A lot of his clients are concerned his clientele list got out, and that makes them nervous. Many have cut ties."

Snowden's list had got out. I had it, but we hadn't turned it over to the authorities. Raven, Mitzy, and I launched cyber warfare on Snowden's clients. I wanted to take them down by hitting their bottom line.

If they didn't have the cash to feed their depraved appetites, then Snowden lost clients. The goal was to take down the entire organization, and we were working on it, one stone at a time.

"I wish we'd done more to save more kids." I puffed out a sigh and tilted my head back to stare at the crumbling majesty that had once been present in the estate Xavier appropriated for our headquarters.

Everything decayed with the relentless march of time. I had billions at my disposal and owned several homes that rivaled this place. Someday, those would fade. It was unrealistic to think otherwise.

Everything changed.

"Unfortunately, Josh did little to impact Snowden's sex-trafficking organization." Xavier picked his way around my men, who still ran drills in the virtual landscape Mitzy created. I followed in his wake.

"And where is he? Will he be joining us?"

Xavier shook his head. "Josh is out of this. He wants no part in this world, not after what we did to him. Besides, his slave, Clara, is nearly due. Did you hear they're expecting twins?"

"No, kidding?"

I found that interesting, considering Josh was a twin. His twin brother, Jake, introduced me to Kate Summers, and through her, I found the vivacious Mitzy and stole her for myself.

"I can understand him wanting distance from all of this." An unexpected twinge rippled through me.

Everyone around me seemed to be finding their one true love and was settling down. Skye and Ash were building their family. Ryker and Tia were engaged. Bent had Piper; no kids yet. Thick-headed Bash found the love of his life. He'd also discovered he was a father to a very feisty teenager. Even Xavier found Raven.

I had no one.

Xavier cleared his throat. "He rescued scores of boys and girls, but the sad truth is that operation in Bangladesh was only the tip of the iceberg."

"True."

Josh accomplished the impossible after we gave him no choice. Keeping his distance had more to do with that than the pending delivery of his twins.

Snowden funneled thousands of young girls through his

business. He sent scores of boys to their deaths in his death matches. We appropriated Josh, due to his unsavory history, for that job. We saved many, but there were still so many more.

"I'm concerned about how we're going to isolate Snowden from his guests." That was my biggest concern.

Xavier gestured for me to follow him. "We know his security plan."

"How?"

Xavier returned a grin. "Let's just say I've been working at this for a very long time."

"Meaning?"

"Meaning, I have a man on the inside. Your team has been briefed on their movements. We're not separating him from his guests. We disable his security, then take him. Trust me; his business associates will not interfere."

"How can you be so certain?"

"Because I know what kind of men we're dealing with. They're rich, bored, and scared of losing everything. They won't be a problem and will likely hand Snowden right over. As long as we let them go."

I wanted to believe him, but it seemed too easy. I trusted no one. That itch between my shoulder blades was acting up. I'd learned to pay attention to what that meant. It was a warning. Xavier, however, seemed unconcerned.

"And how many are we looking at?" I expected resistance. A man like Snowden didn't get where he was, or stay there, without a robust security detail.

I had two teams of six men. Xavier's babysitting team added four more. With me, we had seventeen total going up against how many?

"My source says thirty armed guards. A third will be disguised as help. We take out the perimeter guards quietly, cut down the odds, then take out his personal guard."

"The odds are stacked against us. They'll outnumber us two to one."

"We know their positions on the outer wall, outside the main house, and in the garden where the guests will be. Stealth will be key. Take them out and keep moving. Once you have Snowden, nothing else will matter."

There would be a whole lot more involved, but that was obvious. I had men proficient in black ops, plus we had Mitzy and her team guiding us. We should be able to take down Snowden's security as long as we weren't detected along the way.

I needed to have faith.

For that reason, and that reason alone, I gave in to Skye's concerns…sort of. I wasn't going to lead my teams. Instead, I was going to hang back at the beach while my men took out the outer layer of security. Moving in behind my team, I'd slowly make my way forward.

I didn't have to be the one to capture Snowden. We planned for a helicopter extraction when all was said and done. There would be plenty of time to kill Snowden.

"How much time do we have?" Fatigue pulled at my bones. Not because I was tired, but because being this close to my goal had taken nearly a lifetime. Years of preparation and planning would all come into play over the next few hours.

"We take off in ninety minutes. Final briefing on the insertion is right before takeoff."

Insertion.

It was a fancy term for donning full scuba gear, climbing into a helicopter, then jumping out of said helicopter to plunge into the dark waters of the South China Sea where we would swim underwater for a mile, using our DPVs.

Easy peasy.

My stomach churned.

I didn't like swimming. That made scuba diving a challenge. Throw in having to use rebreathers, and a mile swim underwater in the dark, and I was moments from a full-blown panic attack. Not that I'd share that with anyone.

Whatever it took, I was getting this done, even if that meant swallowing my vomit because I felt like I was going to puke. I needed someone to calm me down.

"I'm going to find Skye." My sister was my anchor.

"I'll be here." Xavier leaned against the wall and watched our men who were still immersed in the VR simulation.

I trotted down to where her team had set up.

No Skye.

"Hey, Ryker."

Ryker looked up from playing cards with Tia and Eli. A quiet man, I had never had a conversation with their trauma surgeon. He gave me a nod, then went back to his cards.

"What's up?" Ryker pulled a card out of his hand and set it on the floor in front of him. "You guys almost done?"

"Last minute drills in VR. Where's Skye?"

Tia gestured over her shoulder to a window opening up onto one of the courtyards.

"She said she needed to get some air."

"Thanks." I headed out into the courtyard. "Skye? You here?"

"Over here." Her tiny voice led me to a corner where the once impressive gardens had gone rogue.

"Whatcha doing?" I joined her in the corner and sat on the concrete bench.

She had picked several flowers and gripped their long stems. Skye saw beauty in places I only saw decay. She had a beautiful mind and a wonderful outlook on life.

"I needed to get out of there. I thought it would be easy, but it started to feel a little overwhelming. I came outside for fresh air and to pick flowers."

"They're pretty."

Skye handed them to me. I buried my nose in the petals and inhaled the floral scent. Hesitantly, I placed my hand to her shoulder. The fine hairs on my skin lifted, but I gritted my teeth, pushed past the sensation, and slowly lowered my hand until my palm brushed her skin.

"It's going to be fine."

"Is it?" She held very still while I touched her.

The muscles of my jaw bunched as the all too familiar revulsion flowed through me when I touched her. Not that Skye disgusted me.

Far from it.

She was a veritable angel.

I hated the response of my body. I hated the pain I'd caused her. I hated myself. None of it had been my fault, although it took years of self-medicating with drugs and fucking countless men until I realized the truth.

We were both working through our triggers. Skye had no problems with me touching her. She never had.

I placed a little more pressure on her shoulder, and she put her hand on mine.

"We're healing, Forest. Someday, it will all have been a dream, a nightmare that no longer controls us. Tonight, we slay our demons."

Our demons.

That's what we called our foster father, Clark Preston, and John Snowden. The trauma they caused left triggers we were helpless to fight.

She had her triggers, and I had mine. Her husband worked with her on moving past hers. It was the one thing I admired most about Ash. I'd idolized him when he was nothing more than my rock idol. I may be an Angel Fire fanatic, but when he married my sister, I learned the true depths of his heart.

The man had incredible compassion. Not many men would be able to handle a wife who couldn't have sex without triggering a PTSD flashback. Well, Skye could have sex, but she couldn't have the kind that brought her pleasure. It took Ash a very long time before he could give Skye an orgasm.

Not that I was all up in my sister's sex life, but Skye and I were close. Those triggers came from a past we shared. We talked about a lot of intimate stuff.

Skye had her husband to help with her issues, and she tried to help me with mine, but the darkness within me wasn't something she could fix.

I was left to fend for myself and wrestle my demons alone.

"Tonight..." I squeezed her shoulder then let go. "Tonight, we bring Snowden down."

"I'm scared." She turned to face me. "I can't explain it, but there's something in my gut—"

"I feel it too."

There was a churning sense of unease I couldn't ignore like we were missing something. It was a sense of apprehension that left me unsettled.

"But let's not give voice to our fears, my summer sky. Let's not give power to those demons." I swept my arm out behind us, where my men readied themselves. "We've got a top-notch team. From the men on the ground to our tech team in Command. We've planned for every contingency."

"I know. The scared little girl in me is trying to crawl out. I knew there was a risk of regression the closer we got to him, but I thought I was strong enough."

"You are strong enough."

"If you say so."

Snowden had wanted to take me to the death matches when I'd been a skinny teenaged kid, but he planned much worse for Skye. The man had done things to her, forced her to submit, and embrace his power over her. She did it to save me, but something broke inside of her when none of it mattered. She hadn't been able to save me from Snowden.

All the abuse, the forced sex, the men we'd been rented out to, all of it were things we talked about as a part of our healing. We never spoke of what Snowden had done to her, how she tried to save me, and how she failed in the end.

Chapter Ten

FOREST

I FELT BETTER AFTER TALKING WITH SKYE.

This was our journey; we would write the final chapter of a dark past tonight.

As the sun dipped toward the horizon, we headed toward the helicopters. The humidity made the drysuit unbearably hot, and sweat beaded my brow. The sun might be going down, but the Philippine air didn't care. It held on to its heat with a relentless determination to make my life miserable.

Fortunately, we would fly with the doors open, and I welcomed the relief the wind would bring.

A glance told me I wasn't the only one suffering. Not that we had a choice. We needed to be ready to enter the water the moment we got to our destination.

"Love you, sis," I said one final goodbye.

"Don't die on me." She wrapped me in an uncharacteristic hug.

Maybe it was my drysuit that insulated me from her touch, but I didn't flinch. I wrapped my arms around her tiny waist and kissed the crown of her head.

"I promise."

She looked up at me. "I mean it, Bean. Don't die."

"I promise, my summer sky."

"Please take care of yourself. Don't do anything stupid."

Her medical team would stay behind. They would only be activated if one of our guys needed their unique skill set.

My plan was for Skye's team to be bored to tears.

I climbed inside my designated helicopter and took an outermost seat.

Ben, Chad, Bay, and Mel were right by my side. I expected they wouldn't be further than arm's length from me the entire time; me and my nannies.

We split Bravo team between the two helicopters. Three of them joined us, and three went with Alpha team in the other helicopter. The whine of the engines filled the air, kicking up dried leaves and dust as the rotors spun up.

Slowly, we lifted off the ground, and I reminded myself I should wave goodbye to Skye.

It was something Sara would have made me do. Funny how thoughts of my assistant filled my mind.

I bet she was having the time of her life with little Zach. Did they make it to the zoo? Did she take him to the aquarium?

Those were a complete waste on a kid that small, but Sara seemed to think it mattered.

Was she cuddling with him on the couch? What would that feel like? Cuddling with Sara?

Where did that come from?

I never thought I'd have a family with kids of my own running around. And I most certainly never saw myself with a woman. They were too fragile for the things I craved.

I needed the strength of a man when it came to sex; someone strong enough to beat me, or at least put up a good fight. Sadly, few men fit that bill.

But a woman?

I filed the odd couch-cuddling thought away. Besides, I wasn't interested in Sara in that way.

I admired her. She never once put her needs ahead of mine.

The woman was kind and selfless to a fault. She took care of my sorry ass, and I didn't make it easy on her.

Part of taking care of me meant she coached me on how to act around people, like reminding me to wave goodbye when heading out on what could be considered a risky operation.

But that's where it stopped.

It had to. I had nothing to offer a woman like Sara. I had little to offer a man other than a rough fuck, which often left bruises behind.

With thoughts of Sara whispering in my mind, my goodbye to Skye turned more exuberant. Sara would be proud.

Down below, Skye blew me a kiss. I did a dorky thing and caught it. When I placed it over my heart, her eyes widened, then she folded her hands over her heart.

I bet that misted her eyes. Skye was a tough cookie, but she had a sentimental side I kind of liked.

The helicopter spun in the air, taking Skye from my sight. I made a mental note to thank Sara for reminding me that little things did make a difference.

With dusk deepening as the sun sank below the horizon, we flew away from the mainland to our designated insertion point somewhere in the South China Sea.

The wind cooled me down. All around me, my men checked their gear. Ben put on his harness then gave me a look. With a huff, I stopped daydreaming about Sara and got to work prepping my gear.

"Five minutes out!" The pilot's voice crackled through our headgear.

Ben and I completed our buddy checks, and then he turned to Mel.

We had an odd number of men.

Ben, Mel, and I buddied up while everyone else worked in teams of two. With all our gear, we weren't actually jumping out of the helicopter. Of course, our rebreathers, BCDs, fins, and lights were on us, but our scooters—our diver propulsion vehicles—would be lowered down separately.

There was too much risk getting hit on the head as we rappelled out of the helicopter.

Four of our men rappelled out of the helicopter first. We lowered our gear down to them. The downdraft from the helicopters churned the relatively calm waters, kicking up waves and sending blinding spray through the air. It made the entire process complicated, but we'd done this before.

Every step of tonight's operation had been a part of our training. I left nothing to chance.

Finally, it was my turn on the rope. I lowered down with Ben to my left and Mel to my right. If we hadn't had our masks on, the spray kicked up by the helicopter would have blinded us immediately. Instead, a watery veil covered the lens and made everything a blur.

That was okay because we weren't staying on the surface. While the last remaining men slid down the ropes, Ben, Mel, and I submerged.

We were fortunate there was little current; otherwise, we risked being swept away while the rest of our men joined us, but we made allowances for that with a down line trailing from the nose of the helicopter.

Twenty feet below the surface, we gathered on the line, and I counted heads. A few minutes later, we did a final count as the last buddy pair joined us.

This was my mission, but I was not the lead. That task fell to Chad and Bay, two SEALs with extensive underwater experience. Seventeen was a large number of divers to keep in a tight formation, but we practiced for this and made it work.

We distributed the DPVs, and everyone clipped into their device. With thumbs raised, we signaled our readiness. Then Chad and Bay took off. Ben and I followed directly behind with Mel flanking us.

Alpha team set up to the right, and Bravo team gathered on the left. Except for my nannies, they buddied up, two by two, three rows deep.

We were an impressive force.

It took less than an hour to navigate to our insertion point on the beach of Snowden's private island. We emerged from the ocean with the sun well below the horizon and water pouring off our suits into the pitch blackness of night.

We tied all our DPVs together, submerged them, and anchored them to the seafloor, then swam the remaining distance to shore.

This was it.

Endgame had begun.

Once on the shore, we removed our dive gear. An outer barrier reef protected the cove, which left its waters mirror-smooth. Tiny waves lapped at our ankles. Thick cloud cover blotted out the moon, leaving us peering into the dark.

With seventeen men, we had a lot of gear to hide. The best place was beneath the inky water, and we made use of the most effective cover in our environment.

Like the DPVs, we removed our gear and sank it under the still waters of the cove. The gentle lapping of the waves and the faintest breeze rustling the thick vegetation were the only sounds except the soft crunching of our boots over the sand.

Our initial plan had us scaling the walls, cutting through the serpentine wire, and dropping in on the other side. As a result of the VR simulation, Bay noticed a series of drainage pipes.

We adapted the plan.

Our entrance to the estate would come by way of a small and slimy, claustrophobia-inducing, drainage pipe. I could handle a twenty-foot crawl through a narrow tube. I put in my earbud and checked our comms.

Viking One to Overlord. Over.

Copy. This is Overlord. Read you loud and clear—Eagle Eyes in position. We see you. Mitzy's clear voice popped in my ear. Somewhere overhead, a drone circled, giving them an eagle's eye of what happened on the ground.

What do you see?

It was time to confirm the intelligence Xavier's inside man had dug up.

I hope you hid your gear. Mitzy's voice squawked through the comms.

Cut the chatter. Where are our bogies?

Ten patrolling the outside walls. Two at each corner. Six up front. Guests still arriving, but there's a score or more gathered in the interior courtyard. Three boats at the dock. It looks like the party has started.

I swore I heard Mitzy huff, but she went on to give the positions of Snowden's security team.

An advantage of crawling through the drains was that we no longer needed to worry about the men outside the walls. They became a secondary consideration, which shifted the odds, if not in our favor, at least we had fewer men to take out.

Once we had Snowden, his security wouldn't risk his life. We just needed to get to him before the men outside the walls discovered the breach.

Copy. Moving into position. Viking One out.

I gave a thumbs-up to my team. We completed a quick comms check as we made our way down the beach.

The drainage pipe reeked, and I turned up my nose. Things got better and better as I belly crawled over something slimy. But this was much easier than scaling twenty-foot walls and cutting through serpentine wire while exposed to Snowden's men.

Still in our drysuits, we wiggled on our bellies, one man at a time, through the slimy pipe, and gathered on the other side behind tangled vines.

Then we stripped.

The benefit of drysuits, versus wetsuits, was that we could wear regular clothing underneath.

Kitted up in black tactical garb, there was no way we would blend with the guests. Getting close to Snowden would prove difficult, but once we disabled his security, blending wouldn't matter.

We strapped on our weapons, pulled on black hoods, and fixed night vision goggles over our eyes.

Phase Two had begun.

Chapter Eleven

FOREST

My team's job was to wait. Once the bulk of Snowden's security had been taken out by Alpha and Bravo teams, my nannies and I would move in on the crowd.

The five of us settled in, blending with the shadows, while the two teams went to work.

Mitzy insisted on nonlethal intervention. Skye agreed. My teams were equipped with tranquilizer darts in addition to their weapons.

I thought we should shoot all the bastards. A bullet between the eyes seemed an easy way to die, and I had no sympathy for their lives. They protected a monster, therefore, lost any compassion I might have had.

Skye felt otherwise, and Mitzy simply threw a fit. In the end, tranquilizer darts were less likely to be heard and blow our cover. Mitzy thought she won that argument, but logic won out instead. To keep her quiet, I let her celebrate the win.

Alpha and Bravo teams split to the North and South.

Conquered by the Spanish, much of Philippine architecture reflected the rich heritage of Spain. Snowden's estate was no exception. Built to resemble a fortress, it had towers at each corner, high concrete walls covered in stucco, and broad walkways on top for armed men to patrol.

The main house faced eastward to greet the rising sun. Built around a central courtyard, every room took advantage of the prevailing breezes which blew in and through arching windows protected by intricate cast-iron grates. The elegant central courtyard provided a gathering place for the residents, complete with dazzling fountains and lush gardens.

Snowden's guests gathered in the courtyard.

Light strains of classical music drifted through the night, along with the deep rumblings of male voices and the softer sounds of women.

The back of the courtyard did not open into the house but instead extended the outside living space into expansive gardens. It was there where we waited for the signal to push forward.

Static crackled over our comms.

Alpha One: Northwest wall, no resistance.

No resistance?

I cocked my head and glanced at Ben. He shrugged. With the change in plans, we expected to encounter fewer armed guards. Most of Snowden's security concentrated on the outer wall, looking out, not in.

When they moved inside, Mitzy would let us know.

Bravo One: Southwest wall clear. No resistance. Heading up.

Alpha One: Heading up northwest stairs. Overlord, check heat signatures. We've encountered no one.

Overlord: Alpha One, no visuals inside the compound, except party guests in the courtyard. Garden's clear. Same count. Ten outside the walls. Two at each corner. Six up front.

That seemed light, but I trusted Mitzy's count.

Where were the rest of Snowden's men?

Alpha and Bravo team took out the men manning the north and southwestern towers. Reporting their progress, they moved silently to the front of the compound.

My nannies and I huddled behind the thick vegetation. I wanted to be out there with my teams, but without military training, I was labeled a liability and held behind.

"No resistance?" Ben spoke to Mel in a hushed whisper.

"Raising the fine hairs on your arms?" Mel's rough whisper sliced through the darkness.

"What's wrong?" I turned to Ben.

"Not sure. Something's not right."

"How so?"

"Eight men on the walls. Six up front. Ten outside? We're missing men."

"You think he's light on security?" Bay huddled close.

I shook my head. "No way would Snowden shortchange his security detail. Maybe they're inside?"

"With the guests?" Chad joined us. "Risky. He wants to wine and dine his guests, get them drunk, and show off his merchandise, not surround them with guards."

We'd discussed this. The women's voices belonged to Snowden's slaves. This event put a sparkle to the ugliness, which was his business. Willing women didn't hang on the arms of men they didn't know, but slaves draped themselves to avoid punishment.

"What do you think?" Ben turned his question, not to Mel, but me.

Alpha team reported in. They took out the men on the northeast tower. Bravo had yet to report back. Once we had the towers under control, we'd move in on Snowden.

It wasn't necessary to take out all his men, only those who were close to him and those with the ability to take us out. We had six of his team incapacitated and waited for Bravo team to report in on their success.

My earbud squawked with Bravo team reporting in. Mitzy's voice followed.

Mitzy: Overlord to Viking One.

I rolled my eyes. Mitzy had fun with our designations.

Me: Overlord, copy.

Mitzy: No more arrivals inbound. I'd say everyone is present and accounted for. Four security moving inside. Two left out at the docks.

Me: Bravo One, take your team and secure the docks. Alpha One, take care of your company.

Alpha One: Roger.

Bravo One: Roger.

I looked at Ben. "You think we're ready to crash this party?"

He exchanged a look with Mel and tugged at his ear. "This feels off."

"How so?"

"Too easy. We've taken out eight of their men and haven't raised the alarm?"

"That was the plan," I said.

We planned on taking out all ten men outside the walls, the eight tower guards, and those at the front of the house greeting the guests as they arrived.

Not alerting them to our presence was the plan.

I didn't understand his concern.

"We go now," I said. "Keep to the shadows, stay on the edges, and keep your eyes peeled."

The four of them exchanged bemused expressions. Then I realized what I'd done. Telling four highly trained men how to do their job may not have been my finest moment. Not that I cared.

I was too fucking close to taking Snowden down.

My nannies and I moved forward with incredible stealth. We headed out of the garden and into the darkness of the open-aired halls lining the inner courtyard.

Festive lanterns lit the courtyard. Lights dangled from trellises covered in a thick carpet of vegetation. Fragrant blooms perfumed the air. The halls surrounding the courtyard remained dark, and we stuck to the shadows.

As silently as I could, I moved from one arch to the next and stopped behind the center posts to peer into the crowd.

I didn't know any of these men but was familiar with every intimate detail of their lives. From their business connections to the names of their wives, their children, their dogs, and their many mistresses, I knew what side of the bed they slept on, what they ate for breakfast, and how to take them down.

No one in this crowd would come out of this evening unscathed. With Mitzy and Raven working by my side, we were ready to wage cyber warfare on these men who thought nothing about ruining the lives of those weaker than themselves.

Each time I stopped to look into the crowd, Ben made a clucking noise to hurry me on. I shouldn't pause like I was, but I couldn't help it.

Where was Snowden?

This was his party, and I couldn't see the man who ruined my childhood.

I remembered him as a frightful man. Large and imposing, he'd been strong and powerful to my teen-self. His appetite for pain had been limitless, and his compassion non-existent.

I looked for him each time I stopped, peering around the columns which formed arches lining the courtyard.

He would be older now. I was sure the intervening years had changed him.

I was bigger, stronger, bolder, and although I knew he would be older, in my mind's eye, I still saw a monster. He had to be in his early fifties. Surely, he had lost his dominating physique and those eyes which commanded a young boy to do whatever it took to keep his foster sister safe.

Anger stirred within me as we drew closer. I channeled all my rage, bottling it up until I could unleash it on Snowden.

Half the time, I didn't know where Chad and Bay were in relation to Ben, Mel, and myself. They would be behind me then suddenly appear to the front of us. When I thought I had their positions nailed down, they would be behind us again.

Working with these men made me feel like an imposter. The only sounds I heard, other than the celebration we closed in on, were the dried leaves and twigs crunching underfoot— under my feet. I felt like a damn elephant trying to sneak up on a mouse.

None of the others made any noise.

But I didn't worry. The party was in full swing. Nobody in the courtyard could hear our approach. The music blared. The soft tinkling of women's laughter floated on the air. The deep bass rumbles of men carried through it all. Their voices grew louder, more boisterous as the whiskey flowed.

Men gripped women adorned in the most expensive ball gowns and paraded their conquests in front of their rivals. They dragged the girls across the dance floor as if the girls wanted to be there. And the girls played their part. No doubt, they would be punished if they failed to please their assigned date.

These women were nothing more than unwilling victims forced to entice men, without scruples, to believe the fantasy that such women would want to hang on their arms and lie in their beds.

Frankly, I was surprised no one was fucking. Knowing Snowden's penchant for orgies, I expected to see several naked women draped on top of the tables, or tied to the beams overhead.

It made my stomach clench and bile rise in the back of my throat.

As we closed in, Bravo team reported an update.

The front docks had been secured.

Mitzy called out Alpha's success as they started taking out the guards outside the walls.

Everything was set. My team approached from the rear while Alpha and Bravo teams came in from either side toward the front.

We waited until everyone was in position.

Me: Overlord, status.

Mitzy: All clear. Good to go.

My stomach felt light, unsettled, and my nerves seemed to go haywire with the go-ahead.

Ben looked at me. His left eyebrow lifted.

The command to rush the guests would come from me. My entire mouth went dry, and I struggled to wet it so I could speak.

This was it.

Me: All units. Go!

We rushed forward, weapons raised, and descended on the guests.

Women screamed.

The men pulled guns on us, pulling us up short. This just became a shit show. We stood our ground against the men, knowing backup in the form of Alpha and Bravo teams would be on the way.

"Where the fuck is he?" I demand of the armed men.

Mitzy: He's not there?

I scanned the crowd, looking for the face of the man I could never forget, the man who haunted my dreams and brought the screams that woke me from sleep.

Then I heard a slow clap.

Up above, and to the right, a spotlight flickered to life and illuminated a monster. He looked smug, not scared, and definitely not surprised.

Snowden stood on the walkway dead center between the two guard towers and looked down on the courtyard.

"My my..." His brittle voice raked against my ears. "After all this time, you've finally come home."

What the fuck?

I lifted my weapon and placed my sights on him. A red laser dot lit up his chest.

He glanced down and gave a slow shake of his head. "My dear boy, you don't want to do that."

"What makes you think that?" The muscles of my jaw bunched as I stretched my finger over the trigger.

"I think you want to tell your men to put down their weapons."

"Not happening. We have you. And you will be coming with us."

"Oh, my boy, you see that's not going to happen." He gave a snap of his fingers.

His men shifted their guns, training them all on me.

Bay and Chad shifted their guns from the men to Snowden. The others held their's on Snowden's men. There were more of them than us, but it didn't matter. There were now three laser dots lighting up Snowden; two over his heart and one smack dab in the middle of his forehead.

"You're a dead man." I couldn't help but growl out the words.

In front of us, the girls whimpered and cried.

"Is that what you think, my boy?"

Each time he said my boy, the fine hairs on the back of my neck lifted. Why did the bastard look so damn smug? We had him.

"You're a smart boy. Look around. Did you think I didn't know you were coming? That I didn't plan for this?" Snowden gave a slow shake of his head. "My boy, I've been planning this moment for years. This whole party is for you."

"Me?"

"Yes. For the day you finally came home to me."

The man was insane. I refused to give him the satisfaction of seeing my surprise.

Mitzy: Forest, what's happening?

I ignored Mitzy's question and focused on Snowden.

Snowden spread his arms out wide. "My boy, don't you see?"

I saw nothing except red. Fury burned in my veins at the audacity of this man. One squeeze of the trigger and he would be dead.

But I held the shot.

The smile cracking his face made me pause. Why did he look like he had won?

"I see nothing but a dead man." The cold metal of my weapon pressed against my cheek. I moved my finger over the trigger.

One shot.

That's all it would take.

"I have a present for you." Snowden's inane chatter continued. "You're going to love this." The fucker sounded far too pleased with himself.

My vision blurred, and I blinked to clear it. Then I heard something that shouldn't be possible.

Snowden gestured toward the front of the house. A commotion sounded then a spotlight lit the area up.

"Sara?" I dropped the barrel of my weapon and gaped.

Sara stood in the middle of five men. They gripped her arms and pushed her to the edge of the wall. In her arms, a tiny bundle let loose an ear-piercing wail.

Zach?

My nephew screeched his displeasure to anyone that might care to listen.

Snowden had Skye's son and my assistant.

To my left, Snowden laughed.

Chapter Twelve

SARA

MEN GRABBED AT MY ARMS AND PUSHED ME TO THE EDGE OF A LOW wall overlooking a courtyard.

Blood roared past my ears, and I mumbled, "No. No. No. No!"

Except I didn't hear anything. Too scared to speak, my mind kept repeating the words on an endless loop in my head.

This wasn't happening.

I had to be asleep.

But a light breeze swept across my skin. Humid air surged into my lungs. Calloused fingers dug painfully into my arms, and the stench of men who hadn't washed in days infiltrated my nostrils.

My toes bumped against the low stucco wall, and I bucked against the men holding me. I clutched Zach tight to my chest and blinked back tears.

Little Zach.

What was going to happen to him? What did these men want?

Terror swam in my veins as my living nightmare continued to unfold. My breaths came in short staccato bursts as my heart hammered away beneath my breastbone.

I held a death grip on Zach, determined he wouldn't be pried from my arms again, then I worried I held him too tight that he couldn't breathe.

I didn't know what to do. I simply clung to him for dear life.

That didn't make him safe.

They'd already taken him from me more times than I wanted to admit. He was mine to protect, and I failed him. I failed Skye, and I failed the man I loved.

Little Zach cried. He was hungry, wet, and venturing toward inconsolable. Not that I blamed him. I felt the same.

Down below, gathered in the courtyard, I stared upon a scene made from nightmares. Armed men pointed guns at one another.

Forest was there.

He towered over the rest of the men.

Despite the black masks and identical black tactical outfits, I quickly picked him out of the crowd.

He pointed his rifle at a man standing on an adjacent walkway.

If I could only go back to the night when Forest and his team left, maybe I could erase this memory, wake up in my bed, and shrug this off as a horrible dream.

If I hadn't buzzed up the janitorial crew who gave me a sob story about their keycards not working, I wouldn't be here.

If I'd been more suspicious of the three-man cleaning crew who were far too young and buff to be simple janitors, Forest wouldn't be staring up at me in shock with fear filling his face.

There was nothing good about me being here. Zach was exactly the leverage Snowden needed to bring Forest to his knees.

I had done that.

It gutted me thinking how any number of different choices could have prevented this moment.

None of that mattered now.

My problem was that I believed in the inherent goodness of people. How could they do this to little Zach?

The crying bundle in my arms was worth everything, and he was in distress. Didn't they care?

One look at Snowden and the answer to that question became painfully clear.

Forest never spoke about what he'd endured because of that man. Everything I learned came from his sister, who I'd grown close to over the years.

Zach cried while Forest's icy gaze turned toward me.

"Sara?" Forest's stony expression faltered.

On the wall to my left, John Snowden cackled with glee.

Skye and Forest rescued me from an abusive home. When they found me, I confessed to the things which had been done to me.

Over the years, Skye opened up about the monster that was their foster father and the man who terrorized them that final summer.

Evil existed.

I met the man who destroyed Forest's life and knew genuine fear.

They'd drugged me during the flight, and I didn't know what they'd done with little Zach.

My throat ripped with my screams as I'd begged for Zach. A twelve-year-old girl brought him to me on the plane.

I remembered the way my arms shook when the little girl put Zach into my arms. Then the guards took her to the back of the plane where they…I cringed with the memory. The men used her in the vilest of ways.

I'd seen abuse. I'd been a victim of it myself. Yet, I had never been in a position where it occurred with the callous normalcy inside that plane.

The girl didn't struggle. She didn't fight. Her body went limp, and her eyes glassed over as her spirit died.

I had been a fool to think evil didn't exist.

And I participated in my abduction like an idiot.

Not once did it occur to me to question why their keycards didn't work. Or why they were there on a Sunday. I'd been too preoccupied with putting the office back in order after Forest's men had blown through.

I didn't pay attention to the janitors as they moved around the office. I should have noticed how they weren't emptying the trash.

How they vacuumed aimlessly and never once moved a chair or passed the vacuum underneath a desk.

I'd been deep in my thoughts juggling what I needed to get done in the morning with the needs of the nine-month-old who was under my care. Zach's little cries for food had me heading to the break room to pull out a bottle and feed him.

Not once did I notice the men angling toward me.

If I had, I might have seen the determined expressions on their faces, or the length of rope one of them carried. I would have seen the hood.

I could have run.

Instead, one man pulled Zach out of my arms while another threw a hood over my head. While I flailed, they tied my arms behind my back. There was a prick in my arm and then nothing until I woke hours later and half a world away.

A shiver traced its way down my spine. This was happening.

Snowden's laughter lifted the fine hairs on the back of my neck. The men surrounding me bumped and pushed me too close to the edge.

I clutched Zach tighter, terrified one of the men would shove me hard enough that I would lose my grip on Zach. Images of him plunging to his death on the tiles below sent a shudder down my spine.

"Oh, I wish you could see the expression on your face, my boy." Snowden's oily voice carried through the still air. It tunneled under my skin and put a hitch in my breath. "The horror is simply delicious. I have your girl and something much more precious, don't I?" He turned his attention to me.

He had this insane idea Forest and I were romantically involved, despite what I said.

Snowden thought he had two things Forest cared about. Sadly, that wasn't true. I wasn't really sure Zach mattered to Forest, but Zach mattered to Skye. That was enough to use against Forest. As for myself? I was nothing more than collateral damage.

Snowden meant for Forest to pay. How? I wasn't sure, but it involved little Zach.

I'd already had far too much of this man's penetrating intensity boring into me as he tried to determine my value to Forest.

Snowden expected to use me to get to Forest, but Zach had been the icing on the cake. I wish I'd been better prepared and able to resist Snowden's interrogation, but I'd been too weak. All it had taken was for them to rip Zach out of my arms.

When Snowden discovered the child was not my son but instead belonged to Skye, he roared in triumph.

That's when I knew this had been a setup.

Snowden planned this entire farce.

As Forest hunted Snowden, his abuser engaged in an elusive game of cat and mouse.

And I gave Snowden all the leverage he needed to destroy Forest.

But what now?

Shock rippled across Forest's face, followed by fury. His muscles bunched. My boss looked ready to explode, and yet he stood stock still.

Forest's men surrounded those gathered, but Snowden had others coming up behind them.

Forest's team aimed rifles at the crowd, and Snowden's men pointed guns back.

I wanted to tell Forest there were more men on the way, but I bit my lower lip as tears rolled down my cheeks.

Women in elegant ball gowns prostrated themselves at the feet of the men. Soft, mewling noises floated on the air. Zach added his agitated cries.

Something inside of me died.

It was a standoff.

Lasers lit Snowden's body. They danced between his temples and skittered across his chest.

"You're a dead man." Forest's words came out in a low, ominous growl.

"Is that what you think?" Snowden looked down at the dancing lights on his chest and laughed. "If you were going to kill me, you would have done it already, but you don't have it in you, do you, boy?"

Snowden swept his arms out wide and gestured at the courtyard below.

"You know, I'm a little upset, my boy. Are you not impressed by the homecoming I've thrown for you?"

"You're insane." Forest's words came out as a deadly rumble.

"Am I?" Snowden lowered his arms. His voice turned icy cold. "I think your manners need work. Don't you remember your lessons, boy? Our time in the basement where you learned to beg for the privilege of pleasing me? Do you remember the cage? The darkness? The bite of my whip? How about the screams of your sister?"

Each cutting word slammed into Forest. The muscles of his jaw bunched, and he flinched with each volley Snowden threw at him.

I hated watching Snowden torment Forest.

Forest's men never once lowered their weapons. Half had their rifles aimed at the crowd. The others pointed at Snowden's heart.

No one moved a muscle except Forest.

The strong, powerful man I knew unraveled. It began with slackness in his strong jaw, followed by slumping in his proud shoulders. His core weakened, and his sturdy legs shook.

"You're a dead man, Snowden."

Forest's deadly words slammed into me, bringing a gasp to my lips. I always thought of Forest as a gentle giant, but something within him snapped.

Forest's low rumble turned ominous. "You just don't know it yet."

"We're all dead men, my boy. But before I die, you and I are going to have so much fun together."

"As I said, you're fucking insane," Forest volleyed back his reply.

"Oh, I think not." Snowden's gaze cut across the distance to me. The man looked entirely too pleased.

I couldn't help but gasp. The man's icy stare knifed into me. The men to either side of me gripped my arms. I nearly lost my hold on

Zach. The man standing behind me grabbed my hair. He forced my head back.

Something cold and sharp pressed against my throat.

My entire body stilled.

"What we have here is a standoff. The only insane thing about this whole situation is how insanely happy I was when I figured out who that little bundle belonged to. I thought it was your secretary's kid, but imagine the thrill when she told me it belongs to Elsbeth."

Snowden rubbed his hands together with pleasure. "Ah, but her name isn't Elsbeth anymore, is it? She changed her name after she killed your foster father. Oh, the memories I have of her tight body wrapping around me. The heat as I sank into her tight pussy, fucking her over and over and over again. It was amazing. I miss your sister, but she is not the one I want."

"Don't you dare speak about Skye."

"Oh, I'll talk about sweet Elsbeth all I want. Skye is a stupid name. Tell me, what do you think she would do for her son? I know what she did for you, her sweet little beanpole, was it? Isn't that what she used to call you? I remember her rocking you in the dark after we were done with you, calling out your name. Oh, the memories."

"You, sick bastard." Forest shifted his weapon, and one of the laser dots moved from Snowden's chest to dance between his eyes.

"You really shouldn't call me names. Have you forgotten your manners? Or what happens when you disobey?"

"One word. That's all it takes. For a man whose life is literally in my hands, you're rather bold."

"Tsk, tsk, tsk. My men have a knife at your girlfriend's throat. Kill me, and she dies. Elsbeth's kid…dies. Is my life worth losing them?"

Two laser beams shifted to where Snowden's men held me.

I should struggle, but I held stock still.

With his men gripping my arms, I was terrified they would yank them apart. If they did that, Zach would fall. My life meant nothing, but I would do whatever it took to keep Zach safe.

"Let me tell you how this is going to go down." Snowden's oily smile spread across his face, splitting it into a grimace. "I sense you don't fully appreciate the situation. You see, you're going to tell your men to put their weapons down. Since I'm a generous man, I'm going to let them go. I'm not interested in them. They can walk right out the front of my house and slip back into the water where they came. Yes, I know exactly how you got here. There is nothing about tonight I don't know."

"That's not happening."

"Oh, it is, and you're going to order them to do it."

"The only thing happening tonight is the bullet I'm going to put between your eyes."

"Do that, and the girl is dead. The child is dead. Tell me..." Snowden's voice lowered to an ominous whisper, "What are their lives worth?"

"They're already dead." Forest gave a shrug, which made me gasp.

Had he given up on little Zach?

"If you kill me, they die. We, at least, agree on that, but what if there was another outcome? This is a welcome home party in your honor, and I feel generous. Do you remember how generous I can be when you do as I say?"

"The only outcome is your dead eyes staring up at the sky."

"You are going to regret your lack of manners. My patience only goes so far."

"This conversation is tiresome."

"Is it? We haven't even gotten to the best part."

"And what would that be?"

"The part where you fall to your knees and beg to serve me. Don't you see, that's what coming home means. It means returning to your roots. You'll serve me. I'll have you on your knees begging to please me."

"Never going to happen."

"Did you forget I had a gift for you?"

I tracked Forest and Snowden's conversation with an icy chill running through my veins. Could Snowden make Forest do what I thought he was going to do?

The man holding the knife at my throat eased up on the grip he had on my hair. Controlling my head, he tilted my face until I met the cold brutality of Snowden's glare.

"As much as I adore Elsbeth, she's not what I want. I have no use for her, but I have a sinking suspicion you care a great deal about what happens to her kid. But what would a party be without a little fun?"

My heart banged inside my chest like a kettle drum. The depravity of this man knew no bounds.

"You see, I'm going to give you a choice."

"From a mad man?" Forest's voice vibrated with fury. "I think not."

"Really? You should rethink that and show gratitude."

"You're fucking insane."

"You keep saying that, and frankly, it's getting tiresome. I'm going to forgive your bad manners because I want to see what you choose."

"Choose?"

"Yes, I really should have said who you choose, not what."

What was Snowden's game? He toyed with Forest.

Taking a deep breath in, Snowden puffed out his chest. He beamed with his victory.

"You can save only one. Save the kid or save your girl. I only have one demand. I want Elsbeth to take whomever you pick. I want to see her face when you go to your knees before me."

My heart skipped a beat, then another, and another. It was as if the entire world stopped and I hung suspended over a bottomless well of despair.

"I'm even going to give you something to show my good intentions."

His men in the courtyard dropped their weapons with the snap of Snowden's fingers. They kicked their guns toward Forest's men, then went to their knees and placed their hands behind their heads.

The bastard planned this. It was the only thing that made sense.

"Go ahead and bind their hands. My men will not shoot you. They won't resist you."

Confused expressions filled Forest's men. A strange churning twisted in my belly. What was going on?

An impossible choice.

Me or Zach.

That was no choice.

Forest would save Zach. He would do whatever it took to save Skye's son.

Snowden got it wrong. I meant nothing to Forest. To him, I was an object, which made me disposable. If Snowden thought keeping me around gave him any leverage over Forest, he was wrong. It would be easier to kill me.

But he knew Forest would do anything to save Zach. That icy chill in my veins ran arctic cold, and I shivered despite the lingering heat.

Odd how thinking about my impending death did nothing inside. I felt empty, devoid of emotion; it was as if something inside of me let go.

This was not how I wanted my life to end, but I wasn't going to fight it. Snowden couldn't have Skye's son. We would all do what was necessary to protect him.

Whatever was necessary.

The man to my left suddenly let go. I reeled, off balanced by the sudden change. He ripped Zach out of my arms and dangled him over the edge.

I screamed and reached for Zach. The knife dragged over my throat and split the skin. The other men yanked me back, and the man behind me grabbed my hair. He forced my head back. The sharp steel pressed against my throat again.

My attention shifted to Forest, and I saw the horrifying moment when he caved. His shoulders slumped, and the barrel of his gun dropped.

"Now, this is a beautiful moment." Snowden preened. "It's so good to welcome you home."

The pain in Forest's expression ripped a hole in my heart. His agony stretched across the distance as he faced an impossible choice.

"You and I have a lot to catch up on." Snowden puffed out his chest and practically crowed with his victory. "You have a lot to atone for, pain you will bear, and you will kneel at my feet, begging me to make you mine. And I'll enjoy every moment. Never think you can beat me, boy. I'm your better...I'm your Master. I own you."

Agony rippled across Forest's face as he looked up at me. Only his eyes weren't on me. They focused on little Zach and his screams.

Chapter Thirteen

FOREST

Snowden was insane.

Choose? He wanted me to choose?

And why did his men throw down their weapons?

Everything was falling apart.

"Cuff them." I barked an order to Ben, who stood beside me.

Ben lowered his weapon then gave a curt nod to his team. Bay, Chad, and Mel lowered their weapons and reached into their pockets to pull out zip-ties.

While Chad circled the crowd, kicking the dropped weapons outward, Ben, Bay, and Mel went to the kneeling men and lashed their hands behind their backs.

Snowden still had plenty of men with guns pointed at us.

Our standoff remained.

"And your other men?" My attention shifted to the walls. I made a concerted effort not to look toward Sara.

My gut churned, and my heart banged inside my chest. He dared to touch my angel? The sweetest woman in the world did not deserve to be here.

What had I missed? Where had everything broken down? How had Snowden known? How did he get to Sara?

Too many questions filled my head. They crowded my thoughts and made it difficult to think.

Zach gave another ear-piercing shriek.

My mind raced as I tried to figure out how to handle this shitshow. I needed to give Snowden what he wanted while my team figured out an exit plan.

"You want to play this game?" I shifted my attention from Sara back to Snowden. "My shoulder blades are itching from the guns at my back. You think having those men drop their weapons does anything?"

"It's a measure of my goodwill." Snowden crowed.

"Fuck that." I lifted the barrel of my rifle and set the laser sight back on Snowden's chest.

Rage consumed me, and it would be too easy to end this right now. There would be casualties. My only question was whether I could live with the fallout.

Would Skye ever forgive me for sacrificing her son?

No reason to think too hard about that. I would never forgive myself.

Sara's shriek had me turning.

Two of the men ripped her shirt. Another one cut away her skirt.

"Your girlfriend is rather pretty. I wonder how long her screams will amuse my men?" Snowden appeared unconcerned by the red dots lighting up his torso. "You can stop that from happening, my boy. All you have to do is—"

"—kill you." I turned my attention back to Snowden.

"I don't think so." Snowden tapped his ear. "I'm going to help you out. Call your team. Tell them to send a helicopter. I want Elsbeth on it. All my men will leave. Well," he gestured toward Sara, "all but the ones holding your girl and the screaming brat. My men leave. Your men leave. You and I stay. I only want you."

He wants me.

Disgust rippled through my body with thoughts of what this man had once done to me.

What were the odds my team could take out the men holding Sara?

Zach's cry rattled my teeth.

The answer to my question was not good enough.

Snowden had me right where he wanted me.

We couldn't take out the man holding Zach without him dropping the kid. A fall from that height would be deadly. Anything I did risked Zach's life.

Sara's fear reached out to me as one of her tormentors took a knife and cut away one of the straps of her bra. I couldn't allow Snowden to degrade her like that.

But how did I save them both?

Think, goddammit! Think!

Ben returned to my side. "Forest…"

"Stop," I said with a hiss.

I was considering the impossible. What if I gave in to Snowden's demands?

Knowing what I had to do, I stopped worrying about what I couldn't change. I would accept what happened, and I would endure. I'd done it before. I would do it again.

It was time to save those I could. I firmed my voice and accepted the inevitability of my situation.

"Tell the rest of your men to drop their weapons. I want them off this island."

Snowden snorted. "I'm not doing that. Do you think I'm stupid?"

"If you want me, you'll do it."

Snowden's eyes widened, then that creepy smile of his split his face when he realized he'd won. "You'll kneel to me?"

I wasn't going to answer that, at least not out loud. The sad truth was yes, I would. I would do whatever it took.

"Tell your men to leave. The women stay. They leave with my men."

"You don't know how a standoff works. You're going to send your men away, then get on your knees."

Snowden would push, but if this was happening, it would

happen on my terms. At least as long as I had terms I could negotiate with.

I didn't know if I had the strength for what came next, but there was no choice about what I would do to save Sara. I couldn't let this monster get his hands on her.

I'd survived Snowden before. I could do it again.

Xavier would find a way to get to me. Faith was not my strong suit, but I had to believe in my friends.

I activated my comm-link and spoke so Snowden could clearly understand. "Viking One to Overlord."

Mitzy: Overlord here. What the fuck is happening, Forest?

"The situation has changed."

Mitzy: Forest!

"Cut the chatter and listen."

Copy. Mitzy's mollified voice returned through my earbud.

With my eyes locked on Snowden, I took a step I never thought I'd ever make.

"Send a helicopter. Skye needs to be on board. You'll land in the garden."

What the hell, Forest? That voice belonged to Skye, not Mitzy.

This was a fucking disaster.

I spoke to Ben, and he updated Xavier, Skye, Mitzy, and the rest of the team. Turning my attention to Snowden, I made my demands.

"If you want me, all your men leave the island. Sara and Zach will go with Skye."

"My men will leave, except for those guarding your girl and the brat. I need some form of insurance."

Ben notified me a helicopter was inbound and would be there in ten minutes. I had ten minutes to figure this shit out.

From the expression on Ben's face, he didn't like my plan. I didn't blame him. A bullet between Snowden's eyes seemed like the perfect solution, but I couldn't risk Zach's life, and I couldn't let those men paw at Sara like that.

"Tell your men to take their hands off Sara."

"And here I was beginning to think you didn't care about the girl."

"I'm warning you."

"Fine." Snowden gave a huff. He snapped his fingers, and the men holding Sara released her. She immediately sprang at the man holding Zach over the edge.

"Give him to me!" She reached for Zach.

"Give her the kid." My words cut across the distance.

Snowden turned his feral stare toward me. There was nothing human in those eyes.

"On your knees."

Fire burned in my gut, and bile rose in my throat. If I went to my knees...

"Give Zach to Sara. You get nothing until they're safe."

"Nothing? Oh, I think you're going to give me a whole lot of something." He reached down and grabbed at his crotch. "I'm already hard thinking about all the things you're going to give me." His cackle ricocheted through the courtyard and lifted the fine hairs on my arms.

I struggled to push back a flood of memories. I didn't have the strength to face them. Ignoring the sudden sinking sensation in my gut proved impossible.

Bowing to Snowden meant only one thing. I didn't know if I would have the strength to endure it, but I would.

I would do anything to keep Sara safe.

"I want all your men to drop their weapons and leave." He needed to know I was aware of where his men were.

"What keeps you from shooting me?"

My gaze cut to Sara.

Tears streamed down her face as she reached for Zach. The tattered remnants of her shirt hung from her body. Her skirt had been ripped from her leaving her exposed to Snowden's depraved gaze. But Zach still dangled over the edge.

Ben spoke to Mitzy. I half followed their conversation as she identified the location of Snowden's men. They had closed in on us and gathered outside the walls. It wouldn't take much for them to overpower us.

I had to save my team. Save Zach. Save Sara.

But I knew Snowden.

He wouldn't let me save them all, and I would pay. In blood, sweat, and yes, even tears, he would make me pay.

I could do this.

I had to do this.

"Have your men head to the dock. I want them on that boat and headed out to sea in the next five minutes."

"Bossy, aren't we, my boy?"

My shoulders lifted each time he used that name, and a shudder ripped through me. The bastard knew it. He used it against me, but I would stand tall.

I would stand until I had to fall.

Snowden regarded me for a moment. We were locked in a battle of wills, determining which of us would cave first. It wouldn't be me. I lifted my weapon and looked through the sight.

If I killed Snowden, I would lose Zach.

With the men in the crowd subdued, my team turned their weapons on the men holding Sara and Zach. They could take out all five men. Sara might survive, but Zach would fall.

Snowden could be a brilliant fucker. He had all the insurance in the world as long as Skye's son dangled over the edge.

Alpha team moved through the crowd separating the women. They corralled the girls in one corner while forcing the men to the front of the house.

Bravo kept their weapons trained on the men holding Sara. Ben, Mel, Bay, and Chad kept a steady bead on Snowden, lighting up his chest with four red dots.

Mitzy's voice crackled in my ear. *Men moving to the docks.*

When had Snowden ordered his men to move? I missed that. Were they still armed?

Snowden tapped his ear. "Your little bird is correct, my boy. My men are moving. See how nice I can be? How generous? All my men will leave. You understand how this works, don't you? Mine leave. Yours follow. We're going to make this an intimate event when you bow to me, aren't we?"

Ben and I exchanged glances.

Snowden had been listening the entire time.

What fools we had been.

I ground my teeth and seethed as the seconds ticked by. We were at a standoff, but Snowden moved his men. Knowing our communications had been compromised, we limited what we said to only the essentials.

Far above us, our drones followed the progress of Snowden's men. They boarded the boats. Alpha team ushered the men from the courtyard to the docks and watched them climb on board with weapons raised.

Snowden refused to allow my team back inside. I grudgingly acquiesced. Alpha team returned to the beach at the back of the estate. Their exit would be via the water. Our second helicopter would pick them up a mile offshore.

Mitzy tracked the progress of the boat carrying Snowden's men as they pulled away and headed to the mainland.

Snowden and I glared at each other until the chop, chop, chop of an inbound helicopter filled the night air. A feral grin spread across Snowden's face as the helicopter landed in the clearing of the garden, then he rubbed his hands together.

"I'm really looking forward to seeing Elsbeth again."

"You say one word to her and I put a bullet between your eyes." I cocked my head toward the front wall where Sara and Zach waited.

Snowden lifted his arm and gave a flick of his hand. The men with Sara backed her away from the edge. Zach was finally pulled back from where he dangled, and I breathed out my first solid breath since this nightmare began.

They moved Sara from the wall and descended the stairs. A movement to my right caught my eye. Skye had arrived bracketed by Ryker Lyons and Tia Meyers. Their mandatory lifejackets flapped around them as they jogged into the courtyard.

I held my hand up, telling them to maintain their position. I didn't trust Snowden.

With a flick of my hand, I had Bravo team split up. Half of them guarded the women huddled in the corner. Chances were one of them, or more, worked for Snowden. I couldn't risk one of them doing something at the last minute.

At the front of the courtyard, three men appeared with little Zach. No Sara.

What the fuck?

My throat burned. My pulse thundered past my ears. I didn't know how to get us all out of this hell.

The men with Zach marched to the center of the courtyard. Snowden presided over us all from his vantage point on the wall. His gaze swept to Skye, and his dark eyes glittered.

Skye refused to meet his gaze. Her full attention locked on her son.

"It's time." The words fell from my lips with a sense of finality. I knew what awaited me, but at least Sara and Zach would be free.

Snowden made a gesture, and the man holding Zach placed my nephew on the ground. The three of them backed off, holding their hands in the air.

I still had ten armed men in the compound. We had the upper hand, but Snowden held Sara, and I didn't know where.

With a nod to Skye, my sister rushed forward. Ryker and Tia advanced with her. They kept their weapons levied on the men backing away. Skye swept Zach into her arms and buried his head beneath her chin with a sob.

Her wide, frightened eyes took me in. We exchanged much in that moment. She knew what I sacrificed.

Hope, fear, anger, frustration.

Desperate emotions reverberated in the space between us.

I wanted to go to her, but I refused to lower my weapon. My arms were tiring, but I kept that damn dot dancing between Snowden's eyes.

Skye retreated with Ryker and Tia guarding their exit.

"Now, Sara." I ground out the words and turned my attention to Snowden. "Where is she?"

"Now, I told you that you could only save one. It's time for your men to leave. They can take the slaves."

"Sara and Zach. That was the deal."

My attention shifted to the score of women huddled in the corner. I needed to save them too.

"I think you got that wrong." His dark gaze cut to the gates where Skye hurried her son to the safety of the helicopter. "There's one more boat. You can take the slaves. I can always get more. But your men need to leave."

"Where's Sara?" It was hard to keep the emotion out of my voice.

"Forest." Ben bumped my arm. "We can take him."

"He still has Sara."

I needed to know she would be safe.

"What are you waiting for, boy?" Snowden's sneer made me want to throat punch him.

"Where is she?" I ground out the words.

"Safe… for the moment. You got the brat. You have the slaves. It's time for your men to leave." He gestured toward the dock. "There's a boat waiting for them."

My attention shifted to the leader of Bravo team, and I gave a sharp nod. I would still have my nannies. But then what?

Bravo team escorted the girls out.

Xavier's men surrounded me.

Mitzy confirmed there were no more men on the island. Her infrared sensors showed my team of five, Snowden, his two bodyguards, and Sara.

Skye made it to the helicopter.

The confirmation came in, but I had them wait. I needed Sara on that helicopter. My nannies would go with her, protecting her instead of me.

I would remain and pay whatever price Snowden demanded. My life meant nothing, and I gave it freely if it saved Sara.

We waited for the second boat to load. Bravo team departed

with the rescued slaves, leaving me and my nannies with our weapons pointed at Snowden.

It was a precarious position. Snowden could duck and dodge. We could lose our advantage.

But then Sara appeared behind him. She struggled in the grip of the men holding her as they brought her to Snowden.

Ignoring the targets we had on him, he yanked Sara to him, putting her between him and the bullets I desperately wanted to plant in his chest.

The ground beneath my feet shuddered as I realized how this would play out.

"Your men had better be on that helicopter in two minutes, or pretty Sara here dies." He put a knife to her throat. "It's time to bow to your Master."

I would never call that man master, but I would go to my knees.

"And how do I know you won't hurt her?"

"You don't, but you know me as a man of my word, and I promise you this."

I wasn't going to like whatever he said next.

"And that is?"

"Simple. Whatever I want, whatever I ask, you do it. You do it with a smile on your face, with your head bowed, and with Master spilling from your lips. You belong to me, Forest. You serve me. You do that, and no harm will come to the girl. I won't touch her. My men won't touch her. The only one who fucks her will be you. But…" Snowden lifted a cautionary finger. "The first time you fight me, the first time you resist or refuse to follow a command, the girl will pay. You could only save one. You made your choice, but I promise if you do as you're told, no one will touch the girl."

My cheeks heated as fury built within me. I was going to kill the bastard, but first, I would bide my time. He wanted me, and I knew what that meant. I understood what I would endure.

But could I trust a monster to keep his word?

"Your word means nothing."

He pressed the knife against Sara's throat, and a bead of dark crimson appeared. "I could kill her, but I'm going to keep her if only to ensure your continued good behavior. The girl can even stay with you. I don't care."

If she stayed with me, then maybe I could somehow protect her. It was impossible to believe anything Snowden said, but there was something I knew beyond a doubt.

He wanted me.

He wanted me willing and compliant.

"Your two minutes begins now. Say goodbye to your men." He arched a brow.

My gut churned with the vileness that was Snowden. I came here to take down a monster and close a chapter on my life. Instead, I was reopening my worst nightmare.

With a deep inhale, I took all the goodness in my life, all the laughter and light, and locked it in the darkest corner of my mind.

Snowden would never have that piece of me.

"Go." I turned to Ben.

"Forest…" His mouth gaped, but I shook my head.

"It's the only way."

"But…" An agonized expression stretched across his face.

I gave a sharp nod. There was no time to argue the inevitable.

"Keep Skye safe."

"We'll find a way." Ben clamped his hand on my shoulder.

I didn't doubt Ben would find a way to free me. What I doubted was what would be left when they did.

I had no illusions about what Snowden planned.

"Ninety-seconds." Snowden let his voice snap. He was a man of his word. I understood that and what it meant. We didn't have time to dick around.

I gave Ben a shove and handed him my weapon.

"Go."

My nannies exchanged horrified expressions, but they understood.

This battle had been lost.

Ben, Mel, Bay, and Chad loped away, devouring the ground with their long strides. They raced to make it to the helicopter, leaving me behind.

I closed my eyes and took my last breath of freedom.

The rotors spun up, and the blades cut through the air.

Wind buffeted me as they took off.

With a final glance, I saw Skye peering out of the open side of the helicopter.

She clutched Zach to her chest. As the helicopter angled away, the words she used to tell me when the darkness overcame me echoed in my mind.

There is light in the darkest places, and hope is as limitless as the summer sky.

I guess we would see.

I turned to face Snowden.

He arched his brows and pointed to the ground.

I went to my knees.

Chapter Fourteen

SARA

When I watched Forest fall, something died inside of me.

Behind me, Snowden gave a low, throaty chuckle. The sound was ominous and foul. His smug laughter curled around me and filled me with despair.

"Do you see that, my dear. Your boyfriend knows when he's been bested." He eased the knife from my neck.

"You're a monster." It wasn't wise to speak. I knew this, yet I felt a need to say something.

"Some have called me that. To him, I'll become everything."

"Why? Why do you have to do this to him?"

"Because he's the only one who never broke beneath me. He endured and survived, never admitting defeat."

"So, you'll destroy him? For what purpose?"

"To prove what he already knows." Snowden glanced at me, giving me a long moment to look into his eyes. "Isn't that what monsters do?"

His guarded expression slipped for a moment. In that sliver of time, a profound sadness simmered in Snowden's gaze. He stared down at Forest with ravenous hunger, but something else was there as well. If I didn't know better, I would call it adoration.

The hardened planes of his face emanated strength and brutality. His long, aquiline nose radiated superiority, but his full lips parted with hungry need.

"You should be careful about how you speak to me. I've given my word not to touch you, but that doesn't mean I won't hurt you."

The arch of his eyebrows lifted with the only warning he would give. I couldn't help but swallow against the bile rising in my throat.

"I don't believe you'll keep your word." I practically spat at him. "You're cruel, inhuman, and despicable."

"I'm cruel, very human, but I cleave to my honor. I can be very creative, however. Watch your tone."

His piercing glare cut off my breath. My heart skipped with the fear surging in my veins. My near nakedness made me feel vulnerable, but I sensed some truth in what he said.

Snowden wouldn't touch me, but he planned on using me to hurt Forest. I could get terribly lost in the horrors he promised, but I vowed to remain strong.

For Forest.

I couldn't let this man use me against him.

With a blink, I crawled my way out of the intensity of Snowden's gaze.

"Now, you understand." He spoke as if I understood some profound truth, but my mind reeled with the impossibility of this entire situation. He canted his head to the side and took a long time admiring my near-naked state.

"Or you will." He pointed down to Forest. "He'll suffer every time you disobey. You'll be by my side, fetching and carrying, serving and pleasing, doing whatever I demand. Fail to please me, and it won't be you who pays, but rather him."

My chest squeezed with the vileness radiating off this man.

He leaned toward me. "There are many ways to torture a man. Do you want to be the source of his pain? Or, do you want to be the only comfort he's allowed? And I will allow that. I'll allow it because you're precious to him, and it gives me something to take away."

My eyes widened, not sure I understood.

"That's right, my dear. Please me, and I reward him. He'll need someone to take care of him. Forest thinks to endure what I have planned, but I'll break him. Are you strong enough to do what it takes to be there when it's time to put him back together again?"

"You plan to use us against each other." I finally understood.

"I plan to use you to help each other, but don't worry. I'll keep my word. I won't touch you. I'll keep you safe as a bird locked in a gilded cage. But if he falters, I'll rip you from the cage."

Somehow, I managed to suck in a breath. I felt as if I had run a marathon. I was breathless, and my heart raced.

"Now, if you'll excuse me…" He glanced at Forest, who knelt in the middle of the courtyard. "Forest and I need to get reacquainted."

I didn't want to know what that meant, but when Snowden grabbed at his crotch, I couldn't help but notice the long, hard length of his arousal. The man intended to…

No. No. No!

I couldn't watch, but Snowden's men gripped my arms and forced me to follow them. We gathered under a trellis covered in sweeping vines that blotted out the night sky.

I understood why.

The canopy provided Snowden protection from the guns circling overhead. The helicopter had yet to leave.

Given a chance, Forest's men would take Snowden out.

That gave me hope because it was only a matter of time. But could they see beneath the thick vegetation? Snowden kept me close, and I understood the reasoning behind that as well.

I was his human shield.

Forest's men couldn't see to target Snowden and keeping me close, confused any infrared they may have. The men beside me were huge, but Snowden wasn't much larger than me.

"It's nice, isn't it?" Snowden stopped a few steps in front of where Forest knelt out in the open. He wasn't speaking to me, but rather to Forest.

"You on your knees…It feels like old times." Snowden stretched his arms over his head, interlocking his fingers and cracking his knuckles. "Like we're finally right where we belong."

Forest glared at Snowden and rocked back on his heels. Deep breaths huffed out of his chest.

He barely controlled his anger. His muscles bunched, and I could see him getting ready to charge Snowden. But then his gaze cut to me. With a sweep of his eyes, he took me in, head to toe.

I felt more exposed beneath Forest's gaze than I had with Snowden, and I didn't know why. Snowden showed no interest in me. Forest? It wasn't interest but rather pain.

I stood to the side of Snowden, a step behind, where his men bracketed me. They no longer touched me, but their presence wasn't something I could ignore.

A madman, Snowden's promise not to harm me wasn't something I placed any faith in. There would be pain, degradation, and rape. I could feel it settling in the air between us.

"Cuff him." Snowden pointed at Forest.

A big man, surely Forest could take Snowden and his men out, but he turned his eyes to me, and I knew he would do nothing to jeopardize my safety.

Didn't he know this was just a fucked-up game?

I wasn't safe.

Forest couldn't keep me safe.

Forest obediently placed his hands behind his back and allowed Snowden's men to bind his wrists.

The lights from the helicopter flashed in the night as it circled us. I knew Forest's men worked to get a line on Snowden, a shot they could take without placing me in danger.

At least little Zach would be safe.

Snowden must have tracked my gaze because he looked up into the sky.

The helicopter should have gone by now. I could only imagine what was going through the minds of everyone on board.

Oddly, Snowden didn't look the least bit worried. A malignant and anticipatory smile spread across his face.

What were we missing?

Right now, Skye would be clutching her son tight to her chest.

The terror of his abduction slowly easing as she checked for injuries. Zach was bruised, but Snowden hadn't harmed him.

Xavier's men had to be fuming. How powerless did they feel? Safe up there while Forest knelt on the ground down here.

I could feel their tenseness, the lock of their jaws as they stared down the scopes of their rifles. The frustration they felt ate at me because I wanted them to find that shot.

I also wanted them to hurry up and fly away. They didn't need to see Forest like this.

"Bring him here." Snowden took a step back while his men lifted Forest off his knees and practically dragged him under the edge of the protective canopy of lush vegetation.

They forced Forest back to his knees and returned to their positions on either side of me. Standing over Forest, Snowden propped his hands on his hips.

"I want your surrender, boy."

"I'm on my fucking knees. I'd say you have it."

"I see the fire in your eyes. You have it in that head of yours to fight me."

He was right about that.

Forest's eyes churned with fury. First chance he had, all that anger would be unleashed on Snowden. I didn't want to be around when that happened.

"I'm going to break you, tear you apart so badly that you'll beg for me to stop. Your wounds will remain raw and open, oozing with your misery. You'll never be able to close them. I hold this power over you. You'll embrace it, and even though you'll want to kill me, you'll love me instead. I bring order to the chaos in your head. You'll serve me, please me, and you'll do anything for me. I'll always be with you, swimming in that head of yours."

"You have me on my knees." Forest ground out the words. "But that's all you'll ever get from me."

"Oh, you're going to give me so much more. I'm going to rip out your heart, and then I'm going to feed it to you while you beg for my kindness."

My attention shifted between the two men.

How much worse could things get?

There had to be an endgame to Snowden's drawn-out speech. It was torturous to watch, nearly impossible to endure because I knew this was only the beginning. Snowden had something up his sleeve.

What would my role be in all of this?

Snowden intended to use me to keep Forest in line. I knew this, but how?

Forest wasn't like ordinary men. His mind didn't work like normal people.

I didn't think Snowden truly understood what kind of gift that could be. And to Forest, I was nothing. Snowden got that wrong. Forest didn't love me. He wouldn't go to his knees for me as he had done for Skye.

Theirs was a love so profound it made my heart ache. I was glad he had someone in his life to love and who loved him back, but the love of a foster sister was nothing compared to that of a lover, and Forest didn't have that.

He never would.

I didn't know what my future held, but I prayed Forest found a man with the strength to love him. He deserved to know what real love felt like.

"I'm going to start by taking something precious from you. Consider it your first lesson in obedience. Pay attention, boy. I can do anything I want. Take anything I want. You can't stop it. And you can't stop me; but obey me, and you can prevent those you care about from getting hurt."

Snowden pointed to the helicopter.

"Your friends seem unwilling to leave us to our reunion. Let's take care of that, shall we?"

He gave a signal

I glanced around, looking for who it was meant for. The men standing beside me didn't budge.

A loud pop sounded.

A low whoosh followed.

The sky brightened, and I peeked around the thick canopy.

A trail of fire shot from one of the towers.

They'd fired a rocket.

Forest saw it. He watched with me, paralyzed with fear.

My heart leaped to my throat, and I choked on a scream.

Canting hard to the side, chaff shot out from the helicopter. Countermeasures against a rocket mortar, they were meant to confuse the heat-seeking guidance, but they were too close.

Light flashed.

The tail rudder exploded.

Without a stabilizing force, the helicopter spun out of control. It lost altitude, spewing smoke as it spiraled downward.

They were going to crash.

Forest surged to his feet. Head down, hands tied behind his back, and he charged Snowden.

Expecting the attack, Snowden stepped to the side. The men standing beside me leaped into action. They tackled Forest, taking him to the ground. Forest landed with a thud on his shoulder.

His agonized cry pierced the air.

The helicopter spun out of sight as the pilot fought the inevitable.

They were going down.

I couldn't stop watching. The tail rotor sputtered. Thick black smoke billowed out from the cabin.

I waited for the explosion, and the flames which would follow, but heard nothing beyond Forest's roar.

Snowden brushed the dirt off his suit. He knelt before Forest, placing his face close.

"She's dead, my boy. Elsbeth is dead. Her brat is dead. Everyone you love is gone. That's the price for defiance. I told you to send them away. Their deaths are yours to bear."

Forest's roar turned into soul-breaking sobs.

My heart broke, and I rushed to his side. I didn't care what the men would do. All I knew was that I had to be there for Forest. To hold him, touch him, comfort him in some small way.

Snowden didn't flinch when I took Forest in my arms. He allowed the contact, almost as if he wanted to watch what we would do.

I felt his eyes on us as he studied our interaction.

I probably gave him all the ammunition he needed to use against Forest and destroy what was left of the man I loved.

Forest buried his head against my chest while misery poured out of him. His entire body shook with his sobs.

Slowly, I rocked him. His entire body stilled.

"You bastard!" I screamed at Snowden. "He did everything you wanted. You promised to let Zach go. You didn't need to…to…" I couldn't say kill them. I couldn't admit he had killed Skye and Zach and all the men on board.

I knew this man was evil but failed to understand what that meant.

"I let the brat go, but they didn't leave. Actions have consequences." He shrugged. "This is your first lesson, girl. As long as Elsbeth was out there, he would fight to get back to her. Now, he has nothing out there to fight for." Snowden's hard gaze tunneled into me. "He has only you, and you're right here with me. He won't leave me as long as I have you."

There was no compassion in the darkness of his gaze.

No humanity.

Nothing redeemable.

Snowden's voice softened. "Imagine all the fun the three of us are going to have together."

"You didn't have to do that. Forest surrendered. He gave himself to you."

"No." Snowden's attention shifted to Forest. "He hasn't given himself…yet."

With a snap of his fingers, Snowden's men went to work. They yanked Forest out of my arms and set him back on his knees.

Forest folded over until his forehead touched the ground. His deep sobs sliced through my heart.

"You're a soulless bastard." My words came out barely above a whisper.

Snowden's expression hardened. He came to me, and before I could register what he intended, he slapped my cheek.

Hard.

My head whipped to the side, and my teeth cut the inside of my cheek. The force of his slap spun me, and I stumbled, nearly falling to the ground.

But I recovered.

I stood my ground, and my gaze landed on Forest.

He straightened his spine and sat back on his knees. Tears streaked his face, but there was no emotion left in his expression. His vacant eyes stared through and past me.

"I'll do whatever you want, but don't touch the girl." His low rumble slammed into me.

I placed a hand over my belly because I didn't recognize the man staring back at me.

My tender, sweet Forest was gone.

Chapter Fifteen

FOREST

IN THE BLINK OF AN EYE, THE WORLD AS I KNEW IT ENDED.

Skye was dead.

My sister was...dead.

My nephew...dead.

Xavier's men...dead.

They were all dead.

A piece of me went with her into her watery grave where it mourned her loss amongst a drowning scream.

As for the rest of me?

Something inside of me broke.

Death swam inside of me.

Despair clawed its way to the surface, seeking and finding purchase in the present.

Hope faded away until it disappeared.

All those emotions I'd locked away meant nothing.

Snowden reached right in and ripped out my heart. He gutted my soul and scraped away my humanity.

My gaze cut left, and Snowden followed the path of my eyes to Sara.

Rubbing his hands together, he gave a sharp nod. One of the men took out a knife.

Snowden killed Skye, and now he would kill Sara. I felt it in my bones. I couldn't save Skye. I lured her to her death. I was responsible for what happened to Skye, my men, and her son.

Me.

I killed them.

My gut churned, and I turned my attention back to Snowden. I wasn't brave enough to watch him violate Sara. The knife went to Sara's hip, slid under the fabric of her panties, and cut them away.

Snowden went to her.

He gripped her chin, pinching painfully by the way her eyes widened, and her tears flowed.

Her distress leaped across the distance and arrowed directly to my heart. That's where her pain lodged, with a sharp tearing inside my chest.

My angel closed her eyes, and faint breaths fluttered out of her mouth.

He wrapped a hand in her hair and jerked her head back. Tracing the fullness of her lips with his thumb, he watched for my reaction.

Anger built within me, but I knew better than to react. It would only make things worse.

Snowden's eyes pinched, and he slid his finger beneath her remaining bra strap. Slipping it over her shoulder, he watched me like a hawk as he bared her breasts.

I didn't move.

"Do you think she'll enjoy this?" He glanced at his men and gave a low, throaty chuckle. "I know they would like to sample her flesh. What do you think, boy? Should I let them spread her legs? Or maybe, spread her ass cheeks and fuck her there? What do you think? What would your girl like best?"

A sharp gasp slipped from her lips as he placed his heavy hand over her midsection. Breaths pulsed in and out of her, growing faster and faster as panic rimmed her eyes.

Snowden gave another nod, and the men forced my angel to her knees. Sara's body crumpled. Her bare knees scraped against the rough ground, and she bit back a cry.

We wouldn't survive this.

There was no way.

"Get your fucking hands off her," I shouted. "You want me. Name it, and it's yours, but don't touch the girl."

Don't ruin my angel.

Snowden lifted his hands off Sara. Her sobs split the air. With his hands held palms out, he beamed with victory.

I didn't blame him.

He'd won.

The fucker had won.

Snowden approached me. Triumph filled his expression. He grabbed at his crotch and gave it a good shake, letting me know he was hard, hungry, and intent on slaking his desire.

"Your surrender boy. I want your willing surrender. No fighting. No resisting. I say jump, and you ask how high on the way up. I tell you to suck, and you swallow me whole. I tell you to bend your knees, you bow your fucking head, and thank me for the privilege. When I want you, you jump at the opportunity and spread your ass cheeks wide."

All the evil inside of him spewed outward, covering me in his filth. He was a cancer that infected me. A sickness I couldn't shake. I'd spent a lifetime bringing him down, yet I was the one on my knees.

I wanted to hurt him.

One day, I would kill him.

But I needed to survive this first.

I would survive, or I would die.

What I wouldn't do was surrender.

Snowden tugged at his belt, freed it from his belt loops, and handed it to the man standing beside him. That one wrapped the buckle around his wrist and folded the belt in half to form a loop. He slapped the thick leather against his palm.

Sara flinched.

I swallowed bile.

"I want you to admit I own you." Snowden flicked open the top of his fly. The rasp of his zipper cut through the air as he dragged it down. The entire time, he kept his attention on me.

I ignored Snowden.

I couldn't tear my eyes from Sara's trembling form. She didn't deserve this.

Pure and innocent, she'd been brought into a hell of my making. The man not holding the belt pressed between her shoulder blades and forced her torso down until her cheek pressed against the tiles.

Her gaze flicked to me for half a second.

At that moment, the light died inside of her. Her gaze turned glassy, unseeing, as she retreated inside of herself.

Her body went limp.

Snowden fumbled with his pants, and my attention shifted back to him. He pulled out his engorged cock and fisted the shaft.

"No teeth. Scrape me...bite me..." He thrust his index finger toward Sara. "She pays. Ten strikes of that belt...each time. I know you remember how I like it."

A shudder ran down my spine. My stomach churned, and I fought against the urge to hurl.

There is light in the darkest places.

Skye's words returned to me, and my attention shifted back to Sara. I no longer believed Skye's words.

I had fallen into the darkest pit of hell and dragged an innocent angel down with me.

Memories flooded my mind. Long days at the office when Sara brought in food, making sure I ate.

She took care of me.

I remembered all the mornings when she kicked my ass off the couch because I refused to go home after working through the night.

She brought clothes for me, so I had something clean to wear as I stayed for another day before she physically kicked me out of the office.

The little frustrated sounds she made when I forgot to shake hands or ask something personal when meeting with clients flitted through my mind.

She was always on me about the little things. Things I didn't care about, but she said made a world of difference when dealing with people.

She teased me, took care of me.

Sara made life more comfortable.

A breath of fresh air, she never failed to bring a smile to my face, or erase one of my many scowls. I laughed with her and experienced the world differently through her eyes.

When all I saw was black and white, Sara would breeze by and show me a world full of a kaleidoscope of color.

She frustrated me. Nagged me all the damn time.

I lost track of the number of times I fired her. Anyone but her would have walked away a hundred times.

Not Sara.

I could be a demanding boss, but she stuck with me.

I never asked her why, and over time, I grew accustomed to her presence.

To her smiles.

Her exasperated sighs.

Her fussing over me.

The softness of her laughter.

Snowden came at me with a smile showing his full teeth.

My insides seized as revulsion ripped through me. I closed my eyes to escape this degradation, but he tapped my cheek.

"Welcome home."

I gave a shake of my head. "Let her up. Cover her, and you can have me."

No matter if I escaped this alive, or faded out in death, this would change me forever.

"That easily? I'm a little disappointed. I expected more of a fight. Maybe you've missed me more than I thought?"

My eyes pinched against the pain. "You gave your word you wouldn't touch her. Honor that, and I'll do whatever you say."

I left unsaid what would happen if he didn't. Snowden didn't care if I sucked his cock or let him fuck me in the ass. That wasn't what he wanted.

He wanted to break me. My suffering was what got him off.

"I see you breaking already." Snowden's taunt filled the air. "Open up. Take me in. Do a good job, and I'll let her up."

Hope withered within me. How could I save her when there was no escape?

You wait. You wait for your friends to save you.

That's all I could do. And until they did, until Xavier and his team found us, I would do whatever it took to protect Sara and save her from the worst this monster had to offer.

Snowden had degraded me when I was a boy. He beat me to within an inch of my life more times than I thought possible. I'd endured his unwanted invasion before. I would endure it again.

It was only a body.

I could give him my body.

Of all the horrors I'd survived, I would survive this one too. I'd take the pain, stuff it down deep where it would fester and grow. Somehow, I would use my self-loathing and grow stronger from the pain.

I opened my mouth and closed my eyes, but Snowden's low tsk, tsk, tsk had me opening my eyes again. The fucker wouldn't let me escape this horror by hiding inside my head. He wanted me to be an active participant in his victory.

My fingers curled into fists behind my back. If they'd been free, I would have strangled the life out of the bastard.

I would do it real slow too.

Strangle him until his face turned blue, then I would let up. Let the bastard gag. Watch his face turn beet red. Then I would do it all again.

Each time, I'd increase the pressure until his larynx finally caved beneath my fingers. I'd leave him to suffocate while I watched the light go out in his eyes.

Instead, he watched the light wither inside of me as he shoved his cock in my face.

The first threads of my sanity unraveled as the violation began.

Chapter Sixteen

SARA

I couldn't watch. The best thing I could do for Forest was to turn my head, but I couldn't silence the sounds.

The satisfied grunts coming from Snowden, the knowing chuckles of my guards, or that final horrific shout which had to be Snowden's release, I tried to block it all out. I kept my eyes squeezed shut, but it didn't help because my imagination filled in all the gut-wrenching details.

But then, it ended.

Snowden came with a roar. He praised Forest on doing such an excellent job with an affectionate slap to Forest's cheek.

Naked and afraid, I was thankful for the lingering heat of the tropics, but the bugs had come out. Mosquitoes buzzed me and bit my flesh. I would be covered in welts if I didn't get inside.

Snowden's men had their hands on me again. They lifted me to my feet, where I stumbled between them. Kneeling for so long, my legs fell asleep.

I did open my eyes. I had to.

When I looked at Forest, he turned away, hanging his head in shame. I didn't blame him.

I'd been witness to the ultimate degradation, but I feared Snowden had only begun.

Snowden tugged at his shirt and pulled it over his head. Before I realized what he was doing, he tossed it to me.

"As promised, my boy. For a job well done. No scraping of your teeth, the girl gets to wear clothes."

The shirt reeked of Snowden's vile scent. I didn't want to put it on, but I was wise enough not to fall on my sword over a stinky shirt.

Forest watched as I shrugged on the shirt. I slid it over my body and covered my nakedness. It hung halfway to my knees.

"I think we're going to have fun." Snowden tucked his now flaccid cock back into his pants. "Now, to make our exit." He gripped Forest's chin and bent down. "How do you think we should leave? I don't want your friends following us."

Forest said nothing.

Snowden raised his hand and pointed at me.

The man holding Snowden's belt reared back and struck my leg. The force of the blow lifted me off my feet. I stumbled forward and fell to my knees.

I couldn't help the blood-curdling scream as my entire world erupted in pain.

"When I ask a question, you answer. Do you not understand our arrangement? Or do you like watching her suffer."

"What is it you want?" Forest ground out the words.

I didn't know how he was holding it together. Not after Snowden...

A shiver rippled down my spine. I didn't want to think about what Forest endured.

"How do you think we should leave?" Snowden gazed down at Forest. "They have eyes in the sky, but I don't want them tracking us."

"Leave the way we came in." Forest gave a noncommittal shrug.

"And here I thought we understood each other." He turned to the man who wasn't holding the belt. "Dan, hold the girl down."

Dan came at me, and I scooted away with a shriek.

"Don't you fucking touch her." Forest's roar had the man stopping in his tracks.

"No one will touch her, my boy, but you need to help us get out of here. You know your team. You know how they think. They will follow us, and that isn't something I want. You and me, the girl and my men, we're going to disappear."

Disappear?

If there was one thing Snowden excelled at, it was at being impossible to find. But if we disappeared, how would Forest's team rescue us?

Then I realized that was the point.

I huddled on the ground while Snowden badgered Forest until Forest gave Snowden what he wanted.

The wealth Snowden commanded astounded me. Within half an hour, he dispatched two helicopters. Like the helicopter which had carried Skye, they landed in the garden.

My heart shattered when I realized I hadn't mourned Skye's death. Her son's death. Or the deaths of the men who had stood by Forest's side.

There had been no time to process what had happened, but the pain of their loss knifed through me. I found it impossible to breathe and curled on the ground in a fetal position.

If only I could rewind time.

What brought me out of my catatonic state was the deep rumble of Forest's voice.

"Sara…" The warmth of his fingers fluttered over my temple.

My eyes fluttered open and met his tortured gaze.

"Forest…"

"The helicopters are almost here. I need you to be strong. You need to get up."

"Skye?"

The tightness of his expression told me not to pursue that line of questioning. We would mourn our losses later.

With his uncharacteristic help, I managed to make it to my feet. A glance at Snowden showed him zipping his pants and threading the buckle back through his belt loops.

Forest released me and tugged at his pants.

I closed my eyes, squeezing out the pain because when I collapsed on the ground, the fly of Forest's pants hadn't been undone.

How long had I been out?

What had happened to Forest?

Those were questions I shouldn't ask. The smile on Snowden's face told me everything I needed to know.

Snowden wore one of my guard's shirts. I still had his shirt covering me. My skin itched from numerous insect bites, and a thin sheen of perspiration covered my skin.

Forest wouldn't meet my eye as he tugged his pants over his hips and closed the zipper.

A few minutes later, the sound of a helicopter cut through the darkness—not one helicopter, but rather two.

What happened next confused me. Men spilled out from the helicopters and raced toward our position. They surrounded us, and we all walked back to the helicopters as a group.

The men moved in and around us, weaving in a chaotic pattern I didn't understand. We walked with them. Snowden's guards pushed me. Forest followed Snowden's lead.

Then we separated into two groups. We piled into one of the helicopters and left the island behind.

When we landed, the odd shuffling of people happened again. This time, there were three vans that we piled into. Each time we went under a bridge, our strange caravan would stop. The shuffling of people would happen again.

Then the three vans split up.

Once again, under the overpasses, we repeated the odd procedure. Two cars met us, and we swapped back.

At the next overpass, we lost the van.

This continued several times until I finally realized what was happening.

Mitzy's drone had to still be in play, but there was no way she could follow all the cars.

We were lost in the shuffle.

Snowden was a fucking genius.

I glanced at Forest, who sat meekly beside Snowden in the SUV.

This wasn't Snowden's brilliance.

Forest had been forced to orchestrate our abduction. There was no way for his men to follow us.

We were officially lost.

After a train ride, a boat ride, and a plane ride, we had one final leg before we finally stopped.

Snowden brought us halfway around the world.

We swapped the tropical climate of the Philippines for mountains and impassable snow and entered a fortress.

The imposing monstrosity of stone felt as cold as the frigid temperatures outside. I imagined our world would narrow down to a cold, dank cell somewhere in the basement.

"You did well on the plane, boy." Snowden walked in front of us.

Forest moved beside me; head bowed, spirit broken, body defiled.

I wanted to reach out to him but resisted the urge. From the way he flinched when I drew close, it might be best if I keep my distance.

Or was that an even greater mistake?

Forest didn't need distance. He needed comfort. I wanted to wrap my arms around him and make all of this go away.

As a former rape victim, I knew that would be the worst thing I could do. I remember not being able to stand people touching me. It triggered me, but I also remember the aching loneliness. That descent into my head, the distancing myself from the world, it had nearly been worse than the abuse.

We entered the fortress and were led through a maze of passageways. Instead of heading down to a dank cellar, we climbed ornate stairs.

Snowden led us down a hall and to a door. He pushed it open.

"These are your rooms. The door will remain locked for now.

You and I still have a few things to work out, don't we?" He cocked his head and placed a hand on Forest's arm.

Snowden's thick fingers curled around the back of Forest's arm, stroking him. Revulsion ripped through me at the way he felt Forest's arm.

Forest cleared his throat. "Yes, we do."

"You surprised me." Snowden looked at Forest, then shifted his attention to me. "I expected more of a fight."

"We have a deal." The low rumble of Forest's voice held steady as he regarded Snowden.

"Yes, I suppose we do. Honestly, I like this. I prefer not fighting with you. It makes things more like they should have always been."

Forest glanced at his arm. "You never intended to keep me as a lover. You had other things in mind for me."

"This is true, although I realize it for the mistake it would have been. You would not have survived the rings, and that would have been a terrible loss." Snowden turned to me. "These are your rooms, Miss Sara. You'll stay here with Forest when not serving me."

Serving him?

My wide eyes made Snowden chuckle.

"Leave her alone." Forest's possessive growl had the fine hairs on my arms lifting.

Snowden finally released Forest's arm. He splayed his hand across Forest's chest.

"I said I wouldn't touch her, but she's going to be right by my side, fetching, carrying, pretty much doing what an assistant does. Since she is your assistant, that now makes her mine, and I could use a bit of executive assistant help. Besides, it's more convenient to keep her close by." Snowden gave a wink. "I find constant reminders to be exceptionally effective."

I still wore Snowden's smelly shirt and was naked underneath it. My dignity had been taken, but I considered it an insignificant thing when compared to what Forest had endured and would continue to face.

My brows pinched with confusion as we entered an expansive suite. Anchored by an exquisite sitting room, two doors lead off from the main room. One led to a bedroom. I could see the massive bed from the doorway. I assumed the other led to a bathroom.

What the hell?

Considering our status, I found the opulence of our accommodations unconventional.

Where were our basement cells?

Snowden ushered us into the small sitting room, which held a grouping of couches. Plate glass windows looked out on a snow-covered landscape.

We were in the mountains. From the height of the peaks, I guessed the Alps, but we could be anywhere.

The flight had been brutal.

Unlike my flight to the Philippines, they didn't drug me.

I endured the flight wide awake while Snowden put Forest through hell. I tried not to look, but there had been no escaping what happened.

Guilt swam through me because Forest wouldn't want me to witness his degradation. Not that I had a choice. Part of Forest's pain came from having me present, and Snowden did whatever he could to enhance Forest's pain.

I couldn't leave him to face this horror alone.

Forest rarely met my eye. When our gazes crossed, he quickly averted his eyes with shame.

Bruised and broken.

That seemed to be Snowden's game. He physically abused Forest and systematically broke him down mentally.

Forest took it all. He never once fought when Snowden raped him, and he didn't defend himself when Snowden let our sadistic guards use him as a punching bag.

Forest's pain filled the airplane with misery.

Eighteen hours of torture. He couldn't take much more.

Forest and I stood together, too stunned by the recent change in our circumstances to reach out to each other for comfort.

"I think you'll find your rooms comfortable."

Snowden gave a brief tour, treating us more like honored guests than his prisoners.

146 • ELLIE MASTERS

"There's a king bed in the bedroom. I know you'll want to snuggle. Bathroom is over here."

He spoke about us sleeping together and showering together as if we already engaged in such activities.

A yawn escaped Snowden. "Now, as much as I'd like to spend more time getting reacquainted, I'm a bit put out by that flight. You have the night to rest. In the morning, Paul will show you around."

"Paul?" Forest's voice sparked with interest.

"Yes, he's assigned to your security detail. Mind your manners with Paul. He has a strong arm and my full permission to use whatever measures are necessary to keep you in line."

"Thank you for the rooms." Forest swallowed and let his gaze sweep around the suite. "Our arrangement remains. No one touches her."

"Yes, yes. No one touches Miss Sara, and you do whatever I say." Snowden walked his fingers up Forest's chest. "Now, how about a kiss goodnight?"

The man was certifiable.

He acted like we were guests instead of prisoners.

As Forest leaned down to kiss Snowden, his eyes cut to mine.

I gave a slow blink and turned away. I don't know if I did that to spare Forest having me watch him willingly kiss Snowden, or to spare myself the horror of watching it.

I wanted Forest to resist Snowden. This felt all kinds of wrong.

It was dirty, disgusting, and yet kept me safe. Or at least as safe as I could be as the captive of a madman.

Once the shock wore off, we would need to figure out how to get out of this hell.

If the shock ever wore off, and that was a pretty big IF.

Snowden turned the kiss sloppy. If he kept on…

I didn't want to think about that. Snowden had the libido of a racehorse.

My heart ached for Forest.

We were fortunate, however, because Snowden broke off the kiss. A yawn escaped him.

"Goodnight, boy." He patted Forest's cheek. "Get some sleep.

You're going to need it. We have a busy day tomorrow. Lots of things to discuss."

"Of course, sir."

Snowden left us. The door drew shut, and the distinct sound of a lock turning clicked through the silence.

That sudden absence of sound suffocated me as we stood there, not talking to each other about what had happened. It was unlike Forest not to have something to say.

When I thought of him, his smile had always been the first thing that came to mind. Once you got past his rough exterior and gruff voice, everything about Forest was…soft.

That's not a word most people used when describing him.

Most called him hard, uncompromising, distant, and cold.

But I knew Forest better than most.

A hero who saved orphaned children, he was a champion's champion with the quirkiest humor I'd ever seen. Kindness lingered inside his huge heart.

He'd always been accomplished at putting a smile on my face when I needed it most.

I could see how people considered him cold and unapproachable. He wasn't the kind of man who asked about a person's day or welcomed any of the messy emotions that tiptoed out after such a request, but he saw the important bits and pieces.

If he thought a person was worthy, he would do anything to help them.

Goodness spilled from Forest; it lingered in the softness of the smiles he doled out as if they were the most precious thing in the world. He was the safest person to be around because he genuinely cared about making the world a better place.

I looked at him, my heart breaking because that man no longer existed. Instead, only the shell of the man I once knew remained.

Everything that made Forest the man I loved was gone.

He gave one look at me, then headed to the bathroom. He kicked off his shoes, pulled his shirt over his head, yanked down his pants, and stripped out of his briefs. The actions were automatic, practically robotic, and yet stunning.

He really was magnificent.

"I'm taking a fucking shower." His voice was husky, tired, and every step he took was ponderous and slow.

He left me with my mouth gaping and head spinning.

The shower turned on, and I simply stood in the middle of the room, not sure what I should do. A second later, he poked his head out of the bathroom.

"Come on, Sara. Get in here. We both have filth to wash off."

"I'll wait until you're done."

"No. You're coming in here."

Shock rippled across my face. Surely, he didn't want me to join him?

"I'm not leaving you alone out there." His attention shifted to the locked door.

"Forest…"

"You stay by my side. Do you understand?" He pressed his temple against the doorjamb and let out a deep sigh. "Whatever thoughts are in your head about right and wrong have no place here. Take that filthy thing off and let's wash the last day off our bodies."

"I don't think that's the best idea."

"Please don't argue with me. I don't have the strength to fight you on this. It's just a shower."

Not sure what was happening, my feet moved of their own accord. I didn't know if it was the command in Forest's voice or the bone-weary fatigue in my body, but I didn't question the thought of taking a shower with my boss.

I simply moved.

Forest took my hand in his. He pulled me to him and folded his arms around me. It didn't escape my attention, he was completely naked, although it didn't seem to faze him.

"We'll get through this. I promise. I'll find a way to get you out of this nightmare."

Wrapped in his arms, I felt, if not safe, at least hopeful he would find a way to make the impossible possible.

Forest always came through. Whatever needed to be done, no

matter the cost, he would do it. This both comforted me and tore me apart inside.

The price he would pay to keep me safe was unconscionable.

I never loved him more than I did at that moment. I wanted to kiss him, not in a romantic way—except who are we kidding, I wanted that—but simply to let him know I cared.

My world would unravel if I felt his lips on mine.

Chapter Seventeen

FOREST

I DIDN'T HAVE THE ENERGY TO DEAL WITH THE SHOCK RIPPLING across Sara's face.

Her emotions were too raw, too powerful, too out there in the open.

They were messy, painful things.

And I didn't have the strength to sort through them.

I had two tasks.

That was all I could focus on.

Number One: Wash Snowden's filth from my body.

Number Two: Keep Sara by my side.

No way was I leaving her alone.

We were in enemy territory.

There would be little I could do to keep her safe. Snowden already thought she and I were lovers. He expected something like this—for us to comfort each other.

No reason to let him think otherwise. The more he believed something existed between Sara and me, the more power I held over him.

That shouldn't make sense, but it was the truth.

Snowden wanted my total surrender. He didn't want our

encounters to be a battle of wills, and he didn't care to fight me physically as he took me.

The man was a sadist, but he'd softened since I'd seen him last. He'd weakened. I was in the prime of my life while the sun was setting on his.

Before—I had to think of the first time he controlled me as *Before*. Now, was *Today*—but before he had brutalized me for sport. The more I fought back, the more aroused he became.

I had been smaller then, a boy on the cusp of becoming a man. Tall and lean, I didn't have the strength to fight a fully-grown man.

I had it now.

Our places were reversed.

Snowden knew it. I knew it.

And he knew I knew it.

It made him fear me.

So why take me now?

It wouldn't take much to snap his neck. Each time he fucked me, I held the power to end his life in my hands.

Hell, I could bite off his dick when he shoved it in my mouth if that's what I chose.

He placed a great deal of trust on the hold he had over me, but that was the thing. Snowden had all the control he needed in Sara.

Ours was an uneasy arrangement.

And somehow, I would use his assumptions about Sara against him. I just had to figure things out.

"You need to take off the shirt." I turned on the shower and rotated the valve until scalding hot water poured out of the showerhead.

Her cautious gaze turned to me, then shifted away.

The accommodations Snowden gave us, the comfort he afforded us, came with a message. It spoke to the deviousness of his mind.

It could be taken away in the blink of an eye, or by a single act of defiance on my part.

His most effective weapon was the past he shared with me. I knew how his mind worked. There had been no need to state the obvious. Just like we both knew I could kill him at any moment, we also knew the balance of power had been well established.

The threats he levied against Sara kept me in line. There was no need for him to explain what these accommodations meant.

Behave, and Sara wouldn't be put in a cell.

Behave, and Sara would be able to stay with me.

Behave, and he wouldn't hurt her.

I intended to be the most well-behaved person on the planet.

Sara hadn't moved since I pulled her into the bathroom. I tentatively reached out to touch her cheek and leaned down until our eyes were level.

"It's going to be okay. I promise."

A vale of tears shimmered in her eyes. She was going into shock as the events of the past day played through her mind.

I could see her torment. I felt her pain.

The sad truth, however, was that we didn't have time to wallow in such things.

I brushed away a tear as it slowly rolled down her cheek.

"I need you to be strong." I couldn't survive this if I had to be strong for us both.

What I had to endure would test me.

Snowden wanted me broken, and I had no illusions he would do precisely that.

He had my body to use as he wished, but he wanted my mind. He wanted my adoration and unwavering loyalty.

He wanted to break me, but I knew what he wanted most.

The man wanted my love. He wanted me to want him with desperate hunger.

We'd spent a lifetime circling each other. I chased, and he evaded until he flipped everything upside down and lured me into his trap.

The bastard was a devious fucker.

He would get what he wanted.

I didn't know how I would resist him because he had everything to break me in the form of the sweet angel standing in front of me.

The thing was…I would break.

I would bear that burden.

Sara, however, would not. Somehow, I would get him to release her from this nightmare.

"Sara..." I tilted my head until our foreheads touched. "Don't disappear on me. I need you."

"Forest..." Her breath came out a whisper. "The things he did..."

"Are things he's done before." I let out a sigh and swept my finger along the soft angle of her jaw. "It's just a body."

"He doesn't want your body."

It scared me that she understood the real battle I waged.

"You're right. He wants more."

"And?"

"We'll find our way through. Do you know what Skye always told me?"

Sara gave a shake of her head.

"She told me hope was as limitless as the summer sky. We just need to believe."

"Oh, my God! Your sister." Sara broke before me. Deep sobs wracked her body. "He killed her."

The rage I had so meticulously squirreled away resurfaced. Fire churned in my gut, and my grip tightened against Sara's jaw.

She winced and pulled back.

Horrified at what I'd done, I stumbled back. She cupped her face and looked up at me.

All I saw was red.

A red mark on her jaw.

Fire burning in my veins.

Flames from the rocket.

Snowden would pay.

But I had hope. The helicopter hadn't exploded. It fell out of the sky and into the sea.

Hope.

If it was as limitless as the summer sky, then I had to believe it was as deep as an ocean.

Sara closed the distance and pressed her hand against my chest.

Her fingers splayed over my heart, and I felt a steady lub-dub beating beneath her palm.

As long as I was alive, I would hold on to hope.

"I'm so sorry," she said.

Her touch, soft and gentle, warm and comforting, didn't elicit my usual reaction when a woman touched me. This felt like an extension of my body rather than an unwelcome intrusion.

I didn't shudder. The hairs at the back of my neck didn't lift in revulsion. My gut didn't churn with disgust.

I stared at her hand against my bare skin and shook my head.

What was this?

"Skye didn't deserve—" Sara's voice cracked, but I stopped her before she could say anything further.

Putting my finger over her lips, I gave a slow shake of my head.

I wasn't ready to think about Skye. I'd bottled up my rage and swallowed it whole. It had resurfaced with Sara's words, and I didn't have the strength to deal with that.

"Not now."

That would need to be something for another day.

My existence narrowed down only to those things I could control.

Once again, I took all my emotions and tied them into a tight bundle of pain, regret, and loss. I wrapped my anger and fear around the mess and shoved it back into the bleakness of my mind.

Another day.

Sometime later, I would unravel that mess and deal with it. For now, I would push it as far back in my subconsciousness as possible.

Emotions were my enemy.

To be strong, I needed to be cold, unfeeling, and put my intellect to work on getting us out of this mess.

That meant taking care of Sara and comforting her as best I could. It began by removing the scent of Snowden from her body and mine.

I closed my eyes and placed my hand over hers. The warmth of her touch soothed me on a level I didn't understand.

She was an unexpected sliver of goodness in a living nightmare, and I would use that anyway I could.

Skye always told me there was light in the darkest places. Skye had been that for me when Clark Preston and John Snowden made me wish for the sweet embrace of death.

Was it possible Sara could be my guiding light now?

I wrapped my arms around her and pulled her to me. This would be the second time I brought her into my embrace. Like all the other women in my life, I'd always kept her at arm's length; or further, if I could.

Sara didn't hesitate and wrapped her arms around my waist. We stood together, breathing each other in. I surrendered myself to the moment, and to feeling the softness of her body pressed against mine.

It felt uncharacteristically natural to hold her. Her natural fragrance filled my senses with a calming force. My heartbeat slowed, and my breaths eased. If I could stay here forever, I would.

Even if it was just for show, no doubt Snowden had cameras in every corner of this place.

If I could keep her safe, her light would continue to shine, and when the darkness overcame me, she would be my anchor, my path back to sanity.

She placed her cheek against my chest and let out a low sob.

"I'm so sorry about Skye. Why did he do that?"

Because he could. Because it would hurt me.

But I didn't voice that to Sara.

Snowden didn't take Skye from me to hurt me. He did it to send a powerful message.

I would have done anything to get back to Skye; killing her took her out of the equation. Snowden needed me to be engaged in his little game. That wouldn't happen if I thought I could make my way back to my sister.

Sara didn't voice the second part of that question, which relieved me of the burden of answering it.

But, if he killed Skye, what would keep him from taking her life as well?

My obedience was the key, and maybe something more.

I didn't know if I could give Snowden what he wanted, but I would try. I would swallow my pride and do whatever it took to keep Sara safe.

"Snowden is a monster." I placed my chin on the top of her head, stooping to do so. "I can't worry about what he will or won't do. That's not how I'm going to survive this."

"Forest…" Her voice broke with emotion. "The things he did…"

I smoothed her hair and gave a low, shushing sound to soothe her. "Are nothing compared to what's in store."

"But you…"

"He wants me to suffer, and I will, but it's all a part of the game."

"I'm sorry he made me watch. It's not right."

I pulled away from her, gripped her shoulders, and stooped down again to get eye level with her.

She needed to understand what was at stake and how to survive what would come next.

"You and I, we'll get through this only if we're together." It was time for uncomfortable truths. "He raped me."

Her eyes widened with the memory, then a look of shame overcame her, and she looked away.

I put my finger on her chin and forced her to face me. "He raped me, Sara. He raped me several times, and he's going to do it again. He wants you to watch because he enjoys your pain. My physical pain is one thing, but the emotional pain he inflicts on others is what he truly craves. It's going to hurt. It's going to be uncomfortable. It's going to be hell. But, we're going to be okay. If you understand that, you'll survive."

"How can you say that? When he…when he does those things to you?"

"We don't control anything right now except our reactions. He wants to hurt you by making you a part of this. It's how he exerts his authority and dominance over me. There's. Nothing. You. Can. Do. About. It."

She needed to understand.

I'd lived through this once before. I didn't know if I would survive it again, but I wasn't going to give Snowden his victory without a fight.

"However bad it is right now, it's going to get worse. We won't be prepared for whatever he has planned, and it's going to bring us to our knees."

I knew with absolute certainty things would get worse. Thinking about how that might manifest wasn't healthy, so I focused only on what I could control.

"How can you be this strong?" Her words came out a whisper.

"Because I have you."

Her brows pinched together. "If it weren't for me, he wouldn't be able to hurt you."

"If it weren't for you, I'd already be dead." I didn't mention she would be as well.

There had been no way for us to survive Snowden's trap in that courtyard. Surrendering had been our only option. She didn't understand that yet.

Steam billowed all around us, covering the mirrors and forming a thick fog billowing in the air. I had no illusions against the fact we were being monitored.

This was probably our only safe space. Shrouded in the steam, and our voices muffled by the water, taking a shower together might be our sole refuge.

"Come, I don't know how long the hot water will last. Let's wash away the filth of this day."

Her head shook. "I don't know how you do it."

I had no choice. That was how I did it.

"You're my guardian angel, Sara. You're the light that will get me through. I need you to be strong. Be my light."

She gave a shaky nod as I stepped into the shower enclosure. I wanted to give her privacy as she stripped, but if Snowden watched, he would see. The bastard would know this was the first time we had been naked together.

He thought we were lovers.

That protected Sara.

If Snowden thought I loved her, he would focus on my need to protect her.

I didn't turn my back or avert my gaze as she pulled his filthy shirt off her body. When she stepped into the shower, I pulled her to me and braced for the familiar sensations of disgust.

Skin to skin, chest to chest, she tucked her head beneath my chin and lay her cheek over my heart.

There was no revulsion rippling across my skin.

No disgust rising from the pit of my stomach.

Her softness pressed against my hard body, and something eased within me.

Holding Sara felt like…heaven.

I felt at peace.

Chapter Eighteen

I LOVED TOUCHING FOREST.

There was nothing sexual about it.

Except we were naked and sharing a shower.

Despite that, an uncharacteristic intimacy surrounded us. It was as if we'd been thrown in a crucible, survived the destruction, and emerged newly formed.

We were different.

Our shared experience, as horrific as it had been, and uncertainty of our future, bonded us into, if not a couple, at least a pair of humans struggling to survive.

I barely had my hands wrapped around him before he hugged me tight. Our bodies pressed against each other.

From his steady heartbeat beneath my ear to the breaths surging in and out of his lungs, we connected.

I pressed my hands against his back, marveling at the hardness of his frame. Too broad to reach around him, and much taller than me, my body molded perfectly with his.

Forest kept himself in immaculate shape as a rule, and I got to feel all his rippling muscles as he flexed them beneath the smoothness of his skin.

Much taller than my slight build, his hips hit me mid-abdomen, which placed another part of his anatomy to lie along my belly. Soft and velvety smooth, Forest's penis wasn't what anyone could ever call flaccid. There was simply too much of him.

But he wasn't aroused.

There was no twitching of sexual interest as he held me.

I didn't know what to think about that. A part of me was sad. Sad that I couldn't elicit any interest in him. My pride took a tiny hit. I'd like to think seeing me naked had some kind of effect on a man, but I didn't overthink it. Instead, I simply absorbed the tender moment for what it was.

We were two people finding solace in each other's arms.

This might be the only time I would find myself held by him, and I decided I would enjoy it for what it was.

He comforted me without demanding anything more out of me. Not that I was porcelain thin and would break from our current situation, but I did appreciate his protective nature.

I didn't think I would survive whatever this was without his strength to fall back on. The strangest thing about this was how natural it felt like I belonged with him.

I wanted to melt into him.

The ache in my heart was real, and when he finally let me go, that ever-present longing would begin anew.

For now, I simply breathed in his essence.

Thick and intoxicating, Forest's natural musk infiltrated my nostrils with the scent of pine and woodsmoke, an earthy essence that grounded me.

I could almost believe we would survive our nightmare.

We parted, after a time, and Forest moved to the side to let me stand under the steady stream of water.

I don't know why it surprised me, but the two-person shower came fully stocked with an array of bath products, both masculine and feminine.

I took the floral-scented body wash and lathered my skin, stepping out of the water to let Forest get clean. He needed a good scrub after what he'd endured.

There was no illusion that Forest wouldn't be covered in Snowden's filth again, but this shower felt symbolic. As if water could cleanse our bodies and free us from the unthinkable.

We were prisoners.

And we would endure more from the vileness, which was John Snowden.

How that would happen, as Forest said, was something we couldn't prepare for, but I would strengthen myself against the shock of whatever Snowden planned.

Forest turned around. I'm not sure what I expected in his expression, but his sudden shyness wasn't it.

Despite the odd expression, he refused to avert his gaze and took in my nakedness with what looked to be genuine interest. While his features were devoid of warmth, lacking that spark of desire, he was checking me out.

It was odd to see interest flash in his eyes. I cocked my head, unsure about how to proceed.

"Forest?" I meant to ask him what was up, but I stopped at the sharp shake of his head.

"There's something you need to know." He tugged at his chin.

"What's wrong?"

"Nothing and everything, but I was thinking about... possibilities."

"I don't understand."

"Snowden."

"Yes?"

"It's something he said. It's been bothering me."

"Okay..." He was scaring me, but I didn't want him to see my fear. If I was to be his light, his anchor in the darkness, I had to be strong.

"He thinks we're lovers."

I nodded. "I know."

"But I don't sleep with women."

"Then why does he think we're involved?"

"That's what I'm trying to figure out." He swapped places with me. "Let me wash your hair."

There was a flatness to his voice, a clinical detachment that gave me pause. My initial reaction, *'Um no,'* but Forest never asked for something without reason.

My heart skipped a beat. He, however, didn't hesitate.

When had showering together turned into him washing my hair? Granted, it was just hair, but I didn't need help. Somehow, I'd managed to do that by myself my entire life.

I didn't tell him no. From the look in his eyes, I could see he was ferreting out an answer to Snowden's assumption of our non-existent relationship.

Forest reached around me to reach the dispenser hanging on the wall. It was filled with a clear amber liquid labeled *Shampoo*.

He pushed the dispensing button and cupped his hand underneath until he had enough shampoo to wash my hair five times over. My hair might be long, and it might be thick, but how much hair did he think I had?

"Um, hang on. I need to get it wet first." What the hell was I doing? Was I really stepping back under the water to wet my hair... for Forest?

It sure looked like that was what I was doing.

Holy hell. This was happening.

He nudged my shoulder to spin me around, and then his hands were on me. Well, not me, but my head.

A spot of cold replaced the warm water as he put the glob of shampoo on the top of my hair.

I expected a rough, calloused touch. What I didn't expect was how good his hands felt on me. I couldn't help but close my eyes and bite my lower lip when he massaged the shampoo through my hair.

He made sure to dig in. His dexterous fingers worked some kind of magic, sparking a riot of nerves that shot down my neck where they fired in a random cascade down my back. Despite the thick steam, I couldn't help but shiver.

The man had a surprisingly delicate touch yet was firm enough to send continuous shockwaves shooting through my body.

Oblivious to my reaction, he continued to massage my scalp and work the shampoo through my hair to the roots.

I bit my lower lip and reminded myself this was a platonic, non-sexual encounter, but then I shifted my weight to my rear foot. I backed into Forest. No mistaking the hard length of his arousal jabbing the small of my back.

He grunted, then shifted to the side. I wanted to tell him not to mind, that it was nothing, but something inside of me gave a little cheer.

He may be gay, but he reacted.

To me.

"I've thought about it."

"About what?"

"Snowden."

If that wasn't a mood killer, I didn't know what was. Here I was cheering Forest's erection, and he threw ice water on it.

"What about him?"

"Do you know why I only sleep with men?"

"Because you're gay?"

Duh.

Forest made no secret of his sexual partners. Relationships weren't his thing, just sex.

I lost count of the number of men who tumbled through his bed, but I could count on zero fingers how many had lasted more than a month.

He wasn't a man built for commitment. I didn't know if it was the result of his underlying Asperger's or if he simply had been that unlucky in love. It could be he simply looked for it in the wrong places.

Not that it was any of my business, but I'd seen the hookup app he used. Those kinds of men were out for only one thing: the same thing Forest desired; mutually gratifying sex with no strings.

"I'm not gay."

"Um...you sure about that?"

"Pretty sure."

"But, you date men."

"I don't date them. I fuck them. What I don't do is fuck women, and you want to know why?"

The way he said it, the words twisted with venom. I most definitely didn't want to know. Unfortunately, Forest didn't wait for my response.

"Women are too fragile for..." He hesitated, and his fingers stopped their near toe-curling massage of my scalp.

"For what? Sex?"

I wanted to turn around and have this conversation face to face if only to peek at his cock. I'd seen it before; long, hard, thick, and not mine.

The sight of him pleasuring himself back in his office shower was not an image I would ever get out of my head. Not because it was bad, but because it had been so achingly hot.

"Yes."

"You sure about that?"

"Pretty certain." He grabbed my hair at my nape, twisted it together, and gave the slightest tug.

"Why do you say that? If it's because of your size..." I could not believe we were having this conversation, discussing his sex life, and the size of his cock, while we were naked in a shower together.

He gave a low chuckle. "Not because of that, but thanks."

The way he thanked me for my backhanded compliment of his size reminded me of the banter we used to share. That easy back and forth never failed to bring a smile to my face, even if I often cursed him for his pigheadedness.

"That wasn't meant as a compliment."

"I know. You were simply stating a fact. Something I'm well aware of."

Cocky much? But what did I expect? We were discussing the size of his dick. Any man would crow when complimented on the size of his dick.

"You're a big man, of course, you'd have a big dick, but you're not the first big man in history. There are lots of men the same size as you. They date women and don't break them."

Forest was massive, but I'd seen plenty of wrestlers and athletes who were married or had women hanging off their arms. Some of those women were petite like me, and they didn't walk bowlegged.

Oh hell, that was a thought I needed to get out of my head.

Forest and I didn't have that kind of relationship. He was my boss, and I was his executive assistant. That was where things between us ended.

Except now, we were captives of a psychopath.

However, the whole concept of insert peg A into slot B wasn't lost on me, and I couldn't get my mind to stop imagining how that might feel.

Soft laughter escaped Forest.

A genuine response, I wanted to bottle his laughter up, if only to remind him of it when things turned south. One thing I knew for sure, this happy place we created was nothing more than an illusion.

Things were going to change.

Snowden had only begun to tear Forest down.

"You said 'big dick.'" His low chuckle filled the shower with a dull rumble.

I spun around and pressed the tip of my finger on his breastbone. "Do not let it get to your head."

"Which one?" He glanced down, and I made the mistake of following the path of his eyes.

Down past my finger, following the drops of water as they crawled down his skin, my gaze tripped on a perfect six-pack, made a sideways move to admire the V-grooves which angled from his hips to the apex of his thighs where his erection jutted out between us.

I couldn't help but gasp and jump back.

Forest let loose another rumbling chuckle which lodged itself deep in my chest and settled over my heart.

"Sorry." He took a step back. "It's a natural reaction. I can't really stop it."

"But if you're gay, how…?"

"Told you, I'm not gay. I'm bi."

"Bi?"

"As in bisexual."

It was a struggle to hear him. His voice was so low I could barely make the words out over his natural rumbling tone. The water pouring down on us didn't help.

Bisexual?

I didn't believe it. If he were bisexual, I would know. I would have seen him showing an interest in other women. Hell, with the crazy hours my job required, I practically lived with him. Granted, that was within the confines of work, but I was the person who managed his life.

I knew about all his illicit liaisons. I would know if he slept with women.

A sudden stillness overcame me, and I didn't like the thoughts swirling in my head. If he was bisexual…

All my hopes crashed around me. We spent far too much time together. If he was attracted to women but showed no interest in me, then he wasn't interested in me.

I didn't want to contemplate what that meant.

I was in love with a man who could love me back but chose not to.

Devastating didn't begin to describe the destruction ripping through my heart.

I tried to be strong and pretend his words hadn't crushed the last vestiges of my vain hope, dumb dreams that he could love me back, but my eyes misted.

Tears fell.

Thank fuck we were in a shower where the water washed it all away.

"But, you don't date women." Surprisingly, my voice sounded steady and sure.

"I don't date men either." His response returned to me in a flat baritone, as if that were obvious.

Which it was.

I knew this. Why the hell was I dancing around the obvious?

Because you don't want to get hurt.

He'd already hurt me more than I could bear.

"You just fuck them."

"But I don't fuck women." He took my hand in his. "Why don't you rinse that shampoo out of your hair, and let's talk? I need you to know what happened with Skye."

I knew what happened. Skye told me the gist of it. No real details, but I understood.

Skye and Forest were two foster kids, unrelated, who had been taken in by Clark Preston, a wealthy lawyer. He abused them, sexually and physically, and loaned them out to his friends for a fee.

John Snowden was one of those people. He developed an obsession with both Skye and Forest. He had plans to turn Skye into his sex slave and to make money on Forest in some kind of illegal fight club.

Skye spared me the details, but I inferred the rest based on my own experiences. When people use words like sex and slave, there was little left to the imagination, and I knew Snowden abused Forest.

After being forced to watch Snowden with Forest, there was little left to imagine.

Chapter Nineteen

FOREST

I DIDN'T LIKE TOUCHING SARA.

The only reason I washed her hair was because the poor thing was on the edge of a nervous breakdown.

The shock of the last day, Skye's death, Snowden's violation, all of it was too much.

It was easy to bottle up my emotions. I'd been doing it my entire life, but Sara was a gentle soul.

She felt life with this incredible passion I didn't understand but yearned to experience. Her emotions bled all over the place. They were impossible to ignore, and I needed a little distance from her pain.

Her pain made me weak because I had a moral imperative to make things better for her.

Hell, it was far more than a simple imperative.

I hadn't been lying when I said she made my black and white world fill with a riot of color. I couldn't imagine life without her, but she was a liability.

Which made our current situation untenable.

To save her, I would have to lose her forever.

My thoughts had been to hold her and provide some of that

human interaction she always went on about. She needed the comfort human touch brought about.

I could do without it.

Oddly, holding her hadn't been as awkward as I thought it would have been.

It felt good.

I felt too good—whole even.

But washing her hair?

I'd done it to soothe her with no thought about myself.

Women always went on and on about how good it felt for a hairdresser to wash their hair, how the scalp massage felt so damn good. I wanted to do something, even as small as a scalp massage, to try to ease some of her suffering.

How hard could it have been?

I knew the answer, and I needed to tamp down the shitshow happening with my dick.

It wanted Sara.

Sara!

I fucked men because they were strong enough to handle my needs. Women were too fragile. And Sara?

There was no way I would subject her to the hunger stirring within me. I cared about her too much to expose her to the vileness swirling in my veins.

No fucking way.

It was time for some tough talk and to scare her away.

I braced my back against the wall of the shower and slid down until my butt hit the floor. Glancing up, there was no way to avert my gaze from the perfection of Sara's curvy body.

Her long, toned legs flexed. The graceful flare of her hips narrowed at her slim waist. Her breasts, softness personified, had me aching to feel them against my body, to cup them in my hands, and to feel her nipples tighten as I drew her into my mouth.

My assistant was an attractive woman, one graced with an hourglass silhouette. She crossed her arms over her chest, hiding the perfect globes of her breasts and putting an end to my fantasy.

I'd already seen everything. I towered over her, and the view I'd had washing her hair wasn't one that would leave me anytime soon.

The way the suds had fallen over the soft swell of her breasts and parted around her rosebud nipples hadn't caught my breath. It shattered the foundation of my world.

I'd never thought of her sexually before. She'd always been kind of a nag, to be honest.

Maybe taking a shower with her hadn't been the best of ideas.

I couldn't unsee her delicate perfection or remove the X-rated thoughts swirling in my head.

Her brows scrunched as she looked at me.

"What are you doing?"

"Getting comfortable."

"You're sitting in a shower."

"And?"

"It's a shower."

"Have you never sat in a shower before?" I patted the floor beside me. "Come on. Sit."

"I'm not a dog. You can't bark at me and expect me to obey your commands."

"I wasn't barking."

"Sure sounded like it."

"Will you pretty please sit your damn ass on the fucking floor?"

She crossed her arms under her breasts, which drew my eyes, enflamed my fantasies, and caught the attention of my dick.

The fucker twitched.

Sara caught the movement, and her gaze cut to my crotch, where it lingered.

Just what I didn't need. I bent my knees and propped my elbows on my kneecaps. I would hide the fucker if it didn't behave. This was Sara, after all.

After I bent my knees, her attention shifted to the bathroom door. I knew what she was thinking.

"Hey," I needed to draw her attention back to me and not what might be waiting for us beyond that door. "We need to talk, and it's best to get comfortable. Don't worry about what's out there. He could barge in on us any second, or leave us for the night. Don't worry about what we don't control. Trust me; it'll help."

"Are my thoughts that transparent?"

"Not really. I'm thinking the same thing. Maybe it helps me to say out loud what I'm trying to tell myself."

"Is it working?"

"Not really."

"This is crazy." She blew out a breath.

"Come. Sit." I patted beside me again. "Let's make each other a promise."

"Okay? Like what?"

"When we're alone, we focus on the moment. Not what might happen, or what just happened, but just that moment. You and me, together. We gather up all those moments and use them to get through the others. Can you do that?"

"I can try."

"Good, now sit. I want to tell you about Skye."

My history with Skye formed the man I was today. I loved her as much as I hated the impact she had on the man I was today. Not that any of it was her fault, but there was one truth I never spoke.

It was time.

If I didn't deal with it now, then Snowden will have already won.

Sara slid down the wall and mirrored my pose. She bent her knees, wrapped her arms around them, and propped her chin on her kneecaps.

I tilted my head back and closed my eyes. It would be easier to speak about the past if I didn't have to look at Sara.

"We don't have to talk about Skye if you don't want to." Sara placed her hand on my arm.

I opened my eyes, glanced down at her, then closed them again. I wasn't ready to think about Skye's death.

"I want you to know what they did to me; to us."

"You know, Skye and I talk..." Sara choked up, and she corrected herself, "Talked. We talked about it. I know what happened."

"You don't know it all."

"She told me they forced the two of you to have sex like you were a sideshow in a circus, sold tickets to it, loaned each of you out, beat you, raped you, raped her. There's no reason to—"

"I didn't just rape her, Sara." I ground out the words.

"You were forced to do the unconscionable. The things they made you do aren't your fault. They weren't then, and they aren't now."

"You don't understand…" I pinched my eyes tight. This was the despicable truth I hid deep inside. "I didn't just rape Skye… I liked it."

God, did I love the pleasure flowing through me when I did it.

The first few times, Skye had been beaten until she had no choice. I grew hard in her hands with fear coiling in my gut if I couldn't get it up. But I did. My body responded with the potency of a young man just coming into his sexuality. We were forced to perform. The better the performance, the greater the reward; time spent locked in our rooms. It was the only place they didn't molest us.

Snowden, in particular, got off on making us do things to each other. He fucked us both, me more brutally than Skye, but he loved forcing us to perform for his pleasure. The man was a sick fuck.

Skye could fake what she needed, but I couldn't.

My orgasms were ripped from me, orchestrated by Clark Preston and Snowden, to be as depraved as possible.

I'd been a boy going through puberty and all that entailed. My body reacted to pretty much everything. I was a horny, lust-fueled, pubescent teen forced to have sex every day with my foster sister.

Every.

Damn.

Day.

The beatings and the rapes I endured merely filled the hours between when I could fuck Skye again. I craved her with carnal hunger, and I loved it.

I loved that fucking her was the only release from my living hell. The pleasure coursing through my body became a drug, and I became an addict.

I became the very monster I hated.

I was just as sick as Clark Preston.

Worse.

It was worse because I had to pretend I was forced. Skye didn't know this, and she never would.

A sharp tearing ripped at my heart.

Skye never would know the truth.

I'd lost my chance to confess the darkness within me.

The disgust I had touching Skye came not because I couldn't stand to touch her, but rather because her touch woke the beast within me.

It made me feel things and want things.

Depraved things.

Like Pavlov's dog, I'd been conditioned to respond. I'd been trained to take.

Touching Skye led to instant erections.

I always feared I would rape Skye for real. Not as an unwilling participant but rather as a sex-crazed lunatic.

Slowly, I grew aversive.

My body reacted if I touched her, but I had learned how to train myself to develop an aversion to Skye.

Our foster father turned me into that man.

Snowden only made it worse.

The better my performance, the greater my rewards.

My aversion to touching Skye was far more complicated than she ever understood.

"I was forced to have sex with Skye, but I grew to love it. I looked forward to it. Snowden and Preston did that to me. They turned me into a monster. Skye never understood my aversion to touching her. It wasn't because it was a trigger to the abuse we endured. It was because I wanted more."

"Forest..."

"I want you to hear this."

It surprised me how much lighter my soul felt admitting this secret. I'd never had anyone I could tell before.

"What they did to you—"

"Snowden will do again." I glanced at her, worried about what I had to say next, and scared how she would react.

"I don't understand."

"He never says anything without reason, and I've been going over everything he said. One thing stands out."

"Only one?"

I wanted to vent a small huff of laughter, but Sara needed to understand what was in store. Snowden had no intention of physically hurting Sara. He didn't dare touch her out of fear for what I would do in retaliation.

But he would use her against me, and that was going to hurt her on a level she couldn't process.

"It's big."

"After the past twenty-four hours, nothing will surprise me," she said.

"Never say never."

She needed to understand, and I didn't know how to tell her the disgusting truth.

"I was forced to have sex with Skye. Preston got off on making us. He craved the control it gave him over us."

"Preston is dead, Forest." She placed her hand on my arm. "He can't hurt you anymore."

"But Snowden isn't. He's very much alive, and he's dying to do whatever he can to hurt me."

Her fingers flexed, and she sucked in a breath while I braced to continue.

"I see..." She expelled her breath in a slow, steady stream.

"I don't think you do."

There was no way to prepare her for every possibility, but Snowden's words kept echoing in my head.

"It's incredible that this world creates such monsters." She blew out another breath. "They feed off our fear."

"That they do."

I braced to tell her the rest of it. My suspicions could prove invalid, but I knew Snowden.

The man was capable of vile things.

"So...what do you want to do about it?" She dropped her hand from my arm and twisted her fingers together as she stared forward.

"Excuse me?"

Her head tilted, and she glanced up at me. "The only way to win is to take from him. Does he know you're bisexual?"

"He watched me fuck Skye. I'm pretty sure he knows."

"But you were a kid then, a highly impressionable kid, and I would venture to say...hypersexual?"

I didn't like that word.

My sexual appetite wasn't 'hyper.' It was insatiable. Hypersexual downplayed my need for sex.

When I didn't answer, she gave a sharp nod.

"I take that as a yes. This explains a lot of things, but it doesn't answer the question. Does Snowden think you're gay?"

"I don't know."

"If he thinks I'm your girlfriend, he can't. If he believes you're gay, then he knows we're not seeing each other. Which means..."

"I won't be able to protect you."

She thought about that for a moment. Pressing her head against the tiles, she stared at the falling water for what seemed like forever.

The tips of my fingers were turning into prunes. We'd been in here for too long. The longer we sat, the more I didn't want to tell Sara what needed to be said.

The poor thing would be scarred forever, at least if the shock didn't kill her first.

"We should probably get out and get some sleep." I'd find a way to talk about this with her tomorrow.

"You have me thinking."

"Is that a good thing or a bad thing?" I didn't want to ask because I didn't want an answer, but I needed to know what it was I had said that triggered her into thinking?

"He wants to lord his power over you, make you do whatever he wants."

I nodded. That about summed it up.

"But that's not what he wants." She tapped her chin as if thinking this through.

"It seems pretty cut and dry to me."

"But it's not. Oh, Forest, you need to think like him. We need to know what drives him. What are his motivations? What is it that he wants? Figure that out, and we have him."

"I think it's pretty clear what he wants, and I'll continue to give it to him to keep you safe."

"No. I'm the tool...the excuse." Her head shook. "He needs me in order to control you."

"And it's working. As long as it's in my power, I won't let him hurt you."

"I know...valiant and all, and I appreciate it, but it feels off. I don't trust him."

"You shouldn't. The man is a monster."

"A psychopath."

At least we agreed on that.

Sara was smart. I kept forgetting how quick she could be. It was easy to do. Her intelligence wasn't like mine.

I figured out analytical shit. Computers, mathematics, and puzzles were my things. Sara knew people. She had a crazy innate sense about them I couldn't begin to comprehend.

"Okay, this is what we know." She began ticking points off on her fingers. "He wants to control you. That begins with making you bow to him, serve him, but there's more." Her brows pinched together, and I lost myself in her beauty.

I never really spent the time to admire her delicate features. Her long lashes fluttered when she was mad. Her brows pinched together when she was upset or deep in thought, like now. Her eyes glittered with so many emotions I couldn't begin to decipher. And her mouth, pert and lickable red, was something I wanted to taste.

Only a taste.

I would take too much from her if I let myself have what I wanted.

I focused on what she said.

"He wants my pain. Rape is only the tip of the iceberg."

"Agreed. But what else?"

I didn't know if it was wise to state the obvious, but it might prepare her to endure what would come.

"He's a sadist."

"I get that," she said. "He's going to hurt you. The question is, how."

I had the answer to that. Snowden could be very creative with rope. He enjoyed the whip but loved to use his hand and belt more.

My flesh would become his living canvas, and there would be more.

There always was.

"I don't think we need to discuss the particulars." I struggled not to spiral into hopelessness. Snowden would make me work to maintain my sanity.

"You know how these things work." I blew out a breath, expelling the fear clawing its way out of me.

"I do, but let's get inside his head. If we can figure him out..."

"I don't want anywhere inside his head."

She shifted and turned to face me. I held back a gulp because that brought her tits into view as well as the dark triangle between her legs.

My thoughts about her lips were positively G-rated when compared to what I wanted to do with those tits and her pussy. Those desires went R-rated to triple-X in a heartbeat.

I swallowed and averted my gaze. I shouldn't react, but there was no way to tamp down the desire building within me.

I might be bisexual, but until recently, the only woman I had any sexual interest in had been the one who repulsed me.

I almost convinced myself that I was gay and not bisexual. I loved fucking men, and there had been a reason I kept myself from touching Sara. I'd always wanted her.

I craved the physicality between men. The battle of wills. The fight to establish dominance. The prowess of a real man who could beat me. I wanted that with an indescribable hunger but had yet to meet a man who could scratch the surface of what I needed.

But I also craved the intimacy of holding a woman, of melding my body with hers in the sensual dance that sex could be between man and woman.

They tasted different. Reacted differently. They felt different. They yielded to me. And they smelled different. Everything about it was different. It was tender. They were loving.

I craved both women and men, but I would never have what I truly wanted. It simply wasn't possible.

Sara had me facing an alarming truth. It wasn't one I could deny, and it wasn't new.

I had a thing not just for women, but specifically for one woman.

I always had.

I pushed Sara away because I knew what I could do to her if I ever gave in to my desire. I would break her, and that could never happen.

I never allowed those thoughts to ruin what we had.

Sara and I had the perfect relationship. We simply kept sex and any sexual tension out of the equation.

Or rather, I did.

I couldn't risk losing her if she ever discovered I had feelings for her. Fortunately, those weren't reciprocated.

Sara knew I only dated men, and she didn't react when I told her I was, in fact, bisexual. If there'd been a spark of interest, wouldn't I have seen it? I'd been watching.

But no.

Sara regarded me with a blank expression when I told her I liked women as well as men.

I just hadn't realized until Snowden put a knife to her throat how deep my feelings went.

Sara made me bleed emotions, messy, troubling, and dangerous emotions.

And Snowden was going to use those to destroy the woman I cared about.

I placed my fist to my chest and pressed the area over my heart. I didn't want to hurt Sara the same way I'd hurt Skye.

But Snowden would.

Sara sat beside me, oblivious to the thoughts swirling in my head. Blissfully unaware of how fragile her safety was, she tapped her finger against her chin as she tried to dissect the mind of a madman.

"Sara..." There was no way she could figure Snowden out.

Slowly, she turned to me. Her gaze angled down to my lap, where I hid my arousal with the bend of my legs. I pulled my knees close against my chest.

She didn't need to see how much she affected me.

"What?"

"Let's go to bed."

Her eyes widened, and I quickly interjected.

"I need sleep."

And the erection jutting between my legs needed a little hand love.

"Um...okay."

"Why don't you head out. I'll..." I glanced down at my lap and chewed at my lower lip. "I'll be there in a minute."

She averted her gaze, but I knew she'd tracked mine. Sara was no fool.

Slowly, she unfolded her legs and stood. Without a backward glance, she exited the shower.

I waited while she dried off and for the door to close before I fisted my cock.

I didn't want to leave her alone for too long. God knew what, or whom, waited for her out there, but I needed a little relief.

Sara's scream had me tripping as I raced out of the shower.

Chapter Twenty

FOREST

I raced out of the shower, then skidded to a halt—a man sprawled on our couch. One arm draped over the back of the sofa and his legs spread wide, he took up as much space as possible, dominating the room, and scaring the shit out of Sara.

Sara clutched a towel to her naked body. One glance at me, and she slowly backtracked.

The man held a phone and stared at the screen. He slowly looked up, arrogant prick, as if he had all the time in the world to acknowledge me. To explain who he was and what the fuck he was doing here.

"Forest, I presume?"

"And who the fuck are you?"

The man unfolded his sturdy, muscular frame and stood to his full height. A tall man, he was almost eye level with me.

Almost.

That, in itself, was unusual enough to stir a reaction, but I still had a couple of inches on him.

Fucker.

His dark hair shifted when he stood. Tousled waves spilled over his forehead in complete disarray, which had my fingers itching to run through them, pull them, and yank them the fuck out by the roots.

He gave a practiced flip of his head, which swept the hair off his face. His arresting forest-green eyes, flecked with a tawny gold, took me in with unadulterated lust.

Fuck me. He was magnificent.

His deeply tanned skin glowed with an inner light, and a spray of freckles dusted the bridge of his nose. His megawatt smile, unwelcome but freely given, anchored a face chiseled out of granite: dark eyelashes, straight nose, strong jawline; they attested to his strength.

He was everything I liked in a man—hard, strong, and confident. The way he carried himself, with the strength of a warrior and the self-possession of a predator, made my heart trip in open admiration. The man epitomized masculine perfection, and it took me a moment to take all of him in.

His iridescent eyes crinkled as the seam of his full lips drew my eye. His tongue darted out and licked along the fullness of his lower lip as he regarded me.

It was a cocky and arrogant move. The bastard watched for a reaction, and I gave him exactly what he wanted.

My God, the man was stunning and fuck if my body didn't take notice.

But that wasn't what stopped me in my tracks.

He stirred an animalistic hunger within me. The way he moved, full of sinuous grace, there was no doubt in my mind which way this man swung. He captivated me with his presence, and I'd bet a million bucks he dominated men with the same physical aggression I did.

It would be interesting which of us came out on top.

"Name's Paul. I'm your security for the night."

Easily the sexiest, most viciously enthralling man in existence, he kindled a desperate hunger I couldn't put into words. The air crackled with a flood of sexual tension as we stared each other down.

Like Snowden, he was dangerous.

Unlike Snowden, who hurt beyond reason by using my extremely high pain tolerance to whip me into unconsciousness and fuck me to the point of suffocation, I wanted this captivating man to do all those things and more.

Such was the dichotomy that was my life.

Paul made me ache for the unattainable, but something about him gave me pause.

There was an odd familiarity about him.

Despite the intensity of my reaction to his physical presence, anger spilled outward in a seething, uncontrollable rage.

With difficulty, I drew my outrage back and kept it contained.

Not knowing if this was one of Snowden's tricks or a test of some sort, I didn't know whether to knock the bastard out, nonchalantly ignore him, or pour him a fucking drink and join him on the couch.

"You mean, you're our guard." The words ground out of me, slipping past my wire-thin restraint.

Snowden said he would leave me with Sara. These rooms were supposed to be our sanctuary.

Foolishly, I thought he meant to keep his word. How easy it was for Snowden to give and then take away.

Shit! I knew he would do this, but it still came as a shock when Snowden pulled the rug out from under me.

A guard? What was the man really here to do?

I met him with the full force of my indomitable will. Aggression seemed the best path to match his strength.

"What the fuck are you doing here?"

"I'm here to watch over the two of you." Paul gave a nonchalant shrug and walked to the small kitchenette where he poured himself a scotch. He lifted his glass toward Sara in a mock salute.

She slowly inched her way over to me. I drew her behind me with my arm, protecting her from this unknown threat. I thought I could keep her safe within these rooms, but evidently, Snowden had other plans.

"Get in the bathroom and shut the door." My command

vibrated the air. Tension coiled inside my body as I prepared to do battle and keep her safe from this threat.

"You should cool down before you lose your shit." Paul took a sip. "I'm your security. Mr. Snowden wants to make sure no one inadvertently slips in and has his way with your girl while you sleep. You should remember to thank him. He'll like that." The bastard winked at me.

My fingers curled into fists. I was seconds from popping this asshole in the face.

"Who's to say you're not one of the assholes who want to hurt her?"

He swallowed the remainder of the liquid, and I couldn't tear my eyes from the way his Adam's apple bobbed. Pressing his full lips together, he let out a satisfied moan which set my nerves on edge. How could a moan be so damn sexy?

He fixed me with a lustful and very hungry stare. "Because I like men." His gaze raked me from head to toe. "You're the only one I'm interested in fucking. Not the girl."

I stood before him naked; my hungry cock standing loud, proud, and showing off as it twitched in eager anticipation.

His gaze cast downward, and an appreciative smile filled his face.

"And you…" His eyes widened as he carefully enunciated each word. "You. Are. Something. To. Admire."

"Fuck you." I'd run out of the bathroom so fast I hadn't grabbed a towel.

Behind me, Sara made it to the bathroom door.

Paul shook his head. "Um, no."

"No, what?"

I was seriously considering clocking the bastard and taking him down. The only thing stopping me was whether Snowden would consider that a breach of our fucked-up arrangement, which provided Sara the only protection she had in this nightmare.

"The doors stay open."

"The fuck they do."

"Open, or I take them off their hinges."

"You're not…"

Paul closed the distance between us until he stood chin to chin with me. Fractionally shorter than me, the man was built and knew how to hold his ground. He possessed all the fluid lethality, which screamed he was a man used to being in charge.

My stomach clenched, reacting to the show of force on a level I didn't want to admit.

Snowden disgusted me.

This man?

He fascinated me.

"Didn't you hear what I said? I'm here to protect your girl from those who might think to take advantage of this situation. I'm not interested in fucking her. Now you, on the other hand, …there are a lot of things I'd like to do to you."

To me.

Not with me.

The message was not lost on me. We would not be equal partners.

This man was a sexual dominant, but I didn't cave that easily.

"Fuck off."

"I'd rather fuck you, but I'm sensing a little hostility." With a step back, he took another long, hard look at me.

I breathed out, unaware I'd been holding my breath. He stood close, too close, and there was something about him that stuck deep in my core.

It off-balanced me. Made me want things I couldn't have.

My entire body ached…

For him.

The corners of his lips turned up when my cock gave a little jerk. The little bastard was showing off after being denied its quick fix in the shower. It was ready for that fuck Paul promised.

I was ready for it too.

"Well, I'm sure your boss will have something to say about that. He's not inclined to share." I had more than I could handle dealing with Snowden's unwanted attention. I didn't need this asshole fucking that up.

"Is that what you think?" Paul's eyebrow lifted in question. "Because I'm pretty sure he has plans to pass you around." He crossed his arms over his chest. "I'm fairly certain of it, actually."

Behind me, Sara slowly drew the door to the bathroom closed.

Turning his attention to her, Paul cleared his throat. "I'm serious about the doors. They stay open." He gave a sharp snap of his fingers. "You have clothes waiting in the bedroom. I suggest you hide in there while Forest and I get acquainted."

The fuck he and I would be getting acquainted. No way in hell was I leaving Sara alone.

"Clothes?" Sara's voice cracked, and her breath gave a little hitch.

"Yes, courtesy of your host."

"He's not our host." Sara cleared her throat. "You work for a monster."

"I disagree. Mr. Snowden has been very good to me, and I tend to respect that." He lifted a finger. "I would strongly caution you about making disparaging remarks against him. He can be quite—"

"Horrific? Disgusting? Despicable?" Sara's tone showed more strength than I imagined.

Unlike me, his size didn't seem to intimidate her.

She took a step forward. "You want me to say nice things about a monster? Is that what you want?"

He gave a soft laugh. "What I want is beside the point." His gaze cut to me. "Consider this a warning or a lesson. It's in your best interest not to irritate Mr. Snowden. Be gracious, the niceties he affords you are precious gifts and should be appreciated." He swept his arm out. "Such as a nice place to stay, clean clothes, a bed to share with your boyfriend, a lock on the door leading out of here, and a guard to keep you safe. Be thankful he chose me and not one of the others."

"Telling me he doesn't trust his men doesn't spark confidence," she said. "What's to say we can trust you?"

"Mr. Snowden and I have a unique understanding."

"That's not an answer," she said.

I couldn't have been more thankful for Sara than I was at this moment.

Paul did strange things to me, off-balancing me in a way no man had ever done before. I should be the one asking the questions, but all I could think about was what it would feel like to have Paul's body wrapped around mine.

"I already gave that answer. You don't interest me." He turned his attention back to me. "Forest, on the other hand..."

"What about me?" I finally found my voice. No way in hell was Snowden allowing this cocky asshole anywhere near me.

He ran his fingers through the air as if plucking on strings. "There's a resonance I'm eager to explore."

"Fuck you."

"I'll be the one doing the fucking. In fact, I look forward to it."

His gaze took a slow, meandering stroll down my naked body. The skin of my chest flushed. I tightened my abs and found myself standing a little straighter beneath the scrutiny.

When his gaze finally landed on my cock, he didn't hide his interest. The bastard even made a show of it with a slow, appreciative shake of his head.

"Not going to happen." I tried to stand my ground, even knowing in my gut what the future held.

His smoldering eyes snapped up to mine, capturing them with the ferocity of his lust.

He slowly approached me. "Mr. Snowden is a generous man by nature. He rewards loyalty. He rewards obedience."

Without hesitation, he reached for my cock and took it in his sure grip.

I was so stunned, I didn't react, but instead sank into the sensation of a man who knew exactly how to hold another man's cock.

His grip tightened, and I huffed against the pain while holding back a low-throaty moan as desire washed through me.

With a twist of his wrist, he stroked me. My hungry cock nearly came right there as intense pleasure coursed within me.

Paul took a step back, satisfaction filling his face.

"Yeah, it's going to happen. The question is whether you'll let it happen the way it should, or if you're going to fight what's happening here."

I took a shuddering step back, stunned by my body's reaction to this stranger.

"I guess that depends on Snowden."

We both knew I had no choice if Snowden ordered such a display. To keep Sara safe, I would do whatever it took.

"I'm sure it does, and here's a little tidbit for you to think about while you sleep."

I didn't want to know whatever this tidbit was, but Paul wasn't going to leave it be.

"Mr. Snowden gives me what I want, and I want you. Think about what that means while you cuddle with your girl tonight. Imagine how it's going to feel when I fuck you, or when I fist you until you come all over yourself screaming my name. You and I are going to have plenty of time to explore this thing between us."

"There's nothing between us."

"Don't be coy, the air crackles with our need; it's practically sizzling it's so intense. All it needs is one spark, and only God knows where it will take us. You can't resist a firestorm, Forest. You won't be able to resist me. Deny it all you want, but you can't ignore the sexual tension vibrating the space between us."

"You might get to touch me if Snowden allows it, but the rest of that shit going on in your head?" I pointed at him. "It's not happening. I don't give a flying fuck what you think." I gestured to my groin and lied through my teeth. "This is because I want to fuck my girl. Not you."

Sara gave a tiny gasp.

Paul gave a low laugh. "Well, if that's the case, go for it. You have all night to do whatever you want with her. I suggest you enjoy her while you can, but you and I both know she can't give you what you need, but I can."

"Fucking lunatic." I grabbed Sara's arm and pulled her across the room, keeping myself between her and the sex-crazed lunatic.

Ignoring his orders, I slammed the door to the bedroom shut and pressed my back against it as I struggled to breathe.

"Forest? Are you okay?"

I held out a hand, asking for her to give me a moment. My cock screamed for release, the kind which could only come from a man like Paul.

Fuck me.

The door behind me shuddered as Paul slammed into it.

He spoke from the other side. "You do not want to test me on this. Open the damn door."

"Forest?" Sara's eyes widened, and she clutched the towel to her naked body.

My attention shifted to the bed, where two pairs of clothes had been laid out.

"Get dressed."

Her pert little mouth opened to argue, but I gave a curt shake of my head.

"Now." I could only hold the door closed for so long.

The door shuddered beneath me as Paul kicked it. I was under no illusions he would force his way inside, but I would have Sara fully clothed when he did.

"Hurry!"

Sara didn't need me to break it down and explain. A smart cookie, she understood. Without further argument, she raced to the bed and threw on the flannel pajamas.

Paul threw his body against the door, alternating his kicks with slamming his shoulder against it in his attempt to break it down.

I waited, timing things as best I could, then I opened the door as he came barreling through. His momentum took him into the room where he stumbled, arms windmilling out of control until he came to a stop.

He spun around, fists clenched, arm drawing back and swung at me.

I met him fist for fist, and blow for blow, as we grappled with each other.

Chapter Twenty-One

SARA

I'D SEEN FOREST FIGHT. HE SPENT HOURS IN THE GYM, PERFECTING his technique. Trained by the best of the best, he was proficient in several martial arts and the blood-thirstiest street fighting on the planet.

I thought it was going to be a quick fight because there was no way Paul stood a chance against Forest's skill.

Limbs grappled. Fists flew. Feet kicked. Legs swept the other off his feet. Sprays of spit from fists hitting jaws had me backing up to the other side of the bed. Spit turned to blood as skin split beneath the blows.

The fight shifted into the other room, placing me out of danger. For now.

My instinct was to try to stop them, but weighing a buck twenty soaking wet, I was less than half Forest's weight.

So, I waited.

Nail biting. Teeth clenching. Fingers twisting. I waited for the dust to settle.

And I worried.

What was this going to cost Forest?

Granted, Paul wasn't Snowden, but he worked for the monster.

Did obeying Snowden extend to the lackeys he sent to watch over us?

There was an odd magnificence to watching the men fight. Forest was all nude flesh, a thing of intense beauty when he put his muscles to work. My gorgeous boss had been blessed by the gods and imbued with incredible strength. He moved with fluid lines and deadly force.

He was artistry personified with the flex of chiseled muscles and bursts of wild aggression.

Every one of his moves worked off the previous one, capitalizing on remaining momentum to accentuate the next hit.

He was a force of brutal, unrestrained power.

I found it breathtaking.

How many of his training sessions had I sat through, enduring the exquisite torture of watching my boss work out?

Far too many.

But those hadn't been real. They hadn't been life and death like this.

The aggression spilling from them both tangled in their limbs and filled the air with uninhibited sexual chemistry.

Paul might be gay, yet I felt his inescapable pull. He was simply magnificent and looked like he'd been pulled off the cover of a magazine. Not a pretty boy mag, but one of those rough, scruffy, simply beautiful mountain man kind of magazines. He was rough, ragged around the edges, and pristinely perfect.

From their grunts and moans, I didn't know if they were fighting or fucking. I felt a little like a voyeur watching the exchange. They beat each other with their fists, but a sexual charge punctuated each brutal blow.

Paul's hands were all over Forest, exploring every inch of Forest's toned physique as their arms and legs intertwined during their fight. The low rasp of their breaths filled the air and was interrupted only by the solid smacking of flesh as they traded blows.

Despite Forest's extensive training, Paul held his own. There was no clear winner and looked like the fight would be won not by brute force but rather a war of attrition as exhaustion pulled at them both.

Whichever of them tired first would find himself the loser in this fight.

And then what?

Paul's nostrils flared as Forest scored a direct hit to Paul's jaw. Blood streamed from his nose, and a cut bled beneath his left eye. Paul danced just out of reach, a grin splitting his face as he egged Forest on.

My pulse hammered in my throat. Not knowing who would be victorious left me in a precarious position. Even if Forest won, that didn't mean there wouldn't be repercussions.

Snowden had called them consequences.

"I see you peeking, little girl." Paul glanced in my direction and flashed me his megawatt grin. The man was simply heart-stoppingly gorgeous.

The momentary distraction cost him.

Forest bent low and barreled into Paul's midsection, taking Paul down to the ground.

"Don't you fucking speak to her." Forest's possessive growl lifted the fine hairs on my arms.

I came around from behind the bed to peek through the doorway.

"You like your women soft..." Paul said with a huff.

Forest straddled Paul and clocked his jaw.

"Don't. You. Fucking. Say. A. Word. To. Her." Each word came with a punch to the face.

I cringed at the damage Forest had to be causing. Oddly, Paul didn't seem the least bit fazed. He laughed.

"You like your women soft but your men hard, don't you?"

Paul's words struck a chord in Forest, making him pull his punch. It was all the distraction Paul needed. With a bucking of his hips and some twisting of his legs, he flipped Forest to his back.

Paul straddled Forest's hips and fought to restrain Forest's wrists over his head. It took a moment, but Paul managed to hold Forest's wrists down by using his arms as bars to press Forest's elbows flat against the floor.

He hovered over Forest. Their hips rocked against each other, the brawn of their chests touched with each inhale, and Paul's devilish eyes lifted to me.

"Do you see what he needs, little girl?" Paul didn't wait for my answer. "He needs a man who can best him. You can only give him the soft yielding of your body, but he craves physical domination."

"Fuck you!" Forest bucked against Paul's grip but failed to knock Paul off his body.

"Oh, we're getting to that, but you still need to learn to enjoy the finer points of foreplay. We're just getting started."

"You're out of your fucking mind." Forest's body heaved as he growled with frustration.

Paul had him locked down tight. Forest couldn't shake him.

"Am I?" Paul rocked his hips forward, and Forest's gasp had me taking a step toward the open doorway.

"You feel it now. You're not the only one with a big cock, and I'm fucking hard for you."

Forest's body rippled as he flexed his muscles. He tossed Paul off, and their positions exchanged again with Forest now on top.

It was Forest's turn to trap Paul's wrists beside his ears and lock his elbows against the floor.

All the air vacated the room as Forest lowered down. I held my breath because it looked as if Forest might kiss him. Instead, his low, rumbly voice filled the room.

"If you fuck me, it'll be by Snowden's command and his command only. I'll never let you touch me otherwise."

"Never say never." Paul huffed a laugh. "You know you'll beg for it."

"And if you ever touch Sara, I'll rip your dick off and fuck your mouth with it before making you swallow it whole."

"Wow, is that supposed to scare me?"

"Doesn't matter." Forest released Paul's left wrist and threw the weight of his entire body into his punch. "And the fucking doors stay on."

A loud crack sounded. Paul's head snapped to the side, and his entire body stilled.

My hands flew to my mouth, sniffling a scream, as Forest shook the unresponsive form of our tormentor. With a grunt, Forest lifted himself off Paul and kicked Paul in the gut for good measure.

"Piper would be very disappointed in you, Paul Rains." He spat on Paul's face.

"Is he dead?" My voice squeaked.

"Not even close, but he's going to hurt for days." Forest pointed back to the bedroom. "Let me take care of him, so he doesn't bother us. Go ahead and get in bed."

"But, you're bleeding."

"That's not my blood." He swiped at a spot on his cheek, and it wiped clean.

"You need another shower."

That fight left a sheen of sweat on Forest's body, and more of Paul's blood clung to him.

"I don't want to risk him coming to while I'm in the shower. Sorry, but we're shutting that door and going to bed. You need to decide if that's going to be a problem."

It didn't escape my notice Forest was still painfully aroused. He ignored his erection as he stomped toward the coffee table and retrieved Paul's phone. He looked at it, grunted, then brought it over and placed it in front of Paul's face. The display turned on.

"What are you doing?"

Forest sat down and crossed his legs in front of him. Cupping Paul's phone, his fingers danced over the screen.

"Nothing," he said.

Forest wasn't doing *nothing*.

He glanced up, brows pinched together. "Seriously, go to bed. I'll be there in a minute."

His attention shifted to the phone, and the well-practiced glazed look in his eyes took over as he focused on whatever he was doing.

That didn't mean I was going to leave him covered in drying blood.

Paul didn't move, he was knocked out cold, but the gentle rise and fall of his chest told me he still lived. I supposed that was a good thing.

What kind of trouble would Forest be in if he killed Snowden's guard? What kind of trouble would he be in for the fight?

"Well, you're not climbing into bed with me covered in his blood."

Forest's attention was locked to the phone. I ceased to exist when he got in the zone like this. He could go for hours without eating, drinking, or being aware of anything in his surroundings. As fierce and powerful as my boss could be, he could also be incredibly vulnerable, which was why he needed me.

I took in a deep breath and headed to the bathroom.

Forest wouldn't take a shower, but I didn't need him to wash his entire body. Just the blood spatter on his face, chest, and abs.

When I returned from wetting a washcloth from the bathroom, Forest was done with Paul's phone. He placed it back on the coffee table, then returned to where Paul lay on the floor.

He removed the belt from Paul's pants and used it to secure Paul's arms behind his back. With a satisfied grunt, Forest smacked Paul's ass.

"Who's the big guy now? Asshole."

Not sure if I was supposed to have heard that, I headed to the bedroom. Forest glanced up at me with a confused expression.

"What are you doing up? I thought you went to bed."

"No." I lifted the washcloth. "I went to get something to clean you up. I'm serious about not sleeping with you if you're covered in blood. You can take a shower or let me clean you up."

I was painfully aware of the fact we would be sharing a bed.

Forest left Paul on the floor and headed to the bedroom. I trailed behind him with a backward glance at the unconscious man on the floor.

"What about him?" I asked.

"What about him?" Forest parroted.

"We're just going to leave him there?"

"I'm not bringing him in here, and the outer door is locked. He can sleep it off in there."

"Where you tied his hands behind his back?"

Forest gave a little grin. "Yeah, he's going to be pissed when he wakes up."

"You think it's wise antagonizing him?"

"I think antagonizing him is a foregone conclusion, don't you think?" He rubbed at his jaw where a bruise was forming. Then he made a show of shutting the door behind him. Not that Paul would care about his defiance now.

Forest glanced around the room, then gave a satisfied grunt when he noticed a chair in the corner. He went to grab it and shoved it beneath the doorknob.

"What about Snowden?"

"Paul isn't going to tell Snowden shit."

"How do you know? And what about the cameras?"

"First off, Paul isn't going to tell Snowden shit because Paul wants to fuck me, and as for the cameras, I think we just answered that question."

"It's like you're speaking, but I have no idea what you're saying. We just answered what question?" I scrunched my brows.

"If there were cameras, we'd be inundated with guards right now. I'd be getting the shit kicked out of me and you…"

I understood. "No one came in when you and Paul fought."

"You got it."

"So, no one was watching."

"There's my girl. You're figuring shit out."

Yeah, I was figuring shit out, but I didn't understand his comment about Paul.

Chapter Twenty-Two

SARA

I WORRIED.

I worried about Forest but felt powerless to help him.

We were still prisoners. Snowden would eventually have something to say about what just happened. No way would that fight go without some kind of punishment.

Consequences.

I was beginning to hate that word.

Questions filled my head, things I needed to ask, but one look at Forest's stooped posture and the fatigue filling his face, I swallowed all my questions. Those would have to wait. Instead, I handed the washcloth to Forest.

"Here."

"Thanks." He took it from me and wiped his body down.

Odd how a few days ago, I'd never seen him naked. Now, he stood before me in the nude, entirely at ease, while I couldn't catch my breath. Without another word, he dressed in the pajamas which had been left for him and turned down the covers.

"Let's try to get some sleep." His rumbly tone magnified in the small room, churning my gut with things I wanted but would never have.

If that fight taught me anything, it was that although Forest might think he was bisexual, there was no denying the intense attraction between him and the unconscious man in the other room.

How was I supposed to get any sleep?

"Shouldn't we keep watch?"

Forest shook his head. "What's done is done, and I'll face the consequences when it's time. Sleep is a luxury. Best to take advantage of it when we can."

Pain filled his words, which reminded me of the horrors he'd endured in the past twenty-four hours, and all that would follow when morning came.

I supposed sleep would be his only refuge.

Snowden had a new plaything, and there was no doubt he had barely gotten started with Forest.

I hated it, but there was nothing I could do about it.

We'd lost so much and had yet to stop to grieve our friends, his sister, and little Zach. When would the tears finally fall?

When would Forest break?

"I don't want to make this awkward," he began, "but I need...I need to feel you beside me. Totally platonic..." His gaze shifted down. It was something he did when he lied, but how could that be a lie?

We were platonic.

Forest climbed into bed and patted the space next to him. "I'm so sorry, Sara, you don't deserve any of this."

He blew out his breath, spewing misery, and the intensity of his fatigue into the air. I wished there was something I could do for him, some way to ease his burden.

But what could I do?

I was the reason he surrendered. I was the reason he caved to Snowden's perverse demands.

Sleep?

I didn't think I would sleep, not until I understood how to minimize the impact my presence had on him.

It was too easy to let panic run rampant in my mind. I needed to be strong like Forest, but how in the hell did I do that?

It began by doing as he asked. If he needed me beside him, that's where I would be, platonic or otherwise.

Who was I kidding?

It would be totally platonic.

I climbed into bed, keeping far to the edge with the intent of maintaining as much space between us.

Much larger than my slight frame, Forest took up most of the king-sized bed. My attempts to place distance between us ended the moment I pulled the covers to my chin. Forest reached out and drew me across the bed until his body folded around me.

"I'm so fucking sorry." Tears choked his voice.

Without a word, I placed my hand over his and let him wrap himself around me. His hand was so massive it splayed over the expanse of my belly. His chest pressed against my back, and he tucked my head under his chin. He drew his knees up, folding me into him, spooning with me, while he curled around me and wept.

I had no words for the emotions flooding through me and filling my heart with anguished What-ifs.

This was what I'd always wanted—intimacy with Forest.

A touch.

A hug.

A kiss.

Something more.

I had it now but hated how it had come about.

I hated how it made me feel, like a thief stealing intimacy from a man who'd lost everything: his family, his friends, and his freedom.

I was reaping the rewards of his downfall. What kind of person did that make me?

I had everything I wanted, but it came at a terrible cost. How could I like this when guilt should be consuming me?

But it wasn't.

I found heaven in his arms, but I was a trespasser who didn't belong.

"How are you holding up?" His warm breath blew through my hair, and he tugged me tighter against his hard body. The length of his arousal poked me in my back, but he didn't seem concerned about it. I tried to ignore the persistent jabbing against my spine.

"I'm okay."

"You're not okay, Sara." He nuzzled my neck. "How are you?"

If he was going to get through this, I had to be strong. I couldn't steal his remaining strength by voicing my fears.

"I'm tired."

That was the truth, if not the whole of it.

Softly, he kissed the crown of my head. "Get some sleep. Tomorrow is going to be—"

I cut him off. "Let's not talk about tomorrow." I hugged his arm and pushed myself deeper into his embrace. "Let's pretend we're someplace else, and this is any other night."

"I wouldn't be holding you someplace else," he said with a low rumble. "You wouldn't let me."

Wouldn't let him?

This was all I'd wanted for years; Forest holding me.

"You feel exactly the way I imagined." His voice thickened with sleep. "You fit against me like I knew you would; a perfect fit." His voice grew indistinct as sleep pulled him under. "Goodnight Sara, I love you…"

My heart skipped a beat, and I didn't dare breathe. He said more, but I couldn't make out anything in the mumbling sounds.

Forest slipped from drowsy wakefulness to deep sleep within the span of a heartbeat. His breaths eased, and all the tension in his body softened. I waited until I knew he was deep asleep before settling into a position I could stay in through the night.

Sleep did not find me quickly, however.

Painfully aware of Paul knocked out cold in the other room, I kept an ear out for any sounds which told me he had awakened. But soon, I drifted in and out of sleep. Being curled up against Forest relaxed me until I couldn't fight the fatigue pulling at me.

He held me the entire night, keeping me safe, and protecting me.

At one time, I thought I heard movement on the other side of the door. I listened acutely for several long minutes as something scraped down the outside of the door. I wondered if I should wake Forest and alert him, but my fatigue proved too strong.

My eyes closed as my ears strained to decipher the obscure sounds coming from the other side of the door.

One thought ran through my head as sleep pulled at me. How did Forest know Paul's last name? And who was Piper?

Eventually, I lost my battle to stay awake. I slipped into a dreamless sleep and woke to a room full of light…and an open door.

Forest snored softly beside me. He'd turned to his back and had an arm draped across his face. My bladder pinched, and I slowly slid out of bed.

Not knowing how the day would go, I decided Forest needed his sleep. With an eye to the open door, I figured he must have gotten up some time during the night to relieve himself. He'd even set the chair to the side against the wall. Only there was no door.

Movement in the other room had me pulling up short.

Paul held a mug of coffee and sported a black eye, busted lip, and several cuts below his left eye.

"Do you drink?" He lifted his cup toward me. "I made plenty."

"Um…" I glanced back toward the bedroom. My attention focused on the door leaning against the wall. Its twin, the one leading into the bathroom, was also off its hinges. I turned back to Paul with a WTF expression on my face.

He gave a sheepish grin. It almost softened the sharp lines of his face and made him appear human. I could almost think he might be likable.

Almost.

I wasn't a fool.

He pointed to the doors leaning against the walls.

"Like I said, no doors." He shrugged. "Forest had a chance to keep them. All he had to do was leave them open."

"You took the doors off the hinges while we slept?"

How the hell had I slept through that?

And why had he let us?

"I removed them after I woke. Thanks for leaving me on the

floor like that. Not a cool move. The belt was Forest's idea I take it? Dick move, by the way."

"What exactly did you expect? You were beating up my boss."

"Your boss, or your boyfriend?" His eyes narrowed with suspicion.

My status as Forest's girlfriend may or may not afford me some degree of protection. I didn't know if it did, but if so, it probably wasn't wise to let that go.

"Forest is my boss."

"Ah, I see. A little workplace romance. How long have you two…"

He pointed at me, the bedroom, and made a crude gesture with his fist and first finger of his other hand. His brows lifted, and I swore his pupils dilated.

His interest in whether Forest and I were sexually active made me uncomfortable. I didn't know why that was. It was the assumption Forest allowed, but with Paul there was an interest that knocked me off my game.

"None of your damn business," I responded with a huff and bit my lower lip with the pain pinching my bladder.

"Feisty, aren't we?"

"Why are you still here?"

Why wasn't Snowden enforcing the consequences instead of Paul?

He shook his head. "Don't you remember?"

"You know what I mean."

"I suggest you use the restroom while he's asleep. Once Forest wakes, you won't have time." He turned toward the bathroom and, with a sweep of his arm, ushered me across the room.

I didn't need much encouragement but hesitated.

"How did you remove the doors? Forest put a…"

"Forest didn't look for which side the hinges were on, which are on this side of the doors. I moved the chair so you guys wouldn't trip over it in your sleep."

"How gracious of you." My lips thinned with the sarcasm dripping from my words.

"I can be quite generous when I want to be."

"Like Snowden?"

"Like *Mr.* Snowden. I suggest you start calling him Mister from here on out."

"Why would I give that monster any sliver of respect?"

"Because you work for him now." His eyes pinched. "Didn't he mention that?"

"The bastard said a lot of things."

"I would listen to what he says, little girl. It'll serve you well in the months to come."

My stomach sank a little with the mention of months.

I thought we'd figure a way out of this in a matter of days, but knowing how much difficulty Forest and Xavier had tracking Snowden down, we might very well be in this for the long haul.

"I'm not a little girl. Stop calling me that."

He approached me, coming far too close, reminding me of the disparity in our sizes. He was nearly as tall as Forest and easily as broad. I took a step back, and he grinned.

"Well, you're a girl, and from my perspective, you're much smaller than I am. That makes you both a girl and little, a.k.a, a little girl. Now, why don't you do as you're told? Take care of business and make yourself presentable. Mister Snowden will want you looking your best."

"Why?" I gulped.

"It's your first day as his assistant. You'll want to impress your new boss and image is everything. Now go. I've laid out everything you'll need." Paul swept his arm out again. "And take your time. It doesn't look like Forest is getting up any time soon."

"Why—"

"Why what?"

"Why are you letting him sleep?"

His attention shifted to the bedroom.

"Because he's going to need it."

Not wanting to push my luck, and oddly feeling as if Paul really would let Forest sleep, I headed to the bathroom. At the doorway, I pulled up short.

Paul stared at me, tenderness brimming in his eyes as he glanced through the doorway leading into the bedroom.

I bit my lower lip, resistant.

"It's okay, Sara. I'm not going to do anything while he's in here. This place is his one refuge. Snowden's instructions were quite specific regarding that." Sadness replaced the uncharacteristic tenderness.

I slipped inside the bathroom and turned on the sink to let the water run. I took care of business, washed my hands, then assessed the cosmetics which had been set out for me. I also noticed the business suit; pencil skirt, soft blouse, low pumps, and decorative scarf.

Those were items I would have bought for myself, which had me wondering, how much did Snowden know about me?

Chapter Twenty-Three

SARA

SINCE I'D SHOWERED LAST NIGHT, I DIDN'T FEEL I NEEDED TO TAKE another shower this morning. It was risky, leaving Paul alone. He could harass Forest, but I was more concerned about getting on Paul's bad side and what that would entail for Forest.

I rushed through getting ready.

When I emerged from the bathroom, Forest sat on one couch, and Paul reclined on the other. They looked like two lions deciding who would jump first and rip the other apart.

That odd sexual chemistry vibrated in the air. Not as strong as last night; it nevertheless remained.

Paul sipped from his coffee, and Forest cradled a cup in his hand. He glanced at me and patted the spot beside him on the couch.

"Coffee?" he asked as if it was the most normal thing in the world for him to offer me a drink.

Not once since I started working for him had he offered me any beverage, and if he'd paid any attention, he would know I hated coffee.

"Um...no, thank you." My attention warily shifted between the two men.

Hours ago, they'd been locked in what felt like mortal combat. Now, they sat across from each other and sipped coffee like wary adversaries sizing each other up.

There was a balance of power to be decided between these men. It had yet to happen. When it did, it would be overwhelmingly destructive. I knew that with certainty.

I hurried around the couch and sat at the far end. When Forest patted the spot beside him, I shifted to sit beside him.

Thighs touching, hips pressing against each other, he slung his arm around my shoulder and pulled me into his embrace like we did this every day.

It felt amazing.

Leaning down, he pressed his lips to my forehead, my nose, and then my lips where the kiss deepened without becoming overtly sexual.

I barely breathed, unaccustomed to the sexual energy flowing between us. The man had barely touched me in all the years I'd worked for him, and now he was fluttering butterfly kisses all over my face? And moaning?

It was the sexiest thing I'd ever heard.

I wanted more.

Across from us, Paul blew out his breath. "Trying to impress me?"

"Making a point," Forest said with a low chuckle. "Soft is good."

"Hard is better." Paul gave a dismissive snort. "Finish your coffee, clean up. You stink. And—"

"And what? Tell me, what exactly does he have planned for me today?"

A shiver ran through me, one of those whole-body things. Forest's grip tightened, and he gave me a look which urged caution, concern, and much more. His glacial eyes, typically cold and impenetrable, spoke volumes in that single glance.

This was Forest being strong. He knew his day would be filled with pain, degradation, and worse.

Yet he chose to face it head-on.

"Whatever he wants." Paul's reply lacked punch. Instead of

poking Forest with the horrors of what would come, he sounded almost apologetic.

I wanted to scream at them. How could they sit across from each other when they practically tore each other apart last night?

Forest appeared mostly unscathed, whereas Paul's face was a bloodied mess.

"I suppose that's true." Forest's body stiffened. "Does that excite you? Or are you jealous? Knowing he can have me whenever he wants while you have to wait for the scraps?" Forest didn't beat around the bush.

I cringed, but Paul merely shrugged.

"Sex is sex. Scratch an itch and all of that. I'll wait my turn, take you when he says, how he says, but you and I both know that's not what's going to happen."

"That thought in your head..." Forest made a little spinning gesture with his finger. "Get rid of it. It's not happening. Like you said, sex is sex. You scratch my back, and I'll scratch yours."

"If that's what you want to believe, then sure." Paul suddenly leaned forward.

Forest didn't flinch, but I did.

"I want to fuck you." Paul leaned back with a satisfied smirk. "When *this* happens, it will be me fucking you, not the other way around."

His confidence overwhelmed me. Beside me, Forest stiffened, as if his entire body had gone on high alert. I didn't know if it was because Paul had offended him or something else. I suspected it was something else. The tension between the two men was as hard as steel.

Paul continued, his tone confident and sure. "No reason to deny it. Sloppy seconds, thirds, or fourths, I can't wait to bury myself deep inside of you and show you what we can be together. Something is simmering between us. It's palpable and explosive. You feel it too, and I'm eager to explore it." Paul shifted and made no move to hide when he adjusted the seam of his jeans over his growing arousal.

"Why not just get it over with?" Forest raised a hand and

gestured at the room. "We're just sitting around wasting time. Get your game on and fuck me."

Paul's eyes pinched.

"Ah, I see. You can't just have me when you want, can you? He has to okay it."

"You're a prick," Paul said. "Not wise, considering…"

"Considering what?"

"You'll see."

I blew out a breath. "For the love of God, could the two of you just stop it already."

They both looked at me, almost as if they had forgotten I was present.

"Stop antagonizing Forest." I shook my head. "And Forest, you reek. Take a shower; you need it." I tried to avoid looking at his crotch, but it was useless to ignore the swelling behind the thin fabric of his pajama bottoms.

He needed a minute alone to take care of that.

Not knowing what his day would entail, but able to connect a few dots, Forest could use a little alone time to seek what little pleasure he could.

Forest placed his coffee cup on the table, pressed his hands on his knees, and stood. Turning slightly, he held out a hand to me.

"Come. Join me."

"I'm dressed. I don't need a shower."

"Maybe not, but I need you in the shower with me."

"Forest…"

He gave the slightest shake of his head, warning me not to argue.

I'd spent all that time making up my face, doing my hair, and he wanted to undo all of it by forcing me into the shower with him again?

I couldn't think of anything more uncomfortable than that.

Last night had been different. Shocked by what had happened, we cleaved to each other in that shower, hid from our captor behind the steam, and crossed an unimaginable line.

I suddenly got it.

I took his hand in mine, and he lifted me from the couch. Walking ahead of him, I reentered the bathroom and stood there fidgeting.

Forest stopped at the empty doorway, gave Paul a pointed look, then picked up the door leaning against the wall and closed us in.

With the water running and steam filling the room, he took my hands in his.

"We need to talk."

"We'll get through this." I tilted my head back to look him in the eyes. I wished I could lend him my strength.

"About that..." He shifted his gaze away from mine, almost as if he couldn't bear to look at me.

"What's wrong?"

"Snowden."

That one word could mean so many different things.

"Will you take a shower with me?" he asked.

"Um...wouldn't it be better if you were alone in there?" I tried not to look at his crotch. "You know..."

I couldn't do it. No matter how hard I tried, I couldn't talk about sex, and I specifically couldn't talk about Forest masturbating.

He crouched down.

Forest did that when he was trying to make a point but didn't want to seem overbearing. I kind of loved the tiny gesture.

"Rub one out?"

Heat flooded my cheeks, and it wasn't from the steam.

"Um...yeah."

He released my hands and ran his fingers through the stringy mess of his hair.

"That's kind of what I want to talk with you about."

"Okay?" What was he asking me?

He glanced over my shoulder, and I spun to follow the direction of his gaze. He was checking out the door and the modicum of privacy it allowed.

"Do you remember what I said about being watched?"

"I do, but you said there weren't any cameras."

"There aren't, but there are still eyes and ears watching us, studying us, and reporting back about us."

"Oh."

"It would be best if you didn't hesitate to take a shower with me or go to bed with me. If that makes sense." He covered his awkwardness by speaking plainly, but I felt the hitching in his voice with the rapid spike in my heart rate.

I didn't want to undress and mess up my hair and makeup. Although, why I cared about that confused me.

I went to the effort because of the importance Paul had placed on making myself presentable. If I could become invisible, maybe Snowden would forget about me. If he forgot about me, then I couldn't be used to hurt Forest.

But I understood Forest's need to speak with me privately and what he was trying to tell me about being watched.

I nodded and tugged at the buttons of my shirt.

Two days ago, the idea of being naked in a shower with my boss would have seemed an impossibility. Now, it merely felt practical.

Practical.

Not intimate.

Not sexual.

But, practical.

I hated that.

I hated the simmering chemistry between Forest and the man in the other room. It wasn't fair. There was no spark between me and Forest. Instead, we had an intimate familiarity that wasn't sexual.

Jealousy didn't suit me. It was crazy to be jealous. Forest wasn't interested in Paul above some weird physical attraction.

Forest waited while I removed my clothes. His penetrating intensity made me feel self-conscious as his gaze raked my body from head to toe. If I didn't know better, I would say his erection grew, but that had to be a mistake.

Once naked, I stepped under the spray of water, ruining my makeup and hair. It didn't matter. I'd avoided the shower because I didn't want to leave Forest alone with Paul. Now, I could take my time and wash away my pain.

Forest slowly removed his pajamas. With the steam, everything was indistinct. Not that I needed to see his body. Every ridge and valley of hardened muscle had been indelibly imprinted in my head.

He stepped in, and I moved out of the water to let him have it. There was the briefest shake of his head before he took my hands in his and pulled me close.

We stood chest to chest, hip to hip, and the long length of his arousal pressed against my belly. He leaned down until his forehead touched mine.

"God, Sara, I would never ask this of you, but…"

"But what?"

Ask what?

"I don't trust Snowden."

"Okay?"

"When we touch, it needs to appear natural. We can't let him know…" He released one of my hands and placed his on my waist. "I need to familiarize myself with your curves and get you attuned to my touch. Will you let me touch you?"

Touch me?

Slowly, nearly reverently, his hand moved. He walked his fingers to my belly and slowly inched them up until he barely touched the swell of my breasts.

"There are many ways for him to hurt me. Using you is one of them."

Holy shit!

I finally understood.

I understood what he was trying to tell me and what he wanted.

"Forest…"

He flinched then gave a long, slow swallow. "I know it's too much to ask, and I'm so very sorry you're in this position. It's not my intent to force you to do anything. I think I can keep you safe…and not force you to…" He barely got the words out before his voice broke.

It was all I could do to hold it together. This was everything I wanted, with one big exception. I was the one who didn't want to force him to do something he found repulsive. He tried to tell me what Snowden had made him do to Skye. I hadn't put the pieces together until now.

That's how Snowden would use me, and I remembered Snowden's words. Only Forest would fuck me.

Holy shit.

Forest's body trembled, and the low huffing coming from his chest were sobs.

Was Forest crying?

He was falling apart in my arms.

Chapter Twenty-Four

SARA

WHAT WAS I SUPPOSED TO DO? THERE WAS NO RULE BOOK FOR THIS kind of thing.

"I need you to touch me." He reached for my wrist, then hovered over my hand. "The first time…I don't want the first time to be in front of him. If you hesitate, he'll know. He'll…"

"Hurt us more."

Forest gave a sharp shake of his head. "I know what I'm asking is wrong, but…"

I wrapped my arms around him and placed my cheek to his chest. His heart thundered beneath my ear, and the deep pull of his lungs drew breath deep into his body. His entire body vibrated with disgust, or maybe revulsion.

I remembered what he'd said about Skye, how he'd been forced to have sex with her, but, more importantly, how he grew to crave it.

Is that what would happen to us?

Would my touch repulse him because of what Snowden would make us do?

I couldn't allow that.

We may not be fated to be together, but dammit if we wouldn't come out of this with our friendship intact.

Before we began, I needed to know one thing.

"Forest…"

"Yes?"

"Is there anything remotely interesting about me?"

"What do you mean?"

"Physically? Do you find anything remotely attractive about me? Does the thought of touching me disgust you? Or are you just as interested as I am to know what it would feel like to make love?"

Make love? I sounded like an idiot. Who said stuff like that? Evidently, I did.

"Sara?" His voice broke. "Do you mean…are you interested in me?"

I could tease out the answers to the questions swirling in my head, but I wouldn't do that. He'd lost too much.

"Don't you know?" I asked.

"Know what?"

I tilted my head to look up at him. "That I'm desperately in love with you? That I always have been?"

His face paled, and he took a step back, not in horror but shock.

"What are you saying?"

I pressed my hand over his heart. This was going to be hard to say, harder to admit, but to get through this we had to do it together.

I bit my lower lip, using the pinch of pain to fortify myself. Then, I looked up at him. Very slowly, I took his hand in mine and lifted it until it hovered over my breast.

"Touch me."

"You don't have to do this." His expression looked pained, but sparks of desire flashed in his icy gaze. Heat simmered there, thawing the icy paleness to a deep, tumultuous blue.

A soft laugh escaped me with his hesitation, and I knew. This was our time.

"Don't let him take this from us. Our first time should be ours, on our terms." I released his hand, letting it hover over my breasts.

He would need to decide if I was what he wanted. Meanwhile, I took a slight step back, never breaking eye contact with him I reached between us and took what I wanted.

He gasped as my fingers wrapped around his penis, and his smoldering gaze turned to me.

Hyperaware of everything around us, my grip tightened as his entire body jerked in anticipation.

"Holy fuck." That's all he managed before I slid my hand from root to crown, finally taking in the full, hardened length of him. His hips bucked, and he placed his hand over mine. "Is this really what you want?"

I gave a slight nod. "Is that okay?"

Acutely aware of our surroundings, and our circumstances, this wasn't how I would've envisioned this moment, but I would take it. I would take whatever he was willing to give.

And I would treasure it forever.

Slowly, I bent forward and placed my lips over his heart. My kiss was soft and gentle. I needed this, probably more than I was willing to admit.

I wanted to slide my hands around his hips, grab his ass, and skim my fingers back up and over his lower back while I went to my knees and traced my tongue down the downy patch of blond hair leading from his navel down to the root of his cock.

My one desire was to give him pleasure, the kind he could take freely and enjoy. Not something ripped from his unwilling body.

I wanted to be the one good thing in his life; his light in the darkness.

I looked up at him, willing to sink to my knees, and waited for him to respond. I wouldn't force this on him, but he needed to meet me halfway.

He stared at me, eyelids heavy with arousal, breaths deepening with desire, and lips parting to either begin or end this.

I released my grip, knowing the stimulation would be too much for him if I wanted him to think.

And Forest would think.

He would analyze this from every angle, using logic to arrive at a decision.

What I wouldn't give to get inside his head and shut off his mind.

I wanted him to feel not think.

The look in his eyes swallowed me whole. His jaw flexed, muscles bunching as the possibilities ran through his powerful mind. Slowly, he lifted his hands and gripped my upper arms.

His voice was raw, ragged, and a little unhinged. "You want... me?" His brows pinched together and formed a little furrow between them.

Frustratingly dense when it came to people, his disbelief wasn't a surprise. It still, however, cut deep. Clearly, it never occurred to him, although he'd had over a decade to miss every damn clue.

"I always have." I gave a little nod and glanced down. If he didn't do something soon, my heart was going to break and shatter all over the damn floor.

"How did I not know?" His voice sounded solemn and sad.

"Because you're a dumbass! I've been right in front of you this whole time! Kiss me already."

Forest grabbed me and pushed me against the shower wall.

I didn't have enough time to register what happened before Forest crushed his lips against mine. Raw, potent, and violent, his desire ripped through me.

He pressed me against the tiles, and the realization of what was happening ripped through me. The rawness of my need ricocheted through me, barreling straight to my core, where it pulsed and flared into an intense ache between the apex of my legs.

His fingers tightened painfully on my arms as his lips pressed against mine. My head felt light and fuzzy. Delirious happiness spread through me, warming my heart and made me believe the impossible.

Forest wanted me too.

His mouth was on me, taking and plundering. Ravenous with his need, he filled me with his taste. Dark, warm, and sensual, I was an instant addict.

My hands danced up his body, wrapping around his back as I traced out the ridges along his spine.

Forest was all ripped and sculpted perfection, and I was finally going to get a chance to explore every inch of him.

Only, I wasn't the one in control. Forest lead the charge, taking, claiming, and kissing me into intoxicated bliss. His need was palpable and growing between us with an urgency neither of us could deny.

"Sara…" Low, throaty, and hoarse with desire, my name spilled from his mouth in a way I'd never heard it before. It was raw, carnal, and everything I could have wanted.

He wants me too!

My head spun with that knowledge.

Forest wanted me.

Me!

I would have given a little cheer, except Forest's mouth was on me, kissing me, loving me, making love to me.

And his hands.

His incredible, strong hands moved with confidence. His fingers slid down my arms, then moved to my waist. Encircled by his massive hands, he broke them apart to move up and cup my breasts, kneading them as he kissed me into oblivion.

His thumbs worked my nipples into tight little buds, making my toes curl, and my eyes roll into the back of my head with the intensity of the pleasure racing through my body.

He chanted my name. Saying it over and over as his kisses moved from my lips to the angle of my jaw. He nuzzled the soft spot by my ear, gave a little nip to my ear lobe, then continued down, biting along my neck until he stopped at my collar bone.

"I can't believe this. God, but I need you. I've wanted to have you forever."

I dug my fingers into his hair, loving how it felt exactly as I'd always imagined.

He stooped down, his mouth moving in a relentless path to my cleavage. His nose pressed into the soft swell of my breasts, and he paused, simply breathing me in.

I took in a breath, crazy this was happening at all, then gave a little shriek when his mouth latched onto a nipple. The tip of his tongue darted out, and the delicate skin drew taut, pebbling my nipple, and driving me insane.

My fingers dug into his scalp as I lifted on tiptoe and pressed my breasts into his face. He shifted to the other side and gave the same determined attention to that nipple as the first. Desire rose within me, sparking with delicious crackles of electricity shooting along my nerves.

I'd heard, and dismissed, stories of women coming from nipple play alone, but damn if I wasn't close.

The burning ache between my legs, combined with the intensity he laved on my nipples, increased my pleasure, building it higher and higher.

"Forest, oh God, Forest!"

He went to his knees and looked up at me. A smoky haze covered his hooded eyes, and his pupils were blown out by his lust.

"I need to feel you inside of me." I wasn't against begging.

His lips pressed together, and I swore a frown turned at the corners of his decadent mouth, but it was all lost on me the moment he placed his mouth over my sex. A screech escaped me, and I quickly covered my mouth. Aware of Paul sitting in the other room, there was no need to advertise what was going on in here.

But keeping quiet proved impossible as anticipation rioted through me. Forest stimulated my nerve endings and drove me up an impossible cliff when his fingers found my clit.

Desperation filled me, and my sex answered with throbbing intensity. Dizzy, aching, and wanting more, I fell apart as his fingers stimulated my nerves until I found myself teetering on a precipice.

Just a little more and I would fall head over heels into oblivion.

The heat of his mouth returned as he sucked on my clit. The rough flicking of his tongue over the tight bundle of nerves drove me insane.

My breaths came as fast pants.

"Christ, Sara," he said with his face buried against my sex. "You taste fucking amazing."

The gentle draw of his lips and tongue had my fingers digging into his scalp and pulling at his thick, white-blond hair. My hips flexed against his mouth as I shamelessly ground against him.

Just a little more, and I would fly.

He seemed to understand, gripped my hips, and devoured me.

Blood pounded in my ears as his wicked tongue sent insane sensations rocketing through my body. Every nerve ending lit up.

He found a rhythm and kept me on that edge. With a quickening of his tempo, breaths stuttered out of me as he pushed me to the brink. With his fingers digging into my skin, the flick of his tongue brought a scream from my lungs. I finally tumbled over that precipice and shattered in his arms.

Panting in short, sharp breaths, I flew with the force of the most intense orgasm I'd ever experienced.

Forest rose to his feet and caught me, arms wrapped around me, lips pressed against mine, I rode the waves of my orgasm in his arms and with our lips locked together.

When I could speak, I braved his gaze.

"That was incredible. It was everything I imagined. I need you. I want to feel you inside of me."

I wanted to complete our union and bring him the same dizzying pleasure where we could finally meld our bodies together, joining us as one.

His expression fell, and he gave a slow blink.

"Sara…" He shook his head, and something shifted inside of me.

Was that it? Was he going to say no? Before I could voice my worries, or give light to the fear festering inside of me, he leaned his forehead against mine.

"We can't."

"But why not?" I clung to him, not wanting to know this answer, but needing him to tell me the truth.

He didn't want me. This had simply been a show for Snowden's lackey in the other room.

I didn't know if I could live with that.

I'd loved Forest from the moment he freed me from my abusive foster home. He was my knight in shining armor. As soon as I could, I went to work for him. I never left his side. I couldn't.

He couldn't look me in the eye, and my insides felt as if they were being ripped apart. They shifted inside of me, shredding me from the inside out.

"I'm clean, Sara. I've always been tested, and I use condoms every time I'm with a man, but..." He swallowed thickly and took in a slow, measured breath. "Snowden...he...I..."

Pain filled his expression, and I understood. Snowden raped him without protection. Forest couldn't have sex without exposing me to whatever diseases Snowden may, or may not, be carrying.

It never crossed my mind how thorough Snowden's degradation had been and would continue to be. He defiled Forest in every way.

"Oh, Forest!"

"It's okay." He tried to shrug it off, but I could tell it bothered him.

He told me it was just a body, but it wasn't. It was everything.

His eyes crinkled, and he placed the pad of his thumb beneath my chin. A boyish grin filled his face, as well as a blush.

I'd never seen him so vulnerable, so heart-stoppingly beautiful.

"You like me." His grin grew. "You really like me."

I gave a playful laugh. "Oh, Forest, I don't just like you. I've loved you since I was fourteen. I've been hopelessly in love with you since the moment we met."

"Why didn't you ever say anything?"

"Because...you were gay."

He huffed a laugh. "But I'm not gay."

"You picked a piss poor time to tell me that. Why? Why didn't you ever say anything to me? If you felt the same about me, why didn't you say anything?"

He bit at his lower lip, worrying it between his teeth. Drawing away from me, he rubbed at the back of his neck.

"I didn't want to hurt you, and you didn't seem that interested, to be honest."

"I can't believe we wasted so many years."

He blew out a breath. "Perhaps it's best."

"How? How can it be?"

"I didn't hurt you."

"You didn't hurt me right now, you big lug. I'd say I survived just fine. And might I just say, for someone who only has sex with men, you're quite talented with your fingers and mouth."

His expression darkened. "I was trained well."

"Oh, Forest!" I couldn't believe what I just said. How insensitive could I be? "Shit, I'm sorry. I didn't—"

He pressed a finger to my lips.

"Don't. Don't ruin what was easily the best moment of my life. I want to have sex with you. I really do, and if we ever get out of this, we'll figure the rest out. But don't cheapen what just happened. You're the light that will get me through. When things become their darkest, I'll always have this moment to see me through. You like me." He tweaked my nose, teasing me. "That's worth a million suns to banish the darkness."

"And you like me."

"I like the way you taste, and I love the way you scream. I can't wait to do that again."

I glanced down at his erection. "And what about you? We may not be able to have sex, but there are other things we can do."

"Like what?" His brows lifted with interest, and I loved the way the intensity of his gaze focused on my mouth.

It was my turn to bite my lower lip. I reached between us and took him in hand.

"My turn to see how you taste." Slowly, I went to my knees.

Chapter Twenty-Five

FOREST

I stared at Sara, eyes heavy with desire, my lips parted in stunned disbelief, and my need palpable as she touched me for the second time. It was all I could do not to come right then.

She liked me.

She'd been in love with me since we first met?

It didn't make any sense with what I knew. I didn't believe her.

I would have known.

How had I not known?

"Forest?" Her soft voice floated up to me.

The sight of her on her knees, hand on my dick, her eyes staring up at me with that satiated smile from the orgasm I just gave her was the most beautiful thing in the world. The sweet taste of her still lingered on my tongue.

She made me an instant addict.

I'd never get enough of her, and I couldn't believe my eyes or the sparks of electricity shooting through my body.

She was running her fingers along my shaft.

Touching me.

Holding me.

Loving me.

Her nails lightly danced along the rigid length of my erection while she gripped my balls with her other hand. My hips bucked. I hissed with the exquisiteness of her touch. Then jerked uncontrollably with the urge to fuck.

We couldn't have sex.

I hated that, but there was no way I could expose her to any of the vileness Snowden subjected me too. I sucked in a breath as her head dipped forward.

Soft and succulent, her lips wrapped around the crown of my cock. Warm and velvety, her tongue circled lightly around the bell-shaped tip. Blissfully amazing, she swallowed me whole.

Or tried to.

Slowly, she fluttered her tongue from the tip to the root and then all the way back up the length. My toes curled. My thighs flexed. I tried to keep my hips still.

I was a big man with a big dick and could do some serious damage if I didn't take care.

Her hand moved up and down my engorged length while her other hand cupped my balls.

So tiny.

So gentle.

So different from a man.

Instead of aggressive and hard, she was tender and soft. Instead of quick to the chase, eager to get the deed done, she took her time. Nearly reverent in her touch, she explored with intense curiosity.

Her fingernails gently grazed my balls. It was insanely arousing. No man took that much time to stimulate me.

Rock hard before she started, I didn't think it was possible to get any harder. But I did. I glanced down, thinking I'd see the crown of her head. Instead, she glanced up at me, eyes soft and mouth stuffed with my dick.

Holy hell, that was erotic as shit.

She was trying to swallow me whole and was enjoying this.

Enjoying me.

She liked me.

I still couldn't believe it.

All these years, I hadn't had a clue, yet here we were. In the most unlikely of places, we found each other. This only solidified my resolve to make sure she remained safe.

Her fingers continued their slow tease while her tongue lapped along my length. She swirled it around the flare of my crown, teasing the tip. Each sensuous lick coiled heat in my balls and drove me insane with need.

I wanted to pick her up, thrust her against the wall, and slam into her pussy as hard and fast as I could. I ached to fill her up and welcome the warm embrace as the walls of her pussy wrapped around my cock.

It killed me that I couldn't.

She tried to take me in deep, but there were limits to what she could handle. Too entranced by her efforts, I kept my mouth shut and simply enjoyed this simple pleasure.

Hell, there was nothing simple about any of this.

When she failed to deep throat me, she resorted to teasing me, gently at first, only taking the tip into her mouth.

Each groan, each thrust of my hips, none of it encouraged her to take more. Then her devilish tongue rubbed against the sensitive underside just beneath the rim. I think I saw stars. I practically levitated, rising on my toes.

I reached down and twisted my hands in her hair and tried like hell not to take control.

I didn't want to force her and treasured anything she could give. But then she added a hand, twisting it around my shaft, stimulating me with the friction of her fingers and the delicious heat of her mouth.

My moans filled the bathroom with my pleasure, my frustration, and my desire to make this last as long as possible. Tension built in my thighs with anticipation of the orgasm gathering in my balls. Despite my size, she sheathed her teeth with her lips and glided up and down my cock until I was delirious with pleasure.

Guttural groans erupted from me as her head bobbed up and down my length—the blissful need for release built until I couldn't contain it.

I called out her name, warning her until I swelled with pleasure. My face pulled tight with the need to hold off and pull out, but she bobbed down, placing me deep into the back of her throat.

I warned her.

I convulsed as she sucked on me.

It was all I needed to hurtle off the edge as I lost the battle for control. With my hips bucking, I came in her mouth and shouted her name violently.

Sensation spiraled through me as each wave of my orgasm rocked my solid frame. Her name fell from my lips, a pleasure-induced litany of emotion I no longer kept contained. There was no longer any need.

Sara belonged to me now, and I belonged to her.

As for the rest? I would figure it out.

Snowden only thought he'd won.

He didn't know I was still putting chess pieces in play.

I pulled Sara into my arms and drew her close.

There was no revulsion.

No violent wrenching in my gut as I touched her.

She fit perfectly in my embrace as if she'd always belonged there.

Sara felt like heaven, like I had finally come home.

"How did we not know?" I kissed the crown of her head. "How did I miss what was right under my nose?"

She gave a soft laugh. "I don't know."

A soft knock interrupted our privacy.

Paul called out. "Ten minutes. I strongly suggest you be ready to greet Mr. Snowden when he arrives."

Fuck.

"And so it begins." Softly, I kissed the top of her head.

"Forest…"

"Shh…whatever happens, remember it's just a body."

I needed her to believe the lie. Once Snowden arrived, he would be my primary focus. I couldn't protect Sara if I paid too much attention to her.

Snowden would zero in on that and make things ten times

worse. I did, however, vow there would be one thing he would never use against us.

I wouldn't let Snowden do to Sara what he'd done to Skye.

Whatever it took.

Those words were fast becoming my mantra.

I hoped I had the strength to stay strong. With the way things were stacked against me, there was an excellent chance I would fail.

After kissing Sara one last time, I headed out of the shower, drunk with happiness, head reeling with our admissions of love to each other, and with my mouth still tingling with the beauty that it had been to kiss Sara.

I could get lost in her for days. We had so much time to make up for.

Instead, I braced to face a monster.

I left Sara to dress and approached Paul.

"Any word on what I should wear? It seems silly to dress when the menu of the day calls for rape."

Oddly, Paul's eyes pinched at that comment.

I'd come to terms with what I would endure. Several choices faced me. I could run from my fate, meet it head-on, or pretend it wasn't happening. I intended to meet Snowden head-on.

It would off-balance him.

Paul tossed me a circle of leather.

"A collar?" I shrugged. "Not very imaginative. Is that it?"

He blew out a breath. "Cuffs for your wrists and ankles."

"Of course. We wouldn't want to forget the cuffs."

I dropped the towel and strapped the leather collar around my neck. The four heavy-duty D-rings attached to it told me the day would not be easy.

"I'm assuming naked is the attire of the day?"

"Shut up." Paul's shoulders twitched. He shoved a pair of wrist cuffs at me. "Put these on."

"Nice and wide, love the rings." The cuffs had the same rings as the collar. Sturdy and meant for restraint. Whatever Snowden had planned for me, there wasn't a snowball's chance in hell I'd get free.

Not that I would try.

Instant obedience.

That was the deal.

After I put the cuffs on, Paul slowly approached, a wary expression in his gaze. He made a show of kneeling before me, which put my dick at eye-level.

Thankfully, after the orgasm I'd just had, my dick behaved. Long and soft, the fucker rested.

Paul strapped on the leather ankle cuffs while I stood over him and tried every trick in the book to avoid getting hard.

Not an easy feat since all I thought about was how Paul's mouth would feel on me after Sara had taken me in hers. I was sure it would be different, but different better, or different worse?

"Arms behind your back." His command shot through me.

They were simple words, but fuck if I didn't respond like a rabid animal. My dick gave a little shudder, and it didn't escape Paul's notice. He was still eye to eye with it.

"I see."

"You see shit."

Paul stood and moved behind me.

"Really? The thought of me restraining you turns you on. What else do you like?" He leaned in close and pressed his hand against my back.

"I'd like for you to take your filthy hands off me."

"I bet you're into ropes, restraints, whips, and all the fun stuff." He smacked my ass. "Good for you...I am too. I love whipping a man until he comes. I bet you'd do that for me, come from nothing but the bite of my whip?"

"Fuck off."

His voice dripped sin and lust. "You'd let me tie you up, whip you until you were delirious with pain, and then you'd beg to come for me, wouldn't you? I bet there are far few men strong enough to best you, and we both know Mr. Snowden doesn't count. He doesn't have what I have."

"As I remember, I knocked you out cold last night. If anyone bested anyone, it was me, not you."

His low chuckle was accompanied by the sweep of his hand

across my back and down my buttocks. The fine hairs at my nape lifted, my breath hitched, and blood surged to my groin.

It took considerable effort not to let out a low groan. I'd never responded to anyone like this before. I wanted everything he said.

"We'll have our time, Forest. Don't worry; it'll come. When it does, I'll show you rapture when you willingly submit to your dominant. I'll fuck you right over the cliff. We'll fly together, you and me."

"Again, with the fantasies." I snorted, denying his claim even as my body betrayed me. "You'll do what Snowden allows and nothing more. And I'll fight you every step of the way."

"I wouldn't expect anything less. The harder you fight, the harder you fall. If that's what you need, I'm willing to take you there."

He fastened my wrists behind my back, showing little kindness as he hiked them high and put pressure on my shoulders.

Coming around to face me, he crowded my space. Face to face, we stared at each other. I didn't move a muscle when he leaned in and brushed his lips over mine. It wasn't a kiss, but more of a promise.

"You'll find I can be soft as well as hard. I'll never yield to you, but I can give you what you crave."

"And what is that?"

"A strong hand, purpose, someone you can submit to without losing yourself in the process." His lips lifted in a cocky grin. "Discipline. Pain. Pleasure."

"Easy words for a man who works for a kidnapper, rapist, and murderer. Don't get ahead of yourself."

"I won't. As I said, I'm a patient man when I see something I want. You're nothing like I expected and everything I want. A treasure waiting to be taken."

"And yet, you're not the one in charge."

The lock to the outer door disengaged. Paul stepped behind me and caved in the back of my legs, dropping me to my knees.

I fell with a grunt and turned my head to glare at him. Paul gestured to the door as it slowly opened.

"You'll greet your Master like such, on your knees. Now bow down, forehead to the floor. Mr. Snowden has arrived."

The door swung inward, and the heavy tread of my nemesis rang in my ears. It wasn't necessary to look up; I would know that sound in hell.

How many times had Snowden walked up to me with a hood around my head, arms strapped to my back, and terror flooding my body?

Too many to count.

But I wasn't that little boy anymore. I had grown, matured, and was stronger than ever.

I braced myself to do battle.

Not with Snowden, but with my fears.

Chapter Twenty-Six

FOREST

"Ah, my boy, I have missed you." Snowden's voice thickened with lust. "Now, up! How do you greet your Master?"

I ground my teeth. My vow to never call him Master disintegrated in an instant.

I pushed off the floor and leaned back on my heels. Slowly, I dragged my eyes up his body and tried not to gag. I met the hardness of his stare with the resolute determination to endure.

"Good morning, sir." I ground the words out.

"How did you sleep? I hope you slept well."

"I slept."

He cocked his head, assessing me. I supposed he wondered if I was being flippant and whether that warranted punishment.

I wasn't.

My words were sincere.

My body had recovered from the previous day's abuse.

Sara slept soundly and had been kept safe.

What did I have to be flippant about?

Asshole.

"Is that so?" He eyed me.

"Yes, sir." I kept my tone even, calm, and non-threatening. I wasn't foolish enough to inject anything but respect. "I appreciate you letting me rest and for allowing Sara to stay with me."

Snowden would pounce on that in an instant. My capitulation would come with time. He expected some resistance on my part. But this was the first give I would hand him.

I intended to give him everything he expected and more.

"And where is little Miss Sara?"

"She's getting ready in the bathroom." Paul interrupted our exchange and kicked my heel with the toe of his boot.

I didn't dare look up at him, but he was trying to send me a message to shut the fuck up. I could do that. I turned my gaze down, lowering my head in deference to a monster.

God, how my stomach churned.

"Go get her." Snowden snapped his fingers in irritation. "I don't like being kept waiting."

"I'm here." Sara rushed into the room.

I couldn't see her but caught the hesitation in her voice when she saw me on my knees.

"I didn't mean to make you wait, sir." Her crystal-clear voice rang with ruined innocence.

There was no way to unsee this.

"Sir?" Amusement tickled his tone.

"Unless you would prefer Mr. Snowden?" She, too, managed to lace her words with respect.

Knowing her as I did, I picked up on the strain in her voice as she tried to keep things light. The poor thing didn't understand how dark this would get.

"That sounds just about right." Snowden practically preened. "Did you sleep well, my dear?"

"I slept."

I cringed when she parroted my response.

The false pleasantry was killing me, and I braced for the inevitable.

Torture, rape, and degradation were taking their sweet ass time getting to this party.

Snowden paused and shifted his attention to Paul. "What happened to your face?"

What would our fight cost me?

I mulled the question over in my head, detaching myself from whatever Snowden had planned for the day.

"I tripped." Paul's curt reply offered no details.

"You tripped?"

"That's what I said."

"Hmm." Snowden grabbed my chin and forced me to look at him. He scrutinized my face and pressed his thumb against the bruise on my jaw. "Did you trip as well?"

"Yes." I ground out my response, giving as little incriminating evidence as possible.

"And the doors? They're off their hinges. Why is that?"

"They were squeaky," Paul said. "I removed them." Paul placed his hands behind his back and broadened his stance.

"Is that so?"

"It is. We discussed leaving the doors open, but it seemed easiest to remove them, given the squeaky hinges."

"Squeaky hinges, is it?"

Paul rocked back on his heels. "Yes, sir."

"Is this true, Forest?"

Fuck. Way to work me into a corner, Paul.

"Not really." My sullen reply had Snowden cranking my neck painfully back.

"How's that?"

"He told me the doors had to stay open. I closed the bedroom door. We had words. He tripped, and then he removed the doors from their hinges."

Snowden threw his head back and laughed.

"Words? I'm assuming with your fists?"

"Words," I said, "and fists."

"And who won that little fight?"

"Forest did," Paul answered for me, surprising me with his honesty.

"Hah!" Snowden pointed his finger at Paul. "And you said he wouldn't be honest with me. It looks like I won that bet."

What the fuck?

That had been a test?

Shit, of course, it had. Snowden wanted to know where my loyalties would fall. But if he thought…

He pulled at his belt. "But of course, you said you tripped. I do believe that qualifies as a lie."

"If you say so." I wasn't going to argue with him.

It didn't matter what happened. I could be the perfect little pet, and he would still find something to use against me.

"I do say so." He slowly drew his belt from the belt loops. "I say this calls for ten strikes. Not the most stellar way to begin your day."

I held back a gulp and braced for a whipping. Snowden always had a twitchy arm. He gestured for me to bend down.

I complied immediately.

Whatever it took.

The leather creaked as he wrapped it around his wrist. It whistled as it swung through the air. And it cracked against my ass with an ear-splitting retort. I bit my lower lip and grunted as pain bit at me.

"That's one, my boy. Let's see how red we can turn your ass."

One turned to two. Two to ten. But he didn't stop there.

Snowden was having too much damn fun and striped my ass until I huffed with pain. He wanted me to cave and beg him to stop, but I held my ground. I soaked it all in and repeated my mantra over and over again.

When he took me, a different pain seared my flesh. My eyes glazed over as I retreated into myself and let the darkness consume me.

It was only a body, but it was a body filled with pain.

I focused on surviving.

The day grew long as Snowden paraded me around his fortress. I never asked where we were. That would become clear with time, and frankly, I enjoyed the walk.

Snowden marched by my side, a master of manipulation, he

poked and prodded, trying to find a chink in my armor. He'd already won because my most glaring weakness walked behind us.

Paul kept to Sara's side. I wasn't sure what his guard duties entailed, but he seemed to keep an eye on her. Once, he pushed a man aside who decided to get a little too close.

I didn't like the man but appreciated him watching over Sara.

He deferred to Snowden in all things but seemed to have a degree of freedom I didn't see in the other men. My gut told me this might be true, and if so, it would prove beneficial. I counted on Paul having free access to the facilities.

We wandered to a banquet hall where Snowden gorged himself, feeding me scraps. Paul and Sara joined us at the long table. Or rather, they joined Snowden. I was on hands and knees at his feet.

He choked me often, yanking on the collar until spots danced in my eyes. An expert at torture, he knew exactly how far he could tease the edge.

I toppled several times, pushed past the brink of physical exhaustion, which only encouraged Snowden to see how far he could push the envelope.

When he took me to the dungeon, I balked.

"What's this, my boy?"

One glance inside that room convinced me this was not a place I wanted Sara to see. Not that I could keep her from looking inside. Her gasp turned my insides, and I hesitated.

I cracked.

"Please..." I choked on the word, but I would beg.

"Please, what?" Scorn lit through his voice.

"Please don't make her watch."

"What if that's what I want?"

If it was what he wanted, there would be nothing I could do about it. My shoulders slumped, and I blew out a breath.

"If it's your will, then it's mine too."

Snowden's smug laughter speared my gut, twisting and ripping with his filth.

"It seems we're learning important lessons today." He'd debased me more ways than I could count, making Sara witness every degradation.

I knew what he was up to, how his mind worked, and hoped Sara would find her way through and past the manipulation.

It was only a body.

I prayed this didn't change her feelings about me. We'd only just found each other, and I couldn't bear to lose her.

The disgust she must feel seeing me cave to this monster's will had to be intense. I wouldn't be able to stomach it. It killed me to think I would lose her while desperately trying to protect her.

"Of course…" Snowden practically cooed. "If you want, Paul can take her back to your rooms. She'll be safe there, but not alone. Tell me, do you trust me to keep your girl safe?"

He was testing me. This was the game we played.

Give me two impossible options and force me to choose between them.

Sara could watch Snowden tear me apart in his dungeon, or I could choose to be separated from her, sparing both her and me the degradation of what would happen in that room. But if she wasn't with me, I couldn't protect her. I had to place my trust in Snowden to uphold his part of our bargain.

It was devious perfection.

I turned on him, rage filling my being. "Do you trust me not to bite off your dick the next time you ram it down my throat?" Or snap your neck the next time you force me in your bed?

Snowden's eyes widened, and he took a step back. Real fear filled his face. It didn't last long.

His face turned beet red, and he retook that step, getting as much in my face as he could. I had eight inches on the man, so he had to look up at me.

All it would take to reverse our positions was a simple yank of the damn leash. I'd be on my knees looking up at him and praying he kept our uneasy truce.

"See, that's going to cost you, but I'll answer your question. You're going to be a good boy and suck my dick with a smile on your face. You're going to let me fuck you whenever I want, and you're going to do so much more. Do you know how I know?"

A red haze covered my vision, and I bucked against my restraints. But I gave a shaky nod.

"Tell me. Tell me how I know." He sneered.

"Because I'll do anything for her."

"Ah, now that's true. Not the answer I expected but sums things up pretty nice. Yes, you'll do all that and more because you know one thing about me. I'll keep her safe until you don't do as I want. And if you think about hurting me or killing me, my men will take her out immediately. It'll start with Paul, who will fuck her until she bleeds. Then my men will have their way with her one by one, then two by two, then—"

"Enough." My heart raced inside my chest with images of what he said.

Sara's eyes widened, and she took a step back. Paul caught her and forced her back with a sharp shake of his head, warning her not to bring any attention to herself.

Snowden had his back to them. He didn't see their exchange. He shoved his pinched face in mine as he tested the limits of my will.

Shaken to my core, I swallowed back a sob. This man had me over the barrel of a gun. There was nothing I could do but play his game and bide my time.

I swallowed my shame. It burned like a hot, white poker and pierced my heart, searing my insides with a howl of pain I had no choice but to endure.

Snowden gripped the collar and gave it a little shake. His mouth curled into a satisfied grin.

"That's right. You'll do anything for the girl. I wonder if she would do the same for you?"

"If you touch her, our deal is off. I will kill you."

He gave a shake of his head. "See, I don't think you will. I think you'll realize she'll grow sick of watching you grovel. She'll put distance between you and cringe when you touch her. You think you're keeping her safe, but you're really giving me everything I need to bring you down."

"Then why bother with this game?"

"Because I know something you do not." He slapped my cheek, a soft tap instead of a hard strike. "You never forget your first love. You never forget the man who showed you what love could be like. You resist me, but you know a sobering truth deep down inside of you."

"And what is that?"

His eyes softened, and he gazed at me with affection. "You missed me."

The man was certifiable if he believed that.

Snowden clicked his fingers with a sharp snap. "Now, let's have some fun and stir up some memories. I have a place for your girl to sit. She'll have a perfect view while you and I get reacquainted."

"Send her away."

"I promised not to separate you."

"I don't want her to watch." I couldn't stand to have her see what he planned on doing to me.

"But what about our arrangement?" Snowden was having fun at my expense, the little prick. He was eating this up. My pain aroused him, both physical and mental.

Bile rose in my throat, and I swallowed it down. "Send him with her."

"Paul?"

I gave a sharp shake of my head.

"You trust Paul?"

"No." I fixed Snowden with a fierce stare. "I trust you and our deal." I made a snapping motion with my teeth.

"You'll pay for that." He gave another pat to my cheek. "And now we understand each other." He snapped his fingers again. "Paul, take Miss Sara back to her rooms. Keep her comfortable. Forest and I will be a while."

The muscles of Paul's jaw bunched. He looked like he was about to argue, but Snowden snapped his fingers again.

"I said you could have him, and you will, but today is for Forest and me. We have much to celebrate."

My attention shifted to the dungeon, and I huffed a breath.

Snowden had recreated the basement from Clark Preston's house, the basement where he defiled me for an entire summer when I'd been a boy.

PTSD had nothing on the emotions careening through my body. A skillful and devious master of manipulation, Snowden executed the perfect psychological torture.

He intended to take me back to my darkest moments.

"Welcome home, my boy."

Chapter Twenty-Seven

SARA

"COME." PAUL DREW ME AWAY FROM THE DOOR.

"Don't touch me." I jerked out of his grip.

How could Forest send me away like this? The house of horrors inside that room would drive any man insane. He needed me. I was the light that would see him through.

While Snowden led a defeated Forest down the steps and into a room made for nightmares, Paul grabbed at my arm. His grip was tight, and I couldn't shake him.

"I said, let me go." I tried to rip my arm free, but he was too strong.

Forest descended the stairs and didn't look back. Snowden walked with an exaggerated swagger and puffed out his chest.

My heart broke for Forest.

"You can't help him." Paul kept his tone level but firm.

"He needs me." My voice cracked, distressed, and helpless.

"No man needs the woman he loves watching what's going to happen in there." His words drew me up short.

"Why do you care?"

"Didn't say I cared, just stating a fact." His attention shifted to Forest's back, and he exhaled a long sigh. "He's saving you."

"He needs me."

Forest went to stand before a large wooden X in the center of the room. There was an iron cage—two of them. One was big enough for a man. The other looked barely large enough to hold a large dog.

Holy shit!

My throat contracted against the horrors in that room. All manner of whips, crops, canes, and other things lined the walls. It was enough to make me sick to my stomach.

Who could do that to another person?

A sick fuck, that's who.

Snowden released the cuffs restraining Forest's wrists. Without any resistance, Forest meekly lifted his hands over his head and allowed Snowden to secure his wrists to the wood using the sturdy D-rings.

Paul pulled me away from the door. "Trust me when I say this is for the best."

"What's he going to do to him?" I didn't want to leave Forest with a madman.

Look at me, dammit!

As if he heard my plea, Forest's gaze lifted and met mine. His arctic eyes bore into me, and then he gave a slow shake of his head, followed by a chin bump telling me to go. His eyes closed, and he took in a deep fortifying breath as Snowden bent to secure his feet.

He was helpless.

"You don't want to know. That's why Forest sent you away. The best thing you can do right now is honor his wish and leave. He doesn't want you to watch this. Support him when he's with you, he'll need your strength, and don't ask about what happens in there."

Forest was in the hands of a psychopath, and there was nothing I could do.

Honor his wish and leave.

Paul's words spoke with far too much knowledge. I hated that he was right.

What happened to Forest wanting me to stay with him to protect me?

The truth?

He was the helpless one.

My presence only made things that much harder on him.

"Don't touch me." I pried Paul's fingers off my arm. "You're all monsters." It hadn't escaped my notice that Paul had been upset he wasn't joining Snowden. "You're just like Snowden."

"I'm nothing like him." Paul released me and took a step back. He lifted his hands as if in surrender. I didn't know if he was mocking me or something else.

"Really? Because from where I'm standing, you're exactly like Snowden. The way you talk to Forest, the things you say to him—"

"Are things he needs. You don't know your boss at all, do you, little girl?"

"I think I know him pretty damn well. Much better than you."

"He's a complicated man with complicated needs."

"And you're an expert? You've known him what? A day?" I fisted my hands on my hips. "I've known him over a decade. I think I know Forest."

"Do you know he's submissive?"

I took a step back.

"Yeah. I knew you didn't. That big monster of a man is deeply submissive, but only to the right man. I bet he fucks a lot of random strangers, and I'm pretty sure he's never been in a committed relationship. What's the longest anyone's hung around? One night? One week? I'd bet a million bucks no one has lasted more than a couple months. Forest is the kind of man who tests his lovers. When they fail, he kicks them to the curb."

"You're wrong."

"Am I?"

I took a step back, confused, and concerned. I didn't believe Paul, but he sure hit a lot of things square on the head when it came to Forest.

Paul closed the distance between us. "Forest is complex. His needs are complicated."

"You know nothing about him."

"I know he's been in love with you for years, but never touched you until this morning. That little display in the shower was a first for the two of you. It was cute, sentimental, and full of all the feels."

"How…?"

He lifted a dismissive hand. "Don't worry. Your secret is safe with me. You two finally connected the dots this morning, and he'll be thanking me later for giving you that moment and not breaking it up. I encourage you to continue exploring what you have with Forest. He's going to need the comfort only you can provide. You're soft and yielding. He's going to need that. I'm hard and demanding. He craves what I offer but isn't ready to embrace it."

"You're crazy."

"Not really. You and I—*We*—are the perfect union of what he needs."

"You talk about we when there is no us. You're disgusting. Despicable…"

"And Devastatingly handsome, you left that out."

"You're a prick. Did you know that?"

"I have a big dick if that's what you mean, but sorry little girl, I don't swing your way. I have eyes for only one man. You're right about there being no *us*—I'm not interested in fucking you—but we are the perfect pair to take care of Forest."

"Asshole."

"Such filthy words today. Should I feel special you've been saving them all for me?"

"You're a pile of filth. No better than Snowden."

"I'm nothing like Snowden."

"Really? You want to beat Forest. Destroy him—"

"Yes, I want to beat him, but only because he needs it. I want to whip him until he bleeds, but only to free him from his internal bonds. I want to force him to his knees and accept that surrendering to me, serving me, is what makes him whole. As for destroying him? I want no part in that."

"You're repulsive."

Paul shook his head as if I didn't understand.

"Forest needs to fall apart. That man is so bottled up inside his head, he can't find his way free of the walls he's built around himself to keep others out. You think you have him? That he loves you? He might. I think it's highly probable Forest is in fact in love with you. I've never seen a man sacrifice so much for someone he didn't love. But the thing about Forest is that he doesn't know how to love another person. You're doomed without me."

"Doomed?"

"Yes."

"And you know what he needs?" Our entire conversation was insane. It made no sense.

"I know how to bring about the truths we hide inside ourselves. I know how to free him. When I succeed, he'll be a man capable of the most intense love. He'll love you, unconditionally."

"Then fucking free him from this nightmare. How does a man like you find his way working for a monster like Snowden? How can you stand by and let that cretin do whatever it is he's doing to Forest? How can you stand there and mock Forest? Tell him you're going to rape him? You're insane and don't even know it. You're repulsive."

"This conversation is over."

"Over? I'd say we've barely begun. And you're wrong about Forest."

"I'm not wrong."

"You're an arrogant prick."

"You're repeating yourself. Be a smart girl, and don't antagonize me. You don't want to be on my bad side."

"If you know about Forest and me, that means Snowden knows too."

That would be the one thing which could destroy Forest.

"I told you…" Paul gave an exaggerated eye roll. "Your secret is safe with me."

"But you work for Snowden."

"Our relationship is…complex."

"What the hell does that mean?"

"It means we're not discussing it. But we are discussing Forest."

"I have no interest in talking about Forest with you."

"And yet you will. You want to understand him."

"I understand him just fine."

"But you don't know why the air crackles between him and me but doesn't between the two of you. That's a mystery you can't solve."

"Forest is bi-sexual. He's attracted to men. Of course, things are going to be different." My shoulders twitched as if that was an obvious statement. The truth was far different.

"He fucks a lot of men, but he's only attracted to a particular kind of man."

"You don't know him at all."

"It seems I know him better than you. But don't worry. We'll share him just fine."

"Share him?" My eyes popped with indignation. "You're insane."

"Not insane, but I accept neither of us has the entirety of what he needs. You and I are two sides of a coin. He needs us both to be whole. Once you accept that, accept me and my role, we'll do just fine—you and me. We."

"He. Doesn't. Know. You." My fists clenched as I bit out the words. "You're helping the man he hates. You're standing by while Snowden does horrible things to him. If you think that makes you someone he needs, you're as delusional as Snowden. Forest might feel some sense of attraction to you—you're his type—but it won't last. He knows what you are. Everything you stand for is something he hates. You lost him before you ever began. Forest will eat you alive."

"That you believe that is cute, little girl." He reached for me and yanked me down the hall.

"Get your fucking hands off me."

"Such foul words from Forest's angel." He didn't let go and continued to drag me down the hall, away from Forest.

I dug in my heels, and Paul spun me around to face him. Nearly as tall as Forest, I had to crane my neck, but I wasn't about to back down.

"I said to let me go."

"Do as I say and there'll be no reason for me to touch you. Trust me when I say you're not my type. Resist, and I won't think twice about slinging you over my shoulder and carrying you the rest of the way to your rooms."

To my rooms.

I didn't want to go back there.

"Isn't there someplace else we can go? Outside? A library?"

"No."

"Why not?"

"I don't think that's wise."

"Why?"

"This is not a place where a woman typically wanders around."

"Why is that?"

I barraged him with questions, hoping he'd finally answer one, but he gave me a look which told me how stupid that last question had been.

"Oh, right. Den of sex thieves and murderers."

"Sex thieves?" He gave a smirk. "That's a new one."

"Whatever." It chaffed me that I'd said the wrong thing. "That's not what I meant, and you know it. Sex-traffickers. Thieves. Murderers. Rapists."

"This place is what it is, and it's not safe for you to go wandering about."

"But I have you to protect me." I injected as much venom as I could.

And an idea was forming in my head.

If I went to the room, I wouldn't be able to tell Forest anything about this place.

I didn't know what it would take to escape, but surely, we needed to know something about the layout.

Our little tour this morning had been a blur. I'd been too concerned about Forest that I hadn't paid attention. The least I could do was learn how to find my way around this monstrous place.

"You're going to your room where you'll be safe."

"Safe?"

From murderers, thieves, rapists, and worse. I wasn't safe.

Paul walked beside me, navigating a maze of passageways as he led me back the way we'd come. He ignored me for the most part, our previous conversation abandoned, and scrolled through whatever messages, emails, and social media he had on his phone.

Finally, we arrived in a corridor I remembered and stopped before a door which hitched my shoulders together until they practically touched my ears.

Paul activated the outer lock with a retinal scan. The door unlocked, and he swung it inward, holding it open for me.

I ducked beneath his arm and took in a deep breath.

Great. What was I going to do with myself while Forest...Sharp pains stabbed through my abdomen, thinking about what was happening in that basement. I held my hand to my mouth to stave off the retching sensation filling my gut.

"Can I get you something? You look like you're going to puke." Paul looked genuinely concerned.

The problem I had with Paul was that he was stunning, incredibly perceptive, and even a tiny bit considerate. I found myself staring when I shouldn't. Not that I was attracted to him. Well, I was, there was an inherent beauty to the way he carried himself.

Easy on the eye, I drank him in whenever I thought he wasn't looking. The man might be gay, but that didn't mean I wouldn't stop to admire the scenery.

"I'm good. Thanks."

He went to the small kitchenette and poured two glasses of water. He brought me one then sat on the couch. Dismissing me, he pulled out his phone and disappeared inside the electronic world.

I drank the water, then took the time to explore our accommodations. Well-appointed, we had been given a spacious retreat. There was nothing special, but the minimalistic decor gave the space an understated elegance.

Paul ignored me as I opened every cupboard in the kitchen, walked the perimeters of each of the rooms, dug in the drawers, opened the curtains, and stared out on a bleak landscape of white.

"Where are we?" I propped my hands on my hips and kept my back to Paul.

"Does it matter?" His raspy voice tumbled in the air.

"Is there a reason not to tell me?" I spun around. "It's not like we're going anywhere."

"Then there's no reason it matters. Enjoy the scenery. It's beautiful."

Beautifully stark. Inhospitable. A death trap to anyone without appropriate snow survival gear. It was the perfect trap.

"Shit!" Paul's curse drew my attention. He stood and patted down his pockets. "Shit!"

"Be careful. Your monosyllabic vocabulary is quite telling."

"What?"

"You're a syllable away from devolving into grunts like a caveman."

"Haha, not funny. You need to work on your humor." He glanced at his phone and bit back another curse. "You don't happen to have a charging cord?"

I patted down my non-existent pockets. The slim skirt had a zipper, a button, and no pockets.

"Sorry, but I seem to have left my purse behind when your goons kidnapped me. I'm fresh out of charging cords."

He gave another eye roll. "Yeah, work on that humor, little girl."

I lifted my hands. "Sorry, but I'm plumb out of witty replies."

"My phone's about to die."

"Don't care. Not my problem. But when you grab that charging cord, do you mind bringing me a phone?"

His look could cut steel.

"A tablet?"

He cocked his head.

"A book?" I gestured around the room. "You realize there is nothing for me to do? No books. No games. No puzzles. Nada. Nothing to cook with. No sharp knives to stab you with."

The corner of his mouth almost lifted into a grin with that last comment.

"Come on, Paul. Being a prisoner is one thing, but don't I get something for good behavior? I'm dying here."

It had not escaped my notice we had been alone for going on an hour.

An hour where Forest was trapped in that basement with a predator.

"Shit." He glanced at his phone then waved it at me. "It died."

"It died?"

"That's what I said."

"You waited until it was that low before you started looking for a charger? Who does that?" I tapped my foot. "I keep mine charged above fifty percent at all times. You should try it."

"Again. Not funny."

"I guess you can stare at the walls with me." I gave a shrug. I didn't care if he grew as bored as I did watching the paint peel.

"I need to grab my cord. Come on."

"Come on?"

He moved to the door. "Yeah. Come on."

"I thought I had to stay here? That it wasn't safe for a woman to wander around out there."

"You'll be safe with me."

"I'll stay here. Thank you very much."

"You're not staying here alone."

"Why not?"

"Because Snowden promised Forest you wouldn't. He left precise instructions about adhering to his arrangement with Forest."

"And why do you think that is?"

"Because..." He drew the word out as if my question was the stupidest thing in the world.

"Because, why?"

"Because he wants Forest to trust him."

"That's not what Snowden wants."

"Perhaps not, but it doesn't change my orders."

"Which are what exactly?"

"To watch over you and keep you safe."

"Which I'm certain you're thrilled about. It means you're not with them. It's killing you, isn't it, to be dismissed like that? I bet you thought you'd be right by your boss's side, taking the scraps he threw you."

"He's not my boss."

"Then, what is he?"

"I told you it was complicated." He gestured toward the door. "Your choice, little girl. You can walk on your own two feet, or I can sling you over my shoulder caveman-style. Either way, it's time for a field trip."

"To get me a book?"

"Is that what you want?"

"No. I want a tablet with an entire library of books on it. A stack of puzzles, cards, games, something to dull the interminable boredom your presence brings."

"You say the sweetest things." He snapped his fingers. "Choose, little girl. Feet or shoulder?"

It was my turn to roll my eyes. "I'm perfectly capable of walking."

He held the door for me and ushered me out into the hall. Something occurred to me, and I couldn't resist poking the beast.

"By the way, who is Piper?"

All the blood in Paul's face drained away, leaving him ghostly white.

"What did you say?" His clipped tone had me drawing back as if I'd been bitten by a snake.

"Piper?" My voice wavered. Meek and a little scared by the tone in his voice, I backed away from him.

"Where did you hear that name?" His command shot through me, demanding an answer.

"Something Forest said," I mumbled the words, feeling all the world as if I'd done something wrong.

"And what was that?" Another sharp rap of his words cut through the air.

"He said Piper would be very disappointed in you."

His voice dropped to an awed whisper. "She's alive?"

"Who is she?"

He gave a sharp shake of his head and glanced down the hall.

"No one."

"Doesn't sound like no one."

Paul moved so quickly I didn't see him coming. One minute I was standing in the hall, the next I was back in the room, slammed hard against the wall with the breath knocked out of me. I gasped as he shoved his face in mine. A hair's breadth separated us.

Leaning close, his warm, rich scent flooded my nostrils. "I'm only going to say this once: never say that name again. Not if you want to live."

"Who is she?"

"No one. She's no one." I opened my mouth, but he covered it with his hand. "I'm serious. Speak her name again, and it's the last thing you do. That person is dead."

"I don't think—"

"You don't understand. She's dead."

I didn't think that was true. The way Forest mentioned Piper said she was very much alive. Not just that, but Forest knew her on more than a casual level.

Warned to keep my mouth shut, we headed back into the hall. I tried to memorize our route but got lost after ten turns.

We ran into a lot of people, more than I expected, and he appeared to be a well-liked man. The others deferred to him on an instinctual level; profound respect flowed outward from them. Snowden might be the man in charge, but I had no illusion as to who led these men.

I filed that fact away.

We entered an office where he grabbed a charging cable then marched directly back to my room. The scanner read his retina. The lock whirred open with a click. Paul slowly opened the door.

I entered then came to a stop. Forest lay huddled in the fetal position on the floor, arms wrapped around his legs, eyes lined tight with pain with tears flowing.

"Forest!" I ran to him and surveyed the damage. Welts decorated his flesh. Blood seeped from cuts. Deep purplish bruising covered an incredible amount of skin. I tilted my head toward Paul. "What the hell did he do to him?"

Forest didn't respond except to tighten the grip he had on his legs.

"Don't just stand there," I screamed at Paul. "Help me."

Chapter Twenty-Eight

SARA

"WHAT DO YOU WANT ME TO DO?" PAUL STOOD BY THE DOOR AS IT slowly swung closed. The automatic lock engaged, sealing us in.

"How about you help me pick him up off the floor for starters?" I looked at him incredulous he asked the question.

Forest's body shook. He mumbled something I couldn't understand, repeating a phrase over and over again.

"I'm here, Forest. I'm here." I wrapped my arms around him. "You're safe."

Covered in blood, sweat, tears, and…other stuff, his skin felt cool and clammy.

"He's in shock." I tried to lift Forest, even knowing I couldn't, then turned to Paul, pleading. "Please, help me get him into the bathroom."

In addition to the large, two-person shower, our bathroom had an oversized tub.

Paul came over and pushed me out of the way. I moved with an irritated huff. He knelt beside Forest, hooked Forest's arm over his shoulder, and slowly lifted him to a standing position.

"Help me steady him." Paul strained with Forest's weight.

I did as Paul instructed, not that I helped much.

With his face beet red with strain, Paul tried to steady Forest, but Forest was as limp as a noodle. Paul hoisted Forest into a fireman's carry.

"Now what?" Paul asked. "You want him in bed?"

"No, we need to get him washed up."

"We?" His lips turned up with the beginnings of a smirk. "I thought there was no *we*."

"Don't be an ass." I pointed toward the bathroom. "Take him in there."

I rushed ahead of Paul, still not sure if the tub or shower would be best. Paul took the decision out of my hands and lowered Forest to the floor of the shower. He propped Forest in the corner and straightened Forest's legs out in front of him.

"You're going to need help." He pulled off his shirt, revealing a rippling expanse of washboard perfection.

I backed away. "No way am I getting in there with you."

"He's a big guy, and you're a—"

"If you say little girl one more time, I'm going to smack you."

"I was going to say tiny, but don't get your panties in a wad. I'm not getting naked, just stripping down to my briefs. Remember? I don't like girls. You have nothing to worry about. That's why I'm your guard."

He stepped out of the shower, toed off his shoes, stripped out of his pants, and removed his socks. My mouth gaped, and he huffed a soft laugh.

"Yeah, I get that a lot. Close your mouth, little girl; this isn't playtime."

"You fucking bastard."

"Well, I'm a bastard, and I like to fuck, so I'd say that's a fairly accurate statement. Now, if you're going to help, I suggest you strip and join me."

Strip and join Paul in the shower with Forest? Had the world gone insane?

A low, moan escaped Forest. His head rolled sideways.

"Angle the shower away from him, please." I began to strip. "Run it as hot as you can stand." When I got down to my bra and panties, I joined Paul in the shower and crouched down in front of Forest. Reverently, I leaned in and brushed my lips over his.

Cold and unmoving, Forest's unresponsiveness worried me.

"Did you know Snowden would do this to him?"

Paul refused to meet my eyes. He tested the temperature of the water and adjusted it.

"Paul?" I stood and tapped him on the shoulder. "Did. You. Know?"

"I did." His attention focused on Forest, not me.

"And?"

"And Forest belongs to him. They have a debt to settle between them."

"A debt?" I pointed at Forest. "You call that paying a debt?"

"I call it the beginning."

"The beginning of what?"

"The beginning of the rest of his life."

"And you'll do what? Watch it happen? Join in on the fun? Participate in the gang bang? What exactly are you going to do?"

Paul's lips thinned into a hard line.

"And if he kills Forest?"

"Mr. Snowden's not ready to kill him." Paul fixed his hard stare on me, leaving the rest of what he might have said unfinished.

But I understood. Snowden wasn't ready to kill Forest...not yet. He had his pound of flesh to take first, and then he'd dispose of Forest. I would be included in that.

"I refuse to accept that."

"I wouldn't suggest that you do. Mr. Snowden enjoys a challenge. The moment you break is the moment he wins. Don't underestimate how much pleasure that gives him."

"I don't even know what that means."

He leaned closer. "It means take care of Forest and don't let him fall."

I didn't know how to respond to that.

"Hand me a washcloth."

There wasn't one in the shower, which meant Paul had to get

one. While he did that, I crouched beside Forest again. I took his hand in mine and held it to my cheek.

"We're going to get through this. I promise." I'd never broken a promise before and said a quiet prayer that this wouldn't be the first time.

When Paul returned, he helped me clean Forest. He handed me the soap, and I washed Forest head to toe. When we finished, I did my best to dry Forest until Paul shooed me out of the way. He hoisted Forest back over his shoulder and took him to the bedroom. Paul placed Forest on the bed with far more care than I expected.

He works for Snowden.

This had to be a part of Snowden's plan. Maybe like a good cop, bad cop scenario?

Before I could change out of my wet bra and panties, or think to turn the sheets down, Paul tucked Forest in. With his eye on me, he bent down, placed his lips over Forest's forehead, and kissed him.

He retreated to the doorway and flipped out the light.

"He needs the arms of someone who loves him, someone soft to ease his pain. Tomorrow will be worse."

"Worse than today?"

Paul didn't answer.

I crawled into bed and wrapped my body around his, reverse spooning him. He drew his knees to his chest.

"I'm here."

"Sara..." His groggy voice reached out to me, but that was it. Between one breath and the next, he fell fast asleep.

Chapter Twenty-Nine

FOREST

Sara's concern for me ate at my heart. I was barely keeping my shit together and had nothing left to give her.

I slept like the dead and woke with my entire body aching. There wasn't a single square inch that had avoided Snowden's violation. I'd passed out several times. I'd pushed through and past exhaustion more times than I could count. My endurance had been tested until I failed.

How I got back in bed was a mystery. I remembered nothing but woke naked and clean. No residue—blood or otherwise—remained.

How had she managed to get me clean?

Paul had to have helped. I cringed with what that implied.

A soft knock interrupted my thoughts.

"Awake?" Paul's imposing form filled the doorway. He wore a pair of black boxer briefs and nothing else.

My gaze roamed the expanse of his tight, toned body with more interest than wise. Unable to help myself, I ached to run my hands over the sculpted muscle of his body and explore the ridges of definition beneath his skin. There were other things, insane things I craved. Those I forced deep into the recesses of my mind.

"What's it to you?" I swallowed my attraction and searched for anger to fill in its place.

"I heard noises and came to check." The bastard seemed genuinely concerned. "I wanted to see if you needed anything."

"I gotta piss." Slowly, I extricated myself from the bed, careful not to wake Sara.

Paul didn't move until I drew closer. His musky scent flooded my senses along with that odd electric charge, which crackled between us. He shifted, turning his body minimally, which forced me to push past him.

It was a show of dominance and hell if I didn't respond with an aching hunger. His hand whipped out and grabbed my arm, holding me in place.

"What the fuck?" I tried to jerk free, but he drew close until our chests bumped together.

"Your girl is something special. Don't antagonize Mr. Snowden, or he will hurt her."

"Do you have any idea what I endured yesterday, not antagonizing him?"

I'd groveled and begged. I barely survived Snowden's psychopathic rampage. My body had been violated in more ways than I cared to remember as I acquiesced to his every demand.

"One slip on your part, and you know exactly what'll happen."

"And you care about her, why?"

"I'm not a monster, asshole. She doesn't deserve this; if you slip, and he goes after her, I'm going to kill you."

"You're going to kill me?"

"I'll make you wish you were dead."

"Why do you care?"

Wrapped in the sheets, Sara's soft, delicate features looked peaceful.

My angel.

"She cares about you. That makes her mine to protect." He placed his finger on my breastbone and pressed hard. "Don't fuck up."

I was going to fuck up. It was a foregone conclusion, but why did

Paul care? What was going on between him and Sara? Not having the emotional capacity to broach that subject, I shifted to a more pressing question.

"Did you help her last night?"

"Help how?" He arched a brow.

"Clean me up."

"How do you know she didn't help me?" His smug expression pissed me off.

"Are you saying you would have?" I gave him a look and walked away. Stopping at the doorway to the bathroom, I pointed. "You're putting the door back up."

"No closed doors." Paul crossed his arms, defying me.

"Sara deserves privacy. If you need to watch me piss and take a crap, then go ahead. I won't close the door if that's what you need, but that goes back on." I pointed to the door again. "For her."

"You're not in charge."

"And here I thought you'd say something lame like I'm not the boss of you."

"You're not." The corners of his mouth ticked up. "No man is, and that's how I like it. Once you get your head out of your ass, you'll understand."

"You sound just like him. No wonder you and Snowden get along so well. As for you and me? I don't know who the fuck you think you are, but that kind of respect is earned. As long as I'm a prisoner? As long as Sara's life is at risk? You'll get nothing from me. Now, are you gonna watch me piss?"

"I have no interest in watching you take a leak."

"Then get out of my fucking way." I stomped into the bathroom and relieved myself.

When I finished washing up, Paul had the door. "You want to help me put this back up?"

"What happened to being the one in charge?"

"It's about compromise. I give a little. You give a little."

"And what exactly do you think I'm going to give you?"

"Everything."

"Keep dreaming." I hoisted the door into place, holding it while Paul fit the pins in place.

His cell phone buzzed. When he pulled it out of his pocket, he gave a low curse.

"What's wrong?" My lips turned up in a smirk.

"Damn thing isn't holding a charge."

"Did you plug it in?"

His look could cut steel, and I held back a laugh.

"It's been plugged in all night and is only at thirty percent."

"You probably have a bunch of apps draining the battery."

"Hasn't been a problem before."

"Maybe the charging cord is corroded?"

"And you're some expert."

This brought a genuine laugh. It felt surprisingly good, but I would have to watch Paul. He had a way of making me lower my defenses.

"You do know what I do for a living?"

"Right, you're a damn tech genius. Doesn't mean you know shit about cell phones."

"I know quite a bit about them. If you want, I can look at the cord, troubleshoot it for you. I'm certain Snowden won't be happy if he can't get a hold of you."

Paul rubbed the back of his neck and squinted at me. "No funny business?"

"Funny business?"

"You're not going to fuck up my phone or anything, are you?"

"Not at all. In fact, I insist you watch." I plopped down on the couch and held my hand out.

Paul looked unsure, but I gave a little flex of my fingers, urging him to trust me. When he handed his phone over, I barely suppressed my surprise.

Sara woke a few minutes later. Making her way into the room, she paused at the door and glanced at me on the couch and Paul hovering behind me.

"And this will help?" Paul asked.

"You need a new phone. This one is past its prime. That's why it's slow and why the battery isn't holding a charge."

"Wasn't slow until recently." In my peripheral vision, Paul raked his fingers through his wavy auburn hair. I held back a groan because I had a fucking hard-on for my fucking guard.

My attention shifted to Sara. Her brows pinched together as she watched us. I understood her confusion. Instead of being at each other's throats, we were having a normal conversation.

While Paul watched Sara, my fingers danced across the screen. Give me electronics and no mere mortal could keep up with me.

"Good morning, Miss Sara." Paul abandoned me and walked toward her. "Can I get you a coffee?"

"No, thanks," she said." I'm not a coffee drinker."

"What do you drink?" He joined her in the small kitchenette. "We can stock the kitchen as needed."

Like this was our fucking home and stocking the kitchen made any sense. I expected Sara to keep her distance from Paul, but she didn't turn away when he drew closer. He was entirely too attentive, something I would care more about if I hadn't been busy with his phone.

Chapter Thirty

SARA

I left Forest alone with Paul, excusing myself for a little privacy in the bathroom. I wasn't going to ask about the odd scene between them or the fact that the door was back on its hinges. Instead of prowling around each other, looking for opportunities to attack, they appeared almost relaxed as if they'd come to some kind of truce.

What the hell were we going to do?

Impossible didn't begin to describe our situation.

A soft knock sounded. "Sara?" Forest's deep rumble extended the lifeline I needed to reel in my desperation. I swiped at the tears which had fallen and glanced at my reflection and practiced a smile. "Can I come in?"

"Yes, of course."

He closed the door behind him, and we stared at each other for half a second before he held his arms out.

I launched into his embrace and placed my cheek against his chest. He wrapped me tight, and we stood there for what seemed like forever.

"How're you holding up, angel?"

I glanced up at him. "Angel?"

"It's what I call you in my head. You're my angel." He spoke the words reverently. "My guiding light."

Of course, he would have a pet name for me. If only I'd known how he felt years ago. We'd wasted so much time.

"I like it."

I had no pet name for him. He'd always been just Forest, sometimes Boss when he annoyed me.

He lifted my chin, tipping my face to meet his guarded expression.

How was he holding up?

How did he feel?

What happened to him in that room?

"I should be asking how you're doing." I pressed my palm over his heart. The steady lub-dub anchored me. I could almost forget we were prisoners of a madman.

"I'd rather you didn't." His reply came too fast.

"Why?"

"I don't want to talk about it."

I ached for him to open up, but understood. How did I convince him it didn't matter? Nothing could change how I felt about him. My greatest fear was he would grow distant because of what Snowden did to him. All I could do was wait for him to open up when he could.

But really? If I was a man, would I want my girlfriend to know the details about my rape?

I didn't have an easy answer to that.

When I'd been abused, there had been so much shame associated with the entire experience. The blame I placed on myself, believing I had somehow asked for it, or deserved it, or worse, had taken years to process.

My adoptive parents tried sending me to shrinks, but they eventually understood I would deal with the trauma on my own time.

Forest had to feel something similar.

"Snowden will be here soon." A resigned acceptance filled his tone. "He left you alone yesterday because he was preoccupied with me, but that will change. You need to be ready."

My heart clenched, thinking about that room with all the torture devices in it.

"What did you mean by be ready?"

"Let's hop in the shower. We don't have long before he's here."

The last time we'd been in the shower, we'd stolen time and wrapped ourselves in a protective bubble where we could forget why we were here. We'd found each other and revealed feelings for each other we'd both kept buried.

This felt different.

Bruises, welts, and cuts marred his flesh. I wanted to reach out, comfort him, but sensed this wasn't the time.

He took no time in wrapping his massive frame around me. We stood under the spray from the shower while he simply held me.

Our connection stirred between us, a melding of mind and body. We weren't going to have sex—the limited kind we could share—but that didn't mean we didn't fit together like a lock and key.

I waited for him to speak. That was Forest's way. He thought things through a hundred different ways before revealing his thoughts in an economy of words; short staccato bursts I was left to interpret.

"I need you to do something for me," he said.

"Anything."

"Don't you want to know what it is first?"

"Doesn't matter. I'd do anything for you."

His body stiffened then he slowly relaxed.

"You're pretty incredible, Sara Brenerkie."

"I think the same about you, Forest Summers."

Why were we using our full names? We were developing our language as a couple, nuances in the words we used, which communicated far more than the words themselves.

I felt his love tunnel deep into my heart, where it curled up and settled in.

"Snowden takes everything. He won't be satisfied having only me. You're my executive assistant. If he doesn't own you in some fashion, then he hasn't won."

"I don't understand."

"He's going to put you to work."

"How?"

"Not sure. It may be as his secretary or as his servant. It may be both."

A shiver rippled down my spine. The thought of serving that man sickened me.

"How do you do it? How do you..." We weren't supposed to talk about it, but I couldn't help but ask.

"Because I'll do whatever it takes to protect you. That's the only way this works."

I glanced up at him. His arctic gaze turned down on me. So much pain simmered behind those eyes. He wasn't sharing what had happened for a reason.

How could he be so strong?

If it weren't for me, he wouldn't be in this situation at all.

I bit my lip and buried those thoughts deep down inside of me. Forest wasn't good at reading human emotions, but he wasn't an idiot. He understood.

"You need to do whatever he says, be the perfect secretary. Anticipate his needs like you did mine. Go over and above to do a good job. And above all else, don't try to protect me."

"How can you ask me to do that?" I could play my part, be Snowden's secretary, but going above and beyond? Or worse, ignoring what Snowden did to him.

"I need him to trust you. He needs to watch all hope die in your eyes."

"I'm really confused."

Forest placed his hands on my cheeks and tipped my head back until we were looking at each other.

"We're in this for the long haul. There are things in play that need time to work. I need you to understand we're not getting out of here."

"What about rescue?"

Xavier had to be working on something. Not to mention, Forest had groomed Mitzy into a cyber-tech genius. They had to be searching for us. All we had to do was get the word out to them. Tell them where we were, what they would face. Forest had special ops teams who were trained in hostage rescue.

"If I can sneak out a message—"

"You'll do no such thing." His reply was terse and brooked no room for discussion. "Promise me."

"Forest, if I can get him to trust me, I can—"

"You do that, and we both die. I need you to trust me." He practically begged.

"But we have everything at our disposal. Xavier has—"

"Promise me."

"I don't understand."

"Trust me. It may not make sense, and I can't explain, but I need you to do this. Work for Snowden. Resist at first, he'll expect that, but slowly he needs to know that he's winning. He needs you to serve him as I do."

My eyes widened, and terror shot through my body.

Forest realized his mistake and hugged me tightly. "Oh, not like that. Shit, that's not what I meant. I swear that man will never touch you."

"Then what do you mean?"

"He needs to know you'll do anything to make my life easier, but also that you won't interfere with what he does to me. Does that make sense?"

I think I understood, but I didn't know why.

"He's never going to fully trust you." Forest kissed the crown of my head. "No matter how perfect you are, how compliant, he knows you're mine. And he'll test you. At some point, he'll test your loyalty. If you think you see an opportunity to get the word out or escape, it'll be a setup. You mustn't take it."

"That makes no sense."

"It's the only way. And as far as Paul is concerned, he needs to trust you too. Don't ever let your guard down around him."

"I don't like Paul. I'll never trust him." I paused and wondered if I should broach this subject. I shouldn't, but it bothered me. "The things he says about you, are they true?"

"Don't worry about what he says about me."

"Is it true?"

"Is what true?"

"Are you attracted to him?"

Forest took a moment before answering.

"Am I attracted to him? The quick answer is yes. I find Paul appealing. He marks all the boxes, which is why Snowden picked him to be our guard."

"But it's more, right? More than attraction?"

Forest was the biggest, strongest, most dominating man I knew. He made others quake in their boots and didn't bow to others. I couldn't imagine him submitting to anyone, but that's what Paul kept implying would happen.

His lips twisted into a smirk. "If what you're asking is whether I'm submissive, I don't have an easy answer. I'm more of what you call a switch and tend to lean more toward the dominant side. Have I ever submitted? I have. It's been a part of my self-prescribed therapy over the years. I used to use drugs to self-medicate, then I discovered kink. Sometimes, when my mind grows dark, I need a very particular kind of release. But it's always been under very controlled circumstances."

"You confuse me. I can't see you submitting to anyone."

"I like dominant, aggressive sex with all the things that go along with that, but then there's Paul. He's a natural."

"Natural?"

Forest gave a sharp shake of his head. "His dominance is palpable, intoxicating. Whether he's strong enough to top me has yet to be decided, but I'm pretty sure he's never been a bottom in his life. When we have sex, there's only one way it'll happen."

When; not if.

Forest spoke as if it was inevitable. In our crazy, messed up world, it probably was.

"I need to read up on my knowledge of kink." My voice quieted.

"Is that what you want with me? To top me? I've never done that before."

"Does it interest you?"

"It scares me."

"I'm more interested in holding you, loving you, and making love to you. Tying you up and doing those things doesn't feel like what we want."

What we want?

Interesting use of pronouns.

His consideration for my wishes, needs, and desires was interesting. I turned it around because I wanted to know his thoughts.

"What do you want with me?"

"I want forever."

Forest wasn't a man good with words, and he was worse with expressing his feelings and those pesky emotions, but that was everything I needed to know.

"Can I ask you something?" Forest swept a wet strand of hair off my face.

"Anything." I laid my cheek against his chest.

"Does it bother you that I like men?"

"It never did before." My reply was nearly instantaneous. I glanced up at him, sensing unease in the way his body stiffened.

"But now that you and I are together, does it bother you?" There was a flush in his cheeks I'd never seen before. He bit at his lower lip, and his gaze danced between my eyes as he struggled to say whatever it was on his mind.

"I hadn't thought about it."

"I don't know if I can give that side of myself up." The muscles of his jaw bunched. "I don't ever want to hurt you, but I don't want to promise something I can't give."

The idea I wasn't enough should be soul-crushing.

Oddly, it wasn't.

I'd spent my life in love with a man who I thought couldn't love me back. His need for men was something that was simply a part of him. That wasn't just going to go away, which meant I would have to share him with others.

I waited for a seed of jealousy to sprout, but it didn't. Maybe if it were another woman, I'd feel differently, but I didn't feel threatened by the idea of other men.

"We're a complicated mess, aren't we?" I wrapped my hands around his neck. Tugging him down, I lifted on tiptoe to brush my lips lightly over his. He wrapped his arms around me, drawing me tight against his body.

"That we are."

"I don't want to stop what we've found. I'm not willing to give you up. If that means sharing you with another, or others, we'll find a way to make it work."

"You're an incredible woman, the light of my life, and the hope that sees me through."

If that's what he needed from me, that's what I would be for him. If I were completely honest, I wanted Forest all to myself. I couldn't imagine another person having a piece of him, but I shoved those thoughts as deep as I could. Forest needed me by his side, on his side, and fighting with him.

"Snowden will separate us," he said.

"He said he wouldn't."

"He wants more than my surrender."

"I know."

"Do you?"

"That man is insanely in love with you, and I do mean insanely."

"How do you know that?"

"He looks at you with such longing. I've never seen that before. He might think nothing about giving you to others or letting us stay together. I think he gets off on that power trip, but as long as the person you think of first is him, he has what he needs. And he desperately wants you to love him back."

A knock sounded, and Paul poked his head inside. "You have twenty minutes. I suggest you don't keep him waiting."

"And so it begins," Forest said.

"And so it begins," I repeated.

We rushed through our shower, touching each other only in passing, but needing so much more.

Chapter Thirty-One

FOREST

She wanted to talk about Snowden, but I asked her to leave it alone.

With Sara, I would make it through.

Without her, I would fall.

In hindsight, I wished I'd held that thought closer to my chest.

Paul stayed behind with Sara while Snowden took me away. We spent the morning in that basement where he released years of pent up fury on my body, whipping me to unconsciousness. Then he took me savagely until I bled.

When I thought I couldn't take anymore, Snowden surprised me with a new game. He brought me outside, to a courtyard, where the cold air snapped the last reserves of my strength. Dark, pensive clouds blotted the sun, and lazy snowflakes drifted down where they disappeared on the hard ground.

Barefoot and nude, I shivered and hugged myself for warmth while I waited for whatever it was he intended. The gleam in his eyes told me it would be bad.

He settled himself in the corner of the courtyard where a cover kept the snow off him. Banks of heaters warmed him while I stamped my feet to prevent them from going numb. He signaled two of his men to come forward.

"To the victor goes the spoils." Snowden gave an imperious wave while I tried to sort out this new hell.

The men looked to one another, huge grins splitting their faces. They came at me, circling me, spitting on me, while my attention shifted to Snowden.

That was a mistake.

The first man clocked me in the jaw while the other hit me in the solar plexus. They worked me in tandem, taking turns with their punches while I absorbed the pain and swallowed the rage boiling inside of me.

"Chop, chop, boy. You can fight back. That's what makes this fun. If you win, you may return to your rooms for the day."

If I won?

The first man doubled me over with a punch to my gut.

"But if you lose…" Snowden fixed me with a maniacal stare. "These men win the right to take you however they please."

I barely straightened before the next blow came. Hits to my kidneys stole my breath, but I didn't fight back. This could be another one of Snowden's tests.

In the end, I fell.

True to his word, Snowden gave me to his men. He watched for a time, fisting his cock, while the men took turns. Then he grew bored and left. By dinnertime, I could barely stand.

They dragged me back to my rooms, where they deposited me on the floor. I passed out and didn't know I was alone until the sound of the door opening woke me.

Sara cried out and rushed to me.

Paul crouched beside her, his lips twisting. Covered in blood, cum, and piss, I was a mess.

Without a word, he lifted me to my feet.

"Can you walk?" He wrapped his arm around my waist, and I leaned on him. Half dragging, half carrying, he took me to the bathroom where he put me in the shower and propped me against the wall. Sara followed behind us, hands clutched tight at her waist, fingers twisting with worry.

"Can he stand?" she asked.

"I don't know." Paul leaned in close. "Can you?"

Some kind of noise escaped my mouth, but it wasn't formed into words. I was beyond that.

"He's such a mess. What are they doing to him?" Sara pulled at the hem of her shirt, lifting it over her head.

"You don't want to know." Paul unbuckled the collar at my neck, then removed the cuffs at my wrists. "Can you get the ones around his ankles?"

Sara shimmied out of her skirt and entered the shower in her bra and panties. I moved in and out of awareness because the next thing I knew, hot steaming water fell from the showerhead, and Paul stood beside me. He wasn't wearing his shirt, and our skin brushed against each other.

The two of them worked together, almost as if they'd done this before. My mind drifted, splintering for a time, and I woke hours later with an angel wrapped around my body.

"You're awake." Sara lifted on an elbow and stared down at me. She leaned over and brushed her lips across my cheek.

A knock on the door drew my attention. Paul stood in the empty doorway.

"You have an hour to get ready." He spun away, disappearing from view, while Sara tensed.

I drew back the covers, saying nothing, and swung around until my feet hit the floor. With a groan, I buried my face in my hands and drew forth the strength I would need for another day.

Like the previous one, Snowden took me to the basement. When I could barely function, he took me to the courtyard. He paired me up with only one man, a brute with a crooked nose, and a piercing in his ear.

Snowden took his seat beneath the heaters while the cold weather stole my remaining strength.

But today, I fought.

And I lost.

To the victor went the spoils.

Snowden jerked off while his man took me. It seemed beating me in the courtyard came with certain bragging rights because there was never a lack of opponents. After a week, I hadn't fought the same man twice, and I lost every damn time.

When I was returned to the sanctuary of my room, half the time, Sara and Paul weren't there. I yearned for those moments when I could crawl into the shower and wash away the filth of the day alone. When they were there, I accepted their help. Too weak to resist, the three of us became an odd trio of shower-buddies.

Paul kept silent while Sara fussed over me. Her delicate touches reminded me there was goodness left in the world. Paul's masculine presence reminded me of other things.

Thankfully, my body was too tired to respond. My dick remained flaccid while he held me upright, and Sara cleansed my cuts and washed my body. Her tenderness was the only light in my life, and I sank into her delicate touch wishing for far more than the nightly ritual.

On those rare days when I didn't pass out, I would sit on the couch and watch Paul and Sara as they played cards, or chess, or any of the growing number of board games that seemed to appear in our room as the days passed. When I crawled under the covers, Sara always followed. She curled up against me, snuggling tight, as I allowed myself to fall into a dreamless sleep.

This became my new normal, and with each passing day, Snowden chipped away at my resolve, breaking me down slowly.

Darkness consumed me.

Despair overtook me.

My sanity fled.

Snowden was winning our little war.

I spent my mornings with Sara, going through the motions of getting ready. At night, she attended to my bruises, washed my cuts, and held me while I wept. One might think this would keep us together.

It didn't.

We drifted apart.

Or rather, I slipped away.

Each morning, I put Snowden's collar around my neck and wrapped the leather cuffs around my wrists and ankles. He dangled Sara's safety before me, horrific threats of rape, and worse if I wasn't obedient.

I embraced every deviant desire he threw at me.

He wanted to whip me until I bled?

I bled.

He wanted to fuck me until I cried for him to stop?

I cried.

He wanted to torture me until I begged for it to end?

I begged.

But I withheld from him the one thing he craved above all else.

Snowden didn't care about my surrender. He didn't care about my pain. What he wanted was the one thing I had to give freely, but my affection wasn't his to claim.

It was the only thing that kept me going.

It was the only thing that kept me sane.

Until the day the man waiting in the courtyard was one I knew all too well.

Paul's fingers flexed. He rolled his shoulders and shifted his weight.

"Today is going to be a good match, my boy. I've been waiting to pit the two of you against each other." Snowden reached for my groin. "Paul has been waiting."

Movement in the corner drew my eye. Sara sat on one end of the couch, a blanket wrapped around her, with wide-terrified eyes locked to mine.

I took in a breath.

To the victor goes the spoils, but I was too weak from the beating Snowden had given me. My muscles ached from bone-deep bruising. My extremities had been sapped of their strength from hanging in chains. I had nothing left.

But wasn't that the point?

Snowden took pleasure in the extreme, and he wanted to watch me fall.

"Well," I said, "won't this be fun."

Snowden cackled. His laughter rolled through the courtyard and echoed off the walls. Overhead, clouds blocked the sun. Heavy with snow, they filled the air with a flurry of flakes as I faced Paul, stripped bare and practically defenseless.

"Afraid of meeting me in a fair fight?" I'd bested him once already. I could do it again.

"We play by his rules." Paul lifted his fists. "Show me what you've got."

I stepped forward, resigned to fight.

I didn't know who threw the first punch.

We stood across from each other, sizing each other up, then fists flew. My fist slammed into his face while his fist punched my stomach.

Blood sprayed from the cut on his lip as he knocked the wind out of me. I stumbled against the pain and struggled to take a breath. Weakened by Snowden's attentions, my arms moved like lead weights, lagging a half-second behind where I thought they should be.

Paul's eyes narrowed.

I dodged his fist and brought up my own.

Scoring a direct hit on his jaw, his head snapped back. He shook off the blow, and his penetrating gaze bore into me.

Mesmerized, I missed it when he tilted his head back and slammed it into mine. Stars burst in my vision, and I stumbled back, trying to shake it off.

In a blinding move, he did a roundhouse kick and connected the full force of his body against my solar plexus. Blinding pain shot through me, and I fell back, arms windmilling as I struggled to stay upright.

If I fell, it would be the end.

He followed the kick with his fists.

Flying in fast succession, it was all I could do to dodge. Pain erupted with each impact of his fists, and my vision blurred.

I broke apart from him, cleared my vision with a shake of my head, and dived back in. I grasped his head and yanked down while bringing my knee up to his nose. A blunt crack sounded, and I released him.

Blood poured from both his nostrils. He drew his fist back and plowed it into my stomach. My guts smashed together as agony ripped through me.

I repaid him by punching his jaw, battering it back and forth as I developed a pounding rhythm. It was a rhythm I couldn't keep up.

My arms tired.

My punches slowed.

He danced away, evading my attempts to score a hit.

"Is that all you've got?" I wasn't going to let him beat me.

"I've got that and more." Paul danced from foot to foot, smirking infuriatingly at me. "Don't make this easy on me. I like to earn my rewards."

No need to say what reward waited for him. Paul would finally get his pound of flesh, taking from me like all the others.

I growled, blinded by rage, and threw myself at him. Blood hummed in my veins as anger took over.

Ducking my head, I dove at Paul with the full force of my towering frame. Arms wrapped around him, I knocked him off his feet and slammed him to the ground. Straddling him, my fist connected with his jaw, and pain blazed up my arm.

I grinned with satisfaction until a sudden gush of pain ripped through my body.

The bastard wrapped his fist around my balls and squeezed. He tightened his grip until I saw stars. My gut ached with blinding pain, and I thought I would puke. I howled and rolled to the side. The pain rippling through my abdomen was too intense.

I couldn't see.

I couldn't think.

I lost sight of Paul.

I tried to clear my vision as I huffed against the blinding agony coursing through me.

The bastard didn't fight fair.

Bruised and winded, with my balls in agony, I wiped at the sweat beading my brow.

My head pounded.

My chest heaved.

I brought my fists up, trying to block a flurry of Paul's fists and feet. He launched himself at me, showing no signs of tiring.

He clocked me in the jaw, sucker-punched my gut, then followed up with a kick, which left me reeling.

"Give up already." He danced around me. Agile and light, the man was a force of destruction.

I shot my right leg out to sweep his legs out from under him, but my movements were too slow.

He grabbed my foot and twisted. My leg rotated, and the rest of my body followed. I flew through the air and crashed to the ground. The impact knocked the wind out of me.

Paul pounced.

He straddled me, fists flying as he pummeled my face. He pushed my hands away roughly when I tried to clock him in the jaw and easily held them by my ears.

"Give in, Forest," he said with a shout. "You don't have anything to prove, and you can't win."

The hell I did.

These matches were the only way I could fight back. They were my only outlet for the frustrated helplessness which invaded my world.

I hadn't won a single match, but someday I would wipe the ground with one of Snowden's men. I needed a victory. I needed something before I went insane.

I didn't need Paul to best me.

He seized my arms, trapping them, and bent forward until his face hovered over mine.

Behind us, Snowden moved from his perch on the couch. He walked in a slow circle around us, assessing us, and drinking in my misery. He drew Sara with him, gripping her wrist and forcing her to watch me lose up close.

"I bet they fuck like they fight." Snowden's words carried across the chilly air, penetrating the fog of my thoughts. The bastard was enjoying this far too much. "What do you think, Miss Sara?"

I shut my eyes. I hated for her to see me this weak.

A stillness hung between Paul and me as his powerful legs straddled my hips. When he rocked forward, my dick gave a hungry twitch.

"Stop fighting me," he growled at me. "Give in."

"Fuck you." I spat at him.

"Forest..." he lowered his voice to a whisper. "You're giving him exactly what he wants. Surrender, and I'll make what comes next bearable."

I was too weak to carry on. There was no way I could win, not in my current state.

If I'd been fresh...

If Snowden hadn't beaten me unconscious in the basement...If I'd met Paul on equal terms...things might be different.

My entire body went limp as I surrendered.

"When you're fucking me, remember that in a fair fight, you wouldn't win."

"Is that what you think?" Paul let up on my wrists.

"It's what I know."

The air crackled between us, sizzling with an electric charge which demanded an outlet. My dick betrayed me, horribly turned on by Paul's strength and the dominance he displayed.

"I don't have to beat you in a damn fight, rigged or otherwise. You want what I can give you, you ache for it, and if you ever decide to get out of your own damn way, I'll prove it."

"Fuck you." A feral grin spread across my face. The cut in my lip split wider, and fresh blood spilled into my mouth.

Paul stilled, then suddenly movement erupted out of him.

He hit me with so much force every blow left me huffing in pain.

I supposed he needed to make a point.

But we both knew the truth. His victory was an empty one.

Not that he wouldn't collect his damn reward.

"Well done." Snowden clapped behind us. "I can't wait to watch the two of you fuck."

"Not here." Paul ground out the words.

"Those are the rules, son," Snowden spoke softly, hesitantly. "You beat him here; you take him here."

"I'm not taking him when he's hypothermic with a frigid dick. That is not what we agreed to."

What agreement?

Paul shifted his weight, letting me breathe a little easier.

The cold ground seeped into me, a thief stealing the warmth of my body.

"I'm taking this inside." His tone remained firm.

"If that's what you want," Snowden said.

"It is."

"Fine." Snowden snapped with irritation. "We'll take this inside, but I will watch."

"The first time," Paul spoke with authority.

"You do like to test me, don't you?"

"I'm taking what you promised."

"Fine." Snowden turned on his heels. He practically jerked Sara off her feet.

Paul hopped to his feet and held out his hand.

I refused to take it and stumbled back. Wiping my jaw, I took a minute to size him up.

"You have an agreement with Snowden?"

"I do."

"And what is it, exactly?"

Paul cocked his head. He gestured toward the door Snowden and Sara had disappeared inside. "It's best not to keep him waiting."

"Fuck you."

"Promises, promises." Paul grabbed my arm. I tried to jerk it out of his grip, but he held me fast. "A word of warning and a promise."

"Whatever."

"Don't fight it."

I spat in his face. "Isn't that exactly what I'm doing?"

His hand shot out and wrapped around my throat. "Give him what he wants, and I promise to make this easy on you."

"Easy on me?"

"Yes." He gave a clipped nod and released my neck. His fingers splayed out over my chest. The heat from his palm sank into me, and I hated how I reacted.

The uncomfortable truth was I craved the violent sex Paul promised. It aroused me so deeply I didn't care about the shame of wanting it.

"There is no *easy* in this godforsaken place."

Despite the disturbing direction of my thoughts, I found myself believing in the potential swirling between us. It was in the way Paul looked not at me, but into the darkness shrouding my mind. He embraced it, hungered for it, and there was no judgment, only an acceptance of what was painfully obvious.

"True," he said, "but I can make it more palatable. It doesn't have to be forced."

He had bested me physically, but his real victory was in what I would give him.

"Everything is forced." My dick lengthened as it always did when he was near.

He could have slid his gaze down, making me feel ashamed of my arousal. Instead, he kept his eyes on me. Without words, he confessed this was more than sexual desire. He didn't want just to fuck me; he wanted something more.

"You're not ready to accept this, but I'll make you a promise. Decide if that is enough to give me what I want."

I didn't see how I would give him anything.

I felt it. Damn if the desire to bend to his will didn't surge in my blood. The electricity crackling between us needed to be answered, and it would be soon.

"And that would be?"

"I won't fuck you until you ask me to."

I barked a laugh. "Right, there's one glaring problem with that."

Paul arched a brow and waited for me to continue.

"The sick bastard in there is waiting for you to do just that."

I was miserable and cold. My entire body ached from the punches Paul threw and the whips Snowden had laid into me earlier. Defeat filled me with aching desperation for it all to simply end.

Only it wouldn't.

"Just get it over with." I breathed out a sigh. "Everyone else has."

His hand moved from my chest to my neck. He gripped the back of my neck and leaned in until his lips brushed over mine.

The moment our lips connected, a shock rippled through me. My heart seized as a delicious shiver slid beneath my skin. My mouth opened with a guttural groan as Paul swept his tongue inside. His grip tightened as he deepened the kiss.

I gasped as every muscle in my body clenched and trembled beneath the diabolical skill of a man who kissed with his soul. Every breath, every beat of my heart was swept away by my need for him. A throbbing intensity swelled between my legs as my dick responded.

Paul pressed closer. Our chests collided as he crushed his mouth against mine. Our hips pressed together, and our swollen cocks ground against each other.

Fucking amazing, his taste was familiar, even if we'd never kissed before. His scent flooded my nostrils and seeped deep into my lungs.

He released me.

The sudden absence of his heat made me stagger. Paul gripped my chin and forced me to look at him.

"I promise to make this as easy as I can. I won't fuck you until you ask. Take it, Forest. It's all I can give you. And when you trust me, we'll finish that kiss."

My head swam in a lusty haze as my heart banged inside my chest. I swiped at my lips and returned his stare.

"Fucking hell, what was that?"

"I'm brutal, aggressive, and violent. You crave the pain I need to inflict. In that, we're evenly matched. Despite the thoughts swirling in your head, the need to refuse, you know I'm right. But I won't take it from you."

"And what about now? Isn't that exactly what you're going to do?" I huffed against the lusty thoughts his words revealed, confirming everything he just said. Paul was a man worthy of my consideration. He might be the one.

Hell, if he didn't put my thoughts in a spin.

"I'm going to give him what he expects. And I'm going to give you a taste of what it means to submit to me."

"Yes, now."

Paul marched inside, leaving me alone in the courtyard without guards.

I bowed my head, closed my eyes, and followed Paul inside. There was something profoundly wrong with me because I wanted that taste.

Chapter Thirty-Two

FOREST

I FOLLOWED PAUL INTO ONE OF SNOWDEN'S MANY ENTERTAINING spaces. A row of couches surrounded an open area. Toward the back of the room, thick red velvet curtains covered the wall. He had settled into one of the couches with a full view of the center space. Sara joined him. She sat far to the side, as close to the edge of the sofa as she could get.

Where did she go when not in our rooms? My assumption was she and Paul were with Snowden, and while I ached to know what they did, I never asked.

My attention shifted back to the room.

I saw Snowden, and I saw Sara, but where was Paul?

Warm air spilled down from overhead heat registers. I welcomed the warmth and the tingling as sensation returned to my fingers and toes. Paul had been right about being hypothermic.

No wonder my arms seemed as if they had been moving through molasses. A grin turned up the corner of my mouth. Despite the handicap, I'd still gotten in a few good hits. I'd kind of enjoyed the fight.

Music turned on, a sultry beat, and Snowden leaned back with a sigh.

Becoming more and more attuned to the subtleties of his body language, I read much in that singular sound. Anticipatory, but not actively engaged, this show would be for his benefit. While he took pleasure in subjugating me during our mornings together, he was getting old and tired quickly.

I felt Paul before I saw him. My entire body took notice.

He emerged from the side of the room, flowing from darkness into the light. The play of shadows over his muscular form gave me pause as his brutal presence took center stage. Strong, confident, and assured of the outcome of this encounter, he prowled toward me.

My chest heaved from exertion, and my heart raced, although that was for another reason. Despite my fatigue, he captured my attention. His steady gaze swept over me, assessing, admiring, and hungering…for me.

Sex with men was an interesting thing. There was nothing gentle or soft about a man. It was all about brute force, a clashing of muscle, and a battle of wills that determined supremacy. Sometimes power was shared, an equal partnership where each man sought his release. Paul wasn't one of those who sought the common ground. He came to dominate, to overcome, and to assert his right to do as he pleased.

I took half a step back before I realized my foot had moved. It was rare for a man to affect me like this. I wasn't afraid, but wary of the war we would wage and more than excited by the outcome. Supremacy wasn't something I gave into another man's hands often. The few times I had, had been brief and disappointing encounters.

Snowden shifted on the couch, and the massive leather atrocity squeaked beneath his girth. This show was for his pleasure, not mine, and not Paul's. His need to control me filled me with disgust, but I allowed it.

I let Snowden take from me.

And he took.

With brutal savagery, he violated my body with a recklessness I might not survive.

Then he held me.

Rocked me.

Wrapped me in his arms as if we were lovers. As if I craved his twisted affection. The sick fuck was messed up in the head.

Then he did things like this.

He watched me fight other men. If they won, my body was the prize. If I won, I got to rest until the next time. I had yet to win. The more savage the fights, the better. The more brutal the fuck... well, Snowden craved his pain.

Frankly, I found it exhausting.

Paul took another step.

Half in shadow, half in light, he was the living personification of artistic perfection.

Every movement attested to his strength. His muscles bunched. His corded tendons flexed. He radiated hardness and pain.

And those eyes.

His eyes locked on me with a need to dominate, to fuck, and to claim.

Aroused and unashamed, he took another step toward me while I resisted the urge to run.

Or fall to my knees.

Failure to give Snowden a good show would result in the unconscionable.

The silent and ever-present reminder of the price of disobedience, Sara's presence bound me to surrender to Snowden's sick will and obey his commands.

I hated that Sara had to watch my humiliation.

But this was different.

I wanted this. I wanted to grapple with Paul.

To fuck him.

And to be fucked by him.

I wouldn't go to my knees willingly, but if he took me there, by God, I would fall for him. His wild nature called to me. His strength intoxicated me. This man had bested me on the mat, and that turned me the fuck on.

Anything he wants.

That's what Snowden decreed.

The winner could take anything he wanted, and I lost to Paul.

Eyes blown black with lust, Paul licked his lower lip as he sized me up. I could resist. I could struggle. I could fight. I saw it in his eyes, the need to dominate, and unlike most men, he had the strength to force it. He wouldn't. He made a promise. I would let this happen.

Another truth existed between us.

It simmered in his promise, communicated by a twitch of our eyes, the pulse of our breaths, and in the tiniest shifting of our weight. He moved forward on his lead foot while I leaned back.

He wanted to prove his will exceeded mine. Forced or not by Snowden's crazy rules, Paul meant to measure his mettle against mine.

Who would come out on top in that battle had yet to be decided.

The fight had been nothing but a farce.

He edged closer, taking his time, studying me as I waited for him in the center of the room. I would meet him, and I would let him fuck me. Those were foregone conclusions, determined by Snowden's commands. But Paul had made a promise.

What had yet to be determined was which of us would come out on top after our little exchange.

Taller than most men, Paul stood a couple of inches shy of my towering height. He could almost look me straight in the eye.

Almost.

The way the man moved had me salivating. All sinew and muscle, his body flowed with lithe grace. He reached for his shirt and pulled it over his head. I sucked in a sharp breath as his ripped torso was exposed to my greedy eyes.

That made him grin, and I cursed for revealing any interest. I wasn't supposed to enjoy this, but I would. I'd felt the solidness of his body, and mine responded. Blood raced to engorge my cock.

Snowden chuckled behind me. "That's it, my boy. You like Paul, don't you?"

My cruel captor had to touch me to get me hard. He used my

body's natural reactions to force my cock to swell and rip reluctant orgasms from my body.

But Paul?

I reacted to Paul on an entirely different level.

Snowden's intrusion on what was happening between Paul and me did nothing to deflate my rapidly enlarging cock. If anything, blood rushed to the tissues faster. I was long, hard, and painfully aroused.

My greedy cock jerked.

It ached for Paul.

Paul's astute gaze cut to my crotch, then his focus shifted to my eyes. The corner of his mouth twisted with victory.

The bastard knew he had me.

Fuck him. I didn't care.

I wanted whatever happened between us. Whether that was a quick and mutually satisfying fuck, or something else, I simply didn't care. As long as he fucked me, I was good.

Snowden wanted to watch me submit to a man who had bested me. He got off on it. He got off on practically anything which forced me to do something I wouldn't normally do.

He knew my obedience came at the end of the threats he levied on Sara. At any time, I could overpower him and kill him. He knew this. It made him tentative, although cruel when he took me.

I never fought Snowden. I didn't struggle against him. I couldn't. The consequences for doing so were too extreme, and I did whatever it took to keep Sara safe from the deprivations of his men.

Whatever it took.

Beat me. Break me. Make me his.

I submitted to every single one of Snowden's demands.

But this was not one of my sessions with Snowden.

I turned my attention back to Paul, admiring his physique as I took a step back. Paul won the right to have me, but that didn't mean I would bow to him like I did Snowden. We still had a few things to work out between us.

In my life, I'd fucked a lot of men. They often left me physically satisfied but otherwise empty. Paul stunned me by the sensations which flooded my body. The thoughts filling my mind turned me into a heathen, but something else stirred deep within me.

My emotions struggled to be free.

I would fight. With every fiber of my soul, I would fight. But could he be the one? The elusive man physically and mentally stronger than myself?

His chiseled chest expanded with each breath, drawing my eye to his breastbone and the well-defined planes of his pecs. Tanned and toned, his skin glowed with sun-kissed brilliance. His abdomen popped with the perfection of a six-pack I wanted to run my fingers over, explore with my mouth, and delve into every delicious groove with flicks of my tongue. The V-line angling down from his hips promised carnal pleasure beneath the waistband of his shorts, and I wanted to taste him. Even if that put me on my knees. My thoughts spun in a lusty haze as his biceps flexed, and his broad shoulders bunched.

I wanted him to best me. Not on the mat. Not in a fight. But rather where it mattered most...in my head.

Leather creaked behind me, as Snowden shifted. Sara sat on the far end of the couch, silent and locked within her head. I hated how Snowden forced her to watch. I despised what she must think when I allowed others to abuse and degrade me. But I would rather her watch my shameful displays than endure them herself.

Whatever it took.

For as long as I could endure it, I would spare her that pain.

"Do you like what you see?" Paul broke the choking silence.

His deep voice did things to me. It tunneled under my skin and shot along my nerves, where it lodged at the base of my cock with an insatiable need. My arousal grew beneath his command, and I welcomed it.

His hiss, and the sharp intake of breath which followed, made me smile. He liked what he saw. That shouldn't please me, but it did. It meant I wasn't the only one affected by this charade.

I dared not smile and show Snowden how much I wanted this, but damn if I couldn't wait for Paul to make his move.

"Come here." Paul jutted his chin forward.

There was no way to hide my raging erection, so I didn't try. I stood before Paul, feet centered beneath me, pulse pounding in my ears, and breaths accelerating as my arousal grew.

I ached to touch myself. To fist my cock and give it a good tug, but I resisted that urge, waiting for Paul's next command.

"Look at me." Paul swept his hands down his body. "You want me, don't you?"

My gaze hardened.

Sex had no room for idle conversation. Snowden talked during sex, lording his control over me as he forced me to accept the daily violation of my body.

"What I want is irrelevant." Uncharacteristically, my voice broke. I tried to control myself because I very much wanted this. "You won, which makes me yours. Do as you will."

Paul's gaze cut to Snowden. "I would say you're most definitely not mine. You're a plaything given to me to do with as I please, but you're most definitely not *mine.* "

The way he said *mine* punched me in the gut and stole my breath.

His eyes narrowed. "I doubt any man has bested you. They haven't earned that right, have they?"

It scared me how he saw into the core of who I was.

Snowden's breaths pulsed behind me. I spared a glance over my shoulder and regretted it immediately.

The monster had pulled his pants down. He fucked his fist, hips rocking with each thrust. He watched us size each other up. We hadn't even touched each other, and Snowden was already far gone into seeking his release.

And Sara? Poor Sara had to watch it all.

Disgust rippled through me. The only thing keeping Sara alive, keeping Snowden's men from raping her, or Snowden from touching her, was his belief that he had bested me, and her quiet acceptance of it all.

Paul and I prowled around each other, testing each other's strengths with verbal sparring, but it looked as if Snowden would finish first. His face bunched with exertion. His lips pressed into a hard line, broken only by rapid panting as his fist pumped his cock.

When I turned my attention back to Paul, he surprised me with an uplifting of his eyebrow, followed by a shake of his head. The barely perceptible expression came as a shock. Paul was one of Snowden's men, one of the guards assigned to torment me, but I sensed caution in that singular look.

Behind me, Snowden's huffs deepened then broke apart as his release took him over the edge.

The guarded expression in Paul's face changed, hardening again. Only this time, I saw it for the mask it was.

Paul hated Snowden.

How did I know that?

Snowden's breaths heaved in and out. He snapped his fingers, and a female slave I hadn't noticed came over to clean his mess using her hair and her mouth. My stomach twisted at how easily he degraded us all.

But not Paul.

Paul was not a slave. He was a trusted guard who watched over Sara.

What was I missing?

"You two going to stare at each other or fuck?" Snowden's acidic tone pulled me back to the matter at hand. "I'm surprised, Paul. I thought you wanted Forest. Isn't that what you told me?"

"Yes," Paul answered immediately. "But I thought you'd want me to wait so you could watch."

"Oh, I'm watching." Snowden gestured to the girl lapping his cock as she cleaned the cum from his body. "Watching the two of you together is fascinating. I don't know who is going to pounce first." He made a vague gesture toward Paul. "It's not like you to hesitate."

"Oh, I want him."

"Then what are you waiting for?"

"You said I could have him, however I wanted."

"I did."

"I want him...privately."

"We're not taking this to your room. Fuck him now and get it over with."

"You misunderstand. I'm taking him."

My eyes widened at the way Paul spoke to Snowden.

Snowden tilted his head and let out a cackle. "You want my sloppy seconds?"

"You have him in the mornings. I want him at night. I want his pain. I want him to know there's no escape. Whether serving you, or serving me, he's nothing but a plaything we pass back and forth, and I want the girl."

My jaw clenched. "No one touches the girl."

Paul canted his head. "No one but you."

Rage burned within my gut, and my fingers curled into fists. I launched at Paul, intent on murder.

"Stop!" Snowden's shout slammed me to a halt.

My hands pulled back from Paul's throat, and the bastard grinned at me.

"That will cost you, boy." Snowden snapped his fingers. He pointed to the floor.

I fell to my knees and folded over myself as fear coursed through me. I crossed a line, and I would pay.

Please, don't hurt my angel.

I couldn't speak those words. They would encourage Snowden to do precisely that. I chastised myself for losing my shit. Anger, along with the rest of my emotions, was something I'd bottled up and shoved deep inside. It was the only way I survived each day.

I couldn't react if I didn't feel.

Sara didn't move. My attention shifted to her, and Snowden's gaze followed.

"The girl's off-limits, son. Forest and I have an agreement, don't we boy?"

"Yes." I ground out the word. "No one touches her."

An agreement?

We had an understanding.

If he so much as laid a hand on her, the next time he had me in his bed would be the last. I wouldn't think twice about snapping his neck, and there would be nothing his guards could do about it.

He'd gotten lazy.

As I surrendered more and more, he excused the guards from his room. It was just him and me, and I let him do whatever the hell he wanted.

Snowden moved his hard gaze to Paul. "The girl is not to be touched."

Paul shifted beside me. "But what about him? I want him."

"You can have him. You won that right."

"I want more than this." Paul didn't seem concerned about overstepping his position. He spoke with the assurance Snowden would give him what he wanted.

"Forest belongs to me."

"Of course, but when not with you, he belongs to me."

Snowden gave a dismissive wave. "If that's what you want, then fine. He's yours."

"And the girl?"

"The girl is not yours."

"He behaves best when she's around. I want him, which means she needs to be there."

Snowden laughed. "He behaves perfectly for me, but I see your point. You probably need that leverage."

"Then, we agree. I can have him whenever I want?"

A look of irritation crossed Snowden's face. "If you insist."

"And the girl?"

My fingers curled again, but I resisted the urge to punch Paul in the throat. I could only cross so many lines before putting Sara's life in jeopardy.

"Put her in a cage or tie her to the wall. I don't give a fuck what you do with her, but don't touch her. That's non-negotiable. Do you understand?"

"Got it." Paul's gaze shot to me.

Snowden pulled at his chin. He slid further down into the couch, spreading his legs and grabbing the girl by the head. Forcing her head into his crotch, he closed his eyes.

"Fuck him, already."

The girl's head bobbed as she worked on raising Snowden's flaccid cock. I knew his stamina, and the bastard needed a lot more than these few minutes to recharge. I didn't envy the girl her task.

Paul came to stand in front of me. He rubbed his hands together. "You need this, Forest. Let me show you how much."

I stood before him, insanely aroused, but growing more confused by the second. That confusion made it impossible to keep hold of my rage.

"You're going to give me what I want." Paul ground the words out as he reached for my cock. Without hesitation, he took me in hand. His voice lowered for my ears alone. "I'm going to take this from you now, but imagine how good this will feel when you give yourself to me later."

My eyes closed as I fought the sensations filling me. I'd had men jerk me off before, but I'd never had a man hold me like this. There was no hesitation in Paul's hand. He stroked me like he already owned me.

He leaned close and whispered in my ear. "Close your eyes. Imagine you're somewhere else. It's just you and me with my hand on you, taking control, and giving you what you need. Let go, and I'll make this feel incredible."

His thick musk infiltrated my nostrils. I breathed him in, and a little piece of me died inside because I wanted to do exactly as he said.

But I wasn't someplace else.

I was a prisoner and a madman's plaything.

"If you ever touch Sara…" My breathing hitched, and I let out a low groan as he pulled sensations from my body I wasn't willing to give. My hips bucked, overcome with the urge to rut.

"I have no intention of touching her unless that's what you both want. She's yours, but you're mine. Do you see how that works? Imagine the two of us fucking you? I know you've thought about it. My cock sliding in and out of your ass while you fuck her cunt." His fist tightened and damned if his filthy words didn't nearly tip me over the edge. My hips bucked, thinking about what he said.

"I want you." His words were barely above the threshold of my hearing, but the rumble of his voice penetrated my chest. It lodged someplace deep within me. "Imagine taking her while you give yourself to me."

"Don't. You. Dare. Touch. Her." My words came out in short staccato bursts.

"The only way to keep her safe is to keep her with us. Do you understand?"

All I could imagine was the three of us in bed. Now that Paul planted that seed in my head, I couldn't move past it. Sara's soft moans as my dick slipped into her wet heat. Her breathy sighs as I glided in and out. The softness of her breasts as I sucked on her nipples. The hardness of Paul's chest as he bent over me. His fingers working my ass. The burning sting as he shoved inside. The movement of three bodies finding a rhythm as we chased the unimaginable.

My eyes rolled into the back of my head as I grabbed his arm. I needed to slow this down. I needed to stop the madness. Fuck, I needed to come so badly it was insane.

"Let go." Paul's sharp command pierced the lust-fueled thoughts clouding my head.

Without a thought about what I did, my fingers let go. Paul resumed his punishing stimulation of my cock, expert fingers raking along my turgid length, thumb rubbing the sensitive nerves just beneath the head.

"Shit…"

"That's it." Paul cupped my balls and gave a squeeze. "You see it now. Give it to me. Give yourself over to me."

Sparks gathered at the base of my spine and shot to my cock. I wasn't going to come. I was going to fucking explode.

"It's just a body." I gritted the words out and ground my teeth together.

"No, Forest, it's my body. Give yourself to me."

I tried to deny his words, ashamed this one act could undo me to such an extreme. It was nothing more than a fucking handjob. He was fisting me to orgasm. That was it.

Nothing different than any of the men before.

Nothing different.

Except for how it felt.

How I felt.

And what I wanted to happen next.

My gaze dropped to his chest. It felt less personal to stare at the chiseled perfection while he stroked me to toe-curling oblivion.

His grip tightened. His hand moved up and down my shaft, and I huffed against the pleasure building within me. Stabbing heat gathered in my groin, a frisson of need melded with my disgust for how easily this man drew pleasure from my body.

Ashamed of the release moving too fast toward inevitability, I tried to stare through him. This man was going to ruin me. I fought against the insane need of my hips to jerk and rock against Paul's hand.

"Don't fight it. Surrender to me, let this happen." Sin dripped from his mouth, and I wanted to kiss him.

Devour him.

Come for him.

I fisted my hands and tried to resist the orgasm barreling toward me.

"God, you truly are magnificent." Paul held me with an expert touch, stroking and stimulating until my entire body vibrated beneath him.

I didn't want this to happen. I didn't want him to win what felt like a battle of wills between us, but I couldn't stop the freight train of sensations racing to my cock.

I tried.

God, I tried.

I'd never had normal sex. It had always been a measure of unhinged aggression tempered by my fear of going too far. My childhood had not been kind. I'd been forced without my consent into situations no young boy should ever experience.

There was nothing salvageable about me. The thoughts inside my head corrupted any chance of a healthy sexual relationship.

I could never have sex with Sara. I knew that now. She was too soft, too fragile; I would break her with my corrupt needs.

But a man?

A man with a firm grip who pulled and tugged and...dear God, Paul's hand felt terrific. My toes curled, and I rested my head on Paul's shoulder. I leaned into him and sank into the sensations he pulled from my body.

He cupped the side of my head and placed his cheek alongside mine. He stroked the skin along my jaw with reverence. There was no cruelty, but rather an aching tenderness which made the rest impossible to bear.

Paul shifted his stance. The long, hard ridge of his erection pressed along my hip. His lips pressed against my cheek, firm, grounding, soul-shattering.

"Do you see what you do to me? The need I have to fuck you? Give me your pain, Forest. Let me bear it for you." Soft, melodic, he spoke in a tender whisper, hinting at an intimacy we might one day share.

Snowden couldn't hear, not above the pulsing of my breaths and the low moans spilling from my mouth. I was a rutting beast, desperate for the climax Paul promised. Despite the show for Snowden's sick pleasure, Paul accomplished the unimaginable. He allowed me to believe this was a moment shared between just the two of us. Everything around me disappeared except for him.

A rush of heat filled my groin.

There was no stopping the flood of sensation crashing through me. My hips bucked, and thick ropes of my cum splashed over Paul's abdomen.

He glanced down, then slowly ran his finger over the sticky mess. His eyes were on me as he lifted his finger. Slowly, evocatively, he slipped his finger in his mouth, tasting me. Then he withdrew it and pressed the tip against my lips.

"Open for me. Taste how delicious you are on my skin. Imagine how wonderful it'll be when you finally give in and take me into your mouth."

He left unsaid that I would do so willingly. Not that I cared. Not anymore. I would have him, and he would have me. We were a force of nature that couldn't be stopped.

I nodded, agreeing to his words.

Paul sealed my promise and pressed his finger to my lips.

While I couldn't see Snowden, he watched us. My role in this was to obey without question, and that's exactly the show I gave him.

Paul inserted his finger into my mouth. I licked the tip and sucked, licking his thumb the way I would suck his cock. Paul's eyes widened, then his expression shifted, not in victory but something more profound. There was eagerness, anticipation, physical need, and affection.

I didn't know what he expected or how I was supposed to respond. Retreating into myself, I let everything fall away.

Whatever happened would happen.

There wasn't a damn thing I could do to stop it.

If Paul wanted my surrender, he had it.

I couldn't fight it anymore.

Snowden said he would break me, but Paul made me fall apart.

Chapter Thirty-Three

SARA

FOREST COLLAPSED INTO PAUL'S ARMS AS HE CAME. I WASN'T SURE IF it was exhaustion from the fight, or the intensity of his release, or some combination of both. He wouldn't look at me.

Each passing day had taken him further from me as he slipped away inside that head of his.

How could I help him if he refused to speak to me?

How could I soothe his pain if he kept it all bottled up inside?

How could the fragile beginnings of our relationship take root if he pushed me away?

It didn't matter what Snowden did, or Paul for that matter. I loved Forest no matter what.

I felt helpless.

Paul's penetrating gaze landed on me briefly before focusing on Snowden. A look of irritation flashed in his eyes, but he covered it quickly with a smug, victorious look.

"Fucking amazing as always." Snowden's oily smile spread across his face. "I love how you always bring them to their knees. Every. Damn. Time. You have truly mastered my lessons, but are you going to fuck him?"

His lessons?

"I'll fuck him when I'm ready and have the privacy I need."

Over the past week, I'd spent far too much time around Snowden and Paul. Snowden disgusted me on every level. Paul, I couldn't figure out. I didn't like him, but an odd respect flowed between us. He protected me, and I wanted to know why.

An odd flow of power shifted between Snowden and Paul. While Snowden snapped at his men, there was a deference he extended to Paul. I paid attention to it all while I filed papers, transcribed dictation, and cleaned the corners of his office he never went near.

Paul lowered Forest to the floor. It looked like he whispered something to Forest, but I was too far away to hear. Snowden stood, losing interest in the men and snapped his fingers at me.

"Come along, Miss Sara. We have work to do."

My duties as his assistant began with a steno notebook where I scratched out lists Snowden dictated, drafted letters he sent out by hand, and crossed off his to-do list as he completed various tasks. I fetched coffee, answered his phone, and kept people waiting who were eager to speak to their boss. The structure of his empire slowly took shape and terrified me with its global scale.

Not once did he allow me near a computer. My ultimate goal was to send a message to Xavier, but Snowden kept my outside access to the world blocked.

My time would come.

Forest's words kept running through my head, begging me to trust him, but I feared we were running out of time. How much more could Forest endure?

Our future didn't look bright. Snowden didn't keep much from me. I drafted all manner of letters detailing the inner workings of his operation. I knew supply routes, the flow of money, clientele lists, and so much more. An intelligent man, the message he sent was a powerful one. There was no way he would ever let me leave. I knew too much.

But something was happening to his business.

Just yesterday, another of his affiliates had shut down. Something happened with a bank transfer. I didn't get all the details, but it wasn't the first. There had been four such seizures this past week alone. Accounts closed over money-laundering concerns, or tax evasion, or something else.

Snowden's agitation had been palpable. He nearly lost it. I'd never been hit before, but he came close. He pulled his punch and calmed himself down when Paul leaped to his feet and shouted.

Paul was always there, watching over me and protecting me, even when it was against Snowden. I was never without Paul.

Except for now.

I turned to follow Snowden while Paul stayed with Forest. I felt exposed walking the halls without Paul by my side.

Snowden's phone rang. He held it to his ear and listened for a time before pulling up short and cursing at whoever was on the other end. My shoulders hunched and I took a step back, trying my best to be small, unobtrusive...invisible.

"I don't care what the excuse is. We need that shipment delivered on time."

A shipment meant lives he intended to destroy.

"What happened?"

I followed only half the conversation but got the gist. Instead of his affiliates with banking issues, there was a problem in the supply chain. Transports had been confiscated. There'd been some kind of raid.

A smile spread across my face. Anything which interrupted the flow of people through his operation was a win in my book. I kept my head down, hands clasped in front of me, and lengthened the distance between us. My gut said I was safe, even if the anger turning his face red told me to be cautious.

Our days were always this way, perpetually on the cusp of a maniacal meltdown by a madman, but damn it if Snowden wasn't one of the most talented businessmen I'd ever run across.

As Forest's executive secretary, I'd seen all manner of successful men. Their tempers might run hot, some might say volatile, but at the end of the day, the decisions they made brought success.

Snowden was no different. He ran a multi-national sex-

312 • ELLIE MASTERS

trafficking operation. The money flowing through various accounts staggered the mind.

But some of that flow had slowed.

Now transport routes broke down. There were raids on holding facilities.

He yelled at whoever was on the other end of the phone, barking out orders, then shoved the phone back in his pocket. Ignoring me, he headed back down the hall and toward his office.

I knew the way from the rooms where he kept me to his office by heart, memorizing every twist and turn, but that was it. Whatever grand plans I'd had of learning the layout of this compound had yet to come to fruition.

I couldn't get word out to Xavier.

I didn't know how many men Snowden had guarding this place.

I didn't even know how many floors were in the building.

Useless information filled my head like there were precisely seventy-six steps after the next turn before we came to his office door.

"Get me a coffee," he barked, and I leaped to comply.

Decidedly unoriginal, he was a predictable man. Snowden arrived at nine sharp every morning to collect Forest. He kept Forest until noon. That's when Paul escorted me to Snowden's office. He had lunch brought by one of the many slaves, none of whom spoke to me. While I perched on a chair in the corner of his office, Paul joined Snowden for lunch.

After that, Snowden put me to work. I spent my afternoons doing whatever clerical work he demanded. When his dinner was served, Paul returned me to my rooms, where I either found Forest crashed out in bed, sitting silently on the couch or worse; some days, he wasn't there at all. I hated those days the most.

Forest never told me what happened, and I didn't ask. After today, I had a better understanding of what he endured. That gave me even more reason to get a message out to Xavier.

We need the cavalry to save the day.

I deposited Snowden's coffee on his desk.

He snapped his fingers and pointed to his files. "Get me the

Echo file."

I wandered over to the filing cabinets and searched. A paranoid man, Snowden straddled old and new. He didn't trust computers, afraid a hacker might break through his security and kept most of his records in paper form. I went in search of the Echo file.

His organizational system made no sense. Alphabetical might be one way to start, and while his frustration with my lack of speed in finding the random files he demanded could be volatile, he refused to allow me to reorganize.

Not that my stomach could handle it. Most of what he had included portfolios of victims. He had the bios, pictures, details of sale, and the dreaded red Retired stamp over far too many names. I suspected every victim whoever passed through his operation had a file in one of these cabinets.

It was a goldmine of information which would lock him behind bars for several lifetimes. But it wasn't portable. It would require a truck to transport it all, and time we didn't have.

I found the file and pulled it without looking at the contents inside. I'd done that once.

I didn't know if there'd been a direct correlation, but that day had been one of the worst for Forest. After a few days, a pattern slowly emerged, and I faced a sobering truth. The days I slipped up were the ones Forest stayed away the longest and came back in the worst shape.

I placed the file on Snowden's desk, then went to my chair in the corner where I waited for the next command. My entire goal was to be invisible, unobtrusive, and blend in with the decor.

Despite my executive assistant duties or mockery thereof, Snowden handled most things himself. His paranoia was certifiable, and yet the access he granted me to the inner workings of his operation exposed him to significant risk if I ever got out of this place.

I think that was the point. We weren't getting out of here.

Other than making coffee, fetching files he was too lazy to find himself, and staring out the window onto the stark white landscape, it was a struggle to pass the time.

Chapter Thirty-Four

FOREST

Watching Sara leave fired up all my protective reflexes. I couldn't protect her when I wasn't allowed to be with her. That left me to rely on a man I didn't understand. Paul and I were cautious enemies.

I trusted him, even if I didn't understand why, but we were in the process of becoming…Fuck if I knew what the hell we were in the process of becoming.

"I'd say you survived." Paul's cultured voice vibrated within my chest, lodging itself deep inside where it got far too comfortable and kicked up its feet.

The man played me like a Master, giving indescribable pleasure. No one else had done that before. I got hard for Paul before he touched me.

"Congratulations, you jerked me off." I tried to sound unaffected, but that was a fucking lie. "That's not the first time a man had his hand on my dick."

"I did more than put my hand on your dick, and you know it."

"Fucker." I pushed away from him, only realizing we were locked in some weird embrace. My cum clung to his washboard abs and damned if I didn't want to lick him clean.

"Asshole. You came hard, and you're already thinking about more." The cocky bastard dared to speak the truth swirling between us.

I'd done more than come. He was right about that.

"You give a good handjob. Are you expecting a goddamn medal?" I tried to play it off like I hadn't fallen apart in his hands.

"That's not why you came so hard." He swiped at my cum and brought it to his mouth.

While I watched, he made a show of licking his fingers clean. I suppressed a low groan. How did he make that look so fucking erotic? I wanted to leap at him and lock my lips with his just to taste myself on his lips.

"Stop that."

"Make me."

"Fucker."

"We need to work on your vocabulary. There's no shame in denying what you need, or in accepting that I can give it to you."

My body, such as it was, really was just a body. It responded like a well-trained dog. It never failed to get hard given a little dick love, be it by hand, mouth, or something else.

"I happen to like sex."

"So do I. We're well-matched in that regard."

My dick was a hungry fucker, always eager and ready.

Well, except for Snowden. There was no eagerness for sex with Snowden, but my dick responded to the responses he'd conditioned into me when I'd been far too young.

My dick reacted the same way to his men, but that was something I had on Snowden.

He thought to degrade me, but the truth was I found mutually satisfying pleasure in the hands of his men. He fed directly into my voracious appetite for sex and gave me psychological relief from his torture.

That helped in other ways.

His men couldn't help but like me. I might be a bit quirky, but I had my strengths. They shared things they shouldn't and respected the one skill I had above all others. How many of Snowden's men had handed me their phones to debug over the past few weeks? Word got around that I fixed things, and I was pretty sure they didn't share that with the boss.

They knew I was a tech genius but were too damn stupid to understand what that meant. And while they did their due diligence and watched what I did with their phones, they didn't understand what it was I was doing to them.

Paul, the fucker, helped with this. Code I placed in his phone hijacked Snowden's Wi-Fi network, spreading like a virus as it hopped from phone to phone, collecting data, passwords, and so much more.

Snowden had no idea how fucked he would soon be. Nearly all the pieces were in play.

I turned my thoughts back to the man standing in front of me. "Well-matched? Is that what you think?" I gave a little laugh because I eagerly looked forward to fucking Paul, or rather getting fucked by him.

Could he give me what I craved?

The things he said about him, me, and Sara had my mind spinning. Not that Sara would agree to such a thing. My angel was a timid thing, soft, sensitive, and destructible. Put her in bed with the two of us and she wouldn't come out of it unscathed.

A tingling in my balls had me squeezing my legs together. I shouldn't be thinking about her like that. Shit, we hadn't even had sex yet.

Paul and I hadn't had sex yet.

Not real sex.

"You're thinking about Sara."

"How do you know?"

"I see it in your eyes—the hunger—the ache. She's not fond of me. It'll be hard to convince her, but it'll be worth it to try. The thought of you with her while I fuck you is intoxicating as shit."

"Keep your filthy hands off Sara."

He lifted his hands. "I'm not interested in her, but I'm not against a little threesome."

"That'll never happen." Fuck me, but all I could think about was a Paul and Sara sandwich with me in the middle. Talk about fucked in the head.

I needed to get Paul alone and relieve some of this sexual tension. Until then, I wouldn't be able to figure out the shit going on in my head.

Paul took a step toward me. "He's gone. We can…" His hard gaze cut to my crotch, where my dick elongated with each beat of my heart. Damn, if I didn't want to do just that. My gaze dropped to his raging erection, and I licked my lower lip. Yeah, I wanted to taste that.

"Later." I cringed as that word slipped from my lips. It was an admission that he had me.

"Later, it is." It didn't seem possible, but his voice broke.

He mentioned Sara, and now all I could think about was my dear sweet angelic Sara. It was like there were two people inside my head.

One ached for Paul.

The other ripped in half every time Sara left the room.

My love for her deepened with each passing day, even if I didn't express my feelings. The truth was I didn't know how to love a woman. I was in love with Sara. She completed me, but how did I show her? How did I do that in this crazy place, this nightmare, I put her in?

Later? Shit, I'd just crossed a line, admitting I wanted him.

He grabbed my nape before I could react. Pulling me forward, he placed his forehead against mine.

"I'll protect her because she means the world to you. I do that because you mean the world to me. Think about that when you imagine what will happen later."

A shiver rippled down my spine, lifting the fine hairs on my arms. He pulled back and rested a hand on my shoulder. His eyes met and held mine.

Despite the dark, lust-filled thoughts streaming through my head, I felt at peace.

Paul could have reveled in victory, but he didn't. He didn't stare at my lips, demanding my surrender. His eyes didn't dip to my groin with the desire to touch and stimulate until I fell apart again. He looked into me, confessing more than the sexual desire which sizzled on our combined breaths. He hinted at something which terrified me. It was something beyond physical intimacy.

Paul hauled me against his chest and kissed me with his perfect mouth and bruising lips. He yanked on my nape, a merciless grip which took me by surprise, but that was nothing compared to how he devoured my mouth.

I opened for him, letting him sweep his tongue inside where he hunted for and found my tongue. As reckless as it might be, I was desperate enough not to care. Paul kissed like no man I'd ever known, putting the full weight of his being into the act. All his passion, every beat of his heart, every molecule of air in his breath was caught up in the kiss.

I couldn't help but wrap my hands around his neck as my hunger overtook my senses. The throbbing between my legs intensified as my heart rate skyrocketed.

Paul pressed close, arms winding around me as he deepened the kiss. Then all of a sudden, he released me.

"Until…later." A smirk curled the edges of his lips upward.

The fucker got to me. He had me right where he wanted.

We were going to fuck.

No way that wasn't happening after that kiss.

The more vicious, the better.

The more brutal, the better.

I wanted to rage against him and take out all my anger on him. His skillful control was something I would meet head-on.

I liked to fuck men.

The physicality of it spoke to me on a base level and defined part of who I was.

Snowden thought his silly games were breaking me down, but he didn't know a fundamental truth about me.

He gave me to his men, thinking that would break me. It did precisely the opposite. It fortified me against the fight to come and provided a much-needed outlet to vent the anger simmering inside of me.

Now Paul was something else.

If this was Snowden's plan, I had already lost.

Chapter Thirty-Five

SARA

THE DOOR TO SNOWDEN'S OFFICE BANGED OPENED, AND PAUL STUCK his head inside.

"How's it going?" His gaze cut to me and stopped.

I sucked in a breath beneath the intensity of his gaze.

"You finished?" Snowden waved at Paul to join him.

"For now."

"Did you fuck him?"

Paul's gaze shifted to me, then returned to Snowden. "I'm waiting until he's stronger. I prefer a challenge." The corners of his eyes crinkled.

I wanted to slap that smile off his face. Instead, I kept my thoughts to myself.

"I'm surprised, considering how you've been going on and on about it."

"The rest of it stops," Paul said.

What did that mean? All my attention was on what they had to say about Forest.

"The men enjoy their fun." Snowden nearly pouted.

"It stops."

"There's a waiting list."

"I don't care. You said I could have him, not share him with Tom, Dick, and Harry."

"Don't forget who he belongs to." Snowden's tone turned menacing.

"There's no sport in the fights. He's broken before they begin."

"So?"

"It encourages weakness." Paul's sharp retort had Snowden sitting straighter. "You give them something they're not strong enough to take. What kind of reward is it when they know fighting him is a guaranteed win?"

"Like I care."

"You'll care when they break him beyond repair. Your toy won't handle much more. It's a miracle he's survived this long." Paul leaned forward. "Don't forget our arrangement."

"I haven't forgotten." Snowden bristled with annoyance. "So, you want to fight him when he's fresh?"

"An empty victory is a worthless one." Paul shrugged. "It's why I didn't fuck him. I'm waiting for later." Paul glanced at me, placing particular emphasis on that word, but then he turned back to Snowden.

Snowden caught the angle of his gaze. "You're going to do it in front of her, aren't you?" He lifted a finger and shook it. "You always were a devious bastard."

Paul snorted. "There's another problem, something you should take more care about."

"Maybe you should join me in the mornings? Have a go with the whip and watch him scream. It's fun."

"I'm not into that kind of sharing. I'll take my turn, but not when he's unable to function. The fights stop. I want him tested, and you're using protection from now on."

"Are you telling me to use condoms?" Snowden laughed. "Now that's funny, but I don't need a little brat like you lecturing me about condoms."

"How many of your men have fucked him? Do you trust where they've put their dicks? I don't. I'm using protection. I want him tested and treated. I suggest you do the same."

"If he's tested and treated, there's no need for me to care. I like going bareback."

Paul's gaze cut over to my corner, but I looked away.

I didn't want to listen. All it did was remind me of the torment Forest endured to keep me safe. It was only a matter of time before Snowden tired of his toy. When that happened, our future became our past.

"You worry about the strangest things." Snowden tapped the top of his desk. The low drumming sound made my skin crawl.

"Your health? Mine? It's important."

"Like you care about my health."

"Does that surprise you?"

Like most days, my disappearing act seemed to be working. They spoke in front of me as if I didn't exist. I didn't dare shift in my seat, or otherwise draw attention to myself.

They spoke of passing Forest between them like he was nothing but an object to be used for their sick, twisted games. I swallowed the anger rising within me, but what could I do?

I needed to think like Forest, detach myself from my emotions, and put my brain to work.

"I'll consider it." Snowden gave a grudging nod. "Happy now?"

"Ecstatic."

Snowden changed the conversation. "How's your new phone? Mine's a cluster-fuck."

"It's slow, glitchy, and battery life is a joke. I've replaced it twice in the past week because the batteries won't hold a charge, and others are having issues."

"Sara!" Snowden's bark had me springing to my feet.

"Yes, sir?" I didn't approach, but he had my attention.

"Order a case of new phones." He turned his attention to Paul. "We'll replace the whole lot. I can't have shit like that slowing us down." He pointed to the file I'd placed on his desk. "In more good news, our halfway houses are being raided."

"Um, sir…" My voice came out in a squeak.

Snowden ignored me.

Paul arched a brow. "How many?"

I twisted my fingers, uncertain whether to state the obvious.

"We've lost two dozen. My suppliers are having problems restocking the losses." Snowden leaned back and pinched the bridge of his nose. "Honestly, I don't have time for this kind of crap."

"Any idea how it's happening?" Paul asked.

"One was due to a domestic disturbance. The cops raided the wrong apartment. Another was a fire. Firefighters hacked through the doors to evacuate the building and rescued the girls. The third was more dumb luck. A gas leak led to another evacuation. Don't worry. We're covered. Nothing traces back to us."

"Sounds like an awful amount of dumb luck. You want me to look into it?"

Snowden's attention shifted to me. "Aren't you supposed to be ordering us new phones?"

"Um...I can't."

"And why not?"

Did he forget I had no access to the internet? Forest's words returned to me. At some point, he'll test your loyalty. If you think you see an opportunity to get word out or escape, you mustn't take it.

Was this a test?

What if it wasn't? What if this was our one opportunity to tell Xavier where we were?

I kept my head bowed, my demeanor meek, and my thoughts to myself, but what if I turned Snowden's test on its head?

"I don't have internet access, and honestly, that's probably for the best."

"Is that so?" His eyes narrowed, and his words sliced across the distance separating us. "Why?"

"Because all it would take is an email to a friend," Paul answered the question for me.

"And you think your friends will save you? Is that what you think?" His scornful laugh sent shivers rippling down my spine. "Oh, she's funny." His comment was for Paul, not me.

"At least she's honest." Paul turned to me. "I'll order the phones."

I breathed out, not sure if I should be relieved or sad. Internet access granted me the ability to bring this nightmare to an end, or to make it ten times worse.

"No. We're going to give Miss Sara internet access." He approached, invading my private space. "Will she call for help and risk his life? Or, will she be a good little girl and behave?" He leaned in close, his fetid breath overpowering.

I'll be a fucking angel, you monster.

"Stop scaring her." Paul shook his head. "I'll order the damn phones. You're antagonizing her."

"Honestly, I don't know why we keep her around."

"We keep her around," Paul gritted his teeth, "because he'll do anything to keep her safe."

Snowden plopped down in his chair. "Yeah, there is that."

Paul ordered the phones then sat opposite Snowden. I fetched coffee, water, then booze as the afternoon wore on while the two of them discussed the problems they were having within their organization. At six, a knock on the door announced the arrival of Snowden's dinner. This was my cue to leave.

Paul escorted me out of Snowden's office. Instead of turning left, which led back to my room, he headed right.

"Where are we going?" I hesitated, unsure about this change.

"To my quarters."

"Why?"

"Relax." His cheeky grin made him less threatening, but I kept my guard up. "You're perfectly safe with me."

So he kept saying. He said it often enough to make me worry, and he'd started looking at me differently over the past few days. Not with overt sexual interest, but rather an evolving curiosity.

"Really?" I put on my brave face, knowing it was nothing more than a facade.

"Look, we're headed to my quarters so I can get a box of condoms."

"Oh."

"No comment about the condoms?"

"What do you want me to say?"

"I just thought you'd say something."

"About you raping Forest? I think not."

He huffed a low laugh. "That's not what's going on. You saw us together, but you didn't hear what he said after you left."

I bit my upper lip, dying to know, but unable to ask.

"I made him a promise, and he made me one."

"A promise?"

"Yes." Paul turned the full force of his gaze on me. "I promised not to force him, and he promised to finish what we started… later. The next time we see each other, I'll have him." He cocked his head. "How does that make you feel, little girl? Your man wants me. I bet that pisses you off."

"You'd like that, but you'd be wrong."

"You saying it's not true?"

"He fucks men. Why do you think I'd be jealous?"

"Because I watched the two of you in the shower. I've seen you sleep in each other's arms. He has feelings for you, feelings you reciprocate. No way me being with him won't bother you."

Was that true?

It could be, but Forest and I had talked about this. He couldn't change who he was, and while I may have an issue with Paul, I didn't begrudge Forest's needs. Despite my wishes, there was something between the two of them. The longer they spent in each other's company, the stronger the connection between them grew.

But why did it have to be Paul?

"I can't do anything about whatever you have planned. I can't do anything about what Snowden does to him, so why would I care when you do the same? It's just a body. That's all you have, his body. I have him."

"Go with that. You're right about one thing. My f—Mr. Snowden has his body. I'm going to have it soon too, but don't think for a minute there's not a whole lot more going on."

"I don't care what twisted thing you think you have. You don't know Forest."

"He needs what I can provide. He also needs you. Unlike you, I'm able to share. Like two sides of a coin, he needs us both. You'd better figure out how you're going to deal with that because I'm not going anywhere. From the way you watched, I think you're a little more than curious. Have you ever seen two men fuck? I bet not."

"You're insane, and as soon as we're out of this…"

"You're not getting out of here, little girl. Get that out of your head. Mr. Snowden will never let you go, and when he tires of Forest and hands him over to me for good, the only thing keeping you safe will be the protection I provide."

"Is that a threat?"

"I don't need to threaten you. I'll protect you because it's what Forest wants, and he needs to know he can trust me. You should learn to do the same."

He stopped in front of a door, unlocked it, and gestured inside. His quarters were understated with a minimalistic decor lacking any personal touches. I entered cautiously and stood in the middle of a spartan living room with one couch, one chair, one lamp, and nothing else.

Paul moved past me into the bedroom. I did not follow. Hugging myself, I held back frustrated tears.

How were we ever going to get out of this place?

A few seconds later, Paul returned with a box in his hand.

"Has he fucked you yet?"

"Excuse me?"

"It's a simple question. Have you two had sex?"

"That's none of your business."

"I'll take that as a no." He reached into the box and pulled out several foil pouches. "Here."

I stared at the condoms and didn't move. Paul gave a shake of his head, grabbed my hand, and placed the condoms in it.

"Until I get Forest tested, use protection."

"You're giving me condoms?"

"I hope I don't need to explain how to use them?" Devastatingly handsome, Paul would be a lady killer if he wasn't gay. "But, if you need a lesson…"

"I don't need a damn lesson. I just don't understand."

"In this crappy place, you're his only source of comfort."

"Why would you care?"

"Because he's my priority, and despite what you think, I see that he gets what he needs."

"That makes no sense."

"Because you're not a Dom. I'm not your enemy, and I plan on giving Forest everything he needs, and that means you. Wrap your head around what that means."

My fingers closed over the condoms. I wanted to take the next step with Forest.

"What Forest needs is to be free of Snowden," I said. "Give him that."

"I can't."

"Why? If you care about him like you say you do, why not help us?"

"It's not that simple.

Chapter Thirty-Six

SARA

WE LEFT PAUL'S QUARTERS, AND HE ESCORTED ME TO THE ROOMS Forest and I shared. It didn't escape my notice that Paul basically shared them too. He spent every night on the couch, while Forest and I shared the bed, ostensibly protecting us from Snowden's men.

How much of that was real?

I was beginning to think there was more to Paul than I thought.

"Here we are." He stopped by the door but didn't open it. His stunning features stole my breath as they always did. "I want you to talk to him."

"Talk?"

"Yeah, talk or fuck or whatever you think he needs before I come back." Paul had been very upfront about what would happen when he saw Forest next. "A helpful word, if you'll take it…" He curled his finger around a strand of my hair.

I barely breathed with the intimate touch, although he wasn't touching me. He simply played with a lock of my hair, but Paul had a presence about him, overpowering and all-encompassing.

I thought Forest filled a room, but Paul owned the space around him with his unwavering confidence and absolute assurance of his place at the top of the food chain. I felt a little of what Forest must feel, a sense of greatness as if Paul was the epicenter of an undeniable force.

I tried to shake off the feeling, not sure how successful I was.

"A thing about men is that we don't like to talk. We especially don't like to discuss our feelings, but sometimes we need someone strong enough to make us face them. We especially don't like it when our women might have reason to think we're weak. Forest is feeling a whole lot of things right now. What happened between us back in that room, and what will happen when I return, is messing with his head. He's trying to reconcile everything. He has to face the reality of what it means with you."

"With me?"

"Don't be surprised if he's withdrawn, angry, or sharp. Don't let him push you away."

"You're giving me relationship advice?"

"I think it's pretty funny too, but here's the truth."

"The truth?"

"Use the condoms. Fuck him. Show him that you're with him. He needs you as much as he needs me, and right now, he needs you far more than me, which is why I'm giving you time alone with him. Don't waste it. I'll be back…later."

There was that word again…later.

For a simple word, it had grown into something powerful, carrying an inevitable promise.

"When I take him, you'll be there. Don't interfere, but he needs to know it's okay. That you're okay with what we do and how he responds."

"For the record, we're not okay. I don't support this."

"You sure about that?"

"I don't like you. I don't like what you're doing to him. I don't support you tearing him down." I ticked off each point on my fingers.

"You may not like me, but you respect me. You're curious about what you saw back there because it wasn't the same as what you saw with Snowden. You felt what was happening because you're in tune with Forest, an extension of him. Rather than looking away, you watched. That says something right there. As for tearing him down, I'm giving him what he needs to make sense of everything in his head." He repeated my gesture, counting off each point.

"And yet, you're keeping him a prisoner. You're not protecting him from Snowden, and you're not willing to help us. Until that changes, you and I are not okay. This may be all about sex and domination to you, some twisted head game you're playing with Forest, but it's not working on me. You're no different from any of the others who raped him. You're worse. You're worse because you've convinced yourself he wants you."

"You're wrong, and I'm going to prove it."

"I dare you to try." I crossed my arms, trying to project more strength than I had.

"Talk to him. If he tells you he doesn't want me, I'll leave him alone."

"Oh, I can bet on that."

Paul leaned in suddenly. "Don't be so hasty, because when he tells you he wants me, you'll step back and let it happen. How's that for a compromise?"

"I don't trust you."

"You will."

"He's not going to say it."

"Talk to Forest, little girl. Get inside his head. You've got plenty of time before I return." He opened the door and gestured inside.

True to his questionable word, he didn't enter but allowed the door to shut behind me. I stepped in, hands clasped together, fingers twisting as they did when I was unsure.

Forest sat by the window. When I entered, he held his arm out.

I ran into his embrace and buried my face against his chest, tears streaming for no reason at all. Hell, there were reasons. I just didn't want to face them.

"Hey." He ran his fingers through my hair, pulling through the tangles.

"Hey," I repeated, not sure what to say next.

"How're you holding up?" His deep voice resonated inside my chest.

"It's beautiful outside." I shifted beside him, moving to stare out the window.

"I like the view in here more." His glacial eyes turned a darker shade of blue as he cupped my chin.

I had a pocket full of condoms, but no urge to use them. Somehow, I felt wanting to have sex with Forest made me no different from the monsters outside our door. I wouldn't use him like that.

He looked over my shoulder. "Where's Paul?"

"He's coming back later."

Forest's eyes pinched.

"Later?" His voice cracked.

I placed my hand on his. "That's what he said."

Forest pulled his hand out from underneath mine. "And he left us alone?"

"Yeah."

"I see." His heavy gaze stirred with all kinds of emotion he usually kept bottled up.

Sometimes, it was difficult remembering he processed the world differently. I couldn't imagine the emotional pain he must feel or should feel.

Talk to him.

"How are you holding up?" I didn't know how to broach the subject of Paul.

Forest wasn't much for talking, so my task was nearly impossible, but I needed to know if what Paul said was true. Did Forest need this thing with Paul?

"I'm sorry for bringing you into this hell." He pulled away, but that wasn't going to stop me.

We didn't have much time. I discarded half a dozen starter sentences before deciding to hit the problem head-on.

"Paul wants me to talk to you."

Forest sat a little straighter. "I figured that's why he left us alone. What did he want?"

"You want the long, flowery version or the direct and to the point version?"

He cocked his head and gave me a look like I'd grown two heads. "Direct, please."

I pulled the condoms out of my pocket and placed them between us.

"He gave me these."

Forest picked up a foil pouch. "Condoms?" His brows drew together, and he curled his lower lip between his teeth.

"Yeah."

"Why?"

"Well, he grabbed a box of condoms to bring to the room, handed me a few for us, then said he'd be coming back later."

"I see." His expression fell.

I hoped he would give me something to work with, but Forest turned back to the window. He rolled a condom packet between his thumb and forefinger.

"You have nothing to say?" I asked.

His eyes cut to me, then went back to staring outside.

"I bring you condoms, and you have nothing?"

He flicked the foil packet. It flew halfway across the room to land in the middle of the floor.

"What do you want me to say?"

"I don't know." I started to pace. Digging my fingers into my scalp, I pulled at my roots, trying to make sense of the insane. "I want you to say something. Tell me you don't want to. Can you start with that?"

"But I do." He stood to his full height. "All I think about is making love to you."

"Not me." I fisted my hands. "Paul. Tell me you don't want to have sex with him."

He wouldn't look at me.

My breath caught. Paul had been telling me the truth. It hurt more than it should.

"I'm going to take a shower." I rushed away before he could see the tears rolling down my cheeks.

"Sara..." His gruff voice called out, but I didn't look back. I headed to the bathroom and closed the door.

If only there were a lock.

I turned the water on as hot as I could stand and stripped. It looked like I would spend my evening in the bathroom. It was the only place where I could shut out what would happen in the other room when Paul returned.

I took stock of my emotions.

Pain.

Not of rejection, but of not being enough.

I wanted to be everything for Forest like he'd always been everything to me.

That I couldn't give him what he needed gutted me.

How was I going to deal with that?

I couldn't walk away from him. I'd tried that for the better part of a decade, loving a man who, I had thought, was incapable of loving me back.

But he did love me.

Forest was desperately in love with me.

But he needed Paul.

I leaned against the tile wall and slid down to the floor, where I hugged my knees tight to my chest. I let the tears flow. Cold air blew against my skin. I glanced up as Forest entered the shower. The man was impressive, but he wasn't mine.

He said nothing as he sat beside me. Extending his long legs, his toes barely touched the opposite side of the shower. He tilted his head back, closed his eyes, and breathed in the steam.

My gaze shamelessly shifted to the relaxed length of him cradled on top of his balls. Forest had no shame and none of the body image inadequacies I carried around. He made no excuses for his muscular physique and was just as comfortable letting it all hang out as he was covering it up. It wouldn't hurt so much if he weren't so incredibly perfect—not just his body, but his incredible mind and a heart that held all the pain of the world.

Propping my chin on my kneecaps, I watched the water fall.

Silence descended between us until he finally cleared his throat.

"You're sad," he said.

I looked at him, shocked at how bad he was with reading emotions.

"Is that what you think?"

"You look sad."

I blew out a frustrated breath. "I'm not sad." I felt despair, rejection, inadequacy, abandonment, depression, loneliness, powerlessness, a profound emptiness, and incredible isolation.

"Are you angry?" Concern laced his words. "Did I do something?"

"I'm just frustrated." Now, I was lying. Not that I wasn't also frustrated, but I was hiding my true feelings. Forest didn't need that kind of shit. He had enough to deal with.

I resented the daily violation Forest endured while no one touched me. His sacrifice made me feel powerless, and it was only because of me that he couldn't escape this hellhole.

I was the problem, and until I removed myself from the equation, Forest would continue to suffer.

"Sara..." He placed a hand on my shoulder, and it was all I could do not to shrug him off.

"What?" The word came out harsher than I intended, but there it was. My anger showed its ugly face.

"Talk to me." His plea made me feel a thousand times worse.

Wasn't that my job? To talk with him? Instead, jealousy crept in and filled in all the ugly cracks brought on by my insecurities. As hard as this was on me, I had to remind myself he was the one who suffered. His pain was a thousand times worse.

"Do you ever get lonely?"

"What do you mean?" He seemed honestly confused by the sudden change in our conversation.

"You live alone. Work alone. I'm probably the only person you spend time with—"

"I like spending time with you." He nudged my shoulder.

"That's not what I mean. Do you ever want more?"

"Guess I never really thought about it. I've been too busy trying to take Snowden down to care about anything more. And I've always had you. I'm not lonely. If you're worried about that. People confuse me, and social situations make me uncomfortable, but that doesn't mean I'm lonely. I have you. I have Skye..."

Talk about the elephant in the room. We'd never talked through hers and Zach's deaths, let alone everyone else on that helicopter.

"Ah, Forest...I'm so sorry."

"The helicopter didn't explode."

"Huh?"

"Did you see it explode?"

"I saw a rocket hit it," I said.

"It hit the tail rudder, and the helicopter went into a spin. It dropped out of sight."

"Right. They crashed."

"But, it didn't explode."

"Does that matter?"

"I've been thinking about it, and I think it does."

"What does that mean?"

"I don't believe they're dead."

"But, it crashed."

"Over the water."

My brows pinched with confusion.

"Think about it. If they crashed on land, there would've been an explosion. But in water, there's a chance."

"A chance?" My throat tightened, but I didn't believe it made a difference.

"Yes. They train troops on how to escape helicopter crashes. SEALs train for it. That means it's survivable."

But Skye wasn't trained for it, and Zach was a baby.

"Forest, I don't think..."

"Remember what they were wearing when they landed?"

"No."

"They had on life vests. It's standard procedure. If the helicopter crashed in the water, they could have gotten out."

"But..."

"Think about it. Mitzy had eyes on the whole thing. We had a team in the water, another on a boat, and a second helicopter. It doesn't feel like she's gone. I think I would feel it." He thumped his chest. "I've thought about it a lot, and the odds...well, there's a chance."

A slim chance, and not one I was going to take from him. If he wanted to believe Skye was still alive, that wasn't a bubble I would burst.

"Snowden hasn't won," he said. "It may seem that way, but we're in the best position we've ever been in."

"The best position?"

"Yeah."

"And how's that going for you? This is the exact opposite of the best position." I tried to make it a joke, but it came out harsher than intended.

"It's going far better than you might think." A smug smile filled his face.

Chapter Thirty-Seven

SARA

FAR BETTER THAN I THOUGHT? I STARED AT FOREST LIKE HE HAD two heads.

"That's not funny."

"I'm serious." He had a big grin on his face.

"So, getting tortured day in and day out, the rapes, and all the rest are your definition of things getting better?"

"The torture part is kind of a drag, but I'm dealing with that. Snowden thinks he's breaking me down, but he's not."

"How can that be? After everything he does to you."

"To my body...the things he does he does to my body."

"It's more than that, and you know it. The fights...the men..."

"Snowden made a miscalculation."

"How's that?"

"Those silly fights he set up helped me to blow off steam. I release my aggression there, and it saves me from taking things out on Snowden. If I did that—"

"He would take things out on me." I turned the water a little hotter.

"Right, and that can't happen."

"If it weren't for me, you'd already have found a way to escape."

"Not really."

"Huh?"

"I'm right where I want to be."

"You're not making any sense. You're living a nightmare because of me."

"This is the best possible place for me to be. I couldn't ask for a better opportunity. Think about it for a second." He looked at me as if his words made sense. "Where are we?"

"I have no idea." That was one of my greatest frustrations. I'd developed practically zero intelligence during our time here.

"We're inside Snowden's stronghold. This is the epicenter of his operations."

"I don't get it."

"Come on, Sara, you're smart. Think."

I stared blankly at him, and he rolled his eyes. Bringing my hand to his mouth, he brushed the backs of my knuckles with his lips.

"I'm in the center of everything, with access to everything that has anything to do with his business."

"You're a prisoner. You have access to nothing but pain. We know nothing."

"Well…" The grin on his face was one I knew entirely too well. Forest had something up his sleeve. "That's not entirely true."

"Forest?"

"We just need a little more time." He squeezed my hand and placed it in his lap, where he massaged the soft spot between my thumb and first finger.

"More time for what?"

"To map everything out."

"I'm so confused."

"Have you heard anything that indicates any problems?"

Light bulbs started popping in my head. Forest had done something, and I had an idea I knew what it might be. Not that I understood how he'd accomplished it, but damn if that man didn't have a brilliant mind.

"You've been stalling while…" I made a vague gesture. I honestly had no idea what Forest had done.

"That's my girl. You're figuring it out."

"Honestly, I'm not, but I know how your mind works. You're up to something."

"And soon, we should start seeing results."

"What exactly are you expecting?"

"Interruptions in his operations. It'll be almost anything. Whatever Xavier can figure out."

"Wait, you're in communication with Xavier?"

"I'm completely cut off, and please tell me you haven't tried to get word out." He shook his head. "I asked you to trust me."

"I've done shit. I've done nothing but watch him abuse you, tear you down, degrade you, and…"

"Some days are worse than others, but I'm surviving."

"So, everything with Paul is fake, right?" Hope bloomed within me. If he played Snowden, then he was playing Paul as well.

Forest bit at his lower lip and refused to meet my gaze.

"Forest?" Please tell me you're playing Paul.

"Why did he give you the condoms?"

"Excuse me?"

"You heard me."

"Because he's a sick twisted fuck."

"What did he say to you?"

"He said he was coming later, pushed condoms in my hand, and left."

"He's never left us alone before."

"So?"

"Please try to remember. What did he say?"

"Why does it matter?"

He ran his thumb against his jaw and didn't answer.

The green monster of jealousy nipped at my heels and the purple monster of inadequacy, or whatever color that beast was, shredded my confidence.

"Please tell me you're not interested in him." Please tell me I'm enough.

A low growl rumbled deep in his throat. It was a dangerous

sound, menacing, and feral. Forest took my hand in his, gripping tight when I tried to withdraw.

"I have you because of all of this. We would never have found each other, but…"

The dreaded but.

I hated that word.

"Paul?"

"Yeah." He ran his fingers through his hair.

"You want to see what happens with him." The next time I saw Paul, I was going to throat punch the prick for being right. The cocky bastard knew, and I hated him for it. Something died inside of me with Forest's admission.

"I need to know. I'm sorry if that hurts you, but…"

His admission gutted me.

"I get it. It's not like I don't know you like men. Don't hate me for wanting you all to myself. I've never dated someone before, let alone shared him with anyone."

"I don't know if I'd call it sharing. It's more compartmentalizing. I fuck men for the physical release, but I'm not interested beyond that. You're different."

I don't know why that mattered, but in some strange way, it did.

"Different?"

"You're a part of me. I don't know if that's what love is, except I feel it deep in here." He thumped his chest.

"And Paul?"

"Different, but not the same."

The bottom dropped out from beneath me again.

"You can't love me if you're…" I swallowed a sob and pressed my hands to my cheeks. "It doesn't matter, though, does it? Paul said he'd be back, and he'll be back."

Frustrated anger rose within me, not at Forest. As much as I hated his admission that I wasn't enough, it didn't change our circumstances. Forcing Forest to choose between the two of us simply made no sense.

Nothing here made sense.

"I'm just going to leave the two of you alone to—"

"To fuck."

"Right."

"You make it sound ugly." He ran his hand through his hair, a gesture I was beginning to recognize. "Out of all the things I've endured, out of all the things Snowden has done to me, this is what you find disgusting?"

"I didn't say that."

"No, but I see it in your face."

"What you see isn't disgust."

"Then what is it?"

"Knowing I'm not enough for you, that I can't be everything for you, don't you see how that could hurt? How it could destroy me knowing you don't really love me."

"But I do. God, I love you with every fiber of my being. What do you want me to do? I'm not giving up on us."

"There is no you and me. There never was. That's what hurts so much. I think it was just the trauma that made us think our feelings were more than they were."

"What are you saying?" His voice sounded strained.

That I loved him enough to let him go.

"Nothing, I guess."

"Sara...don't."

"Don't what?" My voice broke. It was simply too hard to keep my emotions under control.

"Don't do this. It's not like that."

"It sure feels like it." I sucked in a painful breath. "It's not like we ever really started anything. You're free to do what you want." And who he wanted. It just wasn't me.

"But, I'm not."

"What?"

"Free to do as I want. We have to play this to the end."

I hated how jealous, possessive, and fucking crazy I sounded. Forest liked men, but we weren't talking about nameless men and gratuitous pleasure. This was about Paul, and call me a jealous bitch, but I needed Forest to like me more.

He bent his long legs and wrapped his arms around them,

mirroring my pose. "Say what you want, but this whole fucked-up mess exposed what's been there all along, what I was afraid to admit. Don't pretend it's not true. I love you, and I haven't done all of this to lose you."

All of what?

"What have you done?"

He took my hand in his and placed it over his heart. "I'm tearing him down, piece by piece, destroying what he's built over a lifetime."

"How?"

He tapped the side of his head. "By getting in his head, making him think I'm powerless. He's let down his guard, given me access to everything without even knowing it. We won't be here forever, but it will still be some time. Time to get everything in place."

"What are you planning?"

"I have no idea, which is kind of great when you think about it. I have culpable deniability, but I trust in Xavier and my team. They're out there doing what they can, and soon, if not already, they'll know where we are. But Xavier won't act until he's assured of complete destruction. All we have to do is survive. I'll give Snowden whatever he demands to buy that time, and you need to do the same."

"But what about Paul? He works for Snowden."

"He hates Snowden."

"How do you know that?"

"Because Snowden lied to him."

"What did he lie about?"

"He made Paul believe his sister was dead."

"Piper?"

"Yes, and I'll use that to turn him, but I need him to trust me first."

"When were you going to tell me any of this?"

"Knowledge is dangerous. My goal is to keep you safe. I need Paul to do that, because I can't do it on my own, not when Snowden…"

Not when Snowden had Forest under his thumb.

"I get it." I was such an ass. "Which is why you and Paul…"

"He's a wild card. I can't explain except to say there's something visceral, violent, and inevitable between us. Since I can't run from it, I'm going to embrace it and use it to our advantage. I'm sorry if that hurts you, but I can't stop it. It's going to happen because Snowden wills it. I'd rather it be in an environment I control, away from Snowden, but what happens with Paul doesn't change how I feel about you. I'm not in love with Paul, but he offers something I've never experienced before."

"I'm trying to understand. I'm more naïve than I'd like to admit. I don't get the whole domination thing. It doesn't make sense to me."

"Well, the few, rare, times I've come across a truly dominant male, I've found peace in the quiet that comes from handing over control. Please don't think less of me."

"I want to accept all of you, but I'm going to need a little patience. Truthfully, I'm jealous you share something with him you don't share with me, and I know how needy that makes me sound."

"It means you care for me, but I think about it another way."

"How?"

"Why do you think he left us alone?"

"I honestly don't know why. I think he wants us to have sex."

"There's more to Paul than you see. If he wanted to take advantage of his position, he'd be here doing exactly as Snowden expects, but he's not his father. It's not about taking, but rather giving. The resonance between us goes both ways. Paul isn't inherently cruel, at least that's not the vibe I'm getting."

"Wait. Father?"

"Didn't you know?"

"What the fuck? How long have you known?"

"I just put the pieces together."

"This is the kind of shit you don't keep from me. He's Snowden's son? Why would I know that if you just put the pieces together? And you think you can turn him?"

"I'll turn him." He spoke with confidence.

"How? How are you going to turn a son against his father? Against that monster? Snowden is grooming Paul to take over."

"The crimes of the father are not those of the son."

"You're insane. You know that, don't you? Fucking Paul isn't going to change any of that."

"Getting fucked by Paul is a foregone conclusion. Controlling that interaction is power. As it is, I'm interested. More importantly, I can use it."

"I don't understand." With a flick of my wrist, I turned the water ice cold. This shower was over.

Forest yelped when the icy water hit him and darted out from under the spray. I exited and found my towel. I left the bathroom to change, then pulled up short.

Paul was here.

"You."

"Who were you expecting, little girl?"

I wrapped the towel around my body and marched into the bedroom to dress. If there'd been a door, I would have gladly slammed it shut.

Paul rapped on the doorframe. "Bug up your butt?"

I spun around, yanking a shirt over my head. "Do you care?"

"Not if you're going to be a bitch about it." He glanced back toward the living room. "From the intact wrappers on the floor, and your less than stellar mood, I'm assuming the two of you didn't fuck."

"I'm not having this conversation with you, and stop calling me little girl."

"When you stop throwing tantrums, we'll talk."

I walked right up to him and poked my finger against his chest. "That dominant bullshit doesn't work on me."

He glanced down at my finger then returned the full weight of his gaze to mine, where he obliterated my little tirade with one well-timed smirk. "Don't knock it until you try it. I have a feeling you and Forest will make quite the pair under my control. You just have to take a leap of faith."

"Asshole."

"Reverting to name-calling?" He crossed his arms, effectively removing my accusatory finger from his chest. "Very mature.

Fortunately for you, I'm not allowed to touch you. Otherwise, I'd toss you over my knee and spank some sense into you."

Heat filled my cheeks with his arrogant words. "You try that, and I'll cut your balls off."

"I see why Forest likes you so much. You're feisty."

"Sara, come back." Forest's deep voice boomed from the other room. He came to a sudden stop when he saw Paul standing in the doorway.

"Well, this should be interesting." The corner of Paul's mouth ticked up.

Chapter Thirty-Eight

FOREST

SEEING PAUL HAD AN INSTANT EFFECT ON ME. HEAT SURGED TO MY cock. His magnetism stretched across the distance, where it grabbed my balls and had me sucking wind.

My dick gave a hungry twitch.

And I had a serious problem.

He stood between Sara and me.

No way was I getting past him unscathed. My body trembled in anticipation of the promise we'd made while my heart broke for the pain this would cause Sara.

"Well, it looks like we're all here." Paul took me in with a languid sweep of his gaze. "Drop the towel." His deep voice had me obeying instantly.

My towel fell to the floor as I shifted my weight. I would meet him on a solid base and show him submissive didn't mean weak.

He made a point of focusing on my dick, which showed off its eagerness as it lengthened for him.

Slowly, his gaze traveled upward, lingering on the hard, defined lines of my abs and chest. Unhurried, but relentless, he took in my broad shoulders, moved up my neck, swept across the hard edges of my jaw, and settled on my lips. I slowly pressed my lips together, wetting them with my tongue, then his gaze finally settled on my eyes.

He uncrossed his arms and flexed his fingers. Rolling his shoulders back, he kicked off from the wall and took a step into the room. My weight shifted back before I realized what I was doing.

The man certainly wasn't wasting any time, but he paused.

"I'm sensing a bit of friction." He snapped his fingers. "Get out here, Miss Sara." He pointed to the couch. "And sit down."

A huff sounded from behind him. "You're not the boss of me."

"No? We'll see about that. Don't make me repeat myself. You won't like the consequences."

"You're not touching me."

"I don't need to when I have him. Now get your lovely little ass out here and sit the fuck down."

Sara crept out from the bedroom. Her eyes cut to mine, then dropped to the evidence of my arousal. Pain flashed in her eyes, but then she drew her lower lip between her teeth, and I saw something else. She slowly moved to the couch, her eyes more on Paul than me.

"Be very careful how you speak to her." The threat in my voice had Paul's head snapping toward me. "She's not a part of this."

"Is that what you think?"

"Don't test me on that. She doesn't belong to you."

I would protect Sara at all costs, and that included keeping Paul's hands off her.

"Here's a truth I want you to understand. I'll test you. I'll do it because that's what you need. You're right. She doesn't belong to me, but you do. I'll never force her to do anything she doesn't freely choose, but it's my role to pave the way for what we all need. You're the foundation of our unlikely trio. You support Sara while I provide the focus you need. So, yes, she's very much a part of this, excluding her isn't an option."

"What does that mean?" Sara folded her legs beneath her.

His gaze cut to her on the couch. "Only that this is uncharted territory, which means we begin as equals and explore with open minds. How we move forward is the question each of us needs to answer."

"There's nothing equal about any of this," she said.

"Ask Forest. He'll explain how it works."

"He has no choice in this. He's a prisoner…"

"He chooses when he bends his knee and submits to my boss. He chooses to place you above himself. I'm in awe of the sacrifices he makes every day. I'm also not afraid to admit I'm jealous of what the two of you share, but I'm not threatened by it. My question is whether you feel the same? Is your love as strong as his? Or are you threatened by what he needs from me?"

"Paul…" I ground out his name. "You're crossing a line. Leave her alone."

"Would you rather we fucked in private and hid that from her? Because I can tell you how that ends. We all lose."

"I'm warning you. Leave her out of this."

"That's not how this works…It's not how I lead and make no mistake who is in charge. We do this with her consent, not without." Paul turned to Sara. "So, what's it going to be?"

"Like I have any say." She wrapped her arms around her knees and drew herself into a tiny ball. "You're going to do what you want one way or another."

I ached to wrap my arms around her and tell her how much I loved her. Paul didn't change any of that.

"Here's a little thing about power, little girl. Truly powerful men aren't afraid of handing over control. It doesn't lessen who they are, nor their status. I will walk away if that's what you decide. How's that for giving you control?"

"I don't believe you." She hopped to her feet. "You're no different from the monster out there."

Paul gave me a look, which said I needed to control my woman. I glanced at the towel at my feet and considered picking it up to cover myself. When my eyes cut to his, he had noticed the direction of my gaze.

If I picked up the towel, I undermined his authority. Everything would change. Or, I could support him. I kicked the towel to the side then looked at him as if saying Are you satisfied? His lips pressed into a hard line, and he gave a curt nod.

"If Sara tells you to leave, you'll leave? Is that what you're offering?"

I hoped Sara understood what that would mean, praying she could find some way to trust Paul. I needed this.

"Yes, but only under the condition that the two of you talk."

I went to Sara and took her hands in mine. "Just say the word." I pressed my forehead against hers.

"Do you think he'd leave?"

"I trust him. I wish you could too, but yeah. I believe he'll leave."

"Is this..." She choked up then cleared her throat. "Do you want this?"

"Not if it means losing you."

She squeezed my hands and blew out her breath. "I don't know how to do this. I've never been with anyone before, but I guess if I think about it, I've always had to share you with other men. This isn't easy for me."

"Perhaps another time." Paul placed his hand on my shoulder. He slid his hand down my shoulder, ran it over my bicep, and gripped my forearm.

My body reacted to the touch, and a ripple of desire shot through me.

Paul headed to the door. He stopped with his hand on the electronic lock. "When he asks, I'm going to tell him I was called away unexpectedly. You may want your story to be similar."

"Understood."

I released Sara's hands and pulled her tight against me. My erection remained. Stoked out of quiescence by Paul's parting touch, there was no way to hide it from Sara. Not that I would. I wanted to share what Paul and I had with her, not hide it.

The door lock cycled, and Paul pushed the door open.

"Wait." Sara's voice cracked and trembled. "Don't go."

Paul hesitated and looked at me.

"Sara," I said, "it's okay."

"I can't take this from you. It's not fair to you." She closed her eyes and licked her upper lip. Placing both hands on my face, she lifted on tiptoe and brushed her lips against mine. Soft and velvety smooth, my eyes practically rolled into the back of my head.

I held her tight, lifting her off her feet to deepen the kiss. She was all sunlight and heaven wrapped in my arms.

The door slowly swung shut, and I cracked open my eyes. Paul stood at the door, legs spread, arms crossed over his chest. He took in our kiss, and a genuine smile crested his face.

My only problem was that I didn't want to let Sara go. She decided that for me, pushing against my chest until I lowered her to the ground. Peeking up at me, her attention shifted to Paul.

"Are you sure about this?" Paul didn't move from the door.

"Not in the slightest." She did that thing with her fingers, twisting them together. "I don't trust you, but I trust Forest. I'm going with my gut on this. Please don't make me regret it and don't hurt him."

"I make no promises."

Fuck! That voice. The violent promise of excruciating pain had my balls drawing tight and my dick bouncing with anticipation. Sara didn't understand what it took to silence my mind. One look at the desire swirling in Paul's eyes, and there was no doubt he did.

She looked between us as our gazes locked. "Um...I'll just be in the..."

"Stay." Paul's command made her jump.

"Um..." She looked to me, uncertain, but I nodded.

"I don't want you to feel you need to leave, but I won't make you stay."

She lifted on tiptoe, her eyes cutting toward Paul as she placed her sweet lips on mine. "I love you."

"I love you more." I closed my eyes and breathed her in. Soft and gentle, I ached to hold her, to lie with her, and to make love to her.

And I would.

Just not right now.

"Sit on the couch, or take the chair, but don't interfere. Forest, come here."

Paul's command shot through me, lighting up all my nerves and sending a shockwave of heat rolling through my body. Anticipation rippled through me and quick on its heels was the promise of inevitability.

"You're under my control now." The timbre of his voice changed, turning rough, ragged, and as hard as steel.

I sucked in a breath, excited for what came next, and gave Sara's hand one final squeeze. She wasn't running for the bathroom, but backed up into the small kitchenette, as far as she could get in the limited space.

Heat surged to my dick as I approached Paul. Each heartbeat betrayed my desire. Long and hard, there was no hiding my eagerness.

Not sure how he would begin, or what he would ask, I prepared myself to obey his commands and hand myself over to his will. The moment I drew within striking distance, his arm snapped out, and his hand encircled my throat. My eyes widened as he cut off my air and spun me until my back slammed against the wall.

Without warning, he kissed me, crushing his lips against mine. His free hand reached between us and clamped around my dick. Black spots danced in my vision from the excruciating pain between my legs and lack of oxygen starving my brain, but I didn't care.

The firm, wet heat of his mouth was on me.

This was happening.

He kissed with an all-consuming passion that stole my breath and sent me places in my head I never thought to go. He caught my lips between his, kissing firmly as he brought my body to life with his skillful licks and stabbing bites. His teeth cut into my lips, tugging until I huffed in pain, and his hand moved from my dick to my balls where his punishing grip had me seeing stars.

He held me, not with arms encircled around me, but with the vice of his hand around my throat, controlling every aspect of the kiss. He hungrily ate at my mouth, taking what he wanted, and I barely had a chance to kiss him back.

Pressing against me, the engorged lengths of our cocks moved against each other with only the fabric of his pants separating us. It was a promise of where this kiss would end.

I wanted him to take me with the brutal aggression only he possessed.

"Goddammit, fuck me already." I croaked out the words between licks and bites.

Paul released my balls and punched me hard in the gut. "Did I give you permission to speak?"

Shit, but that did things to my head. Pain filled my existence, slipping into all the cracks and crevices as agony rippled through my midsection and pulsed in my balls. He reached between us and squeezed my dick. Black spots danced in my vision with the violence of his grip.

"You're not ready for me to fuck you."

I growled with frustration but didn't dare speak. He gripped my jaw, holding my head back against the wall.

"You're going to beg for it."

"I am begging for it."

He reared back, and his fist slammed into me. I huffed against the pain. Sara stifled a gasp behind her hand and scooted further into the corner.

"Want to keep flapping your lips, or are you going to shut up and kiss me back?"

I wanted the kiss and lunged for his mouth. The thing I loved about men was that I didn't need to hold back my aggression. I gave as good as I got, the rougher, and more violent, the better as far as I was concerned.

But I wanted him deep inside of me, punishing my flesh with hard, angry, combative sex; a clashing of male on male which would drive me to oblivion.

His dark, musky scent flooded my senses and drugged my inhales. The potency of his skin on mine, the heat of our bodies colliding, Sara's fluttering gasps as she watched, it flipped a switch inside of me.

Pleasure burst from my core and settled with a tingling ache in my balls. Paul's fist tightened and released. Each contraction lifted me on my toes as I huffed out a breath of delirious pain.

His mouth kissed mine and caught the urgent rhythm of my exhales. He breathed in my pain and returned it to me with the control he exercised over my body.

His hand moved up and grabbed a fistful of my hair. His lips collided with mine, turning the kiss ferocious and fierce. I bucked against the pain, needing to fight and assert my dominance, but Paul intensified the kiss, violently sucking and biting as I groaned and begged for more.

His hand yanked on my hair in time to the fisting of my cock. The two sensations warred with each other, dividing my attention until I was delirious for it to stop, but aching for him to push me harder, make it hurt more, and deepen the sensations flooding my body.

I slammed my hips forward. He ground his cock against mine, hips moving in a devilish dance as if we were fucking each other with only the thin barrier of his clothing between us. I reached for his waistband, but he slapped my hand away.

"No." The chastisement brought me up short, and my body stilled. "You don't get to control this." Paul ripped his mouth from mine and stared at my lips before turning his attention to my eyes. "Do we have an understanding? Because I can stop. I'm wondering if you can do the same."

I glared at him and removed my hand from his briefs. It didn't go far, my hand settled on his hip, and I thrust forward. "If you don't fuck me soon, I will take over."

"You think you can?" His brow lifted in challenge, and his fingers released their death grip on my cock.

I slammed my hand over his, covering his fingers and closing mine. I wasn't going to lose the momentum of the orgasm promised by this man's hand.

"I know I can. Don't make me. I want this."

"Say that again." His sharp command cut through the air.

The muscles of my jaw bunched, but I was too far gone to

argue. I wanted this. We'd passed the point of no return when we made the promise to finish this later.

Later was now.

"No."

"No, what?"

"Shit, don't…" Don't make me say it.

"Say it." The hardness in his eyes said we weren't moving forward until I did.

"Fine." I hated admitting it, and it was worse to say it out loud, but damn if the thundering in my heart didn't push me over the edge. Paul was an irresistible force. "Please don't stop. I want this too much."

"Who's in control?"

"You are."

Paul dove for my mouth, crushing his lips against mine as I stopped breathing. His hand tangled in my hair. His fist pumped my cock. He licked and curled his tongue into the corners of my mouth until I didn't know which way was up. If he didn't have me slammed against the wall, I would have fallen apart.

The swollen need between our legs, the passing seconds as he touched me, kissed me, were only promises of what would come.

"Touch me, Forest. Show me what you want."

"With fucking pleasure." I didn't know why I hadn't thought of that before. Then I realized the undeniable truth between us. I'd been waiting for permission.

With any other man, I took what I wanted, how I wanted, and when I wanted it. With Paul, I waited for permission.

I shifted my hand off his and ran the backs of my knuckles along his turgid length. My mouth was dry, eager to take him in and swallow him whole.

Paul lifted his lips from mine. "Touch me." His eyes closed in pleasure when I wrapped my fingers around the swollen length of his cock. "Hold me the way you like being held."

"You don't want me to hold you like that." I stroked the underside of his cock, frustrated by the fabric separating us. I lifted my hand and placed it over his, squeezing tight. "I like it hard and filled with enough pain to make my balls draw up until I want to puke."

His grip tightened beneath mine until I hissed with the pain.

"And what about whips?"

"The best warm-up around, but we're past that, wouldn't you say. I like ropes and restraints, the tighter, the better. Make me scream."

"I'll remember that for later."

My hips jerked as his grip twisted unexpectedly and shot pain down my shaft, where it gathered in my balls.

"Fuck me already." I slammed my head back against the wall, frustrated and aching to come. My erection strained harder as his fingers curled around my cock. I'd never get tired of the feeling of Paul taking me in hand. I'd fantasized about the guilty pleasure too long, and it didn't seem real that I'd finally have a chance to feel him inside of me.

Paul ran his thumb over the crown of my cock, rubbing the slippery wet spot as he bent his head and bit at my neck. My eyes closed, and a tight groan slipped free.

The sharp edges of his teeth sank into the soft skin between my shoulder and neck. Pain shot through me. He bit so hard and deep I swore he drew blood. Not that I cared. Agony centered my thoughts on him. My balls tightened, and my hips bucked.

"Stop playing with me already." I was moments from shooting hot cum all over his abdomen.

"If you think I'm playing, you're in for a rude awakening." His fist clenched viciously around my cock. He pulled me off my feet as he yanked me toward the bedroom. Paul glanced over at Sara, who'd been silent during the entire exchange. "You're welcome to watch if you want, or join in if you prefer."

Chapter Thirty-Nine

FOREST

Sweet Jesus, I needed relief. Lust clouded my thoughts, and I'd forgotten about Sara, but the moment Paul mentioned her, all I could think about was needing her with us.

She wasn't ready for something like this, but I needed to know she was okay with what was happening.

I had only a moment to quickly glance in her direction before Paul dragged me to the bedroom. He released his hold of my dick, and I faced the bed.

My pulse kicked into high gear as he hooked his thumbs beneath the waistband of his pants and slid them down his hips.

"I bet you can't wait to taste me." His smirk sent a shot of heat to my aching dick.

"The thought has crossed my mind."

"Mine too."

I arched a brow, wondering if he would allow it. A shadow darkened the doorway, and I twisted around to find Sara peeking inside.

We'd talked about this, but I needed to know she was okay. I reached for her, not sure if she would take my hand. What was happening here didn't involve her, and yet I wanted her to be some small part of it. Even if that was only to tell me everything would be okay.

Paul reached for a foil packet and ripped off the end as Sara stepped into the room. She took my hand.

"Hey." I pulled her to my side.

"Hey." She glanced up at me.

"Are you…"

Sara placed her hand on my chest. She had to feel the raging beat of my heart. "You two kiss like you're fucking. Touch like you're fighting."

It seemed as if she wanted to say something else.

"And?"

Her attention shifted to Paul and dropped down to the condom sheathing his cock.

"It's stunning."

Paul licked his lips, watching the two of us. Then he pointed to a chair in the corner. "If you want to watch, sit there. If you want to join us, remove your clothes."

Her eyes widened, and she looked to me.

God, if that's not what I wanted, but I sensed her hesitation in the hitching of her breath. Sara shifted her weight, then moved to the corner.

Paul gripped my chin, forcing my attention back to him. "He wants us both, Miss Sara. Imagine what it'll feel like when your mouth is on him, and he is on me? Or when I'm fucking him, setting the pace as he fucks you? It'll be glorious."

Sara folded herself into the chair and drew her knees up to her chest.

"But maybe another time." Paul pressed down on my shoulder. "On your knees. I want your lips on me. Get me ready to fuck your ass."

I lowered to my knees, my eyes on Sara looking for any sign of interest, any sign of revulsion. She hadn't reacted to what Paul had said. He knew my most desperate fantasy and put it out there between the three of us where it would either take root and grow or fester and rot until it broke us apart.

She bit her lower lip as I settled on my knees. The thought of taking Paul in my mouth excited me, but I ached for what would come next. Without his hand on me, my dick lost its stimulation and ached for Paul's touch. Would he hold me while he fucked me? Would he allow my release as he took his?

Paul guided my mouth onto his cock, obliterating any thoughts swirling in my head. A low hiss escaped him, and he rocked his hips forward as I took him in.

"Fuuuuck, I knew you would feel good." His fingers curled in my hair, giving him the control he craved. I willingly handed it over to him, allowing him to set the pace and the depth with which he fucked my mouth. "I'll never force you to join us, but the invitation is always open. He belongs to you as much as me, but he deserves to have us both."

With all my attention focused on his cock, I had no way to know if she responded at all.

Paul fucked my mouth. Slow and with purpose, he claimed the pleasure which belonged to him. When his balls drew up and his breaths hitched, he yanked himself out of my mouth.

"Get on the bed." Hoarse and filled with strain, his voice cracked.

I climbed on the bed, going to all fours, but he slapped my ass.

"Not like that. I want you on your back watching me fuck you."

I'd never fucked like that before. I preferred the dissociation of putting my back to another man or staring at another man's back. This felt too personal, but I didn't hesitate. I wanted to watch him fuck me too. I craved that affection, as brutal as Paul made it.

I scooted back on the bed as Paul towered over me. The urgency to come overwhelmed me. I'd cooled off while sucking his cock, but now it felt as if his hands were on me again. They weren't, but the heat of his gaze as he looked down on me was all I needed.

My hand went to my cock, needing some kind of stimulation.

"No." His cutting command angered me, and I didn't let go.

In the blink of an eye, Paul launched at me. He grabbed my hand, ripping it from my cock and held it tight against the bed. "I said no."

My pulse thundered as he straddled me. My thighs were trapped between his as I faced him. I was seconds from blowing my load but somehow managed to calm down. The show of force activated a switch inside my head and hell if I didn't hunger to surrender.

His gaze raked over my body, and I released the tension in my arm. Then slowly, reverently, Paul bent forward and placed a kiss over my chest. He drew back, settling on his heels as his lips kissed a path downward, tracing a circle around my navel and angling down.

"Holy fuck." My hips jerked as his hand found my throbbing cock.

"Yes, Forest, that's the plan, but first…" He bent forward, and my eyes rolled back as the heat of his mouth encased my cock. He licked along the shaft from root to crown then back again. His lips moved to my balls, where he sent sparks shooting through my groin. He went about it assertively, in control of every action, determined to drive me insane.

Unhurried, his soft sucks teased me, quickened my breaths, and had me clawing the sheets.

"I've wanted to do that since I first laid eyes on you. Feel your cock in my mouth, take it as mine as you give it to me willingly. Like you're going to give me the rest of you."

He swirled his tongue across my scrotum. My balls reacted, drawing tight, as my toes curled and my head shook side to side with the overwhelming pleasure. Paul certainly did know how to draw out a fuck.

I'd never had anything last this long with another man, but he drove me from one sensation to another, leaving me riding the cusp of an impossible wave without ever cresting over the other side. He went back to my shaft, flicking his tongue along the underside as he moved to just below the crown, where all the nerves resided.

"You feel that?" He sucked just the tip into his mouth.

"Yeah, I feel that." It felt like the first time, and I didn't know how to process this soft against the previous viciousness of his touch.

"You don't feel that when you're fucking someone's face or pounding into them like a jackhammer." He blew a soft breath along my length. "Sometimes, soft and gentle can be better than hard and fast."

"But I like the pain."

"I know, and I'll give that to you when you need it, but I bet you've never done this with another man."

"What's that?"

"Gone slow."

"Just put me out of my misery already."

"You're not in charge."

"I think we've established that." My fingers dug through the sheets. "Please fuck me."

The stimulation to my glans had me arching into his mouth. I wanted to buck and fuck his mouth but had a sinking suspicion that would make him stop. No way in hell was I stopping this. I was just about ready to…

His weight shifted, and I cried out with frustration with the orgasm he denied me. A soft chuckle sounded as he lifted my legs, bending them at the knees. With my ankles pressed to my ass, he spread my knees and slipped a finger into my anus.

My eyes closed with the stinging sensation as I braced for the burning stretch to come. The slow and steady build-up had turned into the most intense feeling in my body. I ached for him and needed to fuck. I didn't care if it was soft and gentle or hard and fast. I simply needed Paul; however, he chose to allow it.

Paul lowered himself until we were chest to chest, our cocks lying beside each other, and the weight of his powerful body pressing down on me. His lips met mine in a soft caress as he rocked his hips back and forth as if we had all the time in the world to simply feel. The motion heated me up.

My heart sputtered with the uncharacteristic tenderness, the heavy emotion I hadn't expected when fucking another man.

"Please," I begged. "I need you inside of me."

Paul flexed his hips. He gathered spit in his hand and ran it along his turgid length. I could come from watching him handle himself alone. I shifted restlessly beneath him as he collected more spit and spread it around my tight rim.

I breathed out with excitement. "We're really doing this?"

"We are." Paul lined himself up. "Pull your knees to your chest. It'll make it easier, and keep your eyes on me."

My breath cut off as Paul pushed into my body. My tissues stretched and burned, but I'd found my own slice of heaven. His breath cut off as he sank into me.

"You feel fucking incredible."

"Then fuck me already." I trembled beneath him, overwhelmed, and eager to watch him chase his release.

Paul slid out then pushed back in, going slow at first, but that didn't last long. He thrust hard and dug deep until he established a punishing rhythm.

"Holy fuck." I panted against the quickening of his strokes, unaccustomed to the sensations firing inside my body. "I feel you everywhere."

"That's because I am everywhere. I own you now, every piece of you is mine. This is just the beginning."

I flexed, using my muscles to meet his thrusts. He slammed forward, increasing the pace. Soft and gentle flew out the window as his hunger took control. Mercilessly, he fucked with every fiber of his being.

Paul bent forward, grasped my neck, and crushed his lips against mine. His taste flooded my senses, and I wrapped my arms around him as his magnificent body moved over mine. The heat of his skin against mine slicked with sweat, then his arm moved between us, and he took me in hand, stroking my cock in time with his thrusts.

I cried out, desperate to give myself to him in this moment.

"Come for me, Forest. I'm too fucking close."

My mouth opened in a soundless scream as my dick pulsed in Paul's hand. My hips ground wildly with the heat exploding in my groin.

The intensity of my orgasm stole my breath and turned my vision into a flickering of stars. I came and came until there was nothing left, ejaculating between us, mixing sweat and cum as our bodies slapped against one another. Paul thrust violently forward, hammering erratically as he followed me over the cliff. His orgasm ripped through him.

It took a moment before our breaths eased. Arms and legs entangled, Paul glanced down at me. "Now that was worth every tortured moment waiting to take you. Fuck if I don't want more."

"Next time, warm me up with a whip. Restrain me and make me scream."

"You're going to regret asking for that." His soft chuckle made me smile.

"I hope so."

Paul rolled to his side and propped his head on his hand. He draped an arm over my chest. When I looked up, he wasn't staring at me, but rather into the corner of the room. He bent down and kissed the tip of my shoulder.

"I'm going to take a shower while the two of you discuss what just happened and how we move forward from here." He rolled away and slid off the bed. Unashamed of his nakedness, he walked past Sara. "One half of a coin. I'm only one half of what he needs."

She glanced up and gave a sharp nod. Then her attention swung to me. Somehow, I wouldn't feel complete until I had her in my arms. The only question was, would she still want me?

"Sara." I stretched out a hand. It had been a risk having sex with Paul first, but I hid nothing from Sara. I never had.

She unfolded her knees and came to me. Slowly, she threaded her fingers through mine.

"Are you okay?" I needed to know more but would begin with that first.

"That was…"

"Disgusting?" I held my breath, waiting to hear if that changed everything.

"Oh, Forest." She cupped my face and placed a kiss on my lips. "It was different, that's all." She licked her lips. "I taste him on you."

"I'm sorry." This was awkward.

"Don't be."

"You're not…"

A smile crested her lips. "I love all the pieces of you. I should never have asked you to change. I can't take this from you, and now I realize I don't want to. I can't give you…that. But he certainly can."

She was right about that. Sara would never be able to string me up and do all the filthy things Paul could do. He would take me, break me, and put me back together again. I needed the freedom to satisfy the dark urges, which swirled in my head.

"One half of a coin…" It occurred to me what Paul meant. "You're the two halves that make me whole."

"That's what Paul thinks."

"And it doesn't bother you that he and I…"

"It did at first before I watched you. I expected it to bother me, honestly, but after watching you together, …it was intense, a little hot, and definitely not me."

"You liked watching us?" Hope bloomed in my chest. Maybe there was a way to make this work.

"More than I thought." She placed a hand on my chest. "I'm not sure about the threesome part."

"I'd never ask."

"I know, but is that what you want?"

"To share a bed with the two people I adore more than anything in the world? To give them pleasure at the same time? I'm not going to lie. I fantasize about it."

"I'm not ready for something like that, and I'm not so sure about Paul thinking he can boss me around."

"He's wired for it, but I'll talk to him."

"Why don't you clean up? I'm going to find a puzzle to put together." She leaned in and brushed her lips against mine.

"Paul's in there."

"I know."

I couldn't deny my interest. Now that I'd had a taste of his dominance, I wanted more. I could tell he'd been holding back for Sara's sake. If she was encouraging me to go after him, that was more than I could ever ask.

"And you're going to be okay?" I twirled a strand of her hair around my finger.

"An hour ago, I would have said no. I was jealous and threatened by him, not to mention afraid I'd lose you. It's different now."

"How so?"

"Because I don't feel excluded? I guess that's the best word, but more importantly, I don't feel like I've lost you. What we have is different from that. I feel a whole lot better."

I wanted to pull her into my arms, but my chest and belly were covered in cum. I propped up on my elbow and ran my finger over her lips.

"You're the light of my life, my guiding salvation, and the only reason I make it through each day. I love you more than life itself, and I promise to get you out of this horrible mess."

"If anyone can do it, I know you can. Now, out of bed. He won't wait for long."

Chapter Forty

SARA

I watched Forest fuck another man.

The weirdest thing was that it didn't bother me.

In fact, it kind of turned me on.

Not that I was Jonesing to hop in and join that hot mess. The collision of two powerful males, locked in what could only be described as sexual combat, didn't feel like the safest place for a female.

Their exploration of mutual physical gratification intrigued me. It was nothing like any sex I'd ever seen. Whether that was because it was two men, or because of the power dynamic they shared, wasn't clear.

Damn if it wasn't sensual in its own right, and I kind of sensed Paul held back a little for my benefit. Or maybe, he did it for Forest.

Was that something a person eased into with a partner?

I didn't know.

I went with my gut and sent Forest to be with Paul alone. Whatever else they needed to work out between them would be best done without me present. Watching Forest retreat to the bathroom left me alone to process my thoughts. He initially left the door open, but then it closed forcibly moments later.

My suspicions were confirmed a few moments later. Round two appeared much more brutal than the first.

I used my time to dig deep and sift through my emotions. There was no jealousy, which was impressive considering my previous meltdown.

I felt...at peace.

And happy.

Happy to share this with Forest.

He'd always been unconventional. There should be no reason being in a relationship with him should be any different.

We were in an unconventional threesome.

Or rather, two twosomes with Forest sandwiched in the middle. Was there a word for that?

Something heavy thudded against the bathroom door. A body, by the sound of it, whether Forest or Paul was left to my overly active imagination. When the next sounds turned out to be low grunts and groans, I let it go.

So Forest had a plan?

Of course, he did.

The thumping and banging in the bathroom escalated. It felt a little voyeuristic listening to them having sex, which was kind of funny considering that was exactly what I'd done moments ago.

A yawn slipped from my lips, and I decided to call it a night. Leaving Paul and Forest to do their thing, I changed the sheets and crawled into bed.

I felt drained. Like mentally exhausted as if my emotions had run a marathon. So, what did I know?

Forest had hijacked Snowden's Wi-Fi network, piggybacking on the phones of Snowden's men to spread throughout the compound.

That made sense.

I could see him planting some kind of virus on Paul's phone. That virus would have jumped from phone to phone as Paul wandered around.

While I thought we were prisoners, Forest's infiltration had been in place since the day we arrived. Did that explain the odd interruptions in Snowden's business?

Not knowing much about how that might work, I couldn't be sure, but that had to be it. Which meant, Xavier had to have access to Snowden's network. That was the only explanation for how that information was getting out. Xavier had to be pulling Snowden's operation apart brick by brick.

But where was the cavalry?

Where was our rescue?

If Xavier had details about bank accounts and slave transfers, wouldn't he also know where Snowden was keeping us?

I pulled the covers to my neck and rolled to my side as I tried to sort through all the possibilities.

Every day we remained Snowden's prisoners increased the risk of something terrible happening to us. What was Forest waiting for?

I didn't trust Snowden. It didn't make sense he would share Forest with another man, but he let Paul have Forest.

Why?

I understood the fights with his men and even the prize he awarded them. He wanted Forest beaten down.

But Paul?

With my thoughts in turmoil, I drifted into a restless sleep waking only when the bed dipped beside me. Forest tried not to wake me as he climbed in bed. He moved stiffly as if he were in pain. The hitching of his breath told a brutal story.

I didn't move, but when he wrapped an arm around my waist and tugged me to him, I could no longer pretend to be asleep.

"Hey." He nuzzled my neck and kissed the tip of my shoulder. "You awake?"

"I am now." I curled my arm around his and allowed him to fit me against the curve of his body.

"How's my angel?"

"I'm good. You?"

"I'm very good." He kissed the crown of my head. "Thank you for that."

How was I supposed to respond? You're welcome? Like I'd given him some great gift in watching what was going to happen whether I wanted it or not?

Would Paul have left if I hadn't stopped him?

I'll never know. Not that it mattered. I learned what I needed to know. My love for Forest didn't have boundaries.

"You don't sound good." I threaded my fingers with his.

"I'm sore, but in a good, satisfied, kind of way."

"I don't like that he hurts you."

"I need it. That might not make sense, but it clears my head and gives me an escape from the rest of it."

No need to specify what the rest of it meant. I rolled over and traced around the ridges and contours of his chest.

"Snowden hurts you."

"Snowden tortures me. It's not the same."

"I didn't mean to imply it was. I'm sorry."

"No, that's okay. It's different when it's something I want. I can embrace the pain and use it to focus my thoughts rather than simply survive it."

"Speaking of surviving…do you think we'll ever get out of here?"

"That's the plan."

"And?"

"That's all I have right now. It's going to take time; until then, we keep our heads down, survive, and endure."

"And Paul?"

"I'm working on him."

"Do you think you can turn him?"

"I hope to."

"Tell me about Piper."

Forest ran his fingers through my hair and blew out a breath.

"Well, like you, she's a rescue. She went into foster care, and things turned ugly when she entered her preteen years."

I knew what that meant.

"Why didn't you rescue Paul?"

"I didn't get to him in time."

"How did he get here?"

"My assumption is he was taken into Snowden's fighting rings.

Piper was slated for the sex trade, but I intervened before they could take her."

"What do you think happened?"

"Paul survived. How he came to work for Snowden is unclear. My suspicion is Snowden discovered who Paul was, but it's not something I can ask. I need Paul to share that with me."

"I can poke around."

"No." His abrupt response made me jerk.

"But, I can help."

"I don't want you drawing any suspicion. Please, if anything happened to you, I wouldn't survive it. I need you to trust me. I can't…just please, don't do anything."

His desperation knifed directly to my heart. It was too easy to forget the pain he endured to protect me as I sat in our room safe and sound, day after day. While Forest suffered Snowden's sadistic desires, I read books, put puzzles together, and waited for the long hours to pass.

"I promise, but if you need anything…"

"I need to know you're safe, that you're not placing yourself in danger. Knowing that gets me through…" His voice broke. "As for Paul, I'll find a way to tell him about his sister. If he knows she's safe —"

"Um, I may have already let it slip."

"What do you mean?"

"It was after that first night…after you knocked Paul unconscious. When he took me out the next day to see Snowden, I mentioned Piper."

Forest's body stiffened. "You did?"

"He told me she was dead and never to say her name."

A soft knock sounded on the doorframe. Forest rolled over.

"Yeah?"

"It's after midnight. Get some sleep. You still have the morning to get through."

"I can manage my bedtime; thank you very much."

Paul's low growl made my skin tingle. It lifted the hairs on my arms and sent a shiver shooting down my spine. Why did it sound so damn sexy? Tension coiled in Forest's body.

"Just do as I say. Stop talking and get some rest. I have a bad feeling about tomorrow."

Forest rolled to his back. "For shits and giggles, what happens if I don't?"

"You want me to answer that?"

"No." Forest draped his arm over his eyes and gave a low groan.

"I didn't think so." Paul rapped his knuckles on the door frame. "Goodnight, Miss Sara. Please don't keep him up."

After Paul left, I whispered, "What was that about?"

"He got a call as we were drying off. It appears Snowden is plagued with issues with his business." He gave a low chuckle. "I sense he'll be in a foul mood tomorrow."

"Oh, Forest…"

A foul mood meant bad things.

"I mean it! Stop talking and go the fuck to sleep." Paul's shout from his bed on the couch had me clamping my mouth shut.

The man had impeccable hearing. He also had his own quarters, but he slept in ours. Ostensibly to protect us, but I had a sinking suspicion that was only an excuse to stay close to Forest.

Chapter Forty-One

SARA

OUR MORNING BEGAN LIKE ANY OTHER, WITH A FEW NOTABLE differences.

Forest rose from the bed and went into the living room like he always did. I trailed behind him, yawning and wiping the sleep from my eyes. Paul was already up. He stood in the kitchen, where he leaned against the counter with a freshly brewed pot of coffee, a steaming cup in his hand, and another resting on the counter.

Instead of prowling around one another, keeping a wary distance, Forest strode into the kitchen and swiped the mug off the counter. He took a tentative sip, testing the temperature, all while keeping his eyes on Paul.

Their staring match continued for what seemed like forever before a smile cracked the hard planes of Paul's face. He shook his head, laughing softly, then cuffed an arm around Forest's neck. Pulling him close, Paul claimed a kiss then slapped Forest on the ass. He went to the couch where he plopped down and blew out a breath.

"You're cutting it close." Paul lifted the cup to his mouth as Forest circled the couch.

"I've still got time." Forest took my hand in his and pressed a kiss to the back of my knuckles. The tender gesture filled my heart with warmth, but a frown stole that happiness when his grip tightened.

I knew what he was thinking. Paul mentioned Snowden would be in a foul mood.

"Don't push it." Paul gave a warning.

"If you don't stop talking and keep me from my shower, I will be late."

"You had a shower last night."

"With you." He pulled me along and shut the door to the bathroom behind us.

"It's late." I turned on the water to let it heat up. "I'm with Paul."

"Since when are you with Paul?" Forest pulled me to him, a smile on his face.

"When what he says makes sense." I gave a little giggle as Forest nuzzled my neck. "That tickles."

He rubbed the scruff of his beard over my sensitive skin, sending shivers racing along my nerves. I slapped him playfully.

"You like that, my sweet angel? I know where else I can kiss that'll make you scream."

Hot damn if I didn't want precisely that, but time was not our friend.

He continued kissing down my neck, then yanked the soft cotton of my shirt off my shoulder. Nipping with his teeth, he skirted a fine line between pleasure and pain.

"Forest..." Small panting breaths escaped me as he cupped my breast and planted his mouth over my nipple. The heat of his breath and the warm, moist flicks of his tongue had my eyes rolling to the back of my head.

I ran my hands through his hair and gave more than a gentle tug when he bit my nipple.

"Holy fuck!" My back arched.

His gruff laughter vibrated against my breast. "Now that is something I can't wait to try."

He scooped me into his arms and deposited me on the countertop.

"Where are the condoms?" His gaze darted around the bathroom then landed in the trash bin where a couple of used wrappers had been discarded. "Shit, we used—Paul!" His roar was loud enough to rattle the mirrors.

Forest's body flexed around me, all chiseled muscle and sinuous flesh, as he searched for a condom.

My gorgeous boss, the man I loved, rocked forward with an urge he barely contained. His ice-blue eyes took me in their hungry gaze. Need and want combined into a potent force as he gripped my thighs, torn from rutting between them to finding protection.

"Paul!" His voice deepened.

A throat cleared, followed by a low rasp. "My boy, seems like you have a problem." Snowden's oily eyes swept the room to take the two of us in.

All our heat turned to ice.

Forest stiffened, and he shoved me back, turning with a slow, purposeful movement meant to shield me from Snowden's gaze.

I tugged at my shirt to cover my shoulder, then curled in on myself.

Be small. Don't let him notice you.

But how could he not when he'd walked in to see my legs wrapped around Forest's hips?

Forest took a step forward, placing himself firmly between Snowden and me.

"Should I wait?" Snowden hooked a finger over his shoulder. "Or are you done fucking the girl?"

"I'm done." Forest's reply came out a low growl, and I sensed the tremendous self-control he displayed not leaping for Snowden's throat.

"Doesn't look like it. It seems like the main event hasn't happened yet." Snowden's gaze shifted between us. "You know..." He crossed his arms. "I could wait..."

"That won't be necessary." Forest's low tone came out as a threat.

Snowden took a step forward, glanced at me, then sucker-punched Forest in the gut. Forest took the hit with nothing more than a grunt. Fire blazed in his eyes, but he averted his gaze to stare at the ground.

"Watch your tone." Snowden's eyes narrowed as he looked at me. "I wonder how willing she'll be to spread her legs after she sees how eager you've become to please me. Maybe we should have her accompany us today?"

The muscles of Forest's jaw bunched. He spread his fingers wide, then curled them into fists. He repeated the gesture several times.

"Actually," Paul came up behind Snowden, "I need her this morning." He propped his elbow on the door jamb and fiddled with his hair.

"And how was your evening?" Snowden turned.

Paul flashed a grin. "Pretty fucking awesome. I agree with you… the man is fun to fuck."

"I'm glad you're enjoying your toy," Snowden said with a sneer.

Forest's face turned red, but he didn't say a word. I huddled behind him and tried to breathe without making a sound.

"I think it would teach him a lesson to have her watch." Snowden persisted in his madness.

"Probably." Paul pushed off the doorjamb. He examined his knuckles with bored disinterest then puffed out a breath. "I suppose I could push off my work. I just needed to get it done today."

Snowden looked back at me. I could see the gears churning in his head. Forcing me to be present would fuck with Forest's head, but I sensed Snowden didn't want me there. He looked forward to his mornings with Forest alone.

"I suppose she can go with you. Make sure you look into—" Snowden didn't finish his sentence. His attention shifted to Forest, and he pressed his lips into a tight line.

"That was my plan," Paul said.

"Watch her."

"Always," Paul said.

Snowden turned the weight of his gaze to Forest. "Get your cuffs and collar on and meet me by the door."

Forest pushed off from the counter. All signs of his erection were gone. He twisted to move past Snowden's bulk.

"We're going to have fun today." Snowden grabbed Forest's arm.

Forest said nothing as Snowden released him.

Paul made a show of defiance, blocking Forest. Too much testosterone clotted the air, and I was acutely aware I was propped on the bathroom counter. I slowly slipped off and pressed myself against the wall.

"Be a good girl, Miss Sara," Snowden said.

I gulped and gave a shaky nod.

Forest locked away his emotions and trailed behind Snowden.

Paul and I went to work.

The days blended together, starting exactly the same.

Forest and I would wake, steal a touch, maybe a kiss. Snowden collected Forest and returned him hours later worse for wear. Some days were better than others, but the torture ground Forest down. He came back weak, battered, bruised, and non-communicative.

Forest being Forest, minimized his pain. Then lashed out, taking out his aggression with Paul in what I could only describe as sexual warfare. The two of them battled for dominance with angry, vicious sex. Forest had a lot of anger to work off.

Most days, Paul came out on top of their battles, but there was a time or two when Paul let Forest have his way. Those were usually days when Forest seemed most distant. At night, my compassion put Forest back together again.

I was the tender to Paul's rough.

The soft to his hard.

The kind to his cruelty.

We were two imperfect halves holding Forest together.

With each passing day, the hatred I had for Paul faded. In its place, my admiration grew.

Paul and I spent our days together. I performed tedious clerical work or sat and read a book while he worked. We then returned to our quarters to wait for Forest.

Without fail, Forest headed straight to the shower, saying little as he put whatever happened behind him. I'd learned to give him space and curled up on the couch where I waited.

Paul checked in on Forest's mental state. If Forest was okay, we shared a quick meal. If not, Paul took care of Forest as only he could. Forest would rage in the bathroom as Paul provided the outlet Forest needed.

Their brutal aggression and combative sex was a thing of beauty. Two powerful men, grappling with each other, struggling to take, to claim, to rut. It was insanely hot.

I got kisses, hugs, and cuddles from Forest, but we still hadn't had sex. I sensed Forest's shame in that and didn't push.

How difficult must it be for a man to make love to a woman when he was degraded daily by a monster?

Our evenings generally wound down. Forest held me, and eventually sleep would take him away from it all until morning came.

Rinse and repeat, we did it over again, and again, and again, until I thought I would go mad.

I didn't know how Forest was keeping it together.

Chapter Forty-Two

FOREST

I WAS A PATIENT MAN, BUT THINGS WERE TAKING TOO DAMN LONG.

The code I'd installed on Paul's phone should be integrated into Snowden's operating systems by now, opening up a back door for my team. It should also be on every damn device in the facility.

Mitzy should have Snowden's compound fully mapped and should have access codes to every door.

Should have.

But it was still taking time.

Too much damn time.

I walked a tight line with Snowden. All I had to do was bide my time, but Snowden was grinding me down.

It fucking sucked.

The passwords to his network must still elude Xavier's team. That would be the only reason he hadn't acted.

From day one, I put my plan in motion, knowing it would take weeks before that tiny bit of programming would spread.

Time was my enemy.

I couldn't wait until Snowden realized what he'd done by bringing me inside his enclave. Not that getting captured had been the plan, but it worked to my advantage.

Sara told me about Snowden's growing frustration. That was the only confirmation I had that my plan was in motion.

My job was to endure.

Fucking endure.

Paul's soft snores sounded from the other room. He'd taken up residence on the couch. Sara curled in my arms, tucked up tight against me as she slept.

My sleep came in fits and bursts. My mind refused to turn off, and I obsessed continuously over how my team was doing.

How long had it taken before they received the first coded message?

How long before Mitzy discovered I'd opened a back door into Snowden's security systems?

How long was it going to take Raven and her mad hacker skills to break through the firewall, keeping us from what we needed?

And every day, I prayed Xavier understood that we had to wait. Acting too soon would destroy everything, and our one chance would be lost.

In the meantime, I broke beneath Snowden's brutal blows. My body caved to his twisted desires. I allowed Snowden to believe he was winning our little war. The thing he wanted most was the one thing I withheld, but some days I barely had the strength to hold on. The moment I caved would be the end.

So we played our little game.

"Forest?" Sara rolled over. "What are you doing awake?"

"Just thinking." I swept a strand of hair off her face.

"You should try to sleep."

I knew what she was trying to say. I needed my strength to make it through the day, but I couldn't stop rearranging the chess pieces at play in my head.

One misstep and I would lose everything.

"I know." I kissed her forehead.

The smile on her face was a beacon showing me the way home. All I needed was to avoid the jagged rocks between here and there. She placed her palm on my chest, right over my heart.

"Your heart beats so slowly." She closed her eyes. "It's strong and powerful, like you." Sara let her hand rest over my heart as she counted out the beats.

Her touch awakened sensations that were both foreign yet familiar. Heat pulsed in my groin, and I shifted away. I wanted to take her into my arms and make love to her, but there was never a good time. Not to mention what she must think of me.

The things Snowden did were despicable, depraved things.

They turned my stomach.

I could only imagine the disgust she must feel when she looked at me. I couldn't be the man she needed while letting Snowden do what he did to me, but I did it to keep Sara safe and buy the time we needed before rescue came.

Someday, this would all be a distant memory. Until then, we existed in this limbo state as lovers who couldn't make love.

When someday came, I could only hope she'd allow me to take her as I dreamed about doing every damn night. It wasn't fair that I got to be with Paul when I wanted to be with her as well, but there was never a good time.

I wouldn't touch her with Snowden's taint covering my flesh. He disgusted me.

After I washed the filth off my body, Paul gave me what I needed to forget. Instead of a man who'd been beaten and raped, I could become a man who fucked because I wanted it, rather than... rather than how Snowden made me feel.

I needed that more than Paul would ever know.

Unfortunately, that didn't leave much room for Sara. I hated that because I needed her more than life itself.

Thinking about her sent heat shooting to my groin, where it coiled with potent need. Each beat of my heart sent blood surging to my dick. It swelled with the desire I denied it, wanting to slip inside her body and finally taste what we'd been missing.

My mind fogged over as lust swept through me.

All the reasons I'd been keeping Sara at arm's length faded. It didn't change how she must feel about me, but damn if I didn't care. I needed to be with her...and not just a hug or a kiss.

I acted without really thinking about it, moving more on instinct than thought.

Shifting her to lie beneath me, I ignored her tiny squeak as I crushed my mouth against hers. Need overpowered me.

"Forest…" Her breathy moan sounded like heaven.

The way her arms wrapped around me felt like sin.

Her fingers winding through my hair drove me insane.

Anticipation of what we could be together filled me with a thousand regrets for the horror I'd put her through.

Sara wouldn't be here, if not for me.

Raw desire ricocheted through me and gathered in my groin. I grew dizzy with the need filling me.

Her soft fingers gripped my nape. Her breathy moans repeated my name. The addictiveness of her mouth, her sweet essence, made my taste buds riot as I swept in and devoured every crevice.

Our tongues tangled, frantic with need, and that's when I realized she wasn't pulling away.

"Sara?"

There were tears in her eyes.

"Please don't stop. Don't shut down on me."

"Shut down?" Hell, I was ready to rock and roll. "I don't want to hurt you."

"You won't."

I lifted a little, worried the weight of my body was crushing her, but she placed her hands on my shoulders and pulled me back down.

"I won't break."

How many years had it been?

Decades?

I'd only ever had sex with one woman, and very little of that had been soft. My mind spiraled out of the moment with memories I didn't want.

"Forest…" Sara's soft voice drew me back, or maybe that was the hand she put on my dick. "Stay with me."

"My God, your hand feels fucking incredible."

Sure and confident, she slowly stroked my long length.

"I'm not made of china. It's okay if you need to be a little… rough."

Shit, she'd only ever seen me with Paul. What he and I did together couldn't be called rough. It was borderline brutal.

But that was the point, right?

To take back what Snowden stole, I needed Paul's unrestrained fury and uncompromising dominance. The collision of our bodies, taking and breaking, erased the worst of what Snowden did.

I would not do that with Sara. I wouldn't be rough. We would do this slow and soft.

Gentle, with love.

I would savor our first time, not rush her through it.

"Forest, stop thinking so damn hard and make love to me."

"I may not be able to control…"

"I don't want you to control anything."

Her thumb rubbed at the sensitive bundle of nerves beneath my glans. My hips bucked as I rocked into her palm with a low groan.

"Shit, that feels amazing, but if you don't stop, I'm going to come like a one-pump-and-done virgin."

"No, you won't," she said with a giggle. "I plan on drawing this out."

"At least we're on the same page." I bent down and kissed the soft hollow of her throat. I lifted until I could stare into her eyes. I could lose myself there forever. "Do you want to do this?"

"It's all I think about."

"You don't think less of me because of what he does to me?"

"You're the strongest, most selfless man I know. Snowden doesn't define you. He means nothing." She bit her lower lip and slid her hand down my shaft.

I about lost it.

Gripping her wrist, I pulled her hand off my dick.

"I'm serious. I won't last. I've wanted to do this forever, and I agree on the not rushing part." I glanced at the soft cotton shirt she slept in. "We need to get this off."

I wore nothing.

Clothes were a hindrance when I slept.

I gripped the bottom of her shirt and helped her out of it. She wasn't wearing a bra, and I took no time in claiming one of her breasts.

Sara arched against me as I licked and sucked. The pink skin of her areola puckered as her nipple drew into a tight bud. She gripped my neck, lifting herself to my mouth while I tasted and teased.

The rush of her breaths ran over me, tiny panting gasps, as I moved from one breast to the other. My only goal was to give each nipple equal time in my mouth. I didn't know how I managed to control myself because Sara was a delectable feast.

But I did.

I would take my time working her up.

My thumb hooked on the fabric of her panties.

"These need to come off as well. I need to taste you."

She lifted as I slid her panties over her hips, around the gentle swell of her ass, and down her tight toned legs until her delicate feet kicked free of the scrap of fabric.

Bared for me, all it would take was one well-placed thrust, and I would finally know if she felt as good as I'd always dreamed.

But first…

I kissed the flat expanse of her belly, admiring the swell of her breasts, the narrowing of her waist, the gentle flare of her hips, and the trim little patch over her mound. With great reverence, I pressed my lips there and breathed in her heady scent.

"God, you smell like heaven."

"Forest!" She gave a little screech and clamped her legs together.

"What?" I took another deep inhale. Her sweet scent flooded my nostrils and drove me insane. "You smell divine."

"I'm sure I don't—"

I took another long breath.

"Trust me, angel, you have no idea how crazy you make me. Now spread those legs. I want to taste you."

She cried out as I took one long, languid lick along her slit.

She was so different from a man.

Men were rigid and hard.

She was soft and yielding, the perfect complement to me in every way.

I licked along her petal-soft folds, breathing in her scent. The slow glide of my tongue made her squirm as I slowly teased her toward orgasm. I knew what she wanted, and the sensations that would get her off, but slow and determined was my game plan.

I intended to make this last forever.

As I buried my face between her thighs, she dug her fingers into my scalp and slowly flexed her hips against my face. I pushed my tongue into her slit, fucking her with a gentle tease of what would come.

Her juices covered my mouth and chin as I worked her into a frenzy. To take my full length, she would need to be ready. I still worried I would hurt her when we finally fucked.

She drew a shuttered breath as I heated her up.

"Forest..." Her soft sigh made me smile. She wrapped her legs around my shoulders, opening for me.

Adding my hands into the mix, I moved to her clit, licking and sucking the tiny nub as I slipped a finger into her wet heat. She writhed beneath me, squirming with the sensations I pulled from her body, bringing a smile to my face.

I kept my kisses slow, the licks of my tongue soft, and changed the angle to keep her on edge. All the while, I whispered sweet nothings, soft murmurs of my love for her that wound around my heart and made me feel complete.

Whole.

Undamaged.

Desired.

Using my fingers, I pumped in and out, coating her with her juices in preparation to take me in. Her body bucked beneath me as soft mewling sounds escaped her mouth. I circled my fingers inside of her while turning my attention to her clit.

She arched against me and cried out as she came all over my face. Her climax was a thing of beauty, and I lapped up her juices. The muscles of her walls contracted, wrapping around my fingers like a velvet glove.

"God, I need to be in you." My low growl heated the air.

"Yes! Hurry."

"I love your eagerness."

Her need had me clamping my jaw as I bit back the need to rut and take. This was about giving, but my control was slipping. I pulled back and climbed over her body until we stared at each other. Her hands went to my hips, and she gave a brief nod.

"Please…"

Her plea was heartfelt, and there was no longer any need to wait. Except for one thing. My entire body froze, but then she flashed a foil packet in front of my face.

"I may have been overly hopeful and kept one under my pillow."

"Hopeful?"

"Just make love to me already."

I didn't need encouragement. With a rip and a little adjusting, I sheathed myself then spread her knees apart. She took no time in hooking her ankles over my back.

Reaching between us, I parted her folds, then placed the tip of my cock at her entrance.

"Sara…" I breathed out her name as if it was a prayer. "I've wanted to do this forever."

She arched her back, which pressed her soft folds against the tip. I held back a moan and pushed inside, slowly.

Afraid my size would overwhelm her, or hurt her, I took my time sinking in. Gritting my teeth, I held back the overwhelming urge to come as I sank into heaven.

"Goddammit, you're tight."

"The better to fuck you," she said with a grin.

"You got that right."

I moved slowly, letting her body stretch and adjust to my size. My body fought my control as heat blazed through me. The muscles of my torso strained, my jaw clenched, and my eyes glazed over with the need to move. I tried to rein in my control but knew this was a battle I would eventually lose.

Her body pulsed around me, gripped me, and drove me insane.

Blood pounded in my ears, and incredible sensations rocketed through my body as I buried myself in her wet heat.

I stopped to soak in the moment. Our bodies were finally connected. I didn't think she would be able to take all of me, but her body fit mine like a glove as if we had been made for each other.

My heart filled to the bursting point with the union of body, heart, and soul. God, I loved this woman. I loved her with every fiber of my soul.

She stared up at me, hands on my shoulders, and smiled. Our bodies joined together was the most beautiful thing I'd ever seen.

"You okay?" I asked.

"It feels amazing, Forest. You're amazing."

I didn't know about that. I was barely holding on and hated to admit that I needed a moment. Any movement would send me over the precipice too soon.

One pump and done? Hell, I'd barely held on while simply sliding in.

"I don't know how long I can hold on."

"Then we'll just have to do this again and again." Her impish grin made me laugh.

"Oh, I think we'll be doing a whole lot more of this. Shit, I could live right here."

"Now, that would be awkward in the boardroom."

Our light banter helped cool me off a bit. My release pulled back from the brink, no longer threatening an all-out plunge over the cliff. Not that I wanted to stay that way. I needed to fuck.

"I need to move." Yeah, I'd stepped back from the cliff, but that didn't mean I wasn't a needy fucker.

"Please." She tilted her pelvis and cupped my face. "And don't be gentle. I can take what you need to give."

I didn't think it was possible to love someone more.

Drawing back, my eyes closed with the exquisite pleasure shooting through my body.

Her breathy pants, the sharpness of her breaths, made me cautious, but I didn't let it stop me.

Sara would tell me when it got to be too much. With that

thought in my head, I moved and found, not my rhythm, but rather ours.

Sara's cries of Yes! and More! drove me to quicken my tempo. Our breaths melded together as our bodies drew closer to the brink.

"Forest..." Need filled her breath. "Harder."

My hips bucked as I drove into her. Then I felt it.

Her thighs trembled then clamped around me. Her entire body contracted as I sent her over the cliff with a litany of pleasure induced words I could barely make out. Ripples of her pleasure stroked my cock, sending a current of electricity straight to my balls. I lost it as an explosion of heat ripped through me.

Collapsing on top of her with the aftershocks of my orgasm, I was unwilling to move. I wanted to stay locked like this with her forever, drawing this moment out.

I'd never felt this much at peace. It scared the shit out of me because if I lost her, I would never be the same. The strength of my feelings for Sara were powerful things, scary things; things Snowden could use against me.

A soft knock pulled me from the moment. I glanced up with a frown to see Paul standing in the doorway.

"Sorry to do this, but he's coming."

"It's too early."

Snowden shouldn't be here for another couple of hours.

"I strongly suggest you shower."

"Why?" My eyes narrowed.

"He'll go nuts if he smells her on you."

"So?"

"Don't be a dick. I waited as long as I could, but you need to get up."

"You've been listening the whole time?"

"Kind of hard not to hear that." His lips twisted in a lopsided grin. "Sounded like you were having fun."

"Enjoyed the show?"

"I didn't watch, and I won't." His attention flicked to Sara. "At least not until invited. What the two of you do is between you until she says otherwise. I eagerly look forward to that day if it ever comes." He shifted his attention from me to focus on Sara. The two of them were developing an odd nonverbal communication between them.

I wasn't sure how to feel about that.

He extended a great deal of respect to Sara. I should appreciate it, but the truth was I envied Paul.

I hated that he got to spend all day with my angel when I had only a few stolen moments, and most of those were when I felt my worst.

It wasn't fair.

"Forest," Sara kissed the tip of my shoulder, "Paul's right. You should probably get ready." She propped up on her elbow. "Any reason why he's coming early?"

I was naked. The only things I needed to get ready were the cuffs to bind me and the collar which controlled me.

"I don't know."

"But you're worried?" she asked.

"Yeah." Paul rubbed at the back of his neck. "Seriously, you need to hurry."

Chapter Forty-Three

SARA

Forest wasn't moving, so I pushed him out of bed. Or tried to. When that didn't budge him, I pressed my foot to the small of his back and kicked him out.

"Stop glaring at Paul." I gave a little huff. "Get cleaned up."

My instinct was to say, *Let's get you ready for the day*, but none of our days were things anyone would want to get ready for. By the brooding look on his face, Paul shared my concern.

He had me worried.

Snowden's early arrival had me worried.

Forest's nonchalance about all of it…had me worried.

He slid out of bed then extended a hand to me. "Come on."

"You don't have time for that," Paul said.

"I don't care." Forest's gaze swept past me, full of fire and ice. A deadly presence overcame him.

Every time I thought Snowden had Forest beat, Forest surprised me. He didn't look like a man preparing to be used and degraded. He looked ready to do battle.

Generally, he spent what little time we had in the mornings shielding himself against whatever Snowden might throw at him.

He faced every day with a stoic resignation to endure. I rarely saw this fire in his eyes.

Why was he different today?

Resigned for sure, but a little of the old Forest surfaced. My proud Viking king was stepping out of his shell and standing tall.

That didn't bode well.

If I saw it, Snowden might see it too. That could be very dangerous.

I hastily climbed out of bed and headed to the shower. Paul turned sideways to let me pass, but when Forest tried to come through, Paul blocked him.

"Don't be a fuck-up," Paul warned. "Whatever is going on in your head, get rid of it. This is not the time—"

"Get out of my way." A threat of bodily harm curled through Forest's tone.

This wasn't their usual aggression. That generally turned to brutal, combative sex. This was a get-out-of-my-way-or-I'll-rip-your-fucking-head-off kind of threat.

"I see it in your eyes…" Paul didn't back down. "You finally have sex with her, and now you feel like you have something to prove, but you're only going to fuck things up."

"You don't see shit." Forest's disdain had me biting my lower lip.

Tension curled in the air, heating it up, but without the sexual charge that generally existed between the two men. Forest's irritation, his restlessness, and his anger spewed forth. He closed the distance, making a show of force as he got in Paul's face.

"Your emotions are making a mess." Paul didn't back down. "Get your shit locked down."

Woven within Paul's words lingered the threat of what would happen if Forest didn't do as he said, but caution was there too.

And concern.

Paul was trying to talk Forest down.

But what had changed? Why now? Why was Forest acting like an ass?

Was it what Paul said?

"You don't get to tell me what to do," Forest said.

"You want to go over this now? Because we've decided this between us already."

"Fuck off."

Paul leaned in. The men's faces practically touched. "You don't have time to get in a pissing contest with me. First off, you'll lose. You'll lose because I'll put you in your place because that's what you need. Didn't you hear me? He's coming early."

"I don't give a fuck."

"You do, and you know it. Not sure what bug crawled up your ass, but get your shit in gear."

"My shit is locked down tight."

"Then what's the problem?"

"Maybe I don't like you intruding on us while we're fucking." The harshness of Forest's words had me drawing my shoulders to my ears. We made love for the first time, and he made it sound like all we'd done was fuck.

I backed away, mortified at having the most intimate moment of my life turned into something cheap and meaningless.

"You get fucked by me." Paul shot his finger at me. "You made love to her. Don't ever get the two confused. Now apologize."

"Fuck you."

"Piss off, Forest. That's not what this is about, and you know it. Don't turn it into something it's not. You finally made love to her, and now you're fired up to prove you're still a man. He's going to smell that arrogance on you and feed off of it. He'll turn it against you. I'm telling you to cover that shit up."

"Why do you care?" Forest's flippant tone surprised me nearly as much as it did Paul.

"Because she suffers if you fuck things up." Paul took a step back. "Goddammit, Forest, what the hell has gotten into you? Play the damn game."

"Maybe I'm tired of playing the victim."

"You are the victim. There's no playing," Paul shouted.

"Not that you're doing anything about it. You're part of the problem. When are you going to become a part of the solution? Time to get your head out of your ass and stand up."

"Don't speak to me in that tone."

"Or what? You're going to take me to the basement and beat the shit out of me? Lock me in a cage and fuck me until I choke? Shock me until I shit myself? Sodomize me until I bleed?"

"Not cool, Forest."

"Why? Because it's different between us? Is that what you want to hear?"

"It is different between us." Paul's tone softened. "Don't do this."

"That's the lie I let you believe."

Paul grabbed Forest in the nuts. Forest hissed against the pain and clamped his hand around Paul's wrist.

"You've got three seconds to let the fuck go." Forest's low growl rumbled through the room.

"This is our truth. In three-seconds, you'll be as stiff as a board for me, aroused and ready for anything I want. Things are different between us. He takes without your consent, whereas you give me everything because we make sense together. Don't forget who's on top, because I'm not afraid to remind you."

"Because you care?" Forest hissed as Paul tightened his grip. "Is that what you're trying to say? My fucking Dom cares for me?"

"At least we've finally established you acknowledge me as your Dom. There's no going back now, Forest. You are mine."

"If you're my Dom, then what the hell are you doing here? If I mean anything to you, then get off your sorry ass and help us."

Paul's free hand snapped out and choked Forest. He had Forest by the balls and the throat. Forest stood utterly still.

"Stop fucking me like I'm some goddamn plaything your fucking father gave to you. Help me."

"What the fuck did you say?" Paul's entire body tensed.

"I told you to help me." Forest's face turned beet red, and he practically choked, getting the words out.

Paul really was choking him. I didn't know whether to interfere or not. Getting between the two of them never seemed like a good idea.

"Not that, the other…"

"Oh, you mean about your father?" Forest gave a cocky-assed smirk even I wanted to slap off his face. What had gotten into him? "I love how you worship that monster, believing all his filth and lies when he's the one who's been lying to you your entire life. Did you know he killed your mother?"

Paul's eyes widened, and the tendons on his wrist stood out as he clamped down on Forest's throat. Forest made no move to pry Paul's fingers away.

"That's right. The bastard killed her, then sent you and your sister into foster care where she was brutalized and raped. Tell me, how did Snowden discover you were his mutt? Was it before or after he put you in the rings to fight for your life? Your sister would be so disappointed. It's a good thing she thinks you're dead."

"What the fuck do you know about my sister?"

"That she's better off never knowing what her brother became."

"Piper's dead." Paul ground out the words.

Something shifted in the air.

Something ominous and dark.

"That's the lie he's sold you, but she's very much alive." Forest leaned into the chokehold. "I saved her." His eyes sparked with menace. "Now, let me go."

Paul released Forest and stepped back. He was right about one thing. Forest's erection jutted between them. Even with the anger swirling between them, their sexual chemistry remained a potent force.

Their bond mystified me. It was as profound as it was powerful. I expected them to fuck and work off their aggression right then, but the sound of the door lock disengaging caught my attention.

"Fuck." Paul looked at me. "Quick, get in the shower." He turned back to Forest. "You're a fucking prick. Get on your knees."

As I scooted off to the bathroom, Paul grabbed at the front of his pants, hastily drawing the zipper down.

"On your fucking knees!" Paul's shout had me shutting the door, but I held it open a crack and stared as Snowden entered the room.

Paul positioned himself in front of Forest. His hips jerked like he was getting off, but I knew there was no way he was doing what it looked like he was doing. He released a low groan and fisted Forest's hair as he faked an orgasm. Slowly, he turned around and made a show of pulling up his zipper.

"You got here faster than I thought. I'm done with him."

What the fuck?

Chapter Forty-Four

FOREST

UNLIKE COMPUTERS, WHICH I UNDERSTOOD, PEOPLE CONFUSED THE hell out of me.

Except now.

I had him.

I had Paul.

He stepped across that invisible barrier that kept me separated from others and became someone I called friend.

Whether he knew he'd taken that step, or not, didn't matter. His allegiance had shifted to me.

It was in the tic of his jaw, the flex of his biceps, the urgency of his expression, and the fierce protectiveness he showed, not to me but toward the woman I loved.

It was in the command snapping between us. The absolute assurance I would go to my knees.

No cajoling.

No forcing.

No explaining.

It echoed in the obedience I displayed, falling to my knees without thought.

But that wasn't how I knew.

It was the lie he told his father to protect me.

With Paul's flaccid cock flopping inches from my face, he faked a release for his father's benefit.

Words communicated in the flicker of his expression as he looked down at me. We'd become an us.

Snowden might smell Sara on me, but that wouldn't be what he focused on for the next few hours.

He's all yours. I'm done with him.

That lie bound us together.

Paul looked down on me and communicated silently for me to play along.

I sat back on my knees, feeling as if I'd been hit, not in the gut, but rather shot in the heart.

He protected me from Snowden.

My only question was how solid this connection would be. Could it survive the betrayal racing towards us with all the subtlety of a freight train? When he discovered I'd used him to penetrate Snowden's defenses and gain access to his computers and everything that went with that, would Paul hate me?

Would I come out of this with yet another disappointment to add to the long line of disappointments littering my life? Or was Paul the one I'd been searching for, a man strong enough to silence the noise in my head? Strong enough to stand for those he loved when it mattered most?

We would find out.

Paul moved to one of the couches. He collapsed, acting as if that orgasm had ripped out a piece of his strength. The man was a damn good actor. Even I believed I'd just sucked him off. I wouldn't mind it. The man had a splendid cock.

Unlike his father.

Snowden's lips pressed together as he took me in. "Nice of you to warm him up." His gaze shifted around the room and landed on the door leading into the bathroom. "Where's the girl?"

Paul jerked a thumb over his shoulder. "In the shower."

"Hmmm..." Snowden's slimy lips slid against each other and

made a disgusting smacking sound. "I think we should switch things up today. I'm feeling restless."

Paul leaned his head back and stared at the ceiling. "I'd come, but I've got a ton of work…"

"I have something special in mind." His hard gaze turned to me. "Get your cuffs and collar, boy; it's going to be a long day."

I ground my teeth together but didn't engage. If I looked at Snowden, he wouldn't see a beaten man but rather a man ready for war. I was so damn tired of playing this game.

If Xavier didn't hurry shit up, I was going to choke the life out of Snowden, damn the consequences. But I was supposed to be meek and defeated. It was time to put on my game face.

I got off my knees and put the cuffs and collar on. I was such a fucking good boy for this monster.

When I returned to the living room, I went to my knees, where I waited for further instructions.

Uncharacteristically, Snowden sat on the couch across from Paul. Instead of getting to his feet, he seemed to be in no hurry to begin the daily violation of my body.

One thing to be thankful for was his lack of stamina. In the few hours he spent with me each day, he barely got it up more than once or twice. Most of our time was spent with me lashed in some godawful position while he rained devastation down on my body with his whips, floggers, paddles, and other things.

I was an impulse away from biting off his disgusting dick and snapping his neck. Give me a knife, and I'd cut out his cold, black heart and chop it into a million pieces until nothing remained.

But my revenge would have to wait. I waited for a damn signal from Xavier that the cavalry had arrived.

Days had turned to weeks, and we were now to the point of counting months. I couldn't last much longer, and Sara's safety remained tenuous at best. I hated giving him a second more of my time, but there was nothing I could do. I'd already set events in motion.

Snowden took me in, his appraisal oily and thorough, until I felt covered in filth from his look alone. The man was getting under my skin, making me squirm without needing to touch me at all.

He licked his lips. "We've had some great fun, haven't we?"

The muscles of my jaw bunched. Answering him only led to pain, and not answering led to more pain. Dread balled up in the back of my throat.

Snowden very rarely went off-script. Our mornings together were entirely too predictable, like his eagerness to string me up and start inflicting pain.

What was he waiting for?

"Tell me, boy." His caustic tone sent a shiver down my spine. "Do you like it when he has his dick in you?"

Paul shifted on the couch. "I don't know about like, but I—"

"No one was asking you." Snowden's retort snapped through the air, biting off the rest of whatever Paul had been going to say. "I was asking him."

I shifted back on my heels as Snowden leaned forward. "Do you like it when Paul fucks you?" He shifted his attention to Paul. "Does he get off?"

"Wouldn't be any fun if he didn't."

"At least we agree on that. He's always been a greedy boy, coming at the drop of a hat. I could blow on his cock, and he'd get hard, give it a little squeeze, and he shoots his load all over my hand. I think he likes it. Being forced is your thing, isn't it?" His attention shifted back to me.

Truthfully, he'd hit that right on the head.

I didn't know what he was getting at, but my entire body was on high alert. I could take him if Paul didn't interfere, but I didn't know which direction Paul would jump when it came down to a choice between his father and me.

More time was needed to drive a wedge between them. I'd only just brought up Piper. That betrayal required more time to mature, and I still didn't understand their relationship. Why did Paul work for his father?

"Did you stick your dick in the girl?" His gaze flicked to the bedroom and the disarray of the bed.

"If you're asking if I've fucked her, then yes." I ground out the words. There was no use in denying it. The entire reason Sara was here was to keep me in line.

"Have you?" Snowden turned his soulless gaze on Paul.

"Gross." Paul flinched. "Most definitely not."

"I find that hard to believe. I figured the three of you were forming some kind of love nest in here."

"Hardly," Paul scoffed. "You know how I feel about females."

Snowden snapped his fingers, and I responded like a trained dog coming to sit at his feet. I kept my head down, my gaze lowered in submission. Bile rose in my throat, and I swallowed the acidic burn.

He grabbed at the collar around my neck. "I am your only lover, my boy. Never forget that. All the rest of this is nothing. I give you to him because it pleases me to watch you bend to another's will. I let you fuck the girl because it makes you obedient. And that is what we're going to do today."

My entire body stilled.

Paul drew in a breath.

Silence hung in the air between us as Snowden's heavy breathing pulsed in and out.

"What do you think, Paul? Want some time with him in the dungeon?"

"I wouldn't want to intrude; besides, I have work to do," Paul deflected.

"It'll wait." Snowden gripped my shoulder. "I want to watch the two of you together."

"Someone has to watch the girl, and I have a project I'm working on."

"I'm not aware of any project?" Snowden dug his fingers into my shoulder.

"Just something I've been looking into."

Snowden's eyes narrowed. "I think I've been entirely too soft on you, boy, thinking you were bending to my will, but I smell it on you. It's strong today. Your fury is boiling to the surface. I wonder what it will take for you to explode?"

I made a tactical decision and looked him straight in the eye.

"Our agreement stands. Whatever you want, I won't resist. I am yours."

"Right, our agreement regarding the girl. It's an interesting puzzle, isn't it? You do as I say, and she stays safe, unmolested being the operative word. It's a shame because she's a beautiful woman, a bit more mature than what my clients typically demand, but still a beauty. She'd be worth a fortune on the open market."

"Touch her, and I'll kill you."

Snowden's lips slid into a grin. "Ah, now there is the boy I know, the little fighter. I bet you stay up late at night dreaming about killing me, but that's the problem. I don't trust you."

I didn't trust him either, and everything he was saying made me trust him less and less. The prick had something up his sleeve.

He'd taken me to sleep in his bed a few times, long nights where his sickening snores kept me on edge. He thought to make me his lover, convince me of some twisted bond we shared, but at some point, he stopped. I believed he decided it wasn't worth the risk. When he slept, he was vulnerable.

"We're going to have fun today." Snowden glanced around the room.

"If you touch her…"

"Someday, you're going to defend me with all the spitfire you waste on her. You. Are. Mine. You always have been. That I give you to another—" His gaze shifted to Paul. "Or let you fuck the girl, is only because I have the power to do so, and with power comes the ability to take it all away. Your time with her is at an end."

The urge to rip out Snowden's throat rolled through me. The only thing which stopped me was the creaking of hinges as the bathroom door slowly opened.

"Ah, there she is." Snowden gripped the hair at my nape and gave a sharp yank until my head bent back. "It's time to play a game." He wrapped his other hand around my throat, pinching off my windpipe. "I wonder what she would sacrifice for you?"

I could reach up, yank his hand off my throat. I could push him back on the couch and beat him to a bloody pulp but doing any of those assured Sara's death. It wouldn't come easy. Snowden would make sure she suffered. He'd make me watch as his men raped and tortured her until death took her to an untimely grave.

With black spots dancing in my vision, I knelt before Snowden and took his abuse. Starved for oxygen, I battled my need to breathe. Antagonizing him would only make this worse. Whatever *this* was.

I closed my eyes and allowed my body to go limp. Snowden wasn't strong enough to hold me up. As I anticipated, he released his chokehold and let me go.

"Get dressed," he snapped the command at Sara. "You're coming with us today."

"I have better things to do." Paul tried to sound put off, but Snowden wasn't biting.

"Whatever it is, you can do it later. We're going to have fun downstairs…together."

"Fine, but she takes forever to get dressed," Paul said. "Go ahead, and I'll bring her down in a moment?"

Snowden got to his feet. "Don't keep me waiting."

Gasping to recover my breath, the only thought going through my head was how I would kill Snowden.

Xavier had a day at most to come through. If he waited any longer, there would be no stopping the fury I would unleash, and I didn't care how many innocent lives would be lost as a result.

Chapter Forty-Five

SARA

A SHIVER RIPPLED DOWN MY SPINE AS SNOWDEN LED FOREST OFF. Something stirred in the air, an odd vibration that signaled danger. The moment the door shut, I turned to Paul.

"What the hell is happening?"

"I'm not sure." He gestured toward the bedroom. "We don't want to keep him waiting."

"Why?" I rushed to the bedroom, calling out over my shoulder. "Why now?"

"I don't know."

"Is Forest in danger?"

"I think so."

"What are we going to do?"

"We're going to the dungeon."

"And do what?"

I couldn't believe Paul would do nothing, not with Forest's safety at stake. While I didn't understand the whole Dom/sub thing they had going on between them, the growing affection between them couldn't be denied. I'd hazard to guess things had progressed beyond simple sex.

"You have to do something," I said.

"Like what?" His tone sounded defeated, but I wouldn't accept that.

"What would make him change things like this? Is he angry? Jealous?" Snowden had a lot to be jealous of, but it had nothing to do with me.

"I don't know." Paul snapped at me.

The only reason I hurried was out of fear for Forest. I raced through getting dressed, pulling on a light cotton blouse and one of the tight skirts Snowden provided. I didn't care if any of it matched.

I returned to the living room to see Paul on the couch. He rubbed at his neck, a gesture I was getting to know all too well. It was one of the few things which signaled his unease.

"Well?" I stood in front of him, ready for whatever. Although what I could do against a madman remained to be seen.

"Tell me about Piper?"

Talk about a shift in conversation.

"I thought we had to leave."

"We've got a minute or two."

"What do you want to know?"

"Is she happy?"

"I think so. She's a sought-after physical therapist and married a really great guy."

"She's married?"

"Yeah."

"Kids?"

"I don't think so."

He rubbed at his face, sweeping his hand down from his eyes to his jaw.

"I've missed so much. He lied to me."

I sat beside him, not precisely touching, but close. "What are you doing here, Paul?"

"What do you mean?"

"With Snowden. You know what kind of man he is. Why are you with him?"

"Where else would I go?"

"Anywhere but here. You're nothing like him."

"Are you so sure?"

"I don't know. You don't seem cruel."

"You don't know me. You don't know what I had to do to survive, and you've seen me with Forest. I've killed. Kids, boys like myself, I killed them. It was them or me, and I didn't think twice about making sure I made it out alive. I like hurting people. I get off on it. That makes me a monster as much as him."

I'd forgotten what Forest had said, that Paul had been taken and put into the fight rings. It was what Snowden had planned for Forest.

"You were a kid faced with an impossible choice. What happened to you is unforgivable, but you can be forgiven. As for Forest, that's different. It's not cruelty. That's kink. The same thing that pulls at Forest pulls at you. There's nothing wrong with it if it's something you both want."

I'd been traumatized the first time I watched them together, but I'd also seen the give and take.

The beauty of it.

"If you say so," he said with a mumble.

"You don't seem convinced."

"Let's just say, I know no other life but this."

"Why do you think he didn't tell you about Piper?"

"You mean, why did he lie to me my entire life?"

"I suppose."

"I guess he didn't want me to leave him and try to find her." He shrugged. "Who the hell knows?"

"Is that why you stayed?"

"I stayed because I had nowhere else to go and if I did…"

"If you did?"

"You don't want to know how I got here."

He'd been stolen, like so many other young boys, and forced to make an impossible choice.

Fight or die.

I could see how Snowden had turned an impressionable young boy, especially when that boy had nothing to live for. If he thought his sister was dead, why would he ever leave? But how did

Snowden find out the boy who was victorious and lived was his son?

"I don't know what to expect when we get there, except he'll probably want me to join in." His lips twisted as if he tasted something sour. "It won't be like what you've seen. To maintain appearances, I'll have to—"

I placed a hand on his arm. "I understand."

"He wants you to watch, which means he intends to hurt Forest. He'll be looking for some kind of reaction from you. Give him nothing and let him focus on Forest. Forest is strong enough to survive."

"I understand."

"Good."

With that, he activated the door lock and led me outside. I knew the path to his and Snowden's offices by heart. I'd counted every step.

Foolishly, I thought I'd somehow memorize the maze of corridors that made up this godforsaken place and use that to escape. After all this time, I still had no idea where an exit might be.

I followed half a step behind Paul as he took me down hallways, stairs, and through twists and turns until we wound up at the door I remembered from our very first day.

The dungeon.

Two men stood guard outside. I didn't remember that from before, but this was only my second time down here.

Paul glanced at me, his expression devoid of emotion. He turned his attention to the two men, and his lips firmed into a thin line. His eyes pinched as he activated the lock. The door swung inward.

Nerves twisted at my stomach, making me feel like I was going to puke.

Tied to a massive X in the middle of the room, Forest huffed in pain. His back was littered in red welts, and a sheen of sweat covered his body. The crack of a whip sounded.

Forest grunted.

Snowden looked up. "Ah, you've arrived."

Paul led me down a short flight of stairs and held out his hand to help me down the last two steps. The door behind us swung shut, but not before the two guards from outside joined us. Paul's attention cut to the guards then turned back to his father.

"I have." Paul's use of pronoun was not lost on me.

I didn't exist.

My role was to remain invisible, something I'd perfected over the past few weeks. Although it was nearly impossible to disappear when I was the only woman in a dungeon surrounded by four men. I placed a hand over my belly to quiet the sudden unease which came over me.

"Bring her over here."

Paul kept his hand in mine and led me around the perimeter of the room. My heels clicked against a non-forgiving concrete floor. We passed several cages. One was tall enough for a man to stand inside, but little else. Another was low to the ground. Rings and straps dangled from the bars leaving little left to the imagination. I pictured Forest forced into that cage, his neck secured to one end while his...

I squeezed my eyes shut.

Madness lived in this room.

The far wall was lined with implements, things to strike, and hit, and inflict pain. Snowden had several items removed from the wall. They had been placed on a table that sat beside him. From the marks on Forest's body, most had already been put to use.

This was what Forest endured every day?

There were other contraptions littered around the room, benches, chairs, and things I couldn't make sense of, but they all screamed pain.

Paul pushed me to the back of the room, placing himself between Snowden and me. It was unclear if Forest knew we had arrived. His eyes were shut tight with pain. He huffed through that last strike and sagged in his bonds.

"Forest and I were just having a conversation." Snowden lifted his hand over his head. The crack of the whip shot through the air, making me jump. Forest's body jerked beneath the blow, and his breath rushed out of him.

The door to the dungeon opened, and two more men walked inside. The original two headed toward us while the other two fanned out.

"Miss Sara…" Snowden turned his hard eyes toward me. His lips curled into a sneer. "Do you remember the deal I have with your boyfriend?"

My stomach fluttered with the fear coursing through me. I twisted my fingers together and looked at Paul.

"Do not look to him." Snowden spat. "He is not going to save you."

Paul held up a hand. His eyes were on the men moving around the room. The door opened, and another four men entered.

"What's going on?"

"As I said, Forest and I were having a chat. It seems he's been a naughty boy." His arm drew back. The whip shot forward faster than I could blink. Forest's body shuddered. A low grunt spilled from him. "Now, answer the question, Miss Sara."

My gaze darted from Forest to Snowden. I didn't dare look at Paul. The men were closing in, moving toward Paul and me.

There were eight of them, and the room suddenly felt ten times smaller.

"He said he'd do whatever you wanted, and I…and I wouldn't be touched."

"Not exactly." Snowden's grin turned feral. "He agreed to obey."

I wasn't going to argue semantics with a madman.

"And he's done exactly that." Paul asserted. "What's going on?"

"Interesting that you should ask." Snowden gave a jerk of his head. The men closest to Paul jumped him while the others rushed forward.

I pressed myself flat against the wall while they beat Paul to the ground. He knocked out two of the men, but he was outmanned. Forced to his knees, they knocked him unconscious.

A man grabbed at my arm, and I screamed as he dragged me to

the tall, narrow cage. I kicked and screamed, terror swirling through me as he shoved me inside the cage.

Snowden walked over, hands behind his back, moving as if he had all the time in the world. His eyes glittered like black obsidian, a deadly visage that made me cringe.

I drew back, but there was nowhere to run. I could barely move.

Snowden drew close, his grin wide, feral, and victorious.

"Your boyfriend did not keep up his part of the bargain."

Behind him, his men attached cuffs to Paul's wrists and ankles. They put a collar around his neck, then drew chains down from the ceiling.

Paul groaned as he came to. He struggled to his knees, then stopped when he noticed the rattle of the chains. His head titled up.

"What the fuck is going on?" Menacing eyes threatened death as they took in Snowden.

"I'd like you to tell me."

"I have no fucking clue what you're talking about. Release me."

"Oh, I'd love to do that, but you see, I have a bit of a dilemma." Snowden turned back to me. His oily smile spread across a compassionless face. "You want to know a secret?"

Chapter Forty-Six

SARA

I DIDN'T WANT TO KNOW ANY OF SNOWDEN'S SECRETS.

His fetid breath blew into my face, and I nearly gagged.

"Did you know Paul is my son?" He sneered at Paul. "My own blood has betrayed me."

I wasn't supposed to know Paul was his son and tried to look surprised. It was difficult with the fear racing through my veins.

Snowden didn't seem to notice. A glassy look overtook him as he stared at Paul, who struggled to his feet. One of the guards sucker-punched him, sending him to the floor again with a grunt.

"That's right. He's my boy. Born without my knowledge, hidden for years, then returned to me through a twist of fate." He walked to Paul, leaving me to struggle to make sense of what could have brought this on. "I knew you were mine because of your tenacity, your killer instincts, and your will to survive no matter the cost. A brilliant, brilliant boy, I was so proud of you. It's a shame you've become such a disappointment and over something that rightfully belongs to me."

"Release me." Paul struggled to his knees, weaving back and forth as blood dripped down his temple. His lip was split, and a cut over his cheek swelled. He spat out blood, aiming it for the guard's foot who'd punched him.

"Oh, I will." Snowden continued his slow circuit around Paul. "But first, I need to know the truth."

"I don't know what you're talking about," Paul ground out the words.

"Well, that's what we're going to find out."

Forest shifted. His entire body moved as if he were in great pain.

"Your piece of shit son knows nothing." Forest's low rumble rolled across the room.

"So you keep saying, but we have a leak in our ship. A traitor in our ranks. A rat eating the cheese. Imagine my surprise when it traced back to my son." Snowden kicked Paul in the ribs. "My fucking son!"

"He did nothing." Forest's voice might be deep, but it sounded weaker than I'd ever heard it.

Defeated.

"I've seen how the two of you look at each other. Honestly, it's disgusting."

"You gave him to me to continue your work and break him. You told me to keep him under duress, never letting up. What did you think would happen?" Paul's shout had me holding back a gasp.

"You were supposed to tear him down," Snowden said.

"I did." Paul's gaze cut to Forest.

"You did far worse. You broke our rule. You care for him."

"I beat him and fuck him. That's no different from what you do down here, but that's it. I don't give a shit what happens to him outside of that."

I expected Forest to react. The bond he and Paul developed ran deep. It couldn't possibly all have been a lie.

"Ah, but it's worlds different when you give him access to your phone. Or did you let her send the message? Did you let Little Miss Innocent notify her people?"

"No." Paul stood his ground and faced down his father. "I did not."

"Then explain how a message from your phone made it to Xavier?"

"I did it." Forest wavered in and out of consciousness.

Snowden clapped his hands. "See, now we're getting to the truth. What did you do, my boy? How did you turn my son?"

"I didn't turn your fucking son. He can rot in hell with you for all I care."

Snowden backhanded Forest, snapping his head to the side.

I held back a yelp.

"Tell me, what did you do?"

His men moved around the room, closing in on me in my cage. Paul's sharp gaze took them in, but he could do nothing with chains wrapped around wrists and ankles.

"Release me," Paul demanded. "I'll get to the bottom of it. I'll beat it out of him."

"I would like to see that. I want to know what he's done." Snowden shouted in Forest's ear. "Tell me everything and the girl lives."

"Don't touch the girl." Forest's words came out a strangled cry.

"Oh, I'm going to touch her. You broke our agreement. She's going to get touched by a whole lot of people."

"Don't…"

Snowden grabbed Forest's hair and yanked his head back. "Or what? What will you do? What can you do? You don't understand your position. I. Own. You."

"I'll do anything," Forest begged.

"This isn't a negotiation, my boy. It's a punishment and a lesson, something you'd better learn because next time, I won't show mercy on the girl."

"What did he do?" Paul swayed on his feet, and the chains over his head rattled.

"I told you, Forest got a message out. Our boy is quite ingenious. My only question is, how? I've pieced together one or two things, and it all begins with you."

"Me?"

"Yeah, you."

Paul tracked the progress of Snowden's men as they gathered around me. Lopsided grins filled their faces. They saw only one thing in me.

"For the last time, I've done nothing. I took him while you rested, babysat his fucking girl while you had your fun with him, I've done everything you asked and more. I haven't betrayed you. Can't you see this is his doing? Driving a wedge between father and son?" Paul's gaze cut to Forest, and his expression filled with disgust. "I'll prove it." He jerked the chains.

Snowden paused, a look of confusion rippled across his face as he considered Paul's words.

My expression echoed Snowden's because I thought Paul was on our side.

"I'll beat the truth out of him, and leave the girl for me. I have an idea about her."

Snowden rubbed his shoulder, and for a moment, I didn't see a monster, but rather an old man. He looked tired.

"Is this true?" Snowden walked to Paul. He stopped in front of him.

"When have I ever let you down?"

Snowden's voice softened, and adoration spilled forth. "You really didn't do it, did you?"

"That's what I've been trying to tell you. We'll get to the bottom of this together, and we'll make him pay."

Snowden snapped his fingers and pointed to the chains. Four of his men went to work, releasing Paul.

"Tell me what happened." Paul rubbed where the cuffs had chaffed his skin.

Snowden told Paul how he'd discovered a breach in their security, a cyberattack on the mainframe. It wasn't clear if he'd stopped it.

"It's Forest's men for sure." Paul turned his attention to Forest. "Why did you think I was involved?"

Snowden's shoulder's hunched. "How else could it have happened? Either he did it, or the girl did it, and the only access they have to anything is through you. You have to understand...I thought."

"I'd never betray you." He turned to me. "No way the girl did it. She didn't have access, and there isn't anything in their quarters he could have hacked." Paul cupped his chin. His arm dropped, and he pressed his hands into the small of his back. His fingers slipped down into his back pocket, where he slowly pulled out his cellphone.

"I know how he did it. We have to move." His eyes widened.

"What do you mean?"

"You were right. It was my phone, but I didn't do it. The only thing he had access to was my phone. I never let him have it, but somehow he got to it."

"How?" Snowden released a hacking cough that tumbled through the dungeon.

"I don't know."

Paul knew exactly how Forest had done it. He'd given his phone to Forest to fix when it started acting up, but for some reason, Paul didn't mention that.

I cocked my head. What the hell was happening?

"Remember when mine started acting up? He must have done something to my phone, and remember how we had to replace everything?"

"Sneaky bastard." Snowden paced around Forest, his eye squinting as if he were calculating how best to hurt Forest.

Paul grabbed the whip out of Snowden's hand and struck Forest without warning and without mercy. He rained blow after blow until Forest screamed.

"That's how you get him to talk." Paul came up behind Forest and whispered in his ear. It was too low for me to hear, even Snowden strained, stretching his neck out and cocking his ear toward them.

Paul made a fist and punched Forest in the kidneys until Forest's legs buckled, and he collapsed.

Turning to his father, Paul gestured around the room. "We need to leave. Spread the word, pack what you can, burn the rest, we're getting out of here."

None of the men moved. Their eyes locked not on Paul, but rather Snowden, who chewed at his lower lip, considering his options.

After a long pause, Snowden pressed his lips together. "Go. Notify the others. We leave by the end of the day."

The men moved, exiting the room. Paul put the whip back on the table and turned to follow the men.

"You stay."

"Don't you want me to oversee…"

"No, I want you to help me teach Forest a lesson. It's time he paid the price for disobedience." Snowden walked toward me.

My back was already pressed against the bars. There was nowhere to run. He pulled on the lock, releasing it, then opened the cage. His hand darted in, gripping my wrist, and he yanked me out. He then dragged me in front of Forest and thrust me to the ground.

"It's time to touch the girl." He turned to Paul. "You're going to fuck her while he watches and make it hurt."

"You want me to fuck her?"

"That's what I said." His eyes narrowed dangerously.

"Fine." Paul made it sound as if it was the most disgusting thing he'd ever do. "Let me tighten Forest's restraints. He's going to go ballistic."

"Fine." Snowden retreated with a wheeze and collapsed into the only chair in the room. "Your girl will pay, my boy. She's going to fucking pay."

I huddled on the floor as Paul went to Forest for a second time. He worked on one cuff then moved to the other.

"I'm going to fucking kill you." Forest jerked in the restraints. The threat meant little with him tied up. I hated seeing Forest powerless, but what could he do? Paul had failed us.

Paul came at me, and something shifted inside my head. We weren't getting out of this alive.

Chapter Forty-Seven

SARA

"YOU DON'T WANT TO DO THIS." DESPITE MY RESIGNATION, I couldn't help but try to reach Paul. "Please, don't do this."

Snowden gave a deep sigh, but a fit of coughing overtook him. Paul glanced over his shoulder and gave Forest one last look.

Paul's shoulders bunched, and his legs flexed.

He sprang forward.

Not toward me.

Paul went for Snowden.

He tackled his father, tipping the chair backward.

Snowden shouted, but Paul covered his mouth.

"The door!" Paul shouted at me. "Lock the goddamn door before the guards return."

It took a moment before everything registered.

Forest had a hand free.

He had a hand free?

Sure enough, the left cuff dangled over his head.

Had Paul…?

"The door, Sara! Lock the damn door," Forest said.

I scrambled to my feet, moving more on autopilot than anything else.

Snowden struggled beneath Paul, fighting Paul's hold.

I raced the few feet to the stairs, then launched up them.

There was a locking bar on the inside of the door. Why anyone would put that there made no sense, but I threw the lever. The bar slid into place, and I turned my attention to the room.

Forest had both hands free and worked to rid himself of the cuffs at his feet.

Paul straddled his father. His hands gripped Snowden's throat, who kicked and flailed beneath him.

"My sister!" Rage filled Paul's face. "What the fuck did you do to my sister?"

"Your sister?" Snowden croaked. "You choose him over me? Your blood?"

"You told me she was dead. I chose you because I thought she was dead. You lied to me."

Snowden grabbed at Paul's fingers, trying to release the chokehold grip.

Forest came up behind him. "Paul…"

Snowden's face was beet red, progressing to a darker shade of purple.

"Paul!" Forest grabbed at the back of Paul's neck and pulled. Despite everything done to him, Forest remained strong as an ox.

Paul refused to release his grip, and as Forest lifted Paul, Snowden's body followed. His face turned nearly black, and his eyes looked like they were about to pop right out of his head.

"Help me get him to the cage."

The two of them manhandled Snowden across the floor. The door thumped behind me, and I jumped. Snowden's men had returned.

"What are the two of you going to do? Keep me locked in a cage?" He sucked in air and clutched at his throat. "You're locked in here with me, and they will break through."

"Doubtful. You were an idiot to install an interior bolt."

"Only an idiot would install one without a catch release on the other side. You have minutes at best before they break-in. Enjoy the last minutes of your life."

"Shut the fuck up." Forest gestured to me. "Get away from the door, Sara."

I didn't need encouragement. If Snowden's men had a way in, I didn't want to be in their way. I raced down the short flight of stairs and ran into Forest's arms. Sweat soaked, worked hard, he stank of pain and fear, but I didn't care. I hugged Forest with everything I had and prayed he absorbed some of my strength.

"What now?" Paul glanced around the room. "There is only one way out."

"This turned into a shitshow fast." Forest glanced around the room. "Pick your weapon of choice?"

Paul bent for the whip, then went to the wall of pain, where he grabbed what looked like a pair of bully sticks. He tossed one to Forest.

"What the fuck, Forest? You tapped my phone?"

"I didn't tap it. I installed code on it."

Snowden barked a harsh laugh. "Wait, you're telling me you didn't know?"

Forest growled. "I told you he didn't know."

"But what is this? He's fighting by your side. How did you turn him? Did you suck his dick better than mine? I know my son; he's not taken by a pretty face."

"Shut the fuck up," Paul spat.

"Ah, this is about your brat sister, isn't it? You're mad because of that?"

"You took her from me." Fury darkened Paul's face.

"I took nothing. He's the one who took her." Snowden pointed at Forest.

"I saved her from her rapist," Forest said with a growl. "Your goons picked Paul up the day I rescued Piper. I had intended to free them both."

"Is that true? Did your men try to take her?" Paul went to the cage and poked Snowden in the ribs with the bully stick. "Were you going to turn her into a slave?"

Snowden shrugged. "Probably, but in my defense, I didn't know you were my kids at the time."

The banging against the door grew louder.

I retreated to the far corner of the room, but then looked at all the things hanging on the wall. I wasn't going to go down without a fight.

"Sara…" Forest took my hand in his. "We'll protect you. You don't have to…"

I jerked out of his grip and grabbed a long metal rod. "I'm not going to just stand here. What are we going to do? There's no way out of here, and the two of you can't hold back that many."

"We'll figure it out. Please, just stay as far from the door as possible. I need to focus."

I glanced at Paul and his arsenal. The man had things dangling from his belt, chains in his hands, and a lethal expression plastered to his face. He meant to go to war or die trying to protect me.

I lowered my voice so only Forest could hear. "What did he say to you?"

"Paul?"

"Yes, when he whispered in your ear."

"He said, Trust me."

"That's it?"

Forest gave a sharp shake of his head.

"How did you know you could?"

"I just did. Now go. I need to focus." He shoved me toward the corner and went to stand by Paul.

I had to pass the cage Snowden was locked inside.

He sneered when I passed. "Once I get out of here, I'm going to fuck you myself, and then I'm going to let each of my men fuck you until you bleed. It's going to be an ugly death, a long, painful death, and I'm going to make him watch."

"You're a monster." I angled away from him and huddled in the corner.

The banging on the door intensified, and I realized they were probably banging on the pins holding the hinges in place. It's what Paul had done the first night of our captivity when he removed the doors.

How much time did we have?

Paul and Forest stood side by side, my two warriors preparing to do whatever it took to protect me. I loved seeing them standing together. Any doubts I had about Paul vanished, and I saw him in a different light. No longer working against us, he had become a part of us.

All my attention focused on the door, the banging, and the little shake it gave when it started to shift.

Tension coiled in Forest and Paul as they put their backs to me to face the threat head-on.

I was laser-focused on them and missed the movement in my peripheral vision.

Snowden launched at me.

The door to the cage stood open.

A feral grin spread across his face as he took me down.

Forest moved.

He raced across the room as Snowden snapped a collar around my throat. He tightened it down.

I grabbed at the leather, unable to breathe, as Snowden lifted a knife over his head.

Forest barreled into him, grabbing at the knife, as the door gave a final shudder. The pins were free, and men wrestled with the heavy door trying to shift it far enough to the side to get in.

Paul whipped the chains at them, breaking fingers, sparing a glance over his shoulder to see what was going on.

Forest and Snowden wrestled while my vision dimmed. I struggled to find the clasp on the collar, but there was no buckle.

No catch.

No release.

Nothing.

It was impossible to breathe.

Paul defended the door, smashing fingers, hands, arms, and legs as the men on the other side struggled to form an opening.

Snowden's knife clattered to the floor. He fell back with a whoosh as Forest pinned him to the floor. Forest glanced at me with wide, terrified eyes, then something in him snapped.

He punched Snowden in the face.

Snowden's head twisted to the side.

Forest punched him again.

A spray of red arced through the air.

Spots danced in my vision as I sipped air. It wasn't enough. I would lose consciousness soon.

Men broke through the door.

Paul went down beneath a tangle of limbs. Others rushed at Forest.

And then I heard it.

The most annoying ringtone on the planet, "The Flight of the Valkyries," blared from Paul's phone. The tune picked up in stereo, ringing from Snowden's pocket.

And then there were more.

The annoying ringtone played on the phone of every man in the room. The sudden confusion gave Forest the time he needed to pick up Snowden's knife.

Forest's lips turned up in a grin. "Looks like the cavalry is here."

Snowden lay on the ground, beaten and barely breathing. Forest rushed to me, but a man jumped him. They went down. My vision grayed out.

And somewhere across the room, a shot fired.

Then another.

Chapter Forty-Eight

FOREST

GOD, I LOVED "THE FLIGHT OF THE VALKYRIES."

It rang on every phone and was precisely the signal I'd been waiting for.

The cavalry was here.

Paul was down.

I'd taken Snowden out.

Bullets were flying.

The guy who jumped me dropped with a bullet in his brain. His dead eyes stared at nothing. The rest of Snowden's men fell as Xavier's men took them out with double-taps to head and heart.

I crawled to Sara. The bastard put a locking collar around her throat and cinched it down. It was choking her to death.

I fumbled for the catch, but I couldn't release it without a key.

"Fuck!"

Hopefully, Paul was smart enough to surrender.

Xavier's men had a shoot to kill order in play.

I needed to get this damn collar off Sara before it killed her.

"Sara?" I shook her, but her entire body had gone limp. Please don't let it be too late.

I had Snowden's pathetic knife. It was suitable for piercing, not cutting through leather, but it was all I had. I went to work, head down, with adrenaline spiking through my body.

"Forest."

I heard a voice.

"Forest!"

I turned to see the grim features of Ben Chambers staring back at me.

"Is she…"

I gave a sharp shake of my head. "Not yet, but if I can't get this off…"

Decked out in full tactical gear, Ben knelt by my side. He aimed his gun into the room, protecting me. Smart as a whip, he handed me a serrated blade, something infinitely better than the flesh slicer I held.

"Try this."

The leather was tight against her throat. I was afraid I'd cut her trying to get the leather off, but if I didn't try, she was going to die. I bent to the task at hand.

"There's a man…" I huffed. "Auburn hair…tall, like me, somewhere by the door. Don't kill him."

Ben shifted to Snowden. He flipped Snowden to his front and zipped his hands behind his back, then trotted off to the front of the room. I couldn't spare a glance but said a silent prayer for both Paul and Sara.

It had been far too long since she'd moved. Her lips were blue.

Furiously sawing through the thick leather, I balanced the knife's edge between too much pressure, which could slice her neck and too little, which wouldn't cut through fast enough.

Ben returned, towing a man behind him. I looked up to see Paul worse for wear, but alive. He had a split lip, and his left eye looked questionable. It had swollen shut. He had a limp that hadn't been there before and held his arm awkwardly against his chest.

Ben squatted beside me. "Give me that. You're making a hack job of it." Ben cut through the leather in three clean swipes of his knife. The collar fell away, but Sara didn't move.

"Is she breathing?" I asked.

Ben put his ear to her chest and gave a shake of his head.

Before I could move, Paul went to his knees beside her head. He pinched her nose, tilted her head back, opened her mouth, and pressed his lips against hers. He forced a breath into her mouth.

Ben nodded. "Her chest moved. Do it again."

"Does she have a pulse?" I rocked back on my heels, never feeling as powerless as I did at that moment. If I lost Sara...

Paul breathed for her again.

Ben pressed his fingers to her neck. "It's slow but steady. Keep breathing."

Snowden moved behind me. He coughed up blood and rolled to his side. "I hope she dies, fucker."

I launched at him, full of fury, knife up, and slashing for his throat. It didn't matter if he was more valuable to us alive than dead; the fucker was going down.

"Whoa!" Ben grabbed my wrist moments before I dealt the killing blow.

"Let go," I said with a growl.

"Think about this. You can't take this back. You do this, and you're a killer."

It was what Skye had tried to save me from, the sacrifice she made so I would live.

"I. Don't. Fucking. Care."

Sara jerked behind me and coughed out a breath. "Forest..." Her hand sought blindly and found Paul's.

He looked at me. "You're not a killer. Get over here. She needs you." The command in his voice had me moving before I realized what I was doing.

Ben shuffled back while Paul pried the knife from my hand.

Sara's eyes blinked.

Once.

Twice.

She focused on my face, and a smile brightened her eyes.

"What happened?"

Answers would come later. I fell back on my ass and pulled her into my lap. I rocked her against my chest and didn't mind the tears which flowed down my cheeks.

"We're free," I said.

"What?"

"The cavalry came."

Her brows pinched together. "Did I hear the Valkyries?"

I couldn't help but laugh. "Yeah, pretty fucking awesome."

I turned at a gurgling sound. Paul stood over his father. Blood spray arced across his chest. Snowden twitched on the floor by his feet.

"What did you do?" I glanced at Snowden.

He clutched at a gash across his throat. His mouth opened and closed like a guppy, but no sound came out.

Paul threw down the knife. "He doesn't deserve to rot in prison, and unlike you, I've killed before."

I struggled to process what just happened.

"All clear." A voice shouted from the door.

"That's our signal." Ben climbed to his feet. He extended a hand to Sara. "Name's Ben Chambers. You may not remember me."

"I remember you." Sara brushed the hair off her face. "You were in Manilla."

"I was." He glanced down with a frown. "It wasn't supposed to go down like that. Are you okay? In need of medical attention?"

"I'm good. Thank you. I've got two overly protective men looking out for me." She glanced over where Paul stood, a soft smile on her face, then her gaze tilted down. "Is he…"

"Yeah. He's dead." It didn't feel real. After a lifetime of going after a monster, I expected to feel joy that he'd been taken out. Instead, a profound weariness overcame me.

I was tired.

I needed a shower.

A change of clothes.

A breath of fresh air.

It had been weeks since I'd seen the sun.

Sara stared at Paul.

He glanced back, and time seemed to stand still. Something was exchanged between the two of them in that look. An understanding? The first glimmers of affection? My heart hoped for so much because I knew we could be great together.

Once we were done mopping up this shit, I hoped we'd be okay.

As for Paul? I needed to get to him. I needed to get him alone where we could work through this in a way that made sense to us both.

He had a lot of shit to deal with, and I would be right by his side.

"Paul, you killed him?" Sara's whisper was tragic.

She pushed off my lap, and half ran, half stumbled to Paul. His eyes widened as she threw her arms around him and hugged him tightly. "Are you okay?" She looked up at him, eyes glistening with tears. "I could kiss you."

His eyes flicked to mine, and a smile ghosted across his face. "I may have already kind of kissed you."

"What?"

"It was just mouth to mouth, but you have an excellent mouth."

"You're kidding, right?" She turned to Ben and me. "He's kidding?"

Ben shook his head. "He laid it on you. I'm a witness to it."

"Forest?"

"Are you complaining?" I asked.

She pressed her fingers to her lips, then glanced at Snowden's body. "Whose blood is on my lips?"

Paul pulled her hand away from her mouth. "Mine. It won't kill you, and next time I kiss you, I promise not to do it with a bloody lip."

"Next time?"

"Yeah," he gave a little shrug. "Next time."

Her eyes widened. When she turned to me, she mouthed, *Next time?* It was all I could do not to laugh.

Ben ignored our little exchange and went on and on about how guilty he felt about leaving us behind. How his team had secured the facility. I cut him off.

"Enough. No more about leaving me behind. I'm the one who told you to leave. My call. My responsibility. I don't want to hear another word about it. All that matters is that you're here, and I must say your timing was impeccable."

Sara took Ben's massive hands in hers. "It's true. You had to follow orders, and it looks like you're a hero."

Ben had given a quick debrief on the helicopter crash during his constant talking.

As I suspected, it went down in the water. His hero status came from saving Zach when the kid got separated from Skye after they hit the water. Skye had a life vest on, as well as the rest of the crew. Zach did not. Ben and his team were SEALs. It wasn't possible for them to die in something as mundane as a helicopter going down over water.

"Don't know about that." Ben tucked his chin and looked away.

"You saved little Zach."

"Now that was a clusterfuck. Um, pardon my language."

"You're kidding, right?" She hooked a thumb toward me. "You do know who I work for? Forest has the mouth of a sailor. Fuck is pretty much every other word he says."

"That's not true," I said, mumbling.

"Is too." Sara released Ben and propped her tiny fists on her hips.

Ben rubbed his hand over the top of his bald head. "I guess things turned out in the end."

"Sure did." Sara's eyes brightened. "Nobody thought things would go down the way they did, but we also didn't expect Forest to tear down the entire organization from the inside."

"You should've seen Xavier lose his shit when Mitzy figured it out." Ben gestured to his team. "I'd like you to meet the rest of my men. This is Chad, don't let him charm you with his baby blues. Bay is a bit of a trickster. And Mel...we call him grumpy."

"It's nice to meet you." Chad, with his baby blues, swept my Sara into a hug.

"Never thought anyone would tame the Nordic beast. I'm so happy you're safe." Bay swung her in a circle. "Looks like he's sweet on you, too. Can't wait to hear the stories."

Mel said nothing, but he cracked a smile and planted a kiss on her cheek.

"There will be no stories." I wasn't going to share anything remotely personal with Xavier's men. Sara was mine, and the story of how we came together belonged to us. Besides, we were wasting time with all the hugging. Chad, Bay, and Mel moved on to Paul, doing the chest bump, back thump thing.

Sara laughed at Bay's comment. "Nordic beast? Now that's a new one."

"Oh, we've got plenty more." Bay gave her a wink.

"You think we could stop all the chatter and get the *fuck* out of here?" I made sure to emphasize the expletive and looked Sara right in the eye when I said it. She gave me an exaggerated eye-roll, but a smile brightened her face.

I would never get tired of that. I put that smile there.

And I had a lifetime to do it again, and again, and again.

"Helicopter is waiting." Ben notified us our ride was ready.

Xavier had men streaming into the compound, securing shit before Snowden's men could destroy anything important.

My skin itched, and my nerves buzzed. Snowden may be dead, but I wouldn't be able to get rid of his oily touch until I put this place far behind me.

I'd love to torch the place, but there were too many records that needed to be hauled out. I expected we would fill a lot of holes with the information there. The names of every slave sold by Snowden and the men they'd gone to were in those records. Our task would be to find them, free them, and put their masters behind bars.

I went to Paul. He'd kept his distance after everything went down.

"You ready to get out of here?" I placed my hand on his shoulder.

"I should stay and help out." He refused to look at me.

There would be some utility in leaving him behind. Paul knew which files were the most important, but we didn't need him to stay. I had more than enough people to do that job.

"We'd rather have you with us." Hopefully, Sara wouldn't mind me speaking for her.

"We?" His gaze darted between Sara and me. "I figured you'd leave now that..." His Adam's apple bobbed.

I locked my arm around his neck and pulled until our foreheads touched. "Fuck that. I need you. We need you." I said a silent prayer that Sara would say something.

"Nothing is holding you to me. No threats. No nothing."

"Nothing but a promise. I'm a switch at heart, but for you, it's different. I'd like to explore more of that...without the threats."

"Are you good with that?" His question wasn't for me, but rather Sara.

"Two halves of a coin." Sara's soft voice drifted between us. She lifted my hand, then took Paul's and pressed our palms together. Her hands looked tiny holding ours together. "We're only half of what he can be without us both. And I agree, even if I don't understand all of it, Forest needs you. He needs a man who can take him to that place in his head where the noise disappears."

Paul shifted his gaze. "Are you sure about this?"

She gave a little shrug. "A few weeks ago, I would have said, *hell no*, but there's something binding us together, a chemistry between you and him, between him and me, and even between the three of us. We make sense together."

"You said We." The corner of Paul's mouth lifted in a smirk.

"Don't let it get to your head." She gave a soft laugh, some secret joke between the two of them I didn't understand.

Paul put his arm around me, then his other around Sara. He pulled us together into a somewhat awkward hug. Sara and I leaned in until we were all connected.

"I want to be a part of whatever this is, but not at the expense of what the two of you have."

"You think there's not enough of Forest to go around?" Sara gave a little snicker. "I think we'll manage."

"I suppose we will." Paul released us and took a step back.

We stood over the body of Paul's father, a father he'd killed. I gestured to Ben to clear the room. He stood guard at the door with his men, which left me alone with Sara and Paul.

I placed my hand on Paul's chest. "Are you okay?" I glanced down at the body.

Sara covered her mouth. My poor, sweet angel had seen far too much. I wish I could rewind time and put her back in my office, an ivory tower where nothing bad could ever touch her. Although, if I did that, I wouldn't have her standing by my side now.

Paul blew out a breath. "I wasted my entire adult life feeling like I owed him for pulling me out of the fights. He demanded obedience, and I was young enough to believe everything he said. I gave him my loyalty, my obedience, and never asked the questions I should have. You know what would've happened if he made it to a courtroom."

"You didn't need to kill him. I would have."

"But you're not a killer. You're a fighter, a tough-as-shit bastard who's impossible to take down, but I've seen your soul. You wouldn't have come back from that."

"He's right, Forest," Sara said. "It would've destroyed you. As big and blustery as you are, you're a gentle and kind soul. You save people. You rescue them. You don't kill them. You're a savior, not a murderer."

"That's funny," I said.

"How so?" she asked.

"You sound like my sister."

"Really?"

"What does that mean?" Paul asked.

"It's a long story." I swallowed against a lump in my throat. I was getting choked up.

"You're getting mushy on us." Paul leaned in and pressed his lips to mine.

It was a slow and gentle kiss, a promise made between lovers for a lifetime of more. My entire body trembled, as did his. When he released me, he glanced at the door. "Your men are getting antsy. How about we blow this joint?"

"I'd rather blow you."

He grinned. "Let's blow this joint first, then we'll see about the other."

"Is that a promise?"

"Always." His lips pressed together, and he glanced down one last time at his father. "I have no regrets about killing him. I thought I should feel something, but I don't. I only have one question."

"What's that?" I asked.

"When can I see Piper?"

Sara reached for his hand. "I can't even begin to imagine how you're feeling right now, but we can arrange for her to meet us at Xavier's estate, or you can wait until we get to Insanity. It's going to be a shock for you both. I'd suggest waiting. She'll need time, and you need time as well. Tread gently with her. She doesn't know who her father was."

"What's Insanity?" Paul looked at me.

"Not what," I said, "but where. Insanity is our home."

Our home.

I liked the sound of that.

The idea of the three of us living as one made me ache in the most profound way. I needed them both in my life.

"Ours?" Paul's eyes snapped to mine, and a flood of emotions filled his face.

"Ours," I said with conviction. It was the only way. "We'll figure out living accommodations later, but there's plenty of room for you both."

I wanted to build a big-assed bed for the three of us, but that might be too much to ask of Sara. I could always add a suite of rooms for Paul beside mine. My mind churned with ideas.

"Both?" Sara gripped my chin and forced me from thoughts about what else I would build.

Paul and I needed a dungeon.

"Yeah." I shrugged.

"Are you leaping before you look?" She gave me one of her looks.

"What the fuck does that mean?"

"I have my own place."

"So?"

"He says it like I'm a sure thing." She exchanged a look with Paul, who snorted.

"What the fuck are you talking about? Where else would the three of us live?"

Paul huffed another laugh.

"What's so funny?"

"A bit presumptuous, don't you think?" Sara asked.

"Presumptuous? What's presumptuous about it?" What the hell was wrong with her? It was the only logical solution.

"Usually, you ask a girl to move in with you after you've dated a bit," she explained. "The key word there being ask. We've technically had zero dates, and you forgot about asking…so…"

"So, I don't give a fuck. No need to ask when you're obviously moving in with me. End of story. Paul will stay in one of the guest rooms until I build a suite adjoining ours."

"What if I don't want to live with a bunch of rockers?" Sara continued. "Insanity is…well, it's a bit insane."

"It's home."

"Right, it's a group home full of rock stars." She propped her hands on her hips and looked at Paul. "It's this massive compound Forest built to keep his rock idols close. They're like his pets. He's infatuated with them."

"I'm not infatuated."

"In addition to everything else he does," she continued, "he manages their band. They have individual suites and live in this massive communal home."

"What's wrong with that? Your apartment is too small for the three of us, besides my view is to die for, and…"

Paul gripped my chin and crushed his lips against mine. Strong and determined, he silenced the rest of what I had to say with a sweep of his tongue. Dark, masculine, intoxicating, my toes curled, and my dick twitched. Ending the kiss far too soon, he pulled away with a grin.

I was definitely building a dungeon.

"She's busting your chops. Insanity sounds amazing, but I agree. Typically, you ask before you assume someone is moving in with you. As for me, I'm officially homeless, so I gladly accept. You need the supervision, but Sara is right. You should woo her a bit, take her on a couple of dates, and ask real polite for her to move in with us." He gave her a wink.

Us.

"I'm not taking her on dates." My sullen reply was met with a firm grip at my nape. Paul drew me close, eyes sparking with dominance.

"You want to discuss that in private?" The heat in his eyes told me exactly what kind of discussion that would be.

Big-assed dungeon.

And completely soundproofed.

Maybe instead of an adjoining suite, I could build a whole new building for the three of us, give us a little privacy.

"Stop that," I said.

"Stop what?" His eyes twinkled with amusement.

I reached down and adjusted myself. "You're making me hard."

"From the kiss or…"

"Does it matter?"

"Not really, but good to know." He glanced around.

"You guys gonna stand around and talk all day?" Ben shouted from the door, watching our interaction.

"Three dates?" I tugged Sara to my side.

"Sounds reasonable," she said. "You need a lot of help in the romance department."

"Until you say yes to living with me, I'm staying at your place. I hope you have a couch big enough for Paul."

"It's a small couch."

"Then I'd better hurry up and convince you. Insanity is your new home."

"I'm thinking a night at the opera for date number one."

"The opera!" I covered my ears. "No opera. You might as well drive spikes into my ears."

She laughed. "Okay, how about a concert?"

"Sounds perfect. Angel Fire should be playing someplace." If they were still on tour, I had no doubt Ash canceled everything when his wife and son had been fished out of the South China Sea.

"Of course, they are." She slowly shook her head. "What was I thinking?"

"You didn't mean them?"

"There are other bands."

"Not good ones."

Ben made a show of tapping his foot and rolling his eyes.

I took Sara's hand in mine. "Let's blow this joint."

"With pleasure."

We walked out of there together, Paul, Sara, and I holding hands.

Chapter Forty-Nine

FOREST

A HELICOPTER TOOK US TO A JET WHERE WE ALL BASICALLY PASSED out for the sixteen-hour flight. Or rather, I passed out. It would take days to recover from what Snowden had done to me.

When I woke, Sara and Paul sat together at the front of the plane. They had their heads together and looked at me when I shifted to a more comfortable position.

Paul wandered back to where I sat.

"How are you doing?" he asked.

"I'm exhausted."

"You've been through a lot."

"Looks like you and Sara are chilling."

"Yeah, she's pretty remarkable." He leaned closer. "You know what?"

"You want to fuck me in the lavatory and join the mile-high club?"

"Is sex all you think about?"

"About ninety-nine percent of the time."

"It's a wonder you get anything done."

"I'm good at what I do. But if you want to do the mile-high thing…my dick is ready."

He laughed. "Your dick is always ready."

"Well, I was asleep, and I had a dream about you, so it's technically not my fault. Are you complaining?"

"Not in the slightest."

"What did you want to say?"

His gaze flicked toward the front of the plane to where Sara watched us.

"You're worried about Sara? Don't be. She's a tough cookie."

"Not exactly worried…"

"Then what?"

"A little confused. Excited maybe?"

"Why?" I sat up straighter.

"It didn't totally suck giving her mouth to mouth."

My heart skipped a beat. "Say that again."

Hope rose within me, and possibilities churned in my head.

"It wasn't disgusting, and I haven't been able to stop thinking about it."

"As in not so totally disgusting that you wouldn't mind doing it again?"

"I'm not against it."

"It? As in kissing her again, or as in more?"

He shoved me. "I'm not answering that, and if you breathe a word of that to her, I'll whip your ass until you can't walk for a week. Plus, I'll take that very eager dick of yours and put it in a cage." He shoved his finger in my chest. "That's not a threat, but a promise."

"I like it when you're bossy. My balls just drew up, and I'm super hard now." I lowered my voice.

"Get up." He punched my shoulder.

"Why?"

"Because I'm hard now too."

"Ah…" I rubbed my palms together. "I'm at your service."

"I like it when you're needy." We headed to the back of the plane and ignored the snickers from Xavier's men.

After getting my brains fucked out at thirty-thousand feet, I crashed back in my seat, laying it out flat where I fell into a dreamless sleep. Sometime later, Sara gently nudged me awake.

"We're here, Forest." Her angelic voice filled my heart to bursting.

Indeed, the sounds of the plane's engines had wound down. I'd been so out of it that I slept through the landing.

The doors cracked open and thick, humid air spilled into the plane. Xavier's men gathered their gear and filed out. We had nothing to collect. I ducked my head to keep from hitting the bulkhead and shuffled out behind Sara. Paul carried up the rear.

Bright blue skies and a gentle breeze greeted us. The familiar scents of salt, sea, and tropical flowers floated on the air. I shielded my eyes against the sun and breathed the smell of freedom deep into my lungs.

A small group of people waited for us on the tarmac. My eyes latched onto one person out of them all, and I couldn't help but smile.

"Forest!" Skye ran, dodging between Xavier's men in her rush to get to me.

I barely made it down the stairs before she launched into my arms. I held her tight as she buried her head against my chest, then my entire body went still.

I felt nothing but joy.

No revulsion.

No disgust.

No wretched PTSD tickling at the edges of my mind.

She started to pull away, but I hugged her tighter.

"I missed you, my summer sky."

"I missed you, Beanpole."

"You tried to die on me." I released my grip to hold her at arm's length. "How's Zach?"

She pointed behind her, where Ash held the tiny infant. Ash walked toward us, his eyes on the arm I wrapped around his wife, my foster sister, who was my everything.

"Sara!" Skye wriggled out of my hug and launched at Sara. "Oh my God, I was so worried."

"I thought you were dead." Sara wiped at her tears as they hugged. "I thought Zach…"

"The highlights…we crashed, but everybody got out, and other than getting a little cold, Zach did just fine."

"I'm so sorry…"

"Stop. We don't focus on regrets, or what we might have done differently, or what horrible people did to us. We're survivors who win by living our best lives. I'm just so happy you're safe."

"You're happy? *I'm* happy. I thought you were dead."

"Well, I'm hard to kill. Now let's get you inside and out of those horrible clothes."

When Skye passed me, I grabbed her hand and pulled her tight against me again. Ash drew close, a weird expression on his face. I didn't care. This was the first time I'd hugged Skye in over a decade without feeling repulsed by it and grotesquely turned on.

It was a moment I wanted to last forever.

"Zach!" Sara gave a little yell and held her hands out.

Ash deposited his son in Sara's arms, then gave a little jerk of his chin to me in greeting. He knew I hated the man hug and back thumping gig.

I surprised the hell out of him when I hugged him and thumped on his back. Sara would be proud of me, but she had her face buried in baby kisses and missed it.

"It's really good to see you." Emotion overwhelmed me. I had expected Skye would be waiting for me but was thrilled to see Ash.

I didn't have very many friends and considered Ash to be one of the very few who got me.

"Shouldn't you be on tour?" I asked. "What kind of a public relations shit storm have you left me?"

"Well, considering my wife and son were shot down, I'd say you owe me a little public relations smoothing. But don't worry. We only had to cancel one show. It's going to cost you, but it's not a disaster." Ash's eyes narrowed when he saw my fingers threaded through Sara's. "Looks like we have a lot to talk about, loverboy." He thumped me on the chest. "It's good to see you, bro."

Loverboy?

I laughed at that. I deserved it and didn't mind it at all. For once, I was the one madly in love. I would own that title and embrace everything it meant.

"It's good to be seen," I replied.

He shifted his attention to Sara. "Now, here is a pretty face I don't get to see often enough. Your boss likes to keep you to himself. Hug me." Ash spread his arms out wide, waiting for Sara to come to him.

"It's good to see you, Ash."

When his arms wrapped around her, I held back a possessive growl. It was Ash, but still. I didn't like her in another man's arms. If those were Paul's arms, it would be different. I had no issues with him touching her.

Skye glanced at me then back to Sara. A ghost of a smile curled her lips, but she said nothing.

Ash finally released Sara then looked at Paul. "And who is this?"

"That," I said with a little more possessiveness than intended, "is Paul, Piper's brother."

"Her brother?" Skye gasped.

Ash's eyes widened.

"Yeah." Paul rubbed at the back of his neck.

"Well shit, she thinks you're dead. I guess you're not." He thrust out his hand. "It's nice to meet you. We had a shit of a day looking for your damn pen."

"What?" Paul looked confused.

"Long story." Ash huffed a laugh, then turned to me and held out his phone. "I estimate you have about one second to send Piper a text telling her you found him. Take any longer than that, and she'll kill you."

I took the phone and drafted a text.

Piper responded immediately. You found him?
Me: Yup.

The phone rang.

"Hey."

"Omg, Forest, put him on." Her screech had me yanking the phone away from my ear. I held it out to Paul. "It's for you."

He looked at the phone like it was going to bite him and took a step back. I put it on mute.

"Look, Piper is a bit much, but I don't think she's going to bite your head off." I thrust it out to him.

"I don't know what to say." He continued to stare at the phone.

"Start with hello," Sara took the phone from me and walked it over to Paul. "That's usually a good place to begin."

Paul took the phone. "Hello."

Sara placed her hand on his arm, tenderness showing in her expression. I stared at them with hope. If they could forge a relationship between them, there might be hope for what I wanted. It wouldn't be something I pushed. They'd have to find their way to each other without me, but when they did, I would tie us all together.

Skye came up behind me. "What's the story with those two?"

"What do you mean?"

"Well, I can't tell which one you're staring at."

"I'm staring at them both."

"Both?" Her eyebrows lifted.

"Yeah." I draped my arm over her shoulder, loving how good it felt to hold her in my arms.

"Well, it's about time," she said.

"What do you mean?"

"Sara's been in love with you forever. I like her, but both?" She didn't look like she believed me.

I never dated women, and I'd only ever fucked men.

Now it looked like I was not only going to date a woman, but Sara was moving in with me. I was still fucking men, well one man.

Everyone around me seemed to be settling down. I never thought I'd be one of them. Now, I had two people I loved.

Maybe I should take Sara to Vegas, or better yet, Niagara Falls? Tie her to me forever with a ring around her finger like Ash did with Skye.

I nodded, liking the idea.

This whole three-date thing? Sara was being a pain in the ass about it. She did it to make a point, which was one of the many things I loved about her. She never took any of my shit.

As for Paul? Beyond the sex, there was no question I accepted him as my Dom, but I really liked the guy. I didn't know what he had planned after everything that happened, but I hoped he decided to stick around.

I couldn't imagine a life without him in it, sitting down at the beach with Sara, bouncing our kids on our knees as Sara spread the food out on a picnic blanket. Hell, we could have three kids or more.

Our kids?

Ours with Sara.

It made perfect sense.

My heart squeezed with the emotions spilling through me. I never imagined I'd have a future with anyone, and now I was thinking about kids?

"Hey, Beanpole. Are you okay?" She squeezed me as I watched Sara with Paul.

"Yeah." I looked down at Skye.

"What's going through that head of yours?"

"You may be my summer sky, but they are the light in my darkness. I'm going to marry them."

"Them?"

"Well, Sara to make it official. Paul and I have another arrangement to sort out."

"And Sara's okay with that?" She looked at me, quizzically. "Are you his Dom or something?"

"He's mine," I said that with pride.

"I see. I'm happy for you, Beanpole." She gripped my hand in hers and looked down at our interlocking fingers. "It feels good to hold your hand."

"It feels even better to hold you."

"It's really over, isn't it?"

"Yeah, it is." I tugged her to my side and kissed the crown of her head.

Sara returned Zach to Ash and glanced around the airfield,

looking like she was interested in her new surroundings, but she was giving Skye and me some space.

Paul spoke to his sister for the first time in over a decade. Sara went to him and hooked an arm around his waist. He reciprocated, and she leaned against him. I loved seeing them standing side by side. In them, I saw my future.

It was time to put the past behind me.

I wasn't a victim.

I was a survivor.

There was strength in that.

Frankly, I was ready to let it go. What Snowden did to me—had done to me—no longer mattered. I'd survived when it mattered most.

Skye no longer had to worry about me.

I found Sara, and I found Paul.

I beat Snowden at his game.

I had won.

Several cars drove up, and Xavier jumped out of the lead vehicle.

Mitzy and Raven spilled out behind him. I braced for Mitzy's leap into my arms and caught her as she flung herself at me.

"Forest! You're alive. Oh my God, you are brilliant. When I started getting pings, and then I realized it was you…" A rush of words escaped her as she recapped how she discovered my signal then used it to map out Snowden's operation.

Xavier shook his head at Mitzy's antics.

"It's good to see you," Xavier said.

"Likewise."

"We've got a lot to talk about, but first, how about we get everyone out of the heat?"

It sounded like a good plan. I made introductions all around, getting various reactions when I introduced Sara and then Paul.

I wanted to keep the three of us together, needing Paul's steadying influence by my side, but there wasn't room to put all of us in one car, not with Mitzy and Raven stealing seats.

I didn't worry about it too much. Ben took control of Paul,

who appeared oblivious to his surroundings. He kept his head down, fingers clutching the phone, as he talked nonstop with his sister.

I didn't see tears. Paul was too strong to cry in front of others, but I sensed he was overwhelmed. For that reason alone, I gave him space.

Xavier debriefed me on the ride to his estate.

There wasn't a single piece of Snowden's operation still in existence.

It was all finally gone.

Which meant I would be busy.

We had thousands of rescues who needed our help. The foundation Skye and I built would be bursting at the seams, and that was a good thing. We had years of experience working with victims of human trafficking and sexual abuse.

Life wouldn't be easy for our new rescues, but we could only make things better. Those with no family would find one with us. Those who had families waiting for them would be reunited. They would all receive the counseling and skills they needed to rebuild their lives.

All because of a few lines of code I'd inserted on Paul's phone.

Xavier leaned forward. "As much as I hate to say it, we got far more than we ever imagined because he took you. Everything is coming down."

"Agreed."

"Are you okay?"

"Once everyone stops asking me, I will be."

"Understood. If you need to stand under my whip, the offer is open."

A fierce dominant and expert Master, Xavier knew how to meet the needs of the men under his care. He understood me, and what it was going to take to put all the broken pieces together again. There had once been a time when I'd felt his pull, but I only wanted one man standing over me.

"Thanks, but I've got someone."

"Paul?" He gave a nod of approval. "Extreme circumstances

build unique bonds. Interesting choice, but I'm happy if it works out for you."

I took Sara's hand in mine, needing her connection. "Extreme circumstances also have a way of showing you what's been under your nose all along."

"Can I second that?" Sara cupped my cheek and pressed her dainty lips against my lips.

I was definitely putting a ring on Sara's finger.

Xavier's astute gaze took in the way I held Sara's hand, but he made no mention of it and continued. "Ben and his contacts in the FBI will handle what we're handing over."

"Not all of them will make it to jail." I wanted all the fuckers to get their due; jail, or otherwise.

"No, but they'll all see justice." Xavier made it a promise, and I had no doubt he would follow through on it.

I leaned back and took in a deep breath. "Everything is finally over."

Xavier put his hand on my shoulder. "I think what you meant to say is that everything is finally beginning."

I lifted Sara's hand to my lips and kissed the backs of her knuckles.

I had to agree with Xavier.

I couldn't wait to begin my new life.

Chapter Fifty

PAUL

Six Months Later

As the sun dipped below the horizon, I watched for the elusive green flash. Legend said if a person saw the flash, they would never go wrong in matters of the heart.

I contemplated whether that might be true for a man like me.

Was I taking the right step?

"Aren't you heading down?" My sister, Piper, flounced over to where I looked down on the private beach beneath the cliffs. She was a tiny thing, a perpetual bundle of energy, full of the biggest smiles and the best hugs. I pulled her to me, draping my arm over her shoulder as I stared out at the horizon.

"Nah." I kissed the crown of her head. "I'm gonna stay here."

"You sure? Everyone is down there." She glanced at me, her eyes full of supposition and questions she wanted to ask, but wouldn't. "You should come. You keep to yourself too much."

I didn't keep to myself.

Forest was with me nearly every second of every day. If we

weren't fucking, fighting, or fucking some more, he dragged me to the office, showing me off to anyone who cared to listen, and some who didn't. Where Forest went, Sara was always near. The three of us were inseparable, which meant I was never alone. I should go down there, get to know the band better, but I had the two people who meant the most to me in the world. That was enough for me.

There was a lot of work to do after tearing apart my father's business. I was still dealing with a lot of emotional shit. Forest kept me busy, which helped.

He was my boss now, which was funny considering how our roles reversed when we weren't at work.

"You think too much," she said. "If you need to talk…"

"I'll talk to Forest." I didn't want to share that shit with my sister.

She was concerned and insisted on mothering me, not believing I was okay with killing our father, but I was done talking about him. He twisted the affections of a young boy who found himself in a living hell. He made me believe he had saved me when the truth was far different. The horrible things I'd done for him, in my mind, had been justified. Now, I had to face the consequences of my actions. The bastard had been a sick fuck, and it would be years before I worked through all my issues.

I had no problems putting the bastard down. Piper thought I should.

I didn't.

The past held no interest for me, not with Forest beside me. He promised a bright future, and I wanted to become the man I saw when I looked in his eyes. My redemption came in the forgiveness Forest gave me and in the love he smothered me in day in and day out.

I didn't need to make friends. I had Forest, and I had Sara.

Angel Fire was gathered down on the beach for a cookout. It was rare for everyone to be home, so they made a point to hang out and reconnect, which turned into a big ordeal, leaving me slightly overwhelmed. Forest and Sara were down there, snuggling with each other, as I waited for my mystical sign.

It had been six months since Forest brought Sara and me to the insane home he shared with what I could only describe as the most unique family. The palatial estate, aptly named *Insanity*, had been built by Forest as a recording studio for the rock band he managed. It was later adopted as a permanent home by the band. Ash, Bash, Spike, Noodles, Bent, and Forest now called it home.

The band family was growing. Ash and Skye were working on kid number two. Bash had his woman and a teenage daughter who, as I understood things, had moved in recently. Spike and Noodles remained unattached bachelors. Then there was my sister, my wonderful, glorious, ever perky sister who I thought I'd lost so many years ago.

"Well," she said, "I have to get down there. Bent's waiting for me, and you know what happens when I'm late."

"Yeah," I snorted. "But you like it when he smacks your ass." I gave her an affectionate squeeze.

I didn't think it would be long before the two of them started popping out kids. In an odd twist, my sister turned out to be quite the kinky little submissive. We were alike in so many ways.

"It's pretty neat about Forest and Sara, isn't it?" She looked up at me, eyes searching to make sure I was okay with their recent engagement.

"It's fucking fantastic."

My excitement wasn't faked. I'd gone with Forest to buy Sara's engagement ring, helped him pick it out, and planned the whole proposal. Hell, I'd been the camera guy with a goofy-assed grin snapping ten-thousand photos as Forest bent his knee and stammered out nearly unintelligible words.

"And you're not worried?" she asked.

"Why would I be?"

"I just want you to be happy."

"I am." I was insanely happy with how my life was turning out.

I had a man I loved who was deeply submissive to me. We fucked like we were fighting; brutal, aggressive, bordering on insane, but it was also beautiful and perfectly right. I had a lovely woman I called my friend, who loved Forest with the same passionate intensity as I did. Sara and I got along well. We complimented each other, joined by our love of Forest. He was the glue that held us together.

My affection for Sara confused me because it felt a lot like what I felt for Forest. She was a part of me, just like Forest was a part of me. I couldn't imagine a life without her in it, and I didn't know how to process those emotions.

I didn't understand how my body reacted around her and wrote it off to some strange extension of my feelings for Forest. I'd never been with a woman before. I thought that was just how I was built but damned if my cock didn't twitch when I watched her and Forest make love. They were glorious together, and I couldn't get enough of watching their bodies slide together in their passionate coupling.

We still got looks from the others. Our unlikely threesome confused everyone.

Not that I cared.

I couldn't be happier for Forest and Sara. Forest was a genius, but in many ways, remained a concrete thinker. Tying Sara to him with a ring mattered to him, and I had plans for the wedding.

"Don't worry about me, Sis. I'm the happiest I've ever been." Or would be if I went through with tonight. I turned my attention back to the setting sun. It was almost ready to disappear beneath the horizon.

"Sister's prerogative."

"What's that?"

"It's my job to worry about you." She lifted on tiptoe and kissed me on the cheek.

"Don't."

Forest had just completed construction on a separate residence adjoining the main complex, and we were moving into it tonight. I'd already moved my things into the second bedroom. We were starting a new chapter together.

When Forest mentioned he was building a separate house for the three of us and planned on constructing a dungeon for the two of us, I stepped in and took over. The bastard was the most troublesome submissive, but that's what I loved most about him. As far as the dungeon was concerned, tonight would be the first time he saw it.

"You shouldn't stare at the sun," my sister said, chastising me.

"You need to get your ass on that gondola and get down to the beach, or Bent will paddle it cherry red."

She winked at me. "Why do you think I'm still talking to you?"

"Are all submissives this bratty?" I gave her a shove toward the gondola. "Don't think I won't tell Bent what you said."

Piper stuck her tongue out at me, but she climbed inside the gondola and gave me the finger as it slowly moved along the rails, headed to the beach below.

I turned my attention back to what was left of the sun. Only a sliver remained, and while I shouldn't stare at it, I kept my eyes on it.

A burst of green less than a second long blinked at me.

The green flash.

I pulled my phone from my pocket and texted Sara.

Me: It's time.

Three dots danced on my screen, then her reply popped up.

Sara: I'm so excited. Do you think he'll say yes?

I hoped.

Me: Just get your ass up here.

I didn't add '*Or, I'll swat your ass,*' but damned if I didn't think it. My cock gave a little jerk with images of putting Sara over my knee. She wasn't into kink, but I couldn't help but hope. It was simply the way I was born. Thoughts of dominating Sara and Forest kept me up most of the night and starred prominently in many fantasies.

As I had been Forest's wingman, getting Sara's engagement ring, she had been mine, helping me set everything up for tonight.

Most times, she left Forest and me alone. Brutal barely came close to describing how Forest and I fucked. The man had a lot of aggression to work through. Fortunately, we were evenly matched, and if I didn't beat Forest on the mat, I took him down a notch beneath my whip, putting him exactly where he needed to be. Sara didn't get the sadomasochism Forest and I embraced but was coming around to our D/s dynamic.

Not that she never watched.

Like me, she was a voyeur. The girl had a little bit of kink in her. I loved watching her and Forest fuck, and she loved watching me fuck Forest. It was my hope to bring all of that together, melding all of our needs into one.

We were a perfectly twisted threesome.

The gondola made its way down to the beach. My sister climbed out, and Forest and Sara piled in. Tamping down my excitement, I put on my game face. The moment Forest saw the look in my eye, there would be no question as to how the rest of this evening would progress.

The motor cranking the gondola up the cliff face groaned as I suppressed a groan of my own. Just thinking about having Forest under my command made me instantly hard. I wasn't going to get very far with a raging erection. Fortunately, as the Dom, I could do something about that.

I waited for them at the platform. When the car drew into view, I caught Forest looking for me. When our eyes met, his face broke into a huge grin. I gave a slow shake of my head, letting him know I had assumed my role. His eyes widened, and he glanced back down behind him.

I knew what he was thinking. We were discreet as a rule, mindful that our dynamic belonged to us alone. We didn't subject the others to our kink, not that we hid it, but we were careful to respect those around us. With everyone on the beach, and far out of earshot, it was time for the kid gloves to come off.

Tonight would be brutal. I intended to test the limits of Forest's submission. If he passed my test, the rest would follow.

When the gondola arrived, Sara stepped out first. She knew what I planned and took a step to the side. My gaze locked with Forest's. His Adam's apple bobbed. He swallowed and bent his head in deference to the power I held over him.

I closed the distance, grabbing his throat as I slammed into him and claimed my kiss as I intended to subjugate him. Forest staggered back, overwhelmed, but then he pushed against me, leaning into the grip I held on his throat as if challenging my authority. This was our dance, and I happily obliged him. My fingers around his throat squeezed, and I reached for his balls with my other hand. He hissed against the pain as I squeezed.

I waited for the moment the switch flipped in his head. When he went from challenging me to submitting, when the tension in his body melted away and he surrendered to me, I didn't hold back.

I ripped at his clothes. Shredding his shirt, I bared his muscular chest and twisted a nipple until his low throaty groan edged with pain. My dick was so hard it practically punched a hole in my jeans. I worked my belt free and lowered my zipper. If I wasn't so damn hard, I might have put my belt to better use, but I needed him now.

I moved Forest by the throat, pushing him away from me, then forced him to his knees. My grip shifted to his hair, and I yanked him forward until he swallowed my dick. Then I fucked his mouth, taking what I needed without mercy. I came aggressively, shouting his name.

When I pulled out, Forest's arousal tented the fabric of his pants. It was going to be a long, uncomfortable night for him because I didn't intend on giving him release until the very end. He could be a greedy fucker and often manipulated me into letting him come when I intended to withhold his release. The man loved to challenge me and forced me to reassert my position as his Dom every day.

"Come." I tucked myself back in my pants and found a use for that belt.

I wrapped it around Forest's neck, cinched the buckle, and jerked him to his feet. I'd never put a collar on him before. His eyes widened, and he hesitated, but I didn't give him room to think. That was my job. I freed this Titan of a man from the incessant thoughts in his head by overpowering him.

With a jerk of the free end, I headed to our new home. Forest followed behind me. Sara trailed behind us, watching closely, but giving us the space we needed for our dynamic to flourish.

Someday, I hoped to eliminate that tiny separation.

When we got to the door of the dungeon, I removed the makeshift collar. A proud man, he allowed me to put it around his throat because of the dynamic we shared, but that wasn't what I wanted from him.

We traded power in the moments we stole from the world, times when we descended to our most base desires, but in the past six months, it had become clear to me how much I admired Forest. He had a heart big enough to hold the world and was driven to save so many lives.

He'd saved mine.

A questioning expression crossed his face as I removed the belt from his neck. I let it drop to the floor and addressed him. I wanted to establish ground rules. I needed him to understand what I wanted was far more than what we would share inside that room, but I waited for his reaction.

"You ready?"

"Fuck yeah." His voice took on that low gravelly rumble I loved. It was a bit hoarse and needy. He was turned on, ready to fuck, and hell if I couldn't wait to do just that.

But first...

I opened the door and gestured him inside.

Sara gripped my arm as she entered behind Forest, a show of support. Her eyes were glassy and her expression hopeful.

Forest took three steps before he saw the rope circle I had placed in the far corner of the room. In the center, a sturdy St. Andrew's cross waited. Inside the circle, just off center, I'd placed a red-velvet chair, a Master's chair. Resting before it, a matching velvet pillow sat on the floor. Three items were resting on the cushion of the Master's chair.

"Paul..." His voice broke, and he glanced over at me. I stood one step inside the room, waiting for him to take it all in. Sara moved off to the side, giving us space.

"One day, I hope I walk in here and find you kneeling for me. Until then, I'll do everything to earn the right to claim my title." I went to him and placed my hand between his shoulder blades. "You mean everything to me. I want to be by your side, supporting you..." It was time for my voice to crack. "Loving you."

"Mastering me?" Forest's body gave a little jerk.

"Becoming yours as you become mine."

"Mine?" He barely whispered the word and took half a step forward, toward the circle.

"If you'll have me." I gave a little grin. Breaking Forest down was an art form I'd mastered, but getting him choked up? This was a first.

He stepped to the outer edge of the rope.

"Be careful."

He looked back at me. "Why?"

"If you step over that line, if you step into that circle, you belong to me. One hundred percent mine. Not just here in the dungeon, but in everything."

A smart man, Forest understood. I couldn't profess my desires any stronger than this.

"And what are those?" He pointed to the three small items on the cushion.

They were nonfunctional but profoundly symbolic.

"A ring," Sara piped up. She moved forward and took Forest's left hand in hers. "One to lie beside mine." She traced around his middle finger.

After their wedding, I hoped to one day have my ring sitting beside hers on his hand.

"You knew about this?" He turned his hand over and threaded his fingers with hers.

"I helped him pick it out." She bit at her lower lip and looked up at me, eyes bright and with a smile curving her dainty lips.

"Do you know what he's asking?"

She nodded. "I do."

He turned to me. "Does she *really* understand?"

I understood his concern. I was offering Forest a profound commitment, stepping up as his Master rather than his Dom. My authority would weave in and around every facet of his life.

"She does."

I'd spent hours talking with Sara about my hopes for our future, and I sought out her permission first, a blessing of sorts. She was a part of what we would become. None of this worked without us committed to one another.

Sara freed herself from Forest's grip and came to me. Lifting on tiptoe, she cupped my cheek. I expected a chaste kiss on my cheek. When her buttery soft lips pressed against mine, I staggered back, stunned, and overcome.

Tentative at first, I expected her to end the kiss—a touch-and-go experience—but she spread her hand over my chest and pressed her mouth against mine.

Six months ago, I brought her back from strangulation with mouth-to-mouth, an experience which had me questioning much about my sexuality, but that had been it. Other than the random hug, Sara and I rarely touched.

This was new, and I liked it.

A lot.

With a possessive growl, I yanked her against me and wrapped my arm around her waist. I took over the kiss, nipping and demanding entrance. Forest's low laughter had me stopping in my tracks.

"Be careful, angel," Forest said with a chuckle. "Paul only knows one speed: hard and fast."

I slipped my tongue inside her mouth, loving her sweet taste. What followed was a languorous, exploration as I tasted and explored the wonders of kissing a woman for the first time.

An explosion of heat swept through me, warmth licking along my nerves, shooting sparks of electricity through my body. Her tiny body fit perfectly in my arms, and I deepened the kiss, demanding more as I chased her tongue and claimed it as my own.

I wanted to slap the knowing smirk off Forest's face, but I was too busy kissing our girl. This was his fantasy, me and Sara wrapped in each other's arms. I didn't think he cared if he was involved. The fucker would eagerly sit on the sidelines, fisting his hungry cock, while Sara and I went to town.

We'd get there, but first, Forest and I had our future to discuss. With regret, I released Sara. I found myself surprised to find she was out of breath. Her cheeks pinked, and she gave me a shy, timid little smile.

"Wow." She pressed her fingertips to her lips.

"Yeah." I echoed her words and found myself wondering how the rest of her might taste. How she might feel. I swiped at my face, realizing what it was that I wanted.

"About fucking time," Forest added.

"Shut the fuck up." I turned on Forest. "Don't forget who's in charge."

"Um," Sara glanced at Forest, then looked to the door. "I think that's my exit cue."

"I warned you." Forest gave her a wink.

"Warned her about what?"

"That kissing you would rock her world." He gave me a smirk and rocked back on his heels.

"Is that so?"

"I also told her to be careful."

"And why is that?"

"Because you kiss like you fuck. Raw. Powerful. Relentless. All-consuming."

If I didn't hear the reverence in his voice, I might think he was complaining. What he said was true.

"Yeah, I think I'll just go now." Sara's voice trembled.

"You're not staying? After that kiss?" Forest's eyes widened in shock.

I could see the wheels churning in his head. We'd get there, but Sara and I needed time to process that kiss.

We'd talked about her leaving. I needed Forest and me to be alone for what came next, but I wasn't against switching things up.

"If you want to stay…"

My offer was sincere, even if it went against what I needed with Forest. Hard and fast was a snail's pace when it came to the desires Forest stirred. I intended to make this brutally painful for him, a display of dominance he would carry with him forever.

I could scale it down. Sara knew how we fucked, but she didn't know all of it. She hadn't seen me break him down.

She pressed her fingers to her lips and gave a slight shake of her head. I'd done the best I could explaining the things I would do to the man she loved.

Her attention shifted from me to Forest. "I love you."

"I love you," he said.

"And Paul loves you too," she said.

It was true. Those words were out there between us now. He either hadn't heard, or didn't want to respond, but damn if Sara didn't force a response. His tumultuous gaze turned to me. He held my eyes for a moment before lowering his gaze.

"I know."

Sara moved to the door but stopped and returned to me. She gripped my hand and lifted on tiptoe again. This time, her lips brushed my cheek.

"Take care of him."

"I will." I pulled her to me and kissed her forehead.

When the door shut behind her, I turned back to Forest. He stood his ground, chest heaving, dick straining for release, and hands fisted to his sides.

"Fuck, but if you wanted to get me hard, kissing her like that did the trick." Forest reached for his groin but stopped when I gave a sharp shake of my head.

"I know." I wanted to hold her, strip her, maybe even fuck her. Now that she was gone, my attention focused on the man in front of me. "Best you forget about her and focus on me. Why don't you take a look around?"

He glanced around the room, his gaze lingering on the rope circle for half a beat before moving on.

We had the entire basement for our playground. Other than the velvet Master's chair, there was nothing soft inside this room. It wasn't all dungeon, although, for our purposes, it would act as such.

Forest liked to fight.

I took half the room, over three thousand square feet, and built a full gym, including a mat where we could fight. The other half of the room was filled with all manner of contraptions fit for a dungeon.

There was nothing soft and gentle down here. This was a room built for pain. The predominant colors were black, gray, and silver. The smell of leather permeated the room, and the walls and ceiling had been covered in the finest acoustic panels money could buy. We were locked in our own world down here, where Forest could scream his head off without bothering anyone.

In addition to the St. Andrew's Cross, I had several benches, tables, and other items that would challenge Forest. I tried to build this space with as few things which might trigger Forest from his childhood and the basement my father had tortured him in, but there were some things I couldn't avoid.

He wandered over to several cabinets and opened the doors. Inside was every implement I could find designed to inflict pain, plus a few others he might not be expecting.

"A cock cage?" He picked up a wire cage and looked at me with confusion.

I never withheld orgasms from him, but we would explore all manner of things on our journey.

"If you have something you want added, let me know."

"What about removed?" He lifted the cock cage. "Do I need to be worried about this?"

I got that to get a rise out of him. I grinned at Forest and watched his reaction. "You think I won't use it?"

"Just...not what I was expecting."

I pointed at it. "That's for punishment."

"You don't think the whip with the chains is punishment enough?"

"Not when I know you'll get hard from the whipping."

He gave a cheeky grin and ducked his head. I had him. He glorified pain.

He ran his fingers down the many whips hanging on the pegs. His brows lifted at the more edgier devices.

There wasn't a single cage in the room. I had no use for such a device. Slowly, he made a circuit of all the room, stopping to test the sturdiness of the restraints that would hold him down.

"Looks like you've thought of pretty much everything."

"Do you like it? We can always add more." I was rather pleased with the results.

"And this? This is what you want?" He circled back around to the rope on the floor.

"It's what you need."

"Is that so?"

"It is."

He needed to work this out in his head. The decision would ultimately be his.

"That's a pretty fucking big commitment, Paul."

"In here, you call me Sir."

"Understood." He nodded as if he'd been testing me. "That's a pretty fucking big commitment, *Sir.*"

"Lifelong."

He stumbled back. "What?"

I took a step toward him. "Lifelong. That's what I want."

Forest glanced at the circle and swallowed thickly. "Lifelong…" His voice dropped to his rumbly whisper, and threaded through it was awestruck wonder. He took a step toward the circle. "Shit, that's…this changes everything."

"Careful," I warned. "You cross that line…"

"Yeah, I got it." He pointed to the chair. "What are the other things on the cushion?"

"The ring is to wear beside Sara's wedding band. Cuffs aren't practical for day to day wear. Most people will only see leather knotted friendship bracelets, but they'll be your constant reminder…"

"Right. Shit." He reached down to adjust his cock.

Hard.

Stiff.

Needy.

He was painfully aroused.

I'd give anything to know what he was thinking right now. I wasn't sure how he would react. Forest ran his hand through his hair and spun in a slow circle as he took everything in a second time. "And Sara?"

"I asked her first. As for what I want…"

His voice dropped to a whisper. "I want it too."

"You do?"

"Yeah, I do." He gulped. "Shit. This is…it's pretty intense."

"It's no wedding ring, but it's all I have to offer."

"It's everything." He bit at his lower lip. "And Sara knows what this means? She's okay with it?" His brows scrunched together. "Shit…this is huge."

"I wouldn't offer this without her full support." I pointed at the circle. "Like I said, someday I hope to walk in here and find you kneeling in that circle for me. Until then…"

"Fuck that." He lifted his foot to step over the circle, and I yanked him back.

"Forest!"

"What?"

"This isn't something you rush into."

"I'm not rushing anything. I'd say it's about damn time."

"What?"

He jerked free. "I'm already yours." His gaze cast out over the room. "I have one request."

"What's that?"

"Don't ever hold back. Take me and break me." His entire body trembled. "Take me where I need to go." Forest gripped my nape and pressed his forehead against mine. Our breaths mingled as the intimate moment stretched. I breathed him in, then placed my hand on the flex of his bicep.

"With pleasure."

Our gazes locked, and Forest stepped over the rope, choosing to become mine.

I pointed to the cushion on the floor.

This glorious man gave me everything. He saved me, and I would spend the rest of my life saving him. I would break him over and over, and lead him into the darkness he both feared and desired. There, I would put him back together again as only I could.

My heart filled with joy as I watched Forest fall.

***

I REALLY HOPE YOU ENJOYED FOREST'S STORY. HE IS, BY FAR, MY most favorite character I've written to date, and I have a surprise for you.

You'll see Forest in my new hostage rescue series: The Guardians Hostage Rescue Specialists. You saw some of his Guardians briefly in this book, the men of Alpha and Bravo teams. They've been faceless so far, but it's time to let them shine.

Forest isn't done saving the world. His team of elite hostage rescue experts is on task, ridding the world of evil one devil at a time while they save innocent lives.

I hope you're looking forward to an amazingly HOT series of ALPHA men and the women brave enough to guard their hearts.

You can grab book 1: Rescuing Melissa for FREE by signing up to my newsletter. Click HERE.

I've also written a treat. A short story with all the Gang. How about an Angel Fire Christmas story? I know you'll love it! Grab your story and click below.

An Angel Fire Christmas

Sneak Peek of Rescuing Zoe

BOOK 1: GUARDIAN HOSTAGE RESCUE SPECIALISTS–ALPHA TEAM

Once upon a time, there was a girl.
A happy, vibrant girl
Who didn't believe nightmares were real

But the girl woke up
A terrified, frightened girl
Trapped in a living nightmare.

That girl is me.

ZOE

IT'S BEEN TWO DAYS SINCE THEY ADDED THE LAST GIRL. ANNA arrived much as we all did, struggling, snarling and full of fight. She survived her first beating. She's quiet now. Recovering from her injuries. Now she whimpers and cries, much like me. Just like the rest of us.

Like Anna, I fought when they took me, and like her, I suffered.

I'm smarter now.

We all are.

In the oppressive silence, and cloying blackness which smothers all hope, we're not ready to die. And while nobody knows where we are, or where we're going, we are headed somewhere.

We're fed, watered, and they remove the foul smelling bucket of waste once a day. I think. Measuring time is difficult, but we know one thing. They want us alive when we get to wherever it is they're taking us.

To monsters who wait for us.

To the beginning of a living hell.

After Anna's arrival, the metal floor of our prison vibrated. A low, persistent drone shook the shipping container. Sometime later, hours maybe—It's hard to tell how much time passes in here—a soft up and down, side to side, rolling motion confirms our fears. We're being shipped to the next destination in our descent into hell.

The days pass with the relentless march of time. We can't stop it, slow it, or reverse it.

Time is meaningless when minutes last hours, hours last days, and the world no longer makes sense. With only suffocating darkness to pass the time, each day I lose more and more of my sanity.

My fingers plait a tiny braid. I make one for each day, or at least I think the time between one opening of the shipper container and the next is one day. It's when they feed us and water us like the chattel we've begun.

There are ten braids now.

A loud *bang* and I nearly jump out of my skin.

Men's voices rumble outside.

It feels like a lifetime when they shoved me kicking and screaming into the darkness.

I scurry back, not wanting *them* to touch me. To hurt me. The girls who got too close were dragged out. Not all of them returned. Those who did, are shadows of their former selves. We lost three girls before Anna. She was the last to be shoved inside this box.

That was two days ago.

When the doors open, all we see is more darkness. Light from the moon penetrates the towers of stacked shipping containers, casting shadows upon shadows. I prefer the formless blackness to the shifting shadows. Not once do they open the door during the daytime. It's always night.

Always dark.

A hand reaches in and takes the waste bucket. Footsteps recede while someone else places a large bowl of water just inside. We wait for the man with the bucket to return and toss it back inside.

Covered in filth and grime, the bucket no longer bothers me.

When water comes, no one touches it. We fear what might be in it more than dying of thirst.

We wait.

We wait until the doors close. Until the metallic thunk of the locking lugs tells us we're safe, once again locked inside our stifling prison. Only then do we move.

One girl.

One girl finds the bowl in the blinding darkness.

One girl takes a sip.

And we wait.

If she doesn't pass out from whatever drug they may have laced it with, we share the water. Small sips which do nothing to quench our thirst.

But it keeps us alive.

We survive together, thirteen strangers bonded by a nightmare.

Each girl takes her turn to test the water.

Today, it's my turn.

I lift my head from my knees and reach for the bowl. Dipping my finger into its contents, I croak out a scratchy, "W-water." There is no food. Gnawing hunger claws at my belly, but it's thirst which drives me.

Sighs sound all around me in the dismal darkness. It's been too long without water. The only thing carrying me through, the only reason I hold onto hope is that I believe we're more valuable alive than dead. I know what fate awaits us. We all *know*. But it's still better than death.

I take a long pull, swallowing water down a scratchy throat which still hurts from all the screaming during my abduction. It feels as if I *broke* something inside, because my voice is nothing but a breathy whisper now.

As the first girl, I'll drink more than the rest. That way the drug, if it's there, will be more likely to take effect on me, thus saving the others. I scoot back against the wall and slide the bowl to Bree. She came the day after I arrived. Our fingers interlock as I tip my head back to wait.

If nothing happens, Bree will take a sip and pass it to Chloe. Chloe will pass it to Dawn, and Dawn will pass it to Eve. On down the line, we'll share until the last drop is gone.

Then we'll wait for the door to open again.

We don't have the strength to fight. Not that I'll waste my energy on these men. I'm saving mine for the real monsters to come.

Not sure if my eyes are open or closed, fetid darkness folds around me. My thoughts wander, like they do every hour of every day, to the last moment I was happy. But I struggle to remember happier times.

I don't focus on the men who snatched me off the street.

Instead, my thoughts go to brilliant blue skies and white sand beaches of Cancun. Crystal clear, tropical waters sparkle beneath a bright sun. The festive Spring Break party atmosphere lets a smart girl lower her guard. I lost my freedom in the span of a heartbeat, on my very first night in paradise.

I thought I could walk from the beach to our hotel by myself. I gave no thought to the vulnerability of a pretty young girl walking alone. But I didn't *think* I was alone. People were all around me, partying, with far too much liquor flowing in their veins.

I felt *safe*.

But I was too easily separated from the crowd. They yanked me into a filthy van. Took me to a filthy house on a filthy street. There I was stripped, examined, and left to huddle on a filthy floor with a filthy flea-infested blanket. Then they shoved me inside a filthy shipping container twenty feet long with ten other girls.

Has it really been ten days? The braids in my hair don't lie.

What are my friends doing now? Did they call the police? Do Mexican police even care about an American girl who disappeared? Or do they think I got drunk and passed out in some foreign bed with some nameless boy?

I'll never know. What about my overly protective brother? Austin must be going ballistic, worrying about me? And my father? He must be out of his mind.

"How do you feel?" Bree keeps her breathy voice soft. We aren't allowed to speak to one another. That freedom, among many things, was violently taken from us.

"Good so fa…" I struggle to complete my thought as darkness overtakes me. My eyes droop. My muscles relax.

"It's drugged." Bree's voice sounds far away and defeated.

Hands reach for me and drag me over a rough metal floor as I dream of a happy, vibrant girl who doesn't believe in nightmares.

AXEL

"Alpha-one to Alpha-three," Max's voice crackles through the radio. "Axel, you gotta see this." His tone makes my skin crawl.

"Copy that." I hold my position, weapon leveled on four men lying face down on the dirty floor. Zip Ties bind their wrists at the small of their backs and tie their ankles together.

Legs bent. Backs painfully arched. Shoulders straining. They're furious with my handiwork. Took less than thirty-seconds to truss them up, but I've been hogtying cattle all my life. For the record, humans are much easier to subdue than a calves.

"You got this?" My attention shifts to my teammate, Griff.

"Go ahead. I got this." He spits into the eye of one of our prisoners. Bastard curses in Spanish. "Sorry bud, a little spit in your eye is the least of your worries." Griff gives the shithole a love tap to the kidneys with the tip of his steel-toed boot.

Our angry friend's thick muscles bunch. Fury darkens his face. He, and his buddies, aren't going anywhere, and I think they're finally figuring that out.

I don't move until Griff gives the okay.

We're a six-man team. Knox and Liam stand outside, guarding our retreat. Griff's with me. Max and Wolfe moved through, looking for the target.

"Alpha-three to Alpha-one, headed to you." My radio squawks as I radio my intention to move my position.

"Copy that." Max sounds frustrated, it vibrates in his clipped reply.

Two days we've been on assignment while our target suffered at the hands of these men.

Our target? I grind my molars until my teeth throb and the muscles of my jaw ache.

Our target is my best friend's little sister, an annoying little scrap of a girl who made my life miserable with her hopeless crush. Last year, I finally set Zoe straight. I was a dick about it.

Firm.

Callous.

Mean.

I was an asshole about and broke her heart, but there was no other way. She needed to move on.

And now she's been taken.

"Status." That voice belongs to our mission commander.

CJ's been at this game twice as long as any of us. Famous for bringing a serial killer down, along with his copycat wannabe, he freed half a dozen women while on vacation. In our community, CJ is a legend.

I work my way deeper into the building, knowing he follows our progress via the helmet and body cams streaming our every move. Our successes and failures are broadcast in realtime back to command.

It's dark. We cut the electricity to the entire block. The flashlight mounted on my helmet provides all the light I need as it pierces the dimly lit hall.

"Do you have the package?" CJ's voice crackles with impatience, locking my molars tighter together. We can't afford to be late and this feels all kinds of *too fucking late*.

Cancun is famous for kidnapping rich Americans and pretty American girls. Zoe is exactly what they look for, a willowy blonde knockout with bright bottle green eyes. It's her most striking feature.

I pass down a hall. Weapon up. Scanning left to right. Finger on the trigger guard.

Max and Griff cleared these rooms on their way in, but I never assume. Those who do don't last long in our line of work.

Methodically, I scan the long hall, clear each room as I go, and make my way to the last room at the end of the hall. I meet Wolfe there with a lift of my chin. He responds in kind.

The room's empty.

"Fucking hell." My nose wrinkles at the smell of blood, sweat, and human excrement. The stench is enough to make me gag. Breathing through my mouth only makes it worse. Now I taste the foulness as it floods my senses.

Zoe was in this room.

Past tense.

Mission failure.

Ratty blankets form amorphous lumps on the dirty floor.

Lumps.

Pleural.

Not unexpected. We know the men who took Zoe are part of a human trafficking ring. That's why we're here. We're the hostage rescue specialists paid very well to bring stolen girls home, preferably safe and sound. Although we were only hired to recover Zoe, we'll save them all. Mr. Summers won't have it any other way.

There's easily a dozen or more blankets strewn about. A dozen lives taken. The foul taste of failure coats my tongue. I'm not used to the bitter tang.

Guardians never fail.

Tell that to Zoe. Tell her how this isn't a colossal fucked up failure.

If she's still alive.

My helmet light pierces the gloom, revealing dried blood and fetid urine stains. They kept the girls in here like animals. The blood comes in various forms, dried pools on the floor, stains on the blankets, and splatter marks on the wall. Urine stains are everywhere.

These men are sloppy. Damaging their merchandise cuts into their bottom line. By the looks of this place, all of the girls suffered. Some more than others. Zoe suffered.

In my six years as a team guy, I've seen a lot of fucked up shit. When I left the Navy, I thought the worst of human depravity was behind me. How wrong I was. This is some fucked up shit.

I used to hunt dangerous men, relieving them of the burden of their pathetic lives, or returning them to whichever prevailing authority waited to extract their pound of flesh.

Now, I retrieve the fallen, the broken; those who've been taken. I'm a Guardian, a hostage rescue specialist dealing with a catastrophic mission failure. The girls are gone. From the looks of it we're hours late, maybe even a whole day late.

This job isn't any easier than my team days. In many ways, it's far worse. Revulsion coils in my gut, thinking about what these girls endured.

Girls. Young women. Innocent victims.

That's not an emotion I ever felt for the targets I disposed of during my time in the Navy. I dispatched lives without a bit of compassion or lick of guilt cluttering my conscience.

"What did you want me to see?" I turn my attention to Max, our team leader. He could've told me about this shit instead of dragging me from my position.

"You tell me." He gestures to another room. The door sits off its hinges, propped haphazardly against the wall. The low beam of his flashlight barely lights up the doorway. I push past and look inside.

"Christ!" My heart rate quickens before I can force it back to its slow plodding pace. The veins in my temples bulge as fury fills me. "Fucking pigs."

Max follows me into the room. He ordered me to tell him what I see.

"It's a procedure room." My nose wrinkles at the stench. There's more blood here than in the other rooms. Layers of dried blood pool on the floor beneath an examination table. It tells the tales of multiple victims enduring unspeakable acts.

"Well? What do you think?" Max watches me closely. Like the rest of the team, he's aware of my personal connection to this mission.

"It's a gynecologic exam table."

"No shit Sherlock."

As team medic, my medical skillset comes in handy in the rare instances when one of us needs a little patching up in the field, but there's no reason for my medical skills here.

The back of the exam table is set at an incline. Two metal poles with heel cups extend from the end. Unlike a normal exam table, this one comes with shackles. Shackles bolted at the high end for the chest. Shackles to secure wrists a little lower down. Another runs across the hips to hold an unwilling patient as they thrash. Finally, there are two more straps at the feet.

"What were they doing? Rape?" Max growls, and I echo his rage.

"Could be. The table definitely places a woman in a vulnerable position, but I doubt their customers would pay for damaged goods." I glance around the filthy room, looking for anything which might explain what they did in here. "Check the trash can."

Max heads over to a waste container. Instead of checking, he picks it up and brings it back to me. I'm smart enough not to reach inside. Who knows what might prick me and transfer disease.

Disease?

My eyes narrow and I pull out my knife. Using that, I dig through the contents.

"You seeing this?" My question isn't for Max, but for our Doc Summer watching from command.

"Yes." Doc Summers' crisp voice tightens. A tough cookie, nothing phases our indomitable lead physician.

"See what?" Max peers into the trash can.

"Those are STD kits. Tests for gonorrhea, chlamydia, and..." I sift through the contents. "IUDs? Doc, am I correct?"

Static over the coms crackles then clears. "Looks like they tested the girls for sexually transmitted diseases and inserted IUDs." Her voice softens. "At least that answers one question."

"What's that?" Max turns the can over and dumps the contents on the floor spreading them out. He does this to send better pictures back to base.

I glance at the trash and count IUD wrappers. "Looks like thirteen."

"Sixteen chlamydia swabs. Thirteen IUDs." Doc Summers confirms. "I'd mark that at sixteen victims."

"Not thirteen?"

"If some of the girls already had IUDs, they wouldn't place a new one."

"How fucking considerate." My stomach twists. They want the pleasure of raping their victims without the unwanted side effects pregnancy brings.

"Search the place." A new voice rumbles through our comm channels. Forest Summers' deep baritone is unmistakable and elicits an ass-puckering gluteal clench.

What the fuck is the CJ's boss' boss doing on Overwatch?

My team worked with Forest Summers on an operation in the Philippines that went to hell in a handbasket in the blink of an eye.

That had definitely been a FUBAR moment. We lost the head of our organization. I'm surprised we weren't all fired on the spot. A couple months later, we rescued him in a brilliantly executed raid, but still that's not something a person ever forgets.

Mr. Summers continues, thinking out loud. "There must be something which says where they took the girls. See what the prisoners have to say."

"With pleasure." Not a fan of torture, per se, I love a good interrogation.

"We're on it, boss." Max gives a nod. He's our team leader. All final orders come from him. I tap the button for the team only comm channel. "Alpha-four, we *need* to know where they took the girls."

With Forest Summers' interest in the mission, *need* means necessity.

"Copy that." Griff loves getting his hands dirty.

If we can get the intel we need, we might be able to salvage this operation.

GET YOUR COPY TODAY. CLICK HERE.

Please consider leaving a review

I HOPE YOU ENJOYED THIS BOOK AS MUCH AS I ENJOYED WRITING IT. If you like this book, please leave a review. I love reviews. I love reading your reviews, and they help other readers decide if this book is worth their time and money. I hope you think it is and decide to share this story with others. A sentence is all it takes. Thank you in advance!

CLICK ON THE LINK BELOW TO LEAVE YOUR REVIEW
Goodreads
Amazon
Bookbub

Also by Ellie Masters

The LIGHTER SIDE

Ellie Masters is the lighter side of the Jet & Ellie Masters writing duo! You will find Contemporary Romance, Military Romance, Romantic Suspense, Billionaire Romance, and Rock Star Romance in Ellie's Works.

YOU CAN FIND ELLIE'S BOOKS HERE:

ELLIEMASTERS.COM/BOOKS

Military Romance
Guardian Hostage Rescue Specialists

Rescuing Melissa

(Get a FREE copy of Rescuing Melissa

when you join Ellie's Newsletter)

Alpha Team

Rescuing Zoe

Rescuing Moira

Rescuing Eve

Rescuing Lily

Rescuing Jinx

Rescuing Maria

Bravo Team

Rescuing Angie

Rescuing Isabelle

Rescuing Carmen

Rescuing Rosalie

Rescuing Kaye

Cara's Protector

Rescuing Barbi

The Dark of You

Military Romance

Guardian Personal Protection Specialists

Sybil's Protector

Lyra's Protector

The One I Want Series

(Small Town, Military Heroes)

By Jet & Ellie Masters

EACH BOOK IN THIS SERIES CAN BE READ AS A STANDALONE AND IS ABOUT A DIFFERENT COUPLE WITH AN HEA.

Saving Abby

Saving Ariel

Saving Brie

Saving Cate

Saving Dani

Saving Jen

Rockstar Romance

The Angel Fire Rock Romance Series

EACH BOOK IN THIS SERIES CAN BE READ AS A STANDALONE AND IS ABOUT A DIFFERENT COUPLE WITH AN HEA. IT IS RECOMMENDED THEY ARE READ IN ORDER.

Ashes to New (prequel)

Heart's Insanity (book 1)

Heart's Desire (book 2)

Heart's Collide (book 3)

Hearts Divided (book 4)

Hearts Entwined (book5)

Forest's FALL (book 6)

Hearts The Last Beat (book7)

Contemporary Romance

Firestorm

(KRISTY BROMBERG'S EVERYDAY HEROES WORLD)

Billionaire Romance

Billionaire Boys Club

Hawke

Richard

Brody

Romantic Suspense

Changing Roles Series:

THIS SERIES MUST BE READ IN ORDER.

WITH JET MASTERS

Book 1: Command Me

Book 2: Control Me

Book 3: Collar Me

Book 4: Embracing FATE

Book 5: Seizing FATE

Book 6: Accepting FATE

Romantic Suspense

EACH BOOK IS A STANDALONE NOVEL.

The Starling

~AND~

Science Fiction

Ellie Masters writing as L.A. Warren

Vendel Rising: a Science Fiction Serialized Novel

About the Author

Ellie Masters is a USA Today Bestselling author and Amazon Top 15 Author who writes Angsty, Steamy, Heart-Stopping, Pulse-Pounding, Can't-Stop-Reading Romantic Suspense. In addition, she's a wife, military mom, doctor, and retired Colonel. She writes romantic suspense filled with all your sexy, swoon-worthy alpha men. Her writing will tug at your heartstrings and leave your heart racing.

Born in the South, raised under the Hawaiian sun, Ellie has traveled the globe while in service to her country. The love of her life, her amazing husband, is her number one fan and biggest supporter. And yes! He's read every word she's written.

She has lived all over the United States—east, west, north, south and central—but grew up under the Hawaiian sun. She's also been privileged to have lived overseas, experiencing other cultures and making lifelong friends. Now, Ellie is proud to call herself a Southern transplant, learning to say y'all and "bless her heart" with the best of them. She lives with her beloved husband, two children who refuse to flee the nest, and four fur-babies; three cats who rule the household, and a dog who wants nothing other than for the cats to be his best friends. The cats have a different opinion regarding this matter.

Ellie's favorite way to spend an evening is curled up on a couch, laptop in place, watching a fire, drinking a good wine, and bringing forth all the characters from her mind to the page and hopefully into the hearts of her readers.

FOR MORE INFORMATION
elliemasters.com

[f] facebook.com/elliemastersromance
[twitter] twitter.com/Ellie__Masters
[instagram] instagram.com/ellie_masters
[BB] bookbub.com/authors/ellie-masters
[g] goodreads.com/Ellie_Masters

Connect with Ellie Masters

Website:
elliemasters.com
Amazon Author Page:
elliemasters.com/amazon
Facebook:
elliemasters.com/Facebook
Goodreads:
elliemasters.com/Goodreads
Instagram:
elliemasters.com/Instagram

Dedication

This book is dedicated to you, my reader. Thank you for spending a few hours of your time with me. I wouldn't be able to write without you to cheer me on. Your wonderful words, your support, and your willingness to join me on this journey is a gift beyond measure.

Whether this is the first book of mine you've read, or if you've been with me since the very beginning, thank you for believing in me as I bring these characters 'from my mind to the page and into your hearts.'

Love,
Ellie

THE END

Made in the USA
Columbia, SC
27 August 2024

41189085R00300